Flesh and Blood

A familiar shape walked among the boxcars. Long dark hair, backpack tucked over her shoulders, flashlight in hand. What little light there was passed through her translucent form. Long dark hair, backpack tucked over her shoulders, flashlight in hand. What little light there was passed through her translucent form.

Numb recognition froze Doc.

The circle of her flashlight beam pinpointed something. She walked toward it, stared at it for a moment, then nudged it with her foot.

In a flash, a thin, dark shape lunged up and grabbed her. Her mouth opened in a silent scream. The flashlight tumbled from her hand and landed with the beam pointed at her. The shape was human, bones with a little skin stretched over them. It clung to her. Fangs, white in the flashlight's beam, tore into her throat. Blood spattered, soaking the front of her sweatshirt. The creature gorged itself as the fight drained out of the girl's body. Her fists stopped battering. Her feet ceased their kicking.

The creature raised its face and turned its cloudy eyes into the light. A rem   vny jaw.

The creat   iona.

The imag

D0453275

FLESH AND BLOOD

House of Comarré: Book 2

KRISTEN PAINTER

orbit

www.orbitbooks.net

ORBIT

First published in Great Britain in 2011 by Orbit

Book design by Giorgetta Bell McRee

A CIP catalogue record for this book
is available from the British Library.

ISBN 978-1-84149-970-3

Typeset in Times by M Rules
Printed and bound by
CPI Group (UK) Ltd, Croydon, CR0 4YY

Papers used by Orbit are from well-managed forests
and other responsible sources.

 MIX
Paper from
responsible sources
FSC® C104740

Orbit
An imprint of
Little, Brown Book Group
100 Victoria Embankment
London EC4Y 0DY

An Hachette UK Company
www.hachette.co.uk

www.orbitbooks.net

For Richie, my best friend,
my biggest supporter,
my loudest fan,
my hero,
my husband.

About the time of the end, a body of men will be raised up, who will turn their attention to the prophecies, in the midst of much clamor and opposition.

—SIR ISAAC NEWTON, FORMER GRAND MASTER
OF THE KUBAI MATA

Chapter One

Paradise City, New Florida 2067

Tatiana needed to die. The thought pushed Chrysabelle on until her shoulders burned and her arms shook. Sweat drenched her thin white T-shirt and dampened her hair, but no matter how many times she pounded her fists into the heavy bag, no matter how hard she punished her body, nothing changed. Her mother was still dead. Tatiana was still alive. And Chrysabelle still owed Mal for the promise she'd made to him.

Over and over, she struck the bag, but the memory of her mother dying in her arms still haunted her. She hit harder, and her conscience punched back, heavy with the guilt of her unpaid debt.

Mal had helped her when she needed him. And she'd done nothing to uphold her end of the deal. She'd barely spoken to him in the two weeks since they'd returned from Corvinestri and most of those words had been on the plane ride home. Her fist slammed the bag. Wasn't his fault Maris was dead. It was Tatiana's.

The comarré life taught that revenge served no purpose. Chrysabelle was starting to think otherwise.

She walloped the bag again, then spun and landed a kick with a loud, angry grunt. She dropped her hands and stared at the bag, not seeing it. Just the mess she still needed to deal with.

She walked away from the bag, pushing hair off her face with her taped hands. She should be downstairs, reading through the journals Maris had left behind, trying to find some vampire weakness she could exploit to Tatiana's detriment. Instead, she was hiding out in the gym. No, not hiding out. Training. For when she next met the vampiress who'd killed her mother. And with the covenant between humans and other-naturals gone, being fight-ready was going to matter.

Just like Mal thought finding a way to remove his curse mattered. Which it did. She approached the bag again and punched her fist into it. Most comarré wouldn't dream of creating such tension between them and their patron. Not that most comarré had a cursed vampire for a patron. If Mal even was her patron anymore. She sighed. Her life was an *unqualified* mess.

'Argh!' She whirled and kicked the bag, flinging sweat. Velimai, her mother's former assistant and now hers, stood in the doorway, watching.

Your mother loved beating up that bag, Velimai signed, her face wistful. Wyspers were mute, except for an ear-piercing scream capable of killing vampires.

'It helps.' Chrysabelle fought a wave of sadness to smile at the wysper fae. They both missed Maris. Her presence filled the house.

Velimai nodded back, her fingers moving. *Ready for dinner?*

'Steak?' Chrysabelle asked hopefully. With no patron and no bite, steak seemed to keep her strength up and maintain her superhuman senses better than all the other foods she'd tried. No wonder it was served so often at most comarré houses.

What else? Velimai signed, smiling.

So long as Velimai didn't sign too fast, Chrysabelle could understand most of what she said. 'I'll grab a shower and be down in five.' She started ripping the tape off her hands with her teeth.

Take ten, Velimai signed as she left.

The hot shower felt good, but alone in the steam, Chrysabelle had too much time to think.

She'd sent Mal blood, not just because it was the proper thing to do for one's patron – however suspect his hold on her blood rights might be – but because she had to drain it from her system anyway. According to Doc, Mal's sidekick of sorts, her efforts were futile. Mal had left the blood untouched in the galley refrigerator of the abandoned freighter he called home. Maybe he thought he'd have to kiss her again if he consumed it. She grimaced at that memory and added more cold water to the spray falling over her. No, neither of them wanted to go there again. What he was doing for blood, she had no idea. She wanted to pretend she didn't care, but that would be a lie. Caring about her patron was ingrained in her makeup. One hundred fifteen years of comarré indoctrination was a tough thing to ignore. The struggle between who she wanted to be and who she had been played out even in daily decisions. How many years would it be before she thought of herself not as a comarré but simply as a woman?

She rinsed the soap from her body, letting the water beat against her skin. Her thoughts returned to Mal. Did he feel like she'd betrayed him? She hoped not, hoped he realized she was just waiting for the time to be right. Going back to Corvinestri could be very dangerous for both of them. Surely he understood that.

She couldn't imagine he was in any rush to face Tatiana again. Not after finding out she was the one responsible for his curse. He probably wanted to kill her as badly as Chrysabelle did.

What must it feel like to have the person you'd married turn on you that way? It was bad enough the vampiress had killed Maris and destroyed the covenant, but for Mal to find out the woman who had been his mortal wife was the one responsible for his years of imprisonment and his curse ...

Maybe Chrysabelle wasn't the only one whose life was a mess.

She cranked the water off, grabbed a towel, and dried herself before wrapping her hair up. She threw on a robe and opened the door. The rich smell of steak made her stomach growl. She headed downstairs, ready to dig in.

After dinner, she settled on the couch with one of Maris's journals, but her mind kept returning to Mal. She needed a distraction.

'Screen on.' The wall across from her flickered to life, and the late-evening news projected into the room with holographic precision.

'... an ex-soldier in Little Havana who preaches outside the abandoned Catholic church. His message? Vampires need to be cleansed.' The anchorman smiled like he didn't expect his viewers to believe in vampires either. Idiot. Newsreel of the ex-soldier flashed on the screen and Chrysabelle peered closer. There was something familiar about his shaved head and the glint of his dog tags, but she couldn't place them. What she did know was that the ex-soldier wasn't human. He was fringe, a less-powerful class of vampire compared to the nobles but vampire nonetheless. Couldn't the anchorman tell? Or had he, like a good portion of his audience, chosen not to believe?

'*A woman at a Coral Gables Publix reported the man behind her in the checkout line had horns.*' The woman's face filled the inset screen hovering beside the anchorman's head. '*He had gray skin and a lot of silver earrings and horns. Horns!*' The woman made looping motions at the sides of her head. '*And it's not even Halloween yet!*'

A shadeux fae picking up eggs and milk was the least of that woman's worries. What would the public do when Halloween had come and gone but the monsters still remained? The Samhain holiday was less than two weeks away.

The camera switched its focus back to the anchorman. '*More and more reports have been coming in from all over New Florida about strange sightings just like this one. If you've seen something unusual in your area, give our tip hotline a call at—*'

She changed the channel to another local news station. '*In a press release today, Mayor Diaz-White announced she will be forming a task force to investigate what can only be described as the paranormal happenings taking place in the city, although the mayor claims every incident can be explained.*'

'Screen off.' The holographic image vanished. Chrysabelle had seen enough. Paradise City was only beginning to wake up to the new reality the whole world now faced with the covenant gone. As the days ticked by, the inevitable clash between light and dark forces came nearer, escalating until there would be no denying what was happening. No matter what the mayor told the people.

Which brought her thoughts back to Tatiana. Did a more evil, conniving, ambitious vampire exist? Chrysabelle doubted it. Tatiana had killed Maris as part of the ritual that tore the covenant away, but Chrysabelle had prevented Tatiana from keeping the ring of sorrows. How long before Tatiana made another attempt to claim the ring? It was safely tucked away, but Chrysabelle had considered destroying it several times in the past weeks. If only she could be sure enough of its power to determine that destroying it wouldn't cause further damage to the world around them.

The swirls of gold tattooed on her skin glittered softly as her thumb rubbed the band on her ring finger. One click released a tiny blade, sharp enough to pierce a vein and drain away the excess blood in her system. Those born into the comarré life, raised to fulfill the needs of the vampires who purchased their blood rights and heavily tattooed with the special gold signum that purified their blood, produced the substance in rich, pure, powerful abundance. Without a patron, the excess blood would sicken her, poisoning her system until she went mad. She'd been on the verge once and that was enough.

She held her wrist up to the light. The veins pulsed thick and blue. The time to drain the excess was upon her. Maybe that was why Mal had been on her mind so much these last few days.

Maris had told her that eventually her system would adjust, but Chrysabelle had twice drained her blood to feed Mal and twice he'd kissed her in return, giving her the infusion of vampire power that was her due. Those kisses had kept her body producing. Kept her thinking of him.

She should drain the blood into the sink, wash it and her thoughts of Mal away. She sighed softly and wished he were that easy to forget. He wasn't. Not even close. She stood and headed for the kitchen. What was one more container in the refrigerator among the others? Her blood was valuable. Whether Mal wanted it or not.

*

Corvinestri, Romania, 2067

'This is going to hurt, my sweet. Are you sure you can withstand the pain?'

'You've already told me it will hurt. And I've already told you I can withstand more pain than you can dream of.' Tatiana glared at Zafir. 'Do you think it was pleasant when that comarré whore sliced my hand off in the first place?' If he knew what she'd endured while in the clutches of the Castus Sanguis, but of course, he had no idea.

'*Laa*, my darling, of course not.' His lush, black lashes fluttered over his olive cheeks. 'I only wished to prepare you.'

'Just do it. I will be fine.' She lay back on Zafir's lab table, her head propped on his folded coat, her remaining hand flat on her chest covering her locket where it lay beneath her blouse. Zafir and his brother, Nasir, were both exceptionally beautiful in a dark, Arabian kind of way, but according to Lord Ivan, who'd sent her here, Zafir was the most circumspect of the talented pair. And in this matter, discretion was of the utmost importance. Few knew her hand had been severed, and she intended to keep it that way. The servants who found out had been dispatched, save Octavian, the head of her household staff. She would not, under any circumstance, be made to appear incapable or disadvantaged. She intended to have Lord Ivan's position of Dominus one day, and nothing, *nothing* would prevent that. Soon she would renew her standing in the eyes of the Castus. Show them she was worthy once again. Reclaim the ring of sorrows – and the power it held – that was rightfully hers.

This new hand was the first step toward that goal.

'*Na'am*, you will do very well, won't you?' Zafir laughed softly.

She wanted to slap his face until that patronizing tone became a cry for mercy. He was no Mikkel, that much was certain. Mikkel's talents in the black arts had been exceptional. Of course, those talents hadn't kept her late paramour alive either. And if Zafir's talents in alchemy were as powerful as he claimed, he might be better than Mikkel. If he failed to do as he'd promised, then perhaps she'd give the brother a chance. At the very least, Zafir was Mikkel's equal in bed.

Life had very quickly taught her that pleasure and power were the only real rewards for pain. Her sweet Sofia's face flashed before her eyes, something that had been happening more and more since her confrontation with Malkolm. Seeing him had stirred up the past. She tightened her grip on the locket, the silk of her blouse cool against her fingers. 'Get on with it.'

'As you wish.' Zafir moved the meticulously crafted platinum prosthetic into place at the end of her right wrist. The gleaming hand lay open, the lines and creases on the palm mirror images of those on her left because it had been modeled after that hand. The hot metal had been quenched in her blood to further seal the magic.

He painted the stump of her wrist with a foul-smelling paste that burned slightly, then he adjusted the prosthetic so that her flesh touched metal. The metal was cool, but her body was warm because she'd fed from her comar before coming to give herself strength.

Using a glass spoon, Zafir scooped pale silver-white dust from a squat glass jar and sprinkled the joined area with the powder.

The pain struck in a searing wave.

A cry ripped from Tatiana's throat and she jerked away from the agony, but Zafir grabbed her forearm and kept it pressed against the metal.

'You mustn't move, my love.'

Fire traveled the length of her arm and bit into her shoulder. Lava flowed through her joints, melting her bones with blinding pain. She clenched her jaw to keep from vomiting.

She could endure this. She'd endured the Castus Sanguis's punishing use of her mind and body, and would again if that's what it took to regain their favor. All that mattered was the unholy power they wielded and that a portion of it become hers. *Pain brings clarity.*

Flames licked her skin. Wisps of smoke wafted from the joint of flesh and metal. Blisters rose, filling with fluid. Her fangs pierced her lower lip, and the taste of copper washed her mouth.

'Almost there,' Zafir encouraged. 'That's my girl.'

Killing him might ease the pain. She was no one's gir—

Daggers dug into the stump of her wrist, grinding through the muscle and burrowing into her bone. She cursed loudly. Then cursed again. And just as she was about to shove the fingers of her good hand into his chest and rip out his heart, the pain subsided to a dull throb.

She yanked her arm away from him. 'Do you have any idea how badly that—'

He laughed triumphantly and pointed. 'How do you like it?'

She followed the line of his gaze to the platinum fist at the end of her arm. She willed the hand to open. It did. She wiggled the fingers – her fingers – and the bright platinum digits waved back. She leaped off the table, pain forgotten.

'Oh, Zafir, this is brilliant.' She stared at her reflection in the palm of her hand. Pain always seemed to make her more beautiful.

He grinned at her words, showing off his fangs. Something about the contrast of those long, white teeth against his dark skin gave her a perverse thrill. He was a handsome devil. *Devil* being the operative word. 'There's more.'

'Such as?'

He threaded his arms around her waist, turning her back against his chest. He nuzzled his mouth, cool from not feeding, into the curve of her neck. 'Think *sword*, my lush wonder.'

'Sword?'

'Yes. A wicked scimitar or a deadly katana. Whatever you like.' His fangs scraped her skin, and she shivered with pleasure.

'Very well.' She thought of the hefty two-handed blade her former husband, Malkolm, had once wielded in his mortal occupation as a headsman. She'd always admired that weapon. She should have used it on him. She sniffed. Now was not the time for burdens of the past. She focused on the image in her head.

Tingles of sensation shot up her arm from her new hand. She held it up toward the light. What was happening? The tingles became pressure and her fingers fused together.

She inhaled, the bitter air of Zafir's laboratory clogging her throat. 'What the—'

'Just wait,' he urged. His grip tightened, as if he thought she might bolt. Or turn on him. Wise boy.

Her fingers melted into a solid shaft as they elongated into a polished knife, then longer still until the blade replicated the image in her head.

'Unholy hell.' She went utterly still, very aware that her mouth hung open.

He laughed softly, sending vibrations through her skin. 'You should not doubt me in the future, my sweet.' His hands slipped lower, only to climb again once he'd breached the hem of her blouse.

She pushed him away with her elbows and broke out of the embrace, all without taking her gaze off the sword extending out from her wrist. She slashed it through the air. Perfectly weighted. 'Bloody amazing. How is this even possible?'

'Does a magician tell his secrets?' He shrugged. 'Of course, such magic comes with a price.'

The blade glinted like sunlit water, but she managed to pull her gaze away to stare him down. 'We discussed no price.'

He whispered something in Arabic as he pulled her into his arms again. The sword shrank back to a hand.

She arched a brow, warm tendrils of suspicion growing along her spine. 'How did you do that?'

'I am not a fool.' He kissed her cheekbone.

Neither was she. The fact that he'd built in his own controls angered her beyond the point of reason. Red tinged her vision. Had Lord Ivan put him up to this? If so, they both deserved to die. No one dictated what she did. No one. 'What is this price you speak of?'

'The only payment I require is more of what you've already been paying me.' He cupped her body against the hard lines of his own. 'If Nasir could see me now, he would be very jealous indeed.'

Barely restraining the urge to tear his throat out, she tipped her head back to let him kiss her neck. How dare he think to control her? 'Does Nasir know what you've done for me?' She'd insisted their relationship remain a secret, telling him she wasn't ready to be scrutinized by the rest of the nobility until her hand was restored.

'Mmm,' he hummed against her skin. 'And give him a chance to tell me how I should be doing things? *Laa*, my darling, I've kept you for myself.'

'Good.' In that much, Lord Ivan's assessment had been correct. Her metal fingers stroked Zafir's chest, drawing circles over his unbeating heart. 'There's something you should know about me.'

'What's that?' His hands strayed to her rib cage.

She straightened. 'No one controls me.' She'd had no control of her life as a mortal and had fought too hard to wrest control of her vampire life to have it taken from her now, no matter how small a thing it might be.

His face stayed buried against her neck, his mouth hungry on her skin. 'Of course not, my precious.'

'Remove the controls you built in.'

He laughed. 'You think I'm a fool? To give you such power freely? No.'

She threaded her fingers into his hair and jerked his head back to look him in the face. 'Bad decision.' Her metal fingers stilled, pressing against his chest. She whispered, 'Sword.'

Zafir's eyes shot wide as the blade pierced him. He jerked once, then disintegrated into a small heap of ash.

Tatiana turned the sword back into a hand and shook her head at the sooty pile on the laboratory floor. 'Let's hope your brother's not as stupid.' She liked intelligence in her male companions, but not so much that their ambitions ran roughshod over hers. She needed devotion, not competition.

She tipped over a few Bunsen burners, staying long enough to be certain the blaze would devour all traces of her actions. Vampire law stated that killing another noble was an unforgivable crime. She'd come to believe the only real crime was getting caught.

She slipped out the door and pulled up the hood of her cloak, staying in the shadows of the small overhang. This part of

Corvinestri was deserted as far as she could see down the cobblestone streets. Zafir was not a wealthy, high-ranking member of the St. Germain family, and his neighborhood reflected that, something that suited her purposes rather well.

Ensconced in a dark alley, she waited a little while longer until tongues of flames licked the windows. Lights came on in the house next door. Perhaps the stone wall adjoining the two buildings had already grown hot. From her hiding place, she scattered into a cloud of black wasps and resettled herself with great dramatic flair on Zafir's doorstep.

She made a show of knocking. 'Zafir? Zafir, are you home?'

After a moment of restless waiting, she banged on the door. 'Zafir, you must get out!'

Neighbors began to trickle out of their homes.

Satisfied with the amount of witnesses, Tatiana tipped her head back and yelled, 'Fire!'

'I didn't get anything. You?' Mal leaned against the rusted railing of the old freighter. His gaze followed the silver ribbon of moonlight on the water, beyond the other abandoned freighters crowding the decaying port, past the expensive electric lights twinkling on the curve of shoreline where the wealthy mortals lived, and out into the great black sea. Four miles away floated artificial islands sewn with crops of wind generators. The low moan of the turbines hummed just beneath the ever-present drone of the voices in his head.

'N-nothing,' Doc answered, clearing his throat. His black-as-midnight skin wore the sweaty sheen of a creature struggling against his true nature. And losing. 'Not a drop. The butcher on Hibiscus won't sell to me anymore. Says there's too many freaks running around and he doesn't want to get a rep.'

'Bloody hell.' Mal's body clenched with hunger. The voices amped up their whining. *Feed, kill, drink.* He glanced at the leopard shifter. Full moons were difficult on the cursed varcolai. Doc shouldn't have gone for blood, but he'd wanted to run the streets, see if a good sweat could help him shake the powerful urges pulling at his body tonight. By the looks of him, the run had done him as little good as Mal had said it would.

'Been two weeks,' Doc said. He shifted restlessly, his hands trembling like a man fighting withdrawal.

'Seems longer.' Much longer, Mal thought, since he'd had human blood. Comarré blood. *Should've drunk her dry when you had the chance.* And now even pig's blood was getting scarce.

'You could drink what's in the fridge.'

'No.' He couldn't bring himself to drink the blood Chrysabelle had sent, but he couldn't bring himself to dump it either.

'Maybe time to see Dominic. Get some blood from his fake comarré. It's gonna be spendy, but ... ' Doc shrugged, his eyes brassy green-gold, pupils wide open even in the bright moonlight.

'Not yet.' Mal was used to going without. *Weakling.* Dominic was a last resort. Very last. Too many strings. Too much money. Right now, Mal just needed to get Doc through the next few nights. Not being able to shift into his true form made Doc's life hard, except on full-moon nights. Then it was hell.

Mal knew all about that. Hell was his permanent address. Especially since Chrysabelle had failed to fulfill her part of their deal. *Lying, cheating blood whore.* He ground his back teeth together, wishing he could crush the voices as easily.

He'd promised to help her rescue her kidnapped aunt, and she'd promised to get him to the comarré historian to find out how to remove his curse. Maybe in Chrysabelle's mind, a dead aunt negated the deal. He couldn't blame her for being upset, especially since Maris had revealed she was actually Chrysabelle's mother, but Maris's death wasn't his fault. It wasn't enough reason for Chrysabelle to shut him out.

Part of him wished he'd never tasted Chrysabelle's blood. His fangs punched through his gums. A very small part. He nodded at Doc. 'You going to be okay?'

Doc shivered despite the near eighty-degree temp. 'Yeah, bro, I'm tight. I just wish—' A tremor rocked his body.

'I know.'

Doc raised a brow. 'You miss her?'

'Yes.' Mal shifted his gaze back to the ocean. Heat lightning shattered the horizon's edges. Doc's mention of Fiona didn't surprise him. The pair were nuts for each other, despite her being a ghost. She was the last human Mal had killed and, of all the voices in his head, the only one to manifest as a ghost. After the many years she'd been stuck to him, Mal had come to tolerate Fi. More than that really. He'd come to appreciate her company. She alone could temper the beast that rose within him and rein in the voices when they took control.

Unfortunately, she'd been another casualty of their trip to rescue Maris, and Doc had taken her death extremely hard. He still believed she would return, but the space on Mal's left arm where her name had once been written remained bare.

'You should go see her,' Doc said. 'Work things out. You might as well drink the blood she sent. You need it—'

Mal's head whipped back around. 'I meant Fi.'

Doc snorted, scrubbing at his goatee. 'Sure you did.' A halo of sweat crowned his shaved head, and his canines jutted past his lip like two toothy daggers.

'You look like hell.'

'I feel like hell.' Doc closed his eyes, visibly steeling himself. The fangs disappeared and the claws retracted, only to reappear a few seconds later. His half-form wasn't going to cut it tonight. The need to change was too strong due to the full moon's power.

'Stop fighting it. Get below and shift. I'll make sure you don't run.'

Doc's curse meant the only full form he could shift into was a common house cat, and in that state he was highly susceptible to larger predators. Like dogs. And Mal didn't want to nurse him through another incident like the last one.

Doc nodded and headed for the hatch.

Mal turned back to the railing and wiped a hand over his face. The sharp angles and hard contours of his true image only served as a reminder of the monster that lived inside him. The monster that needed to be fed. Soon. *Kill, drink, eat, blood.*

The scent of jasmine and spice rose up behind him. He spun around. 'What are you doing here?'

Katsumi bowed slightly from the hips, palms together before her. 'Lovely to see you, too, Malkolm.'

'If you're here, you want something. What is it?' He was too hungry to deal with anyone, especially this fringe. The former wife of a Yakuza crime boss, Katsumi had the missing pinkie and full-body tattoos to prove it. She'd been turned in the 1980s, and her cutthroat style had earned her a serious reputation. If Katsumi had been nobility, she could have given Tatiana some healthy competition for vilest vampiress of the century. Now she worked at Dominic's nightclub, Seven. In what capacity, Mal had yet to fully determine.

Katsumi gave a little half smile. 'So cranky when you're underfed. Which seems to be all the time. Right to it, then. I've come to offer you blood.'

His muscles tightened painfully and the beast inside tugged at the bonds keeping it prisoner. *Take, drink, kill.* 'Go on.'

Her almond eyes twinkled with devious intent. 'I'll provide you with all the blood you need. And by the looks of you, that's not a small amount. On one condition.'

'Just one? You're getting soft in your old age.'

She laughed and adjusted the cuffs of her high-necked dress. Katsumi's ink bodysuit was widely known but rarely seen. 'Is that what's happened to you, my dear noble friend?'

'We've never been friends. What's the condition?'

She slunk closer. Her perfume had none of the sweetness of Chrysabelle's. 'I want you to fight for me again—'

'No.' Under no circumstances would he enter the Pits again. *Yes. Fight, kill.*

'No one has to know.' She lifted her hand toward his face, then obviously thought better of it. 'You can wear a mask, if you like.'

'A mask isn't going to hide what I become.' *Monster, killer, murderer.*

The light in her eyes brightened. 'Then own it. Use it. You've had more human blood in the last few weeks than you've had in the past fifty years. You're stronger than ever. You could win now, win your way back to a place where you can afford to buy whatever blood you need.'

'You mean back to a place where you can profit off me again.' Back in the day, Katsumi had made mountains of yén from Mal's fights. So much that she'd shared some of her take with him. Just enough to buy blood from the butcher. Just enough to keep him in fighting shape. But with Fi inside him, keeping the beast from rising, he'd lost most fights. Which was fine. No one needed to see that part of him. Losing had done nothing to diminish the crowd's desire to gawk at the marked anathema.

'Not again. Not ever. Besides, I don't need your money.' There was plenty of that left over from the sale of the diamond Chrysabelle had given to Doc. Not that Mal had touched that money for anything yet. Or wanted to.

Greed soured her smile. 'But there is something you need. What the comarré promised but didn't deliver.'

'How do you know about that?'

'Dominic doesn't keep many secrets from me.' She cocked her head to one side like a hawk staring down a fat, dumb rabbit. 'So would you fight for the chance to speak to the comarré historian? To finally find a way to end your curse?'

Ice burrowed into his spine and froze him in place. 'You can't offer that.'

'Oh, Malkolm-san, but I can. Dominic knows how to access the one you seek. Fight for me and I will persuade him to show you the way.'

'You can't promise that.' *She lies, lies, lies . . .*

'I can and I do.'

'You give your word?' Katsumi's word wasn't worth squat, but a chance was a chance.

'Yes.'

Fool. He hated himself. So what was new? 'When?'

'Tomorrow night at Seven.'

'I'm not waiting in the holding cells.' Never again.

'And spoil the surprise of your presence? I wouldn't dream of it.' She blinked like she was shocked he'd even suggest it. 'You'll have a room of your own.'

He still didn't trust her. 'How do I know you won't go back on your word?'

'I've broken only one promise in my life.' She held up the hand with the missing pinkie. 'Once was enough.'

Chapter Two

'You will not fail again.' Lord Ivan paced across the hand-knotted Turkish carpet in Tatiana's sitting room. 'You cannot. I know how difficult the task before us may be, but the ancient ones care little for our troubles.'

'I understand that, Lord Ivan.' Tatiana rose from the velvet upholstered chair as she watched him. Ivan was her sire, the Dominus of her family and the last obstacle between her and the power she craved. The House of Tepes had done well under Ivan's rule, but her plans would raise it to levels not known since Vlad Tepes himself had held the title. Before she could do that, she needed to be back in the graces of the ancient ones. That meant possessing the ring of sorrows at the very least. Pleasing the Castus Sanguis was a slippery, dangerous, painful slope, but she'd traversed it before and would do so again if need be. 'I would also point out that I did succeed in breaking the covenant. Surely some credit must be given for that.'

He waved one heavily jeweled hand in the air. 'Yes, of course, but without the ring's power, we are vulnerable. We must be invincible. Unstoppable. No matter what the sacrifice, we must have the ring. The power it unleashes . . . ' He shook his head and turned back the way he'd come. 'The ancient one assures me it is great.'

'Have I given any indication I am unwilling to sacrifice?' She lifted her arm, causing the sleeve of her ivory silk blouse to fall back from her wrist and reveal the metal hand that had replaced her missing one.

He paused, his gaze darting to her new appendage. The gilded mantel clock ticked toward midnight. His mouth softened. 'No, my pet, you have been perfect. As willing as I could have hoped for.' He smiled. 'As I knew from the start you would be.' He drew to her side, pulled her against him, and kissed the hard, scabbed joining of metal and flesh. 'Why else would I have given you the gift of navitas?'

Beneath her calm expression, she seethed. He may have given her navitas, the ritual in which a vampire was bitten by a different sire so they might take on that vampire's lineage, but the pain from the process had been hers alone to bear. 'One might say you offered it to me because I not only shared your ambitions, but because I also have the wherewithal to accomplish whatever might be necessary to realize those ambitions.'

Lines of irritation bracketed his mouth. His hands tightened painfully on her hips and he leaned in as silver tarnished his pupils. 'Calling your sire weak is rash, even for you, gypsy.'

She hated that name and all it reminded her of, but she robbed him of that satisfaction and smiled sweetly instead. 'I would never call you weak, my lord.' She stroked his cheek with her flesh hand. 'Would I have accepted your offer if I hadn't seen how strong and capable a leader you are?' Her palm trailed down to his chest, her fingers sliding beneath the placket of his shirt to caress his hard, muscled chest. 'Of course not, my lord.'

'Good.' The silver in his gaze diminished and a guarded smile returned to his mouth. He lifted her right arm and squinted at the metal prosthesis. 'Otherwise, I might find it necessary to remove the gift I procured for you.' He dropped her arm. 'I assured you I would find someone to fix what had been done to you without anyone else knowing. There was no need to kill Zafir.'

'I didn't kill him, my lord,' she lied, knowing he meant to catch her. 'As I told you, he made unwelcome advances. I pushed him away and a lamp broke. I was lucky to escape that fire myself.'

He eyed her suspiciously. 'And what of your missing hand? Any luck finding that yet?'

'No.' She and Octavian had searched every centimeter of the room where the comarré whore had cut off her hand and every possible escape route but had found nothing. She could only assume the girl had taken it. Or perhaps Malkolm had – but she'd never imagined her former husband the sentimental type. 'Do you think she'll use it against me?'

'It's not her I worry about but her friends. They are an unsavory lot.' His smile came fully alive and he lifted her chin with his fingers, kissed her firmly, then shook his head. 'The path ahead will not be an easy one.'

Was anything she'd done for him? Or anything in her life for that matter? She caressed the Tepes star that dangled from a thick gold chain around his neck. She could see herself in the bold ruby square at its center, a beast of a gem compared to the chip that decorated her locket. 'Nothing worth having ever is.'

He laughed. 'That's my Tatiana. Not afraid of anything, are you, love?'

'No. Nothing.' Nothing he'd ever find out about. Nothing that would ever happen again. She forced a smile as the dulcet tones of Sofia's little-girl laugh echoed in her memory. 'Shall we discuss your plan of action?'

He slipped his arm around her waist and led her toward the door. She knew instantly what he wanted. Since Mikkel's death, Ivan had become exceedingly amorous. If he hoped to woo her as a means to keep her loyal, he was dead wrong. 'Yes, but not just now.' His fangs extended, his face shedding its humanity to reveal his true visage. 'It will make for wonderful pillow talk afterward, I assure you.'

'I look forward to it, my lord.' She laughed, fluttering her lashes, leaning into him and savoring the moment she'd be able to walk over his ashes on the way toward leading the vampire nation into a new age of domination.

Sweaty and miserable, Doc stumbled into the hold that had been modified into a gym and collapsed to his hands and knees on the mats. He gave in and quit fighting the inevitable. By now, the need to mentally command his body to change was gone. Instinct took over and a moment later he found release in his animal form. If you could call the pitiful house cat that was his only option a true form. It wasn't. Not to him. Or any other straight-up shifter.

Never would be either. Even if he had to live with this hellacious curse for the rest of his unnatural life.

He sprawled on his side, panting with the effort of holding off the shift for so long. He lifted a paw. The claws were tiny pinpoints. He hated this form. Just like he hated that for at least one night a month, he had to assume the shape of a creature so small and lame compared to his true self.

Varcolai were not humans born with the ability to shift into animal forms; they were animals born with the ability to take on human shape. Being Doc the human wasn't any more difficult than breathing, and it was a damn sight less humiliating than walking around looking like a house pet. Except when nature sank her full-moon teeth deep and reminded him what he really was under that smooth, vulnerable skin.

Then being human became virtually impossible. So he gave in, shifted to his lesser form and hid from the world.

His pride leader, Sinjin, had cast him out as soon as Doc had told him about the curse. What good was a house cat to a pride of big cats? His cursed form wasn't the only reason Sinjin had ordered the pride to shun him. He closed his eyes against the truth, but that didn't stop it from staring back at him.

There was the little matter of what he'd done to get cursed. He'd dealt in certain pharmaceuticals. Not street drugs, but the kind of amped-up concoctions that othernaturals paid big for. Really big. Hell, that kind of scratch let a player make the rules of the game. But with big rewards came big risk. He'd known that.

Just like he'd known the risk in working for Sinjin's enemy.

With good reason, Sinjin had a major beef with Dominic – owner of the nightclub Seven, powerful alchemist, and New Florida's leading drug lord. Sinjin had owned Seven long before Dominic had come to town, back when the club had been a broken-down scum hole of a joint, but then Sinjin lost the building and the business to Dominic in a poker game. To this day, Sinjin swore Dominic had used his alchemy to win. Dominic denied it, of course, but that hadn't stopped Sinjin from declaring Seven off-limits to the pride. Anyone who went there was subject to pride law.

The other major varcolai clan in Paradise City, the wolf pack, were under no such orders. Their members worked at Seven and benefited from the cash and perks Dominic freely doled out. Doc wondered if it wasn't the anathema's way of punishing Sinjin and his pride a little more.

Damn vampires. Doc hissed because he couldn't curse, but the anger leaked out of him like air from a punctured tire. He might hate Dominic, but he didn't feel that way about Mal. As screwed up as Mal was, he'd saved Doc's life. Brought his torn and broken body home and given him to Fi, who'd nursed him back to health after a pack of street dogs had treated him like a chew toy. Sure, Fi had thought he was her new pet, but once they'd gotten past that little surprise … He bent his head in grief. Cripes, he missed her. If he'd been able to go leopard, he might have saved her life.

Evie, the witch he'd sold the juice to, was to blame. If she hadn't insisted on testing the goods before he split, none of this would have happened. How was he supposed to know Dominic's drugs would turn her to stone? How was that his fault? Talk about killing the messenger. He lifted his back foot to scratch behind his ear.

If only he'd rolled out of there before Aliza, Evie's mother, had figured out what went down. If only, if only, if only …

Damn that albino freak and her whacked-out daughter.

He rolled over and stretched. House cat or not, it felt good to be in animal form. He yawned. He should find a spot to curl up in and sleep until the sun rose.

The stitching along the edge of the mat was frayed, leaving a tail of string right out in the open. He looked over his shoulder. Not like anyone was around anyway.

Satisfied, he bounced to his feet and swatted at it, then sat back on his haunches. This body came with some damn foolish urges, that was for sure.

A small, dark streak sped through the corner of his vision. The musky, meaty smell of rat filled his nostrils. The quivering anticipation of the hunt ran through him hot and electric. *Hell, why fight it?* With a soft chirp of anticipation, he was on his feet and moving.

The rat darted out into the narrow corridor. Even without the overhead solars, Doc's night vision was on point. He chased after the rodent, eager, hungry, saliva pooling for the kill.

Passageways and stairs disappeared beneath Doc's padded feet. Whiskers brushed metal as he rounded corners and ducked pipes. All that mattered was the long-tailed meal and where it went next.

The passageway ahead angled through the heart of the freighter and into the belly of the main hold. The solars grew weaker, dimming as the game took him in deeper. Squealing, the rat slipped between a couple empty boxcars, two of many that formed a maze through the ship's gut.

Doc pursued, turning the corner so sharply his ribs grazed the hard edge of the first container. He barreled through, the scent tangible on his tongue, the kill moments away. He exploded out into the open and skidded to a dead stop. The sight on the other side erased all thoughts of the rat and the hunt.

A familiar shape walked among the boxcars. Long dark hair, backpack tucked over her shoulders, flashlight in hand. What little light there was passed through her translucent form.

Numb recognition froze Doc.

The circle of her flashlight beam pinpointed something. She walked toward it, stared at it for a moment, then nudged it with her foot.

In a flash, a thin, dark shape lunged up and grabbed her. Her mouth opened in a silent scream. The flashlight tumbled from her hand and landed with the beam pointed at her. The shape was human, bones with a little skin stretched over them. It clung to her. Fangs, white in the flashlight's beam, tore into her throat. Blood spattered, soaking the front of her sweatshirt. The creature gorged itself as the fight drained out of the girl's body. Her fists stopped battering. Her feet stopped kicking.

The creature raised its face and stared with cloudy eyes into the light. A remnant of flesh hung from its scrawny jaw.

The creature was Malkolm. The girl was Fiona.

The image flickered and disappeared.

Chapter Three

Chrysabelle smiled with the satisfaction of another day well spent and a new night well begun. Nothing like a long, hot shower after an intense day of training. She tucked her damp hair behind her ears and pulled her white terry robe closer. It would be a long time before she broke the habit of wearing white, but why should she? It was as natural for a comarré as breathing.

The delicious smell of whatever Velimai was making in the kitchen wafted up from the first floor. Chrysabelle leaned on the countertop and stared into the bathroom mirror. Every day, every night the same. She'd wake up, train, shower, eat dinner, and read Maris's journals, looking for an advantage against Tatiana. She was in a rut. Did it matter? She was happy. Mostly. Free to do what she wanted. At least until Tatiana came knocking again. Unless Chrysabelle got to her first. But that would take planning, and so far, she'd yet to come up with anything.

She sighed as the niggling reminder of Mal's unpaid debt wormed through her consciousness again. Something else to be dealt with in time. Not now, but soon. She reached for one of

Maris's journals and carried it downstairs to read until dinner was ready.

This journal dealt with the time leading up to Maris's decision to claim libertas, the comarré ritual in which a comarré might fight her patron for her freedom. If the comarré lost, the patron was granted a new comarré. If the comarré won, she went free. Either way, the loser ended up dead.

Maris had won, but the ritual had left her crippled, unable to walk until years of secret rehabilitation enabled her to regain some mobility. It had also freed her from her patron and allowed her and Dominic, her vampire lover, to leave the noble realm and live a somewhat normal life. At least until Maris had left Dominic. Why she'd done that, Chrysabelle had yet to uncover.

Maris had been exceptional at keeping secrets. Even Dominic hadn't known that she'd regained her ability to walk over the years. In the end, that secret had made it possible for her to kill Chrysabelle's patron and escape without detection, all in an effort to free Chrysabelle so she might live a life beyond the servitude of the comarré world, something Chrysabelle had long wanted.

Maris had gotten her wish. But at what price? Even Dominic had paid highly. His noble family, the house of St. Germain, had declared him anathema for loving the comarré of one of his peers and causing that comarré to claim libertas, during which her patron had been killed. The council had blamed him for the patron's death. And although killing another vampire was an unforgivable sin, he had escaped with his life because he had only been the cause and hadn't actually dealt the killing blow. Not that Dominic was suffering now.

His nightclub, Seven, seemed to be doing very well. The man wore expensive suits, had his own plane. Once a week, he laid a blanket of white roses on Maris's grave. And he might indulge in some things that were not exactly above board, but Chrysabelle couldn't help but feel some affection for the man who still obviously loved her mother.

She returned to the journal but had read only a few pages when the intercom chimed twice, indicating the guard at the main gates was calling.

Velimai came out from the kitchen, wiping her hands on a towel. She threw it over her shoulder and signed, *Are you expecting someone?*

'No, but that's okay. I'll get it.' Chrysabelle got up to answer the intercom. 'Yes?'

'Ms. Lapointe, there is a visitor here, but they're not on your list. Should I let them in?'

'Who is it?'

After a brief pause, the guard responded. 'He says he works for Mr. Scarnato and has a message from him.'

She chewed her bottom lip. If someone meant her harm, why would they bother stopping at the guard shack? Why not find another way in? Although using Dominic's name was a pretty good ruse. 'He's alone?'

'Yes, ma'am.'

'Let him through.'

'Very good, ma'am.'

She checked the closed-circuit monitor that showed the gates into the property. Those gates had to be opened manually, which would give her time to react if whoever was in that vehicle was up to something. Instinctively, she felt for her wrist blades, but she wasn't in the habit of rearming herself once she'd gotten ready for bed. Perhaps that would have to change. She turned. 'Velimai, could you get my—'

Velimai stood behind her, Chrysabelle's sacre in her upraised hands.

'Sword.' Smiling, Chrysabelle took the weapon, careful not to touch the wysper's sandpaper skin. 'Thanks.'

Should I get Maris's sacre as well? she signed.

'No. I plan on keeping her rule of no vampires in the house, so whoever this is won't be coming in.' She slipped her arm through the red leather strap on the sheath and hung the sacre over her shoulder. 'Assuming it's a vamp.'

Good, Velimai signed. *I'll be in the kitchen. Call if you need me.*

'Will do.'

As Velimai headed into the other room, Chrysabelle turned back to the monitor. A sleek black car stopped outside the gates. The window tinting prevented seeing into the vehicle, but the driver put the window down and leaned out, presumably to let her get a good look at him. She recognized him as one of the fringe vamps who had piloted Dominic's plane to Corvinestri on the trip to save Maris. What was his name? Leo? Yes, that was it.

He pressed the intercom button. 'Evening, Ms. Lapointe. I'm alone.'

She leaned on the wall and pushed the button to be heard. 'Good evening, Leo. Get out of the car and walk in. I'll buzz the pedestrian gate.'

He gave a thumbs-up, got out of the car, and walked to the left where a smaller gate allowed pedestrians to come and go.

She punched the buzzer. He pushed through and headed toward the house. She kept tabs on him via the monitor on his way to the front door. She opened it before he could knock.

'Here you are.' Leo handed her a sealed envelope.

She took it. 'Be right back.'

'I'll just stay here.' He backed away but stayed within the pale glow cast by the entrance lights.

Yes, she thought, *you will.* She shut the door and ran her nail beneath the seal. It occurred to her as she read the note within that she had no way of knowing if the handwriting belonged to Dominic or not.

Buonasera, dearest Chrysabelle,

I am sorry to approach you this way, but I find the events of the past few weeks have weakened me more than I anticipated. My heart seems incapable of healing, and my body has followed suit. Please, bella, it shames me to ask, but if you could provide me with the nourishment to return to my full strength, I would consider it a great boon and be indebted to you for my eternity. I know well the value of what you can provide, so if you are not so inclined, I understand and hold no ill will.

Ciao,
Dominic Scarnato

She stared at the note. Then read it again. It meant exactly what she thought it did. Dominic wanted blood. Her blood. Well, what he wanted was comarré blood. She couldn't blame him. Comarré blood meant power and strength unlike anything human blood could provide. Dominic had been through so much and had done so much for her. After they'd returned from Corvinestri, he'd sent his cypher fae, Solomon, to the house to prepare a special ward to erase the house's location from

Tatiana's memory. How he'd done that exactly, she didn't know, but Dominic's alchemy was strong. He was a good man at heart. She would give him the blood. After all, Malkolm didn't want it. Maybe she could even get Dominic to go with her to fight Tatiana. No doubt he wanted her dead as much as Chrysabelle.

The sacre no longer necessary, she unhooked the sword from her shoulder and rested it against one of the large Oriental vases flanking the foyer entrance. She opened the door. 'I'll be right back with a package for Dominic.'

The fringe nodded. 'Very good.'

She went to the kitchen and placed two containers of blood from the fridge into the cryopack she'd previously used to send blood to Mal. He'd sent the pack back empty, but she knew full well he hadn't drunk the blood. Fine. He could be a child. She wasn't going to allow herself to revisit the hurt she'd felt over his rejection. Wasn't going to dwell on the fact that comarré rule held such a rejection to be akin to human divorce. Now Dominic would benefit from what she had to offer. Better than it going to waste. Of course, if Mal did still hold her blood rights, giving blood to another vampire was ... very wrong, to put it plainly. She shoved down the proper comarré thoughts and did her best to ignore the nagging urges of her past.

Part of her – the small, feminine, rebellious part of her that had begun to strengthen these last few weeks – even hoped Mal found out. Maybe it would spur him to action.

She returned and handed the cooler to Leo. 'Tell Dominic I hope he's well, and I'll speak to him soon.'

'Will do.' The fringe nodded, fidgeting a bit, then walked back toward the car.

She shut the door and returned to the journal she'd set aside. An hour into reading, her gaze caught on a sentence.

And so, I had found a way to the Aurelian outside ordinary means.

Chrysabelle read the sentence again. And again. Then she read further, devouring the information. To think, all this time . . .

Journal in hand, she ran upstairs to her suite, skidding down the marble-tiled halls. Before her angled dressing room mirrors, she dropped her robe, turned halfway, and lifted her hair to study the gold markings covering her back. Her signum shone like living stars, glittering and moving with each breath she took.

Holy mother, if what Maris said was true, there was no need to return to Corvinestri to get to the comarré historian.

At last she could tell Mal she was ready to pay her share of the debt and take him to the Aurelian, the one person who might know how to break his curse. The way was written on her skin.

Doc shivered in the freighter's murky hold. Not because of the dark or because of the need to change coursing through his body on this second night of the full moon, but because of the fear that Fiona wouldn't show again. And that if she did, he wouldn't be able to help her.

Of all the hard realizations of his life, the most recent had come to him last night as he lay in bed replaying over and over the ethereal scene he'd witnessed.

He loved Fiona. He'd never said it out loud, but it was the straight-up truth. No one had ever got him the way she had. So what if she was human? Or a ghost. He didn't care. He just wanted her back.

And so he fought the change that had bested him last night, because he needed to speak to her, and holding on to that ability meant holding on to his human shape. If he had to stand here all night, dripping sweat and shaking with the effort, he would.

He didn't have to.

A soft flicker of white broke the darkness up ahead. Doc strained to see, his varcolai eyes catching every stray mote of light. A shape emerged. A girl with a flashlight and a backpack and the most beautiful face Doc had ever seen.

He positioned himself in the beam of light. 'Fiona, it's me, Doc. Can you hear me?'

She faltered, her translucent brows furrowing. She glanced over her shoulder.

Doc waved his arms. 'Right here, Fi. I'm right here.'

She spun her flashlight around. 'Is there someone here?'

'Yeah, me. Doc. Maddoc.' He moved closer. She had to hear him. Then maybe she could tell him how to help her.

Her gaze hesitated on him. Then her eyes widened in what he could only hope was recognition. 'I know you.'

Relief swept through him so quickly he almost shifted right then. 'Yeah, baby, it's me ... Doc. The leopard-shifter. I live here' – he spread his arms wide to indicate the freighter – 'with you and Mal, the vampire. Or you used to live here, until ...' Maybe he shouldn't tell her she'd died a second time.

She laughed. 'Leopard-shifter? Vampire? That's silly. There are no such things as vamp—'

A thin, dark shape lunged up out of the tangible blackness surrounding her and grabbed hold.

Mal. The scene from last night was repeating itself.

Her mouth opened in a piercing scream. The flashlight tumbled from her hand and landed with the beam pointed at her.

'No!' Doc shouted. He reached for her, but his hand passed through her like she was nothing more than a dream.

Not a dream. A nightmare. Last night's gruesome scene replayed in hellish detail.

Mal was almost a skeleton. Just bones with a little skin stretched over them. He clung to Fi and sank his fangs into her throat, tearing the flesh like paper. Blood gushed down the front of her college sweatshirt. He gorged himself as the fight drained out of her body. Her fists flew against him, their pummeling turning into weak flutters. Her feet twitched on the stone floor of the nightmare's ruins.

Helplessness made Doc's hands tremble. Mal raised his head and stared through him with hazy eyes. A remnant of flesh hung from Mal's emaciated jaw. Once again, Fi lay dead at his feet.

Doc dropped to his knees and tried vainly to reach her a second time. Her image flickered around his hand and then she and Mal were gone.

Exhausted by the effort of holding off the change, Doc slumped forward and shifted instantly.

In cat form, he panted, grieving, until sleep crept over him.

A woman's voice calling his name woke him up. Fi? He wasn't sure. He opened his mouth to respond, but all that came out was a meow. The change was too fully seated for him to shift back to human now. He must have been asleep for only an hour or two. He shook himself and ran toward the voice.

Again, the female voice called out for him. Then for Mal.

It wasn't Fi. It was Chrysabelle.

He bounded up the stairs as she continued to call out. He ran down the passageway toward her, but the hatch ahead of him was shut. There was no way he could open it without hands. He cried loudly and scratched at the door.

'Doc? Is that you?'

He meowed in answer.

The door opened and Chrysabelle walked through. 'Why are you locked in here? Where's Mal?'

He rubbed against her legs, unable to help himself. She kneeled down and scratched behind his ears. Man, that felt good. A soft grumbling vibrated from his chest.

The scratching stopped when she stood up. 'Can you take human form? This is very important. I need to talk to Mal.'

Yes and no questions he could handle. And if he was locked in, he assumed Mal had done that because he'd gone out. Doc sat on his haunches and shook his head slowly.

'No human form?' She frowned. 'Do you know where Mal is?'

Again he shook his head.

'Great.' She sighed. 'Just when I think I can help him, too.' She reached down to scratch his neck again. 'Are you supposed to stay inside until you can shift back?'

This time he nodded, even though the thought of running through the docks suddenly seemed like a very good one. There were rats out there the size of small cars. Why was he supposed to stay in?

'When Mal gets back, can you remember to tell him I was here? If he comes home soon, tell him I went to Seven to see Dominic. Maybe he can catch me there.'

Doc hissed.

She held up her hands. 'Sorry, I know you and Dominic have a bad history. Just remember to tell Mal I was here and that . . . that . . . Oh rats, just tell him we need to talk.' She gave him a little wave and shut the door.

Doc stared at the closed hatch and meowed. What had the human said about rats? His stomach reminded him that food was a good idea.

He took off toward the galley. Rats liked the galley. And really, what else mattered besides the hunt?

Chapter Four

'I am deeply sorry about your brother, Nasir.' Tatiana dug the tip of her tongue into one fang until tears came to her eyes. 'So very sorry. I didn't know him that well, but as any valued, upstanding member of the House of St. Germain, he will be missed by all of us.'

Nasir snorted and muttered something in Arabic. 'Really? Missed by all of you? The line of St. Germain is hardly given much respect by the other houses.'

'I have a great deal of respect for the abilities of your house.' She pulled the glove off her metal hand and flexed her fingers. 'What your brother did for me …' She swallowed as though overcome with emotion and hoped that revealing her imperfection would gain her some sympathy. Otherwise Nasir would be reunited with his brother sooner than expected. 'I will be forever in his debt. Your brother was exceptionally talented.'

'He was.' Nasir nodded, all traces of umbrage gone from his face. 'Your sympathies are greatly appreciated.'

'As the Elder of the House of Tepes, it is the very least I can do.' Tatiana smiled softly and took Nasir's hand in hers. 'The very least.' Amazingly, she could actually feel the sensation of his fingers against her metal ones.

She studied the vampire across from her. Nasir was quite possibly more beautiful than his late brother. But could he match Zafir's talents?

Nasir squeezed her hand tighter. 'I still can't believe he's gone. Almost two hundred years we've been together.' He swallowed and stared past her like he was remembering. 'I keep imagining him in that fire, what it must have been like ... '

'Now, now, you mustn't torture yourself like that.' Tatiana moved closer, letting her hand slide up his arm, discovering the delicious surprise that Nasir's bulk came not from his clothing but from an abundance of muscle – at least twice what Zafir had carried on his much-leaner frame. A tickle of pleasure tightened the skin across her belly. 'There was nothing anyone could have done. When I arrived, the fire had already engulfed the basement and first floor.'

Fortunately, Nasir had his own house. Unfortunately, it was in the same wretched neighborhood. 'The fire wiped out everything. Did you share a laboratory with your brother?'

He shook his head. 'No, I have my own. Zafir and I were very competitive in our work.'

Well, that was good news. 'You must go on with yours. He would want that.'

Nasir pulled away slightly. 'I don't know that I can.'

She leaned in, allowing the neckline of her gown to fall open. 'I have endured great loss in my life as well, but I have never let it stop me from achieving everything I put my mind to.'

'How?' Dark lashes fringed his eyelids. 'How did you get past it?'

She hadn't. Her hand reached his hard bicep and trailed across his chest to smooth the lapel of his mourning coat. Bloody hell, he was a rock of a man. 'By surrounding myself with things that brought me pleasure. Losing myself in them. Reminding myself how good it felt to be happy.' She tried to remember what innocence looked like, then fixed the memory on her face. 'Perhaps you would let me help you?'

'My lady—'

'Please, call me Tatiana.' Her breasts brushed his forearm. This was almost too easy. She tamped down the urge to giggle.

A flicker of understanding registered in his eyes. 'When you say *help*, are you suggesting ... I mean, I wouldn't want to take advantage—'

'I could use someone with your talents in my employ. Besides, you cannot take advantage of something freely offered.' She flattened her hands on his chest, feeling his body stiffen under her touch. 'Why should two creatures as beautiful as us be alone?' She stuck her bottom lip out a fraction. 'Or do you not find me beautiful?'

'I find you very beautiful. My brother and I often remarked that not another noblewoman in Corvinestri could compare to you.'

'Then kiss me,' she whispered, giddy with the sound of puzzle pieces sliding into place.

He bent his head and did as she asked, filling her with great satisfaction that her charms were very much intact and that men's defenses against women had evolved so little in so many years.

Each minute that ticked by filled Mal's head with another reason why he shouldn't be here, in a place he'd vowed never to re-enter, about to fight for a woman who was only out for herself.

Then he reminded himself that if Katsumi really could get Dominic to help him remove the curse he was under, life could be ... bearable again. The voices howled at that thought. He pushed them down. No matter what happened, he would not let the beast out. *Yes, you will.* He already had a reputation. He didn't need every fringe vamp out to make a name for himself knocking at his door looking to take on the big, bad anathema.

Son of a priest. What was he doing here?

Fighting. He could do that. Had been doing it all his life.

He paced from one side of the small anteroom to the other, every muscle in his body aching to coil and strike, every bone remembering the damage he'd earned in this place. The pain. The humiliation. *Loser.*

He would use those memories. Let them fester until the rage exploded out of him with an unstoppable force. *Kill, kill, kill.* No, he wouldn't kill. No matter how hard the voices pushed. He wouldn't give Katsumi the satisfaction. A kill paid more, but he didn't care about that. All he needed was for his opponent to concede. A fair win. That was enough. *Never.*

Who would Katsumi put up against him? He had a good idea it would be Ronan, the fringe vamp who was Seven's head of security and the one combatant Mal had never beaten, thanks to the weakness produced by inadequate blood supply. Ronan would jump at the chance to fight Mal again, that was certain.

Ronan would be cocky, ready to trounce Mal like he had so many times in the past. Ronan would want to punish Mal for the blade Chrysabelle had sunk into Ronan's shoulder. Nothing worse than being humiliated by a comarré. Not in Ronan's world anyway. But then, all he knew of comarré were the weak imitations Dominic managed to produce.

What would Chrysabelle think if she knew Mal was about to

step into the Pits? Not that he cared what she thought. Not that she cared what he did. She still hadn't tried to contact him. Probably wouldn't either. Now that she was free, why should she? She'd gotten what she wanted. He was anathema. Beneath her.

Wouldn't she have a fit if she knew he'd finally drunk the blood she'd sent over? Not all of it, just two containers' worth. He hadn't seen a way around it. If he fought while weak and lost, what would be the point of fighting? And if he won after drinking her blood and Dominic was able to get the voices out of his head, he'd let Chrysabelle off the hook for helping him, since technically she would have helped already by giving him the strength to win.

Except, if she found out, she would want him to kiss her again. The voices howled. But they had nothing to worry about, because that was not happening. Just like he was not thinking about the softness of her mouth or the sweetness of her—

A sharp rapping on the door interrupted his thoughts.

He leaned against the wall and tucked his hands into the pockets of his leather pants and did his best I'm-so-confident-I-almost-forgot-I-was-here look. 'Come.'

The soft beeps of buttons being pushed on a keypad echoed through the steel door, then the lock snicked open. Katsumi entered and shut the door behind her. Her hair was wound in an elaborate knot and secured with tasseled picks that coordinated with the red and black silks she wore. She looked like she'd already won. 'Are you ready, Malkolm-san?'

'Don't I look ready?' *Ready to lose.*

Her nostrils flared. Could she smell Chrysabelle's blood on him? He doubted fringe could pick up on things like that. 'You look like a man about to change his past.'

'I'm not here to change my past. I'm here to change my future.' He peeled off the wall. 'Let's go.'

'Not so fast.' She reached into her long embroidered coat and extracted a bag of blood. 'A little something to help you.' She tossed it onto the small table beside him. 'From Dominic's best comarré.'

The voices spun into a frenzy. *Drink, drink, drink.* He didn't need the blood after drinking Chrysabelle's, but refusing would make Katsumi suspicious. He grunted in derision. 'Dominic's comarrés are as real as you are noble.'

The reminder of her fringe status earned him a brief flicker of anger. 'Their blood is still better than the average human's.'

'I wouldn't know.'

'Which is exactly why you need to drink it. Or have you reconciled with the daughter of Dominic's former whore?'

He stopped suppressing his anger. His face shifted into the hard angles and sharp lines only nobility could achieve. His fangs extended. 'Use that term for either of those women again and I'll kill you faster than the sun rises on South Beach.'

Katsumi smiled. 'So, you do still care.'

'Leave. I'll be out when I'm done.'

Her brows rose. 'Drink the blood now.'

'You like to watch. Is that it?' He stepped toward her and went for a more menacing tone. 'I'm not here for your entertainment, *ane-san*.' He laced sarcasm into the Yakuza term of respect for *little sister* to remind her how far she'd fallen. 'Get out.'

She crossed her arms. 'No. I won't have you go in there weak. I have a lot of money on this fight. Drink it or you can forget I ever offered to help you.'

He snatched up the bag, sank his fangs into the plastic, and drank. *More, more, more.* The blood was almost sour, like the barely remembered taste of citrus, so different from the complex, drugging sweetness of what ran in Chrysabelle's veins. Or maybe it had just been so long since he'd had human blood that he'd forgotten the taste. Either way, he couldn't understand how Dominic made any money off his fake comarré if this was the best of what they produced.

Finished, he tossed the bag down and waited. There was no rush of power, no sudden jolt of his heart beating with temporary life, no flush of heat. Had there ever been before Chrysabelle's blood? No, not with human blood. No wonder nobility paid any price to own comarré. The blood in their gilded veins was more addictive than any human street drug.

Which made him a junkie. *More.* He exhaled, trying to drive out the rising need, but failed. *More.* The craving to taste her again surged hard within him, as bitter as the aftertaste left by the inferior product coating his tongue. *More.* His skin craved hers, that warm flesh that spun his head and recalled his days in the sun.

'There now,' Katsumi cooed. 'Isn't that better?'

Yes, more blood, more blood now. Hell, no, it wasn't better. All it had done was rouse the voices and remind him of one more woman who'd betrayed him. Mal cracked his knuckles. 'Let's go before I change my mind.'

'Take your shirt off. The cover charge was double tonight and they expect a show.'

Hate was too weak a word for what he felt. He yanked the shirt over his head. 'Happy?'

She eyed him with a hunger that made his inked skin crawl. 'Very.' She pushed the door open and gestured down the hall. The noise of the crowd awaiting the next fight rushed in, filling his head with flashbacks of worse times. 'You know the way.'

He shoved past her. Behind him were the holding cells for all the others who would fight tonight. *And die. Like you.* Ahead of him lay one entrance to the Pits. Through the holding cells and out the other side was another entrance. Right now, whoever he was about to fight was standing there, waiting for the signal to enter and begin.

If that combatant was Ronan, not killing him was going to take every shred of control Mal had. Which wasn't a lot to begin with. The beast rattled its chains in agreement.

He stopped before the woven steel grate that marked his entrance. A weird dizziness spun through his head. He blinked hard to clear away the fog at the corners of his vision. Just phantom feelings of being here before.

'Feeling all right?' Katsumi asked.

He didn't bother making eye contact. 'Perfect.' Control. He needed control. He shifted back to his human face and inhaled. The familiar stench of death – the tang of dried blood and ash – surrounded him. Behind that were traces of silver and stone and the scents of the audience. The voices moaned for more.

'Good luck, then.' Her footsteps faded as she walked away, replaced by the muted announcement on the other side of the door. A thin, tinny resonance underlay everything he heard. He shook his head to clear it, but it clung to every sound.

'Ladies and gentlemen, the fight you've been waiting for is about to begin.'

A loud cheer went up. He could practically hear money changing hands.

'Fringe versus noble in a fight to the death.'

So definitely Ronan, then. The crowd was going to be disappointed when it ended clean.

'And now, without further ado . . . our combatants!'

The steel grate shot up, leaving faint trails of light behind it. What the ...? He rubbed his eyes before walking into the arena.

A small tremor of panic filled him as his feet crossed familiar ground, but he ignored it. *Time to die, monster.* That was an old feeling from when he'd been weak and desperate for blood. He walked through to a deafening swell of noise. For a moment, it was as if he'd never gotten away from this place. He closed his eyes and focused. This time was different. This time he was strong.

The sharp clang of the other grate rang out from across the pit. He opened his eyes. The sound echoed in his head the way it once had in his dreams. Ronan, also bare-chested, walked through the opposite entrance, raising his arms to the crowd in a foolish display of confidence. Let him parade around like the cock of the walk. His fall would be that much harder. *Drink him to death. Drain him dry.*

Ronan stopped preening long enough to narrow his eyes at Mal. 'I'm not going easy on you this time, old man.'

Mal glanced at the flames shaved into Ronan's close-cropped hair and the gold hoops dangling from his ears. 'Nice hair, Irish. Did you pretty yourself up for me, or did you figure looking like a girl would make losing easier to take?'

Ronan smiled, showing off inferior fangs. 'Blather all you want. I'm going to clatter your arse just like old times.' He leaned in. 'Except this time, I'm going to kill you when I'm done playing.'

'Playing is all you're going to do, whelp.' Mal notched his head from one side to the other, cracking his vertebrae. Another wave of dizziness hit him, and he rolled his shoulders to cover. Chrysabelle's blood suffused him with a strange confidence he'd never felt in this ring before. Maybe that was why he felt so odd, as if he were watching himself from somewhere else. The voices' constant whine muted.

Both entrance grates came crashing down.

The crowd bellowed in anticipation. The stadium setup meant the view was good at any angle, despite the shoulder-to-shoulder attendance. Chains of iron and silver roped off the twenty-foot-wide pit. Silver for vampires and varcolai, iron for fae. Both for remnants if the mixed lineage creatures had unlucky blood.

The announcer continued as he walked around the outside of the ring. 'Tonight in our headline fight, noble Malkolm fights fringe Ronan in a grudge match.' He turned his attention from the audience to the men in the pit. 'Combatants, are you ready?'

Mal nodded. Ronan shot both hands skyward and circled once, like he'd already won. Bloody fool.

'Then let the battle begin!' The announcer chopped his hand through the air.

Mal launched across the arena. A half second later, his shoulder was buried in Ronan's stomach and he was plowing Ronan into the silver chains. The sizzle of skin announced contact.

Ronan shoved Mal away and tore free of the burning metal. He threw a punch, but Mal ducked, speedy with veins full of comarré power.

A wave of vertigo tilted the floor. Mal recovered in time to land a jaw-rattling hit that split Ronan's lip. Blood trickled down his chin before the wound zipped closed.

'First blood,' the announcer sang out to the cheering crowd.

A honey-sweet fragrance filled Mal's senses. The voices shrieked, amping the metallic screech up another hundred decibels. He flinched and froze at the sudden din.

'You bleedin' tool.' Ronan threw a fist that connected with the side of Mal's head.

The punch knocked him to the ground and opened a line of pain across his temple. The crowd noise morphed into a fog of sound that wrapped his head like a wet wool blanket and muffled the voices.

He started to roll to his feet as Ronan's foot shot toward his ribs. 'You'll stay down, if you know what's good for—'

Mal grabbed Ronan's foot and kept rolling, flipping the fringe to the ground and bashing him face-first onto the concrete floor. Ronan lay still.

More blood scent flowed into the air. Sweet. Familiar. Very much like the smell of ... of what? Mal's head felt fuzzy and useless. Like his brain had been soaked in whiskey. Or worse.

A needle of clarity pricked through the muzziness. The blood Katsumi had forced him to drink had been tainted. With what, he didn't know, but if not for Chrysabelle's blood, he'd probably be Ronan's punching bag right now.

Chrysabelle. *Chrysabelle.*

Mal stumbled to his knees. Everything wore a second shadowy image. Saliva pooled in his mouth with a sudden bout of nausea. Katsumi's drugs were starting to win. He had to figure this out before he keeled over. Concentrating, he flipped Ronan onto his back. Blood gushed from the man's busted nose and covered his forehead where the skin had broken. Head wounds always bled like crazy. Ronan moaned and lifted his head, his eyes fluttering open. Mal slugged him again, cracking his skull against the concrete a second time. Ronan stilled.

Mal swiped his knuckle through the blood on Ronan's forehead and tasted it.

Recognition punched him in the gut. He fell back on his heels, staring at the smudge of red on his skin.

Ronan had comarré blood in his system. Real comarré blood, not the excrement Dominic passed off in his club. And there was only one real comarré in Paradise City. Mal licked his lips for a second taste, just to be sure. He'd been right the first time. He knew that blood, because he'd had some himself before coming to Seven.

Rage ignited within him, grain alcohol poured on a spark. The beast roared and Mal leaped onto Ronan. Without Fi, there was no one to help him control the snarling, desperate creature trying to break free. She'd kept the beast at bay for so long but now she was gone. Suddenly, Mal didn't care that the beast raged wild. He opened himself to it, welcoming the assured destruction the beast would bring.

Because for whatever foul deed Ronan had enacted upon Chrysabelle to get her blood, he was about to die.

Chapter Five

With a set of sacres strapped to her back and an assortment of other blades hidden about her person, Chrysabelle approached the public entrance to Seven, having already decided to go past it and enter through a side door. The pair of varcolai wolf-shifters who guarded the club's front entrance were still sore about Mal persuading them to let her in fully armed the last time. Beyond that, Seven was starting to get a reputation among humans as the place to go to see real live vampires – at least among those who believed in vampires, like the typical habitués of Puncture, the strictly human nightclub for those who *wished* they were vampires. That place was probably losing money since most of their clientele now hung out in front of Seven.

Humans were not always the smartest of species. Well, some of them weren't anyway.

The idealized, romanticized, Hollywood vampire who was going to offer them life eternal was a myth. Vampires, fringe and noble alike, had two uses for humans: servants and food. Not always in that order. And while some fringe were more tolerant, that could soon change with the covenant gone. It wasn't a coincidence that the city's murder rate had already begun to rise.

She shook her head as she lingered at the opening to the alley leading to Seven's main entrance. A Gothic-looking crowd of humans hovered as closely as the newly installed velvet ropes would allow. Well away from the main group, a few picketers carried antivampire signs. The wolf bouncers stared straight ahead as if the crowd didn't exist, except for an occasional snarl when one got too close.

A car drove up from the opposite direction and stopped. A well-dressed fringe couple got out. The crowd rolled toward them in a wave. Wrists were offered up amid cries of 'Bite me!' 'Drink me!' 'Let me serve you!'

Chrysabelle turned away. Disgust soured her stomach, not just because of the sycophantic crowd but because part of her understood feeling that way. Being around Mal had put urges in her system unlike any her first patron ever had. She'd certainly never dreamed about Algernon in a way that woke her up drenched in sweat and soul-deep need.

Enough. Mal wasn't interested in her for anything but a chance at freedom, and she was a fool for thinking differently. She was just comarré to him. Born to serve. That was all. If he truly cared, he would have made an effort to contact her by now. She walked on.

The second alleyway appeared to dead-end but if you knew where to look ... Chrysabelle paused before reaching for the concealed door that would give her access to a back entrance into Seven.

Her sixth sense itched. Something felt off. She glanced up, checking the rooftops of the buildings around her. Nothing that she could see, and her night vision was relatively decent, despite not having a recent infusion of vampire saliva. The feeling of being watched still prickled the back of her neck, but she shook it off and pushed through.

The door took her into another alleyway and lastly to the somewhat-secret entrance to Seven. She'd never entered this way before, only exited via this door, and therefore didn't have the access code. The heavy *thump, thump, thump* of the music inside pumped through the club walls like a heartbeat. She wasn't sure anyone would be there to let her in, but she'd give it a shot before braving the front.

There was no handle on the outside. She leaned her shoulder into the door and pushed, but it didn't budge. The hypnotic beat of the music vibrated the metal against her skin. She pounded the door in frustration, knowing no one would hear her knocking over the music.

She glanced back at the way she'd come, looking around for a place to hide her weapons. Better that than turn them over to the bouncers. The street value on weapons like hers, the Golgotha dagger in particular, would assure she'd never see them again.

Suddenly, the music went from muted bass to full-blown clarity. Her head whipped around. Pasha stood in the open doorway.

Not the fae she was hoping to run into. 'Did you hear me?'

He smiled, displaying a mouthful of sharp teeth, and shook his head. Tonight he wore henna paisleys up and down his arms, an enormous henna dragon on his chest, a few scraps of strategically placed leather, and not much else. 'No. I just knew.'

Of course he did. Pasha was a gemini, one half of a pair of twin haerbinger fae, and because he'd kept himself pure by only drinking the blood of his twin, he could see the future. Gemini haerbinger were extraordinarily rare. Mostly because the ungifted twin usually killed the other.

Chrysabelle checked to see if he was wearing gloves. She didn't need any accidental skin contact giving him a reason to enlighten her about how she was going to die.

He wiggled his leather-clad fingers at her. 'Don't worry.'

She looked past him. 'Where's your sister?' Unlike Pasha, Satima had no qualms about drinking whatever blood she could get.

He stared at her, his overlarge eyes unblinking. 'Satima's telling fortunes in Pride.'

Telling lies was more like it. 'Good place for her.' Each of Seven's rooms was devoted to one of the seven deadly sins. Pride suited Satima. Especially since there wasn't a room for Crazy. 'I need to see Dominic. Can you take me to his office without leading me through the club? I don't want to deal with security right now.' Based on her last visit, she knew Ronan, the head of security, wouldn't be too happy to see her.

Wicked light sparkled in his eyes. 'Yes, but you will owe me a favor.'

'No, she won't. I'll take her.' Now, *this* was a fae she didn't mind running into. Behind Pasha, the shadeux fae Mortalis materialized out of the dark hall and gave the haerbinger a hostile look. Light glinted off the silver filigree caps on Mortalis's pointed ears and the tips of his horns. They curled from his forehead to his jawline. Even capped, the horns' points were razor-sharp. 'You get back to work.'

Pasha scowled and disappeared into the dark, leaving behind a cloud of patchouli.

Mortalis pulled the door open and gestured for her to enter. The barbs along his forearms lay flat against his skin, a sign he didn't consider her a threat. 'Are you here about ... the package?'

'No,' she said as she slid past the charcoal-blue fae. 'It's best where it is.' Mortalis had been part of the rescue effort in Corvinestri and had proved himself a worthy ally. She wouldn't have asked him to help her hide the ring otherwise. 'No one knows, right?'

'No one.'

'Good. How have you been?'

'Well, and you?' He started walking. She fell into step beside him.

'All right. Still trying to wrap my head around my aunt actually being my mother and the fact that she's gone.' She sighed. 'How's Nyssa? Is she completely healed?' Chrysabelle felt some responsibility toward the girl. Under torture, Maris had given Nyssa's name to Tatiana, and as a result, the remnant girl had almost died at Tatiana's hands. Fortunately, most remnants were fairly resilient. Nyssa, with her wysper and shadeux bloodlines, was no exception. Noble vampires were foolish to consider remnants an untouchable class of being.

An uncommon smile lit Mortalis's face. 'She is ... beautifully recovered.'

'And?' Chrysabelle smiled back. She had reason to believe the two had moved well past the acquaintance stage since Mortalis had insisted Nyssa convalesce at his home.

'And learning to sign with two extra fingers is like trying to teach a fish to ride a bicycle.'

'I'm sure she's making it worth your while.'

Mortalis rested one six-fingered hand on his stomach. 'Feeding me like a king.'

'Well, you still have the waistline of a prince.' She suppressed the urge to chuckle. Laughing at a creature better armed than you was never a good idea. The twin hilts of a matched set of fae thinblades rose above his shoulders, but the weapons she couldn't see beneath his dark green leathers definitely outnumbered her hidden ones. 'I'm happy for the two of you. You should come over to the house sometime. Velimai would probably like some fae company.'

'I'll talk to Nyssa.' He dropped his arm back to his side, the barbs along his forearm still flat to his skin. 'You're here to see Dominic?' His voice held a hint of surprise.

'Yes. I need to talk to him about my mother.' They rounded a corner. The floor sloped downward, taking them into the underground levels of the building. 'If anyone would have answers about her, it would be him.'

Mortalis nodded. 'Yes. I'm not sure he's here, however. Since your mother's death, he's been scarce around the club.'

'His private quarters are here, aren't they?'

'Yes.' There was hesitation in Mortalis's voice and a frown on his face.

'But? I'm practically his stepdaughter. Whatever it is, I'm sure he wouldn't mind you telling me.' Stepdaughter? Had she really claimed that?

The fae sighed. 'He keeps a penthouse on Venetian Island.'

'I didn't know that.' But of course Mortalis would. He was Dominic's personal bodyguard.

'No one does, which is why I'm still here – to create the illusion that Dominic is as well.' Mortalis glanced at her. 'I trust you'll keep that information to yourself. I'd hate to have to kill you.'

'And I you.'

Mortalis grinned and a rush of crowd noise greeted them as

they started down a flight of stairs. Dominic's office overlooked the Pits. They must be close. She never wanted to see that place again if she could help it. She'd killed her first fringe there in self-defense, and the act had happened with an ease that had both startled and amazed her. 'Busy night?'

He rolled his stormy sea eyes. 'Some special secret fight Katsumi arranged. Invite only, high rollers. She's got Ronan tied up in it, too.'

'Good. I don't really want to see him again. What's he doing for her?'

He held his hands up, fingers splayed. 'I don't know and I don't care. Dominic put her in charge while he's away, so any mess she makes is hers to clean up.'

'You don't like her much.'

He snorted. 'She's too ambitious. Among other things.'

'I know all about that.' She rolled her eyes. Another Tatiana in the making. Chrysabelle trailed her fingers along the concrete. Special luminescent paint gave the walls a soft glow. 'What does Dominic see in her?'

'Not as much as she thinks.' Mortalis shrugged, his hidden weapons giving off a sound like a pocketful of change being rattled. 'But she does get things done.'

He stopped before a door, little more than an outline in the concrete. It swung inward at the push of his hand. Down another short hall, then through a second door that Mortalis unlocked with a key he tucked back into his leathers, and they were inside Dominic's office.

Mortalis turned on a few lights. Electric, of course. Dominic could afford just about anything he wanted.

The fae turned to go, then stopped. 'You need anything? Nyssa says I should work on my hospitality skills.'

'No, I'm fine.' Chrysabelle adjusted her sacres before settling into one of the burgundy silk armchairs across from Dominic's massive antique Renaissance-style desk. His office was a tribute to all things excessive. Marble, gilding, silk, antiques. Any human seeing this room would immediately believe every vampire myth Hollywood had ever perpetuated.

'I'll be back as soon as I find him. If he's here. If not ... I'll be back sooner.'

He left, and she lolled her head back against the chair, closed her eyes, and listened to the braying crowds down in the Pits. Something had them wild. Behind her, a set of gilded French doors led to a balcony that overlooked the arena. Not that she had any desire to see what was going on down there. A mix of anger and sympathy washed through her just remembering what Mal had told her about having to fight there to earn the means to survive. As if he hadn't survived enough in his life already.

And because of her, he had to survive a little longer.

She was a terrible person for not talking to him. She'd promised to help him, then gone silent. He'd had enough betrayal and false promises from Tatiana, he didn't need them from her, too. She would go to him, explain, make him listen by force if need be. She had to let him know that she had every intention of helping him – especially now that she thought she'd figured out how to get to the Aurelian. There were parts of Mal she really liked. She wanted to at least be able to call him a friend. She almost laughed. A vampire for a friend. That was a step in putting her comarré life behind her.

The noise level surged. Someone was winning. Which meant someone was dying.

'What are you doing in here?'

Chrysabelle's eyes snapped open as her head came up and her

hands went to her wrist blades. She'd been so consumed in thought she hadn't heard the door open. Katsumi stood on the other side of the office near a second entrance.

'Waiting for Dominic.'

'He's in his quarters and he's not to be disturbed.'

'Mortalis went to check.' Chrysabelle sank back in the chair and pretended to relax. Her hands stayed poised on her blades. Neither Mal nor Mortalis liked Katsumi. That was good enough for her.

Katsumi glided across the floor, her full-length silk coat fluttering out behind her. The tassels at the end of her hair sticks quivered. Chrysabelle would bet good money those doubled as weapons. 'He's not to be disturbed. Tell me what message you would like to leave for him, then you may stop wasting your time.'

'Trying to get rid of me?' Chrysabelle stood. She was at least seven or eight inches taller than Katsumi. With that advantage in reach, her sacre could turn Katsumi into ash without much effort.

'This is no place for you.'

Sometimes playing dumb was fun. 'There are plenty of women here.'

'I mean because of what you are, comarré.'

'Dominic has comarré working here. None like me, obviously, but I'm sure I'm perfectly safe, even if the head of security is still recuperating.' She lifted her brows. 'Or are you the one I should be wary of?'

'No, of course not.' The ice in Katsumi's gaze belied the calm mask she'd molded her face into. 'And Ronan is fine. Completely healed, despite your efforts.'

'If I'd made an effort, he'd be dead.'

Katsumi sniffed. 'Threats have little effect on me, comarré.'

'I wasn't making a threat. Just stating the truth.' The crowd was chanting now. Sounded like the word *kill*. Chrysabelle glanced toward the French doors.

A small strangled noise left Katsumi's throat.

Needing no more impetus, Chrysabelle walked toward the doors.

Mortalis returned. 'I can't find Dominic. He must be—'

'Go home,' Katsumi scolded. 'Go home!'

Chrysabelle threw the doors open and stepped out onto the balcony. The crowd was frenzied, chanting, fists hammering the air. In the ring, one man lay prone on the concrete floor, blood spattered around him like confetti. His opponent crouched over him, his fists a blur as they pounded the prone man's face into pulp. Rage seemed to pour off the upright vampire in swirling black lines.

The thump of her heartbeat overtook all other sound. She knew what she was seeing – *who* she was seeing – but her brain stalled, trying to spare her the inevitable. Trembling, she grabbed the balcony's glass railing to steady herself.

She inhaled and the familiar sweetness wafting up from the bloody battle below coated her throat. The trembling wound up from her fingers and worked its way into her bones, caging her body in anger.

The prone man was Ronan.

The man covered in black ink was Malkolm.

And at least one of them had her blood running through his veins. Maybe both.

The railing shattered in her grip and sliced her palm. She dropped the shards of glass and backed away, trying to quell her anger. She clutched her hand to her chest. Blood dripped onto her white tunic, matching the straps of her sacre sheaths.

'Wait.' Mortalis held out his hand. Katsumi was already gone.

'No.' She ran past him, out of the office and through the club toward the main entrance, not caring who saw her or her weapons. She was leaving. Now.

A few seconds after she entered the club's main floor, a fringe vamp stepped into her path. 'Hello, fair comarré. Would you care to—'

Her bloody fist shut him up and knocked him out of the way. She was in no mood to be trifled with. By anyone.

Mortalis caught her in the foyer that served as the club's final security threshold. 'Wait a damn minute, will you?'

'No.' But she stopped. 'I'm too angry to be here right now.'

'Why do you care if Mal fights?'

'I don't. What he does is his business. But one of those two in that ring has my blood in them. I smelled it on them. Maybe both of them. If it wasn't Mal, I want to know how Ronan got it. And if it was Mal, then why is he telling me he's not drinking it? He can drink my blood but he can't talk to me?' Anger brought her hands up. 'Just let me go. I need to think.'

'You're bleeding. At least let me wrap that for you.'

'I'm fine.' She turned and strode toward the exit. 'This club has had enough of my blood for one night.'

Chapter Six

Doc woke with a nasty film of fur coating his tongue. He spit, grimacing and tasting rat.

How long had he been out? Sun wasn't up yet, he could feel that much, and the air had that predawn brightness to it. He stretched, sat up, and ran his hands over his stubbled head. By tomorrow night, the moon would be weak enough to stop influencing him. He could go back to being human and miserable, instead of being house cat and miserable.

The fog in his head dissipated slowly, and shreds of what had happened before he'd fallen asleep trickled in. He blinked, trying to bring the memories back faster. This always happened after any time spent in his cursed form. It was like his brain shrank when he changed and everything that wasn't cat-related dropped out. He thought back over the hours before he'd passed out.

Chrysabelle had been here, looking for Mal, but Doc had been locked in and Mal hadn't been here. But before that, Fi had shown up again in her new ghost form. And she still needed his help. Help he couldn't give, but he knew someone who could.

Maybe. The one woman who might be able to help probably wouldn't want to help Doc in any way. And seeing her meant facing his past. Dammit. When was his life going to smooth out and chill?

He sighed and got up, kicking the pile of rags he'd fallen asleep on.

For Fi, he would go see Aliza. He would face the woman who'd cursed him and ask for her help.

The price he'd have to pay for that help would be so out of his budget he couldn't imagine. But to save the woman he loved, he would do anything.

Anything at all.

He staggered to his quarters and assessed himself in one of the few shipboard mirrors. He looked the way he felt. A few hours of sleep and a shower would fix him up. Aliza wouldn't like his visit no matter what time he arrived, but her tune would change when he explained why he was there.

Help for her daughter in exchange for helping Fi.

She couldn't say no to that, could she?

Unlike his dead brother, Nasir didn't snore. Tatiana thanked the fates for small favors. She rolled his sleeping form off her and slipped from the bed, ignoring the robe puddled on the floor beside it, to walk naked to the windows. She pulled the curtains back and stared out at the vile, rose gold horizon.

The coming dusk throbbed in her bones, but not as much as the need to avenge what had been done to her and make things right between her and the Castus. The comarré had a day of reckoning coming, just as soon as Tatiana found her again. Her memory of the girl's location in Paradise City had gone strangely dim. But find her Tatiana would. Then she would take great pleasure in torturing Malkolm's little whore until she gave up the ring of sorrows. Perhaps Tatiana would remove her fingers one by one, working her way up each knuckle until the girl was left with stumps. An eye for an eye, a hand for a hand. That was the kind of justice the Castus appreciated.

Tatiana smiled at her reflection in the glass, then glanced over at Nasir. A good lover always softened her disposition. And Nasir wasn't just good. He was exceptional. Maybe he was trying to make himself indispensable so she wouldn't send him back to that slum he called home. She shuddered. How anyone lived with only two servants she had no idea. Regardless, his skill in bed astounded her. He was completely focused on her pleasure. And then there were those little pots of oils and unguents he kept dipping into and spreading across her body. For a moment, she'd actually felt herself float off the bed, borne only by a sun-warmed breeze.

If those were a testament to his alchemical talents, he had real promise.

She let the curtains swing closed, walked back to the bed, and slid in alongside Nasir. She traced the black curls fringing his forehead. He'd fallen into line so much easier than his brother. Beyond the body-numbing sex, Nasir was much more eager to better his circumstances. And he was willing to be used. She adored that.

Resting back against the pillows, she began a mental list of things she'd need for her upcoming trip to New Florida. With Lord Ivan's backing, funds were unlimited. She'd already sent Octavian ahead to find suitable accommodations and procure a car and driver. Although he was kine like the rest of her staff, he showed remarkable efficiency and a genuine willingness to please her. Both qualities she admired greatly.

Coming up with lodging would be a good test for him. Unlike the Continent, with its wealth of secret vampire-friendly hotels, the Southern Union had none. She was an Elder now, after all. She couldn't be expected to remain cramped up in that ridiculous airplane hangar like the last time.

What else would she need? The Nothos hadn't been as successful as she'd hoped on the last trip, but better they die than her. She'd take at least a dozen this time. Weapons, naturally. She lifted her right arm and admired her gleaming new hand. She couldn't wait to see Malkolm's face when she duplicated his beloved headsman's sword.

Her comar should come, too. No point in being without a blood source if she didn't have to, despite how much she hated having that creature around. So pure and light with that damnable glow, like some freakish reminder of everything she could never have. Gah. But there was no denying the power his blood gave her.

Maybe she should get Nasir a comarré before they left. Her fingers trailed down Nasir's chest.

His eyes fluttered open and he smiled as he reached for her, pulling her under him.

She faked a protest. 'It's almost dusk, and I have much to do.'

'Yes, I know,' he whispered against her neck. 'I can feel the night coming. But *enti qamari* – you are my moon. I could stay forever in your arms.'

Fates help her, she might have to guard herself around this one. 'You flatter me.'

His mouth moved lower. 'I speak the truth.'

A soft moan escaped her throat. 'I ... oh ... we need to ... yes, right there ... talk ... mmm.'

'About what, my sweet?' He scooped two fingers into a

small indigo pot on the nightstand, then drew a path from hip to hip.

Stars burst over her skin. 'About ... Oh. Oh! Um, about a trip.'

'I will go anywhere you wish.' His tongue felt like silk. 'Anywhere.'

'And ... and ... I'm going to buy you a present.' The stars spread across her body in a wave of heat and light. Her eyes rolled back in her head. Bloody hell. She really needed to keep this one alive.

'You are too good to me. Now, no more talking.' His wicked mouth curved into a smile that sent trembles of anticipation through her. 'I am very, very busy.'

Waves of pleasure washed over her, thinning her resistance to the rare pockets of happiness entwined with the painful memories from her past. They surfaced in a rush, and unable to hold them at bay any longer, she wept.

Mal's world narrowed to the arena and the fringe beneath him that somehow, *somehow* had Chrysabelle's blood in his system. Deep in the most primal part of him, Mal's being screamed that she belonged to him. She was his and his alone, and no other vampire who laid a fang on her should be allowed to live.

Smelling her on Ronan painted his vision red and nearly released the beast he'd tried so desperately to control.

Now the beast pulled against his mental chains, the voices chanting along with the crowd for Ronan's death. They hated Chrysabelle, but they loved death and destruction more.

Over and over, his fists destroyed Ronan's face in a blind fury. *Kill, kill, kill.*

However Ronan had come by Chrysabelle's blood, no way had it been with her approval. She'd never knowingly allow

Ronan to drink from her, not after her last encounter with the arrogant fringe. Whatever Ronan had done—

The perfume of Chrysabelle's blood hit him anew, catching him in midpunch and pushing a wave of need through him so strong he nearly collapsed. The voices whined. Only blood warm from Chrysabelle's veins had that kind of effect on him.

Whispers of 'comarré' filtered through from the forgotten crowd and brought his head up. The crowd was transfixed on something above him. Echoes of a familiar heartbeat built in his head. He glanced toward Dominic's balcony. The glass railing was cracked and the French doors open, but the balcony was empty. A streak of red marred the fractured railing.

No way in hell could Chrysabelle have been here. Seen him. Of everything he wanted, that was *not* one of them.

If praying would have helped, he would have willingly set his tongue on fire to do so. He pushed to his feet as the adrenaline drained out of him, leaving him foggy and numb. The beast and the voices went deathly quiet.

His hands hung at his sides, Ronan's blood dripping off them. He had to find her. Talk to her. Figure out why she had been here.

But those were questions for another time. The poison regained his system, and a second later, his legs buckled. He fell to the concrete as cold and lifeless as the fringe he'd just been trying to kill.

Chrysabelle stumbled blindly through the streets of downtown. Her hand ached. Her head hurt. Her stomach verged on rebelling, but sheer will and righteous indignation kept her dinner down. She wanted to scream. To lose her cool. To be very uncomarré.

If Mal thought he still owned her blood rights, which he very well might, then he had every right to drink the blood she'd sent.

But why tell her he hadn't? Was that his way of punishing her for not helping him? Was he that afraid of kissing her again? And how had Ronan gotten her blood? Dominic was at some secret penthouse on some island she'd never heard of. Surely his driver had delivered the blood Dominic had asked for. Or not. Maybe Dominic hadn't even sent that note.

Nothing about tonight made sense, but with enough thinking, she'd figure it out. She needed a plan. Maybe she should go back to the freighter and confront Mal when he returned. Get it straight from the horse's mouth, as it were. No, she might kill him if she did that without calming down.

Calming down. That was a good plan. Although killing him didn't sound that bad either. Blood dripped off her fingertips. She needed to go home and take care of her hand. Killing something sounded much more appealing.

The sensation of being watched gnawed through her thoughts. She looked around and realized she wasn't exactly sure where she was. Great. How far had she walked? Her car and driver were parked a few blocks away from Seven, but she wasn't sure where that was from here. Seven was not, apparently, in a great part of town, but then Paradise City had more questionable areas than safe ones. Figured Dominic would pick this area. He'd probably gotten the building for a steal.

She checked the rooftops of the surrounding buildings, but just as before, they were empty. She rubbed the back of her neck, her hand brushing the reassuring hilts of her sacres. Wrapping her hand through one of the straps that crisscrossed her chest, she walked to the curb and started across the street to loop back the way she'd come.

A whisper of laughter brushed her ear. Several dark shapes flickered past the waning light of the next streetlamp. Dawn was coming and the solar was weak. She turned in time to see more dark shapes in the street behind her.

The slightly musty stench of fringe vampires rose off the asphalt like steam. Considering the blood trail she'd been leaving, it was no wonder she was being tracked. Blood speckled the front of her tunic and the side of her pants. The scent alone must be driving them mad. She bit the inside of her cheek to keep from smiling. A little swordplay was just the thing for her current mood, and if someone got ashed, so much the better. All that solo training was fine, but there was nothing like a little fieldwork to hone one's skills.

The fringe swept closer, dancing in and out of the shadows. She'd done nothing to cover her signum, so they probably knew what she was. Or thought they did. She spun in a slow circle, trying to count how many there were. More laughter. They thought she was easy prey.

How very, very wrong they were.

She gave way to the anger coursing through her veins. It bloomed bright and caustic, filling the marrow of her bones with a sense of indestructibility. Comarré were taught to suppress their anger, to banish it. Anger made a fighter vulnerable. Tonight she didn't care. Comarré rules hadn't helped her very much lately. All that propriety and sense of duty worked within the confines of noble society, but Paradise City was as far from noble society as heaven was from hell.

One after the other, the streetlights popped, shattering glass over the sidewalk in frosty shards. Laughter echoed down the empty road, bouncing off the abandoned buildings.

'Come and get it,' she whispered into the moonlit night.

Oily fringe-shaped stains leaked out of the shadows and closed in. A tall fringe, his hair a spiky mess, jumped onto the hood of the closest car, denting its hood. His attitude announced him as leader. He planted his hands on his hips and smiled at her. 'Well, well. Dinner has come to us tonight.'

A female fringe emerged from the shadows and leaned against the car. She glanced at him, then grinned at Chrysabelle. 'This one smells sweet, Frankie, like candy.' She strolled toward Chrysabelle, winding a strand of screaming-red hair around one finger. 'I like candy.'

The rest of the crew surrounded Chrysabelle, posturing in their worn leathers and hard-edged grins. At least fifteen of them altogether. Not quite the odds she'd been anticipating, but she'd done nothing but train lately. She was ready for this. Sweat dampened the back of her tunic where the sacre sheaths crossed her spine.

These were fringe. Not nobles. They were weaker, younger, most definitely less powerful, but that didn't stop her from sending up a quick prayer. *Holy mother, give me strength. Guide my weapons.*

An eerie sense of calm replaced her fear with a boldness that came from years spent in the sparring halls of the Primoris Domus. She'd felt it before when she'd killed the fringe in the Pits and when she'd fought with Tatiana. Comarré training was like a bad habit, only harder to break. Anger coiled in her belly, a live wire snapping and sizzling.

'Wait up, Ruby.' Frankie jumped off the car and landed beside the female fringe. With their arms slung across each other's shoulders, the pair approached Chrysabelle. 'Maybe we'll keep her as a pet.' He squeezed Ruby. 'What do you say, love? Isn't she pretty the way she glows? Like a sweet, bloody lightning bug.'

Ruby and the rest of them laughed. The crew tightened the circle around her.

Fools.

In a single motion, Chrysabelle lunged her left leg out and reached back to snag the hilts of her blades. They sang out a high, metallic hiss as she freed them from the leather. She straightened her arms and sliced the swords inward, beheading the fringe on either side of her with the sharp sizzle only a hot blade could produce.

Frankie and Ruby jumped back as the heads of two of their crew thumped wet and solid to the ground, their bodies following right after.

Frankie snarled, fangs bared. 'Get her.'

Hands grabbed at her and fingers wrapped around her upper arms. She jerked one arm free and broke a nose with her elbow. A hand tried to push her head to the side. Teeth grazed her arm. She ducked and flipped the other fringe over the top of her, staking him with her sacre as he tumbled past.

Ash floated through the air like dirty snow.

Three down, twelve to go.

Several of that dozen now brandished weapons of their own. Short blades, mostly. Ruby flipped a butterfly knife through her fingers, opening and closing the weapon with a staccato *click-clack, click-clack.*

From behind Chrysabelle, the *shush* of metal cutting through the air warned her to duck. She did, but the dagger sliced through her tunic just above her elbow and opened a long cut as it sailed past. The gash stung, and as if her body just realized that wasn't her only wound, the cut on her palm began to burn anew.

She spun, sacres flying, but the fringe moved out of reach. The element of surprise was gone. Time to get close and personal.

'Give up, comarré?' Frankie motioned to those behind her.

'Get staked, fringe.'

Frankie scowled. 'Been doing a lot of that, have you? Your vampire killing days are over, sweetheart.'

'Really? Because I feel like they've just begun.' Sweet sunlight, she really wanted to take Frankie's head off next.

'Kill her!' he yelled. Several vamps jumped her, knocking her down. She dropped her sacres and twisted as she fell, throwing one off, but a large male leaped on top of her. He hissed, spraying saliva, and reared back to strike.

She palmed one of her bone daggers as something flew overhead and thunked into the female fringe standing over her. The crew member had a half second to glance down at the steel spike protruding out of her chest before she turned into ash. Three more bolts followed, neatly taking down three more surrounding fringe.

A broad shadow muted the moonlight, and the fringe on top of Chrysabelle got yanked off and tossed aside like a sack of bones. She flipped to her feet. The man who'd pulled the fringe off her leveled his crossbow and took out another retreating vamp.

Frankie and Ruby were nowhere to be seen. If the man had taken them out, too, she hadn't seen it. Maybe they'd split at the first sign of trouble.

Miffed her fun had come to an end so quickly, she brandished her Golgotha dagger at the intruder. The man might be human, but his bronzed skin made her wonder. She'd never seen fae that color, but the feral way he stared back, his icy blue eyes unblinking, reeked of fae bravado. Tiny silver hoops winked from his ears and a short black Mohawk ran down the middle of his shaved skull. His knuckles bore the words *HOLD* and *FAST*, and more crudely rendered ink decorated his arms. A harder man she couldn't imagine. Except maybe Mal.

'Are you fae?' she asked. His dirty jeans, soot-black T-shirt, and black leather vest clung to a heavily muscled form. She pulled her gaze back to his face. What human had that kind of aim? That kind of weaponry?

'No.'

'What, then?'

He lifted the brushed titanium crossbow and notched it against his shoulder. 'Just the guy who pulled your roast out of the fire.'

His voice sounded like whiskey and wind. 'My *roast* was doing just fine, thank you.'

'Didn't think I should let those vampires make a snack out of you, but maybe I was wrong.' He racked a slide on the weapon's underside, and the cross arms snapped in against the stock, then he popped the trigger handle into the stock as well, turning the crossbow into something that looked more like a length of flat-sided pipe. He tucked the whole thing into a chest holster beneath his vest. A matching length of round pipe hung on the other side of his ribs. 'I know feeding vamps is a big part of the comarré job description, but they didn't look like paying customers. Excuse me if I interrupted something.' He gave her a short nod and turned to go.

Arrogant enough to be nobility but definitely not fae or vampire, yet he knew she was comarré. Few humans knew that term. She called after him. 'Since you know I'm comarré, you should also know it doesn't work that way.'

He stopped and faced her again. He jerked his chin at the blood-spattered front of her tunic. 'Then maybe you should stop advertising.' He reached toward his back.

She lifted the dagger. 'Try anything and I'll—'

'Here.' He pulled out a handkerchief. 'For your hand.' He

nodded at the weapon. 'You can put that away. I'm not going to hurt you.'

She'd like to see him try. 'Right after you tell me who you are.'

'Creek.' He held the handkerchief out a little farther. 'You have a name?'

'Chrysabelle.' She took the handkerchief. Looked clean. She tucked the dagger away, snapped the handkerchief open, and started wrapping the fabric around her hand. 'You're human?'

He nodded. 'Most days.'

A human male. When was the last time she'd had a conversation with one who wasn't comarré or a noble's servant? She tied a knot in the makeshift wrap, holding one end of the fabric with her teeth. It smelled faintly of spice and smoke. 'You just happened to be in this part of town?'

'I live in this part of town. Grew up here.' His eyes narrowed a bit and made a sweep of her from head to toe. 'Not the best place for someone like you.' His gaze went to her sacres, still on the ground. 'At least you came prepared.'

She retrieved her swords. 'Likewise. Your weapons are interesting. For someone like you.'

'They do the job.' He jerked his thumb over his shoulder. 'You headed back to Seven?'

'Back to? How do you know that's where I came from?' She slipped the sacres into their scabbards, happy for something to do besides gawk at the man before her.

'Where else would a comarré be going? I'm headed that way if you want company.' He shrugged and took off, a slow easy gait that conveyed more grace than a man of his size should have.

If he'd meant to hurt her, he could've tried something by now. Or not bothered to interfere between her and the fringe. And he wouldn't have given her the handkerchief. She caught up to him in a few long strides. Better than guessing which direction the club was in. 'They don't let humans in, you know.'

'I'm not going to party, I'm going to work.'

'You work at Seven?' He must be new. Not that she knew every employee, but he had a memorable look. Not traditionally handsome, but interesting. And human, her gut kept reminding her.

'Not yet.' He slanted a look at her. 'I take it the comarré don't socialize with the rest of the employees.'

'I wouldn't know. I'm not one of those comarré.' She frowned, instantly wishing she could take the words back. He didn't need to know who she was or wasn't. No wonder Maris had never gone out without her signum covered. Wearing your life on your skin left much to be desired. 'My car is parked there.'

Beside her, Creek stayed silent, watching her.

She changed the subject. 'So you're looking for a job there.'

Shifting his gaze back to the street, he shrugged. 'Gotta pay bills.'

'What do you do?' Probably anything he wanted.

He hesitated. 'Private security.' He twisted his head around, looking at her sacres. 'You're good with those. Where'd you pick that up?'

'Comarré school.' She was suddenly too tired to make up another answer and well past caring. 'Where'd you learn to fight?'

'FSP.'

'Is that a local school?'

'It's a state prison.'

A long, quiet minute passed. 'You were a guard?'

'Not exactly.'

He didn't look at her, didn't glance over to see her expression, but she felt the weight of his anticipation to her reaction like a thousand pounds of steel pressing down. If he expected her to freak out because he'd done time, he was going to be disappointed. Living among vampires had a way of tempering the mortal world's big baddies. 'How long were you there for?'

'Seven years, twelve days.'

A long time, but not that long. A serious crime would have meant more. 'What did you do?'

He snorted softly. 'Didn't your mother teach you it's not polite to ask an ex-con his crime?'

'She didn't really get a chance to teach me much. She was murdered.'

He briefly raised a brow before his face returned to passive stoniness. 'My father, too.'

She nodded, knowing that pain and wondering what had happened. They were more alike than she would have imagined. 'Did they catch who did it?'

The muscles in his jaw worked. 'Yes. What about your mother?'

'The person who murdered her is still out there.' She took a breath, feeling a new strength well up inside. 'But I'm going to take care of it.'

He stopped walking. 'If you're going to take justice into your own hands, you need to see your opponents better.'

She faced him, surprised he wasn't lecturing her about becoming a vigilante. 'I did fine back there.'

'You got cut.' Taking a step closer, he lifted his hand toward her arm, then dropped back. He didn't come closer. 'You could do better.'

She didn't move away. 'Better how?'

'You watch too closely. This' – he made a V with his fingers, pointing them at his eyes then at hers – 'is fine for one-on-one, but with a crowd, you gotta learn the infinite stare.'

'And that would be?'

'Instead of watching your opponent, stare through them. Focus on your peripheral vision, let that do the seeing for you. With practice, it will become second nature. You'll notice every move.'

'Hard to practice when I don't have a sparring partner.'

His mouth twitched. Almost like a smile. 'Are you asking?'

Was she? Her heart beat a little faster. Asking him seemed risky for reasons that had nothing to do with his past.

He held his hands up. 'It's cool, don't worry about it.' He pointed across the street. 'Club's two blocks that way, so your car must be close.' He gave her a little nod and took off running, leaving her behind before she had a chance to say anything else.

Chapter Seven

Creek killed the engine on his customized Harley-Davidson V-Rod, walked it through the cargo door of the old machine shop, and notched the kickstand into place. The bike was a sweet machine, but also a constant reminder of the deal he'd struck. Probably just what the Kubai Mata had intended.

He slid the door shut and secured it before grabbing a beer from the fridge and heading up to the loft he'd converted into a bedroom. Not the most luxurious place he'd ever lived, but better than a prison cell.

He climbed the steps in twos, his feet drumming softly on the metal stairs as he thought about the comarré. He couldn't blame her for refusing his offer to spar. If he'd told her he was KM, would she have accepted it? Would she have even believed him? The Kubai Mata were not supposed to exist. Not according to her education. Not according to the education of many. Had to be that way, though. Couldn't give the vampire nation any idea what was about to rise up against them.

Her refusal hadn't stopped him from tailing her to the gates of Mephisto Island. Her driver was careless and made the task easy.

Creek had driven past the gates, given Chrysabelle time to get through, then circled around and entered without too much problem. The guard was some kind of remnant and easily susceptible to the bribe Creek had offered. For a few more bills, he'd learned her house number.

Scaling the estate's walls had posed no real obstacle, and after watching the house for an hour or so, he'd gone home. Her security needed tweaking, although he could sense there were wards of some kind protecting the home. He'd come up with some ideas to tighten things and present them to her soon.

Soon as in right after he found a way to run into her again and explain who he really was. Something he was still figuring out himself. The Kubai Mata were a shadowy group; even the information he'd been given had been very need-to-know. And apparently he didn't need to know much. They'd commuted his sentence to time served and promised it would stay that way as long as he did their bidding, but that's not why he played along. They'd provided his sister, Una, with a full ride to the college of her choice and a monthly stipend for her, his mother, and his grandmother. The women in his life were everything to him. For them, he would do whatever the KM wanted and not worry that the KM were part Freemason, part Templar, part Cosa Nostra, only more dangerous and in charge of some crazy power. Still, Chrysabelle had nothing to fear from him. The KM might make the Illuminati look like the Boy Scouts, but othernaturals and the humans who served them were the only ones who had anything to worry about.

He climbed out the only window that wasn't boarded up to sit on the fire-escape steps overlooking the back alley. Few humans lived in this part of Paradise City by choice anymore. It was a vampire/remnant ghetto now, as full of fringe and fae as it was rats. Nothing like it had been when he'd grown up here. He couldn't imagine a better neighborhood to set up shop in. His sector chief, Argent, should approve whenever he decided to drop in for a visit.

When he did, he'd find that in the two days Creek had been here, he'd already located a well-established vampire club, sussed out its exits and entrances, started cataloging the regulars, and found the comarré. Not bad for a couple days' work.

He took a long draw off the bottle and wished for a nice Cuban. Vampires picked up the smoke too easy, though, and he'd had to give them up for the most part.

The subtle breeze carried a little salt tang in from the ocean, cutting through the neighborhood's general oily stench. The combination reminded him of the Glades, where his mother now lived with her mother, out on Seminole land. Both women and Una wanted him to move out there, to reconnect with his Native American heritage, but truth was, he didn't feel like he belonged there any more than he felt like he belonged anywhere. Maybe when his time with the KM was done. He lay back against the metal stairs, stared up through the lattice of rusted iron and studied the sky. The stars sparkled and shimmered like the signum on the comarré's skin.

She was like something out of a dream. Nothing in his training had adequately prepared him for seeing one of her kind in person. That sunbeam-blond hair, those eyes like the early summer sky, and those strawberry-red lips combined with all that gold ink made for one hard-to-ignore package. He'd known immediately she wasn't one of Seven's brand of comarré. Just like he'd known immediately he wanted to spend more time with her. And not just because of the mission. He sipped his beer and refused to let his head wander in that direction. Being locked up had a way of sharpening a man's desires to a razor-thin edge. He needed to focus on the comarré and forget about his own wants. The comarré and the ring she possessed were his responsibility now. His to persuade. His to protect. His to recover. He tipped the bottle again. A man could do serious harm to himself around a woman like that, tripping over his words and acting a fool. But he wouldn't. Because he was stronger than that. He was KM.

In a small way, he felt sorry for her. Despite being free now, she'd spent her life in service to the vampires. Sustaining the one who owned her. That was the whole purpose of the comarré – keep the vampires happy and fed and away from humans. All the decisions in her life were already made for her.

Kind of like being in prison.

Yet there was more to the comarré than that, a darker, hidden side. He knew about the physical training they went through, the weapons skills that were drilled into them. That much was evident by the way she worked those swords, one in each hand. He whistled low and long. If that didn't get a man's attention, nothing would.

He rolled his head slowly side to side, watching the constellations wink in and out of sight through the cage of metal above him. Those gold tats of hers were something else. Straight-up amazing, if you knew what she'd had to endure for each one, and he did, thanks to the eons of knowledge that had been crammed into his brain in a matter of weeks. Without question, he knew more about the comarré than she did about the KM. Hell, even *he* knew more about the comarré than he did the KM.

He especially understood the pain she'd endured for those marks, since he'd been through the KM rituals. Women supposedly had a higher tolerance for pain, but he couldn't imagine that pale, slender female going through that kind of agony. Especially not for the sake of some vampire. Pissed him off, actually. No woman should have to endure pain at a man's hands.

Una's dark eyes flashed in his mind, her cries and the sound of their father's hand cracking her cheek echoing in his ears. He'd come home at just the right time to save her. Just the right time to crucify himself. He clenched and unclenched his empty fist, feeling the snap of bones under his fingers as if he were there again.

Anger pushed him upright. He hunched his back, remembering the day he'd accepted the KM's offer. He'd walked out of FSP an hour later, proof of the organization's power. He exhaled hard. Out of one prison and into another. But the deal was worth it.

Worth the pain of the day he'd been sealed into KM service. The memory lingered on his skin, sharp and heavy and just as painful. Being bulletproof didn't mean the bullet wasn't going to hurt. Neither did it mean the pain would weaken him. Instead of being something to fear, pain was something to use.

He set his beer on the step beside him and was about to get up and go back inside when he went stone-still. Two vampires strolled into the mouth of the alley, oblivious to his presence. Just to be careful, he used some of his newly acquired skills to stop his heart and breathing. They kept walking. As a safety measure, he'd decided not to make any kills this close to his home, but temptation kissed his fingertips and made them itch for his crossbow.

If the fringe looked up and saw him, he'd take them out. If not, he'd let them pass. Fringe weren't specifically his mission, but if they were hunting humans or him, they were fair game. He wasn't comfortable with them knowing his home base either.

Vamp One said something to Vamp Two that made Vamp Two throw his head back in laughter. As his gaze rose, his beady eyes locked onto Creek. Then the vampire pointed Creek out to his buddy. A second later, two sets of fangs gleamed in Creek's direction.

So much for letting them skate.

Creek vaulted over the fire-escape railing and landed in front of the dentally challenged pair. 'Evening.'

The vampires stared back in silence, perhaps stunned by his good manners.

Without waiting for a return greeting, he yanked his halm off his belt and flicked it open to its full six-foot length. Few understood the power of the quarterstaff, and as a result, few feared the weapon. He liked that. Surprise was always an advantage.

Like now.

He tucked the titanium rod beneath his arm and lunged forward, ramming the sharpened tip into Vamp One's chest, ashing him instantly. Vamp Two took off, but Creek flung the halm like a spear after him. The halm pierced the vampire through the lower back, pinning him to the potholed asphalt.

The creature screeched and clawed at the ground, trying to free itself.

Creek pulled a knife from his boot and strolled toward the thing stuck, buglike, on his halm. With one hand on the quarterstaff, he planted his boot in the middle of the vampire's back. Kid couldn't have been more than twenty, twenty-one when he'd been turned. But that kid was long gone, replaced by a parasite.

'Nothing personal,' he muttered, and drove the blade down into the creature's neck. He jerked the blade toward the ground, crunching through bone and cartilage with a few deft cuts. The remains went to ash moments after he'd severed the spine. He wiped the knife on his jeans, then tucked it away, snapped the halm closed, and retrieved a small pouch from the interior pocket of his leather vest. A pinch of hawthorn powder went over the ashes, and they burned away like a lit fuse, leaving no trace of the kill. He did the same to the first one on his way back to the fire escape.

Fringe were good practice, and he'd need it to protect Chrysabelle and the ring in her possession from the noble vampire currently hunting her. At least until he convinced the comarré to turn the ring over to him. From the dossier he'd read, Tatiana was a tough customer and could not be allowed to possess the ring, whatever its powers were. Must be something else. The Kubai Mata wanted it badly enough to free a murderer from prison and put him to work.

Despite what they'd authorized him to do, he wouldn't take the ring by force. He'd never use force against a woman. He would feel Chrysabelle out, see if she was open to giving the ring up. In theory, the KM were the good guys. Giving them the ring shouldn't be such a hard thing to do. He leaped, snagged the bottom rung of the ladder, and climbed back to the platform.

From there, he swung his booted feet through the open window and back into the loft. In the meantime, he'd live up to the rest of the KM credo and protect the citizens of Paradise City from the monsters now living among them and the ones that were yet to come.

When he wasn't getting to know Chrysabelle better, that was.

Doc missed the growl and hum of the old airboats, but there was something to be said for the silent running of the carbon fiber blades and electric engines of the newer environmentally mandated boats. He notched the throttle back as he swung around an island of trees. The boat lost its plane, the air beneath it disappearing as the boat slowed and made contact with the water again. Ever since the run that had gotten him cursed, he hated the Glades. Hadn't been out here since. There were mostly two kinds of people who lived in the Glades: those with a rightful claim to the land, like the Seminoles, and those looking to hide. His business was with the latter.

The cluster of houses, glass and steel boxes on stilts, broke the horizon line like jagged teeth. Strong morning sun glinted off the buildings. He adjusted his sunglasses. Even with his pupils narrowed to slits, the combination of glare off the water and unfiltered daylight was murder on shifter eyes this early in the a.m.

He approached the houses and grudgingly gave the witches props for living out here. Hard to sneak up on someone who had an unadulterated view in every direction. Not to mention the local inhabitants who did a damn fine job of keeping most people out to begin with. One of those inhabitants, a fifteen-foot gator named Chewie, lounged on the dock of the house he was headed toward, soaking up the morning sun like a teenager on spring break.

Doc's back teeth ground against each other. *Hated* the Glades. He eased the boat toward the dock and got to his feet. Aliza's airboat sat beneath the house, out of the elements. He wouldn't be getting that close yet. He reached into the bag at his feet, pulled out the chickens he'd brought, and dangled them in Chewie's direction.

'Come and get it, you overgrown suitcase.'

Chewie's lids cracked open. Doc tossed the chickens in the opposite direction of the boat, and the gator slipped off the dock with a splash and disappeared into the black water.

The sound of a pump-action shotgun being cocked froze Doc where he stood. He lifted his hands. 'I've got good reason for being here.'

'Then start talking,' Aliza spat. 'My finger itches. And there better not be anything untoward in those chickens.'

He looked up. Aliza stood on the second-level porch, glaring down at him from the shadows of the eaves. Her lack of pigment made her look like a ghost, reminding him again why he'd come to see her. 'The chickens aren't drugged. I'm here because I want to fix things with Evie.'

'Hard to talk to stone.'

He sighed. 'I mean I want to help make things right.'

The shotgun came down half an inch. 'How?'

'There's got to be a way to turn her back, right? I want to help.' With hands still lifted, he splayed his fingers. 'Whatever it takes.'

'Why now? Why after all these years?'

He'd been hoping to explain things in a calmer, more rational manner. Not that that had ever been Aliza's style. 'I have a friend who's in trouble and you're the only one I know who might be able to help her.'

Aliza snorted. 'Figures you'd want something in return. Why should I help you?'

'You shouldn't.'

She was quiet a moment. Hard to argue with truth, apparently. 'What did you do this time?'

'Nothing.' Something splashed in the water to his left. He almost didn't stop a wave of revulsion from rippling through him.

'Then why does she need help?' She peered at him. 'What are you cooking?'

'Nothing. My friend is ... dead. Kind of.'

Aliza lowered the shotgun and pursed her mouth to one side. She narrowed her pale gray eyes in thought. Finally she nodded. 'You can come in. Your behavior determines how you leave.'

Lunatic. He tied up the airboat, stepped onto the dock, and climbed the steps. Chewie was still out of sight. Aliza looked the same as the last time he'd seen her. Maybe her yellowy-white dreads were a little longer, but other than that, she was the same albino crackpot she'd always been.

She motioned with the gun for him to go in. He pushed through the door and walked to the center of the kitchen. The house smelled like swamp and women. In Aliza's case, that was probably the same smell. How she'd ever turned out a daughter like Evie, he had no idea. That girl was beautiful. Or had been, before Dominic's drugs had turned her to stone.

And there she was. In front of the wall of sliding glass, facing out toward the Glades, the statue that had once been Aliza's daughter stared blindly into the vast swamp. Her hands clutched at her throat just like they had that night. He swallowed and rubbed a hand over his scalp as if there weren't anything unusual about such a thing.

The screen door slammed shut behind Aliza. She pointed toward the kitchen table. 'Sit.'

He took a chair that let him keep his back to the wall and twisted slightly so Evie's statue stayed out of his peripheral vision.

Aliza tucked the shotgun under one arm and poured a cup of coffee, then brought it to the table and sat opposite him. 'Talk.'

He explained everything he could about Fi, how she had come to be a ghost through Mal's curse, how she'd gotten killed again, how she'd started coming back, reliving the past ... everything he could think of, except that he was in love with her. No need to give the old witch any further ammunition.

'Your friend's not a ghost anymore.'

'Yes, she is. I saw her with my own—'

'No, she's a shade now. It's different.' Aliza sipped her coffee, wrinkling her brow. 'She's caught in a time loop and will stay that way, dying again and again every night.' She shuddered. 'Shade's a horrible thing to be.'

'Then help her.' He relaxed his jaw and forced out a difficult word. 'Please. I said I'd do whatever it took and I meant it.'

'Hmph. And I suppose in exchange for helping make Evie right, you're also going to want your curse lifted.'

He blew out a long, unsteady breath. 'I've wanted that for a long time. But I'll settle for just helping Fi.'

She arched her thick white brows. 'That so?'

He nodded, ignoring the widening hole in his chest. Having Fi back would be enough. She'd help him forget about the curse. She always had.

'You love her?'

'That's none of your damn business.'

'I'll take that as a yes.' Aliza drained the last of her coffee and sat back, judgment clear in her harsh stare. 'The kind of magic that turns a woman into stone isn't easy to undo. It's heavy. Means sacrifice. Can't just whip that kind of thing out of thin air.'

He sighed, steeling himself. 'What do you need?'

'Some of the drug she took that night.'

'Done.' Evie had scored an eighth of Medusa, a highly potent love potion that gave the user the ability to keep a man hard for as long as she wanted.

Aliza leaned her head forward. 'I'll also need blood.'

With a calm that surprised him, he laid his arm on the table. 'I'm prepared for that.'

She laughed. 'Not yours, fool boy.'

The small, sharp teeth of his sixth sense nipped the back of his neck in warning. 'Whose, then?'

'Dominic Scarnato's.'

If she'd asked for the blood of an unborn child, he'd have been less stunned. 'Do you know what you're asking? I can't just walk up to him and say, "Hey, I need some of your blood." The man is a powerful crime boss. He pretty much runs the supernatural business that goes on in Paradise City.'

'Told you.' She shrugged. 'I need the blood of the one whose magic made those drugs.'

'I can't get it. Pick something else.'

'There is nothing else.' She stood and walked her empty cup back to the sink. 'Come back when you have it.' She leaned against the counter. 'Or don't come back at all.'

Anger made him bold. He jumped up, almost knocking his chair over. 'Anything else? Pot of leprechaun gold? A unicorn horn?'

'Nothing quite that tough.' She crossed her arms and smiled, crinkling the corners of her gray eyes. 'I need the blood by Samhain.'

Samhain was Halloween. Son of a— 'That's less than two weeks away.'

She inspected her fingernails. 'Well, then, you'd better get cracking.'

Chapter Eight

'Do you know what I hate about this place?' Tatiana asked Nasir as she stared out the window of her private jet, watching the horrifically bright landscape blur past the landing aircraft.

'What's that, my love?' He curled a lock of her hair around his finger, leaning into her space.

She hooked her finger around the lock he'd claimed and tugged it from his grasp. 'Besides the fact that this place is full of fringe, fae, remnants, and all sorts of undesirables, besides the fact that the Americas are a mess of human politics and infighting, besides the fact that several people who've tried to kill me reside here, it's too damn sunny. All the time. Why would any vampire in his right mind want to live in such an awful place?' She collapsed back into her seat with the appalling weight of returning to this forsaken land, her eyes fixed on the world beyond the helioglazed glass.

'Well . . . ' Nasir started.

She glared at him, willing him to continue and give her a reason to strike him.

'I was just going to say that it's warm. You know how good that feels to those of our kind. My homeland is very much the same.' He tipped his head. 'It will be dark in a few hours. The day is almost past.'

She returned her gaze to the window. 'If I don't kill something soon, I'm going to be in a very foul mood.'

He leaned in and stroked the side of her neck. 'There are other ways to improve one's mood, my sweet.'

She squinted at him, but it did nothing to improve her ability to suffer foolishness. Perhaps she should have bought him some picture books instead of the comarré. 'You realize there are twelve Nothos on board this plane, as well as a fringe pilot and copilot, and my private bedroom is currently occupied by two comarré? Where exactly did you imagine this mood enhancement would take place? Out here, in front of these aberrations?' She waved her hand over her shoulder toward the monstrosities taking up most of the plane's forward space. The stench of brimstone was enough to ruin anyone's mood, forget that it might never come out of the beautiful leather covering her seats.

'Surely the comarré can spend a few minutes out here with—'

'I realize you've never owned a comarré before, but you must understand that putting them out here with the Nothos would be like asking a feral dog to watch your steak.' Bloody hell, he was an idiot about certain things. She tried to focus on his talents in bed and with alchemy and patted his hand like she'd once done to the child Malkolm had allowed to die.

'Yes, I suppose it would.' He gave her a conciliatory smile. 'Later, then.'

'Later you're going to be out searching for my cover.' She

couldn't go around looking like herself and risk being noticed by that wretched comarré or her shoddy group of friends. Someone local, someone connected just enough to get her in the door ... that's what she needed. Unfortunately, she had to rely on Nasir to bring that someone to her.

The plane taxied toward the hangar, slowing to a crawl as it eased into the large metal building. As soon as the doors were shut and sealed against the invasive sunlight, she disembarked. Nasir followed behind, but the comarré and the Nothos stayed safely ensconced in their separate spots on the plane.

The head of her household staff, Octavian, waited, hands crossed behind his back, posture as crisp and unyielding as his charcoal suit, even in the humidity. Behind him were two vehicles, a sleek black limousine and a rather dodgy delivery truck. He bowed as she approached. 'My lady.'

'I assume you've taken care of things?'

He looked extraordinarily pleased. 'I have, my lady. I have located what I believe to be the center of much othernatural activity. A nightclub of all things.'

'We shall see, won't we?' She gestured toward the nondescript delivery truck. 'And this?'

'For transporting your Nothos.'

'Very good. The pilot and copilot will be bunking here.' She would be ready for anything this time.

'Whatever pleases you.' He swept his hand toward the sleek limousine. 'And this is for you, of course. The house I have arranged has several interior rooms and one side that is sufficiently shaded by large trees, as well as other features you may find useful.'

'A house?'

He smiled. 'A grand estate, one befitting a noble of your status and rank, I assure you. There is even a guesthouse where the Nothos may be kept.'

She pursed her mouth. 'How much did that cost me?'

His smile grew. 'Nothing, my lady. I simply displaced the kine occupants.'

She almost laughed. That Octavian referred to his fellow humans as kine was significant proof of his desire to leave them behind and join the vampire world. 'Displaced?'

'I secured them in the estate's wine cellar.' He lifted one shoulder nonchalantly but failed to hide his pleasure at what he'd done. 'I thought perhaps you might require some sustenance after your trip. The wine selection seems to be above adequate as well.'

Now, this was the kind of brain power she needed around her. She lifted a finger toward Nasir. 'Be a dear and get the bags, would you?'

Nasir grunted. 'Shouldn't he be doing that?'

She didn't turn but simply layered the power of persuasion into her voice. 'Nasir.'

He tromped back into the plane like a good little boy.

She flashed forward until she was inches from Octavian. He didn't flinch at her rapid advance. Didn't stutter a breath or miss a heartbeat. Clearly, he wanted what she had to offer so badly he'd already begun to imagine himself a peer. She stared at him, really seeing him for the first time. Brown hair, brown eyes, but not unattractive for a kine. Ever respectful, he dropped his gaze as her inspection continued. Fit. Young enough to still have hope.

At last he began to tremble ever so slightly. 'Have I displeased you, mistress?'

'No, Octavian. You've done well.' If she'd praised him before, she didn't recall it, but the time to cultivate a higher sense of loyalty in him had come. They were on dangerous ground in this wretched place. She needed every soldier she had.

He flushed and his pulse quickened. Desire wafted off him, smoky and sweet. Her fangs descended, and she made no effort to hide them. Unlike her other servants, Octavian would undoubtedly enjoy seeing them. She smiled. 'Look at me.'

'Yes, my—' He lifted his head and his mouth fell open. He closed it to swallow. 'What else might I assist you with?'

She leaned in, inhaling the perfume of his blood. 'You would do anything for me, wouldn't you?'

'Yes, my lady, anything.' His gaze darted to the ground for just a moment, then returned to her face before he finally turned away again. 'Anything.'

She slipped a knuckle beneath his chin and brought his face up. The heat of his skin melted into hers and awoke a craving she'd never before felt for a mortal. The urge to kill him and put an end to such unwelcome desire coursed through her, instantly at war with the knowledge that he could do more good for her alive. She broke the contact. He looked genuinely bereft. 'I may call upon that willingness very soon.'

'Yes, mistress.' He barely got the words out before a shiver of unbridled pleasure rolled through him.

Power sparked electric in her veins. She wanted to laugh with the giddiness bubbling up inside her. It was going to be so much easier this time. Nasir came down with the bags as she pointed to the car. 'To the estate. We have work to do.'

Darkness weighed on Mal like six feet of packed earth. He woke with a start, clawing at the empty blackness above him and half crazed with memories of his time in the ruins. But that wasn't where he was. He rested on a comfortable bed. No mold or must or damp corroded the air.

He sat up and blinked, his eyes picking out shapes and objects in the dark. He was in a large, well-furnished suite. Where, he wasn't quite sure.

Then it came back to him. The drugged blood. The scent of Chrysabelle pouring out of Ronan. The indicators that she'd been there in the Pits.

He wanted to rail against the barge-load of refuse his life had become, but there was too much to figure out and not enough time to do it.

A table near the bed held an LED lamp. He clicked it on, illuminating the space.

He went very still. He knew this room. Had spent time here. He inhaled, figuring he deserved the torture. The honey-sweet fragrance of Chrysabelle's blood still lingered in the suite, but then, it had been the last place he'd willingly drunk the blood she'd drained for him. And the last place he'd kissed her.

Chin dropping toward his chest, he shook his head at his own foolishness. How had things gotten to this point? Because he was a stubborn fool.

Now, Chrysabelle could be anywhere. Hurt. Suffering. Or worse. Crimson edged his vision. If Ronan had harmed her in any way, Mal would kill him. If he hadn't already.

Fists outstretched, Mal tipped back his head and roared out the anger scraping his insides raw. Katsumi, Ronan, maybe even Dominic for condoning what went on in his club – they all deserved his wrath.

Rapping sounded from the door.

'What?' Mal shouted.

The door opened and Mortalis walked through. Before he could shut it, Katsumi barged past.

'Oh, you're all right. I was so worried.' She wrung her hands, studying him as if he were a lost love come home. What a farce.

Mal leaped to his feet. 'Like hell you were. You're the one who gave me that doctored blood.'

Mortalis held his hands up. 'Hold on. What doctored blood?'

Mal ignored him as Katsumi lifted her chin. 'I may have given it to you, but I had nothing to do with it being tainted.' She laced and unlaced her fingers with theatrical precision. 'I had money on you. A lot of money. Why would I do anything that would ruin my chances of winning?'

Mortalis nodded. 'She's got a point.'

Mal scowled. 'No, she doesn't. Why are you defending her?'

Mortalis, standing slightly in front of Katsumi, gave Mal a glare. 'I'm not defending her. I'm trying to sort this out.'

Katsumi had the audacity to feign hurt. 'I thought I could do something to help, but if you're going to act like such a child, then—'

Mortalis turned to her. 'You want to help? Go find Ronan.'

'He's still alive?' Mal asked.

'Yes.' Katsumi sniffed. 'The fight was declared a draw. No winner. Mortalis brought you here. I took Ronan back to the cells, then went to get a med kit. When I came back, he was gone.'

No wonder she was so bunched up. She'd lost money and a willing fighter. 'Mortalis is right. Go find Ronan so I can finish what I started.'

'You'll fight him again?' Her eyes lit up with appalling glee.

'No, I'm just going to kill him.'

She jabbed a finger at him. 'You want to take him out, do it in the pit. We have an agreement and you owe me.'

'Getting poisoned canceled any agreement between us.'

She started to argue back, but Mortalis stopped her. 'Enough. You have a club to run while your head of security is missing.'

She poked a long, red nail into his shoulder. 'It's Dominic's club. He has a problem with how it's being run, he can tell me himself. I don't need to hear it from his *boy*.'

Boy? Mal raised his brows. Katsumi must have a death wish.

Mortalis stared down at her, his eyes black slits against his sooty skin. 'You'd think a creature with no soul would take a little care around someone like me.' He stepped toward her. 'Unless you need reminding what my kind are capable of.'

Mal crossed his arms. 'Never hurts to have a refresher.'

'Bite me,' Katsumi spat.

Mal sneered. 'Not even the voices in my head are that insane.'

Mortalis laughed. Katsumi didn't. With frost in her gaze, she stalked out, slamming the door behind her.

Mortalis didn't wait for Mal to speak. 'We need to talk.'

'No, we don't.' Mal headed for the exit. He didn't have time to make nice or buddy up.

Mortalis grabbed his bicep. 'You can't just go barreling out there and hope it all works out.'

Smoke trailed up from where the fae's silver rings connected with Mal's skin. He yanked his arm out of the shadeux's six-fingered grip. 'Watch me.'

The fae stepped into his path. 'Katsumi's hiding Ronan. I don't have proof, but I can feel it. No one else claims to have even seen him in the holding cells after the fight.'

Mal shrugged. 'That doesn't surprise me.' Katsumi couldn't let him kill Ronan when there was money to be made. What else did Mortalis know? 'What about Chrysabelle? I know she was here. There was blood on the balcony railing.'

'She cut her hand, but she's fine. She went home.' Mortalis frowned. 'That was yesterday, by the way. You've been out for a while.'

'All the more reason I need to talk to her.' Mortalis might think she was fine, but what did the fae know about comarré? Mal wanted to see her. Had to see her. And he'd had enough blood these past few days that he could face her without dropping fang and salivating like some newly turned vampling.

'I don't think that's a good idea.'

'Duly noted. Get out of my way.'

Mortalis didn't budge. 'No. There's more to this. I know it. The fringe have started to organize. There's talk of putting Ronan in charge.' He exhaled like the weight of a thousand secrets lay on his back. 'Something's going on and I may be your only ally right now, so either listen to me or don't, but I'm willing to help.'

'You work for Dominic.' Mal planted his fingertips on Mortalis's chest and pushed to emphasize his point, causing the shadeux to sway. 'And he's just as guilty as the rest of them, so your help' – he pushed a little harder – 'I can do without.'

Mortalis stood firm. 'Dominic doesn't know about any of this.'

'He tell you to come down here and feed me that line of bull?'

'No, because he's not here, and he hasn't been since Maris died.'

That slowed Mal down. 'Where is he?'

'I'm not at liberty to divulge.'

Chump. Mal shook his head, disgusted. 'You're such a company man, Mortalis. Your clan must be so proud of you.'

Mortalis lifted his head, aiming the tips of his horns in Mal's direction. 'My choices are not yours to judge. I certainly don't judge yours.'

'What's that supposed to mean?'

'You know what it means. You drank her blood.'

Mal cooled a notch. 'Which is why I need to talk to her. To explain.' To stop screwing up his already chaotic life.

'Then I'm going with you.'

'No.' He pushed past Mortalis, headed for the door.

'Tell Velimai I said hello. You know, from one deadly fae to another.'

His hand stopped on the knob. Son of a priest. 'You're driving.'

Chapter Nine

This time of night when the dying sun dusted the sky lavender and the early stars emerged, everything seemed draped in magic. Not the kind that waited around corners or bared its teeth when startled, but peaceful, benevolent magic. The enchanted dusk muted imperfections and smoothed rough edges. Chrysabelle could almost imagine that Maris was still alive, that the humming coming from the kitchen belonged to her. Chrysabelle knew it didn't, but a strange compulsion made her lean up from the poolside chaise and check.

With a smile, Velimai stepped out of the house through the wall of sliding glass panels that were opened to the evening air. In her hands, a tray holding a flute of pineapple juice. She walked forward, almost floating in that way wyspers had of gliding like leaves on water. Chrysabelle's imaginings faded in her wake.

With a wistful sigh, she lay back against the chaise, the journal she'd been reading closed against her chest. Not her mother. And it never would be. Meeting Creek had reminded her how very alone she was in this world. Yes, she had Velimai, but

Velimai wasn't human, and on the days when she ached for the counsel of someone who understood what she'd been through or might grasp what it meant to be comarré, there was no substitute.

The journals came close at times like this. She could hear Maris's voice when she read. Sometimes, though, reading Maris's thoughts overwhelmed Chrysabelle, especially the little notes written directly to her. Those ... those tore at her heart, gnawing on the parts that were trying to heal, keeping the pain fresh. And so the reading went slowly.

Velimai set the tray down, lifted the flute, and placed it on the small table beside the chaise. She tucked the tray beneath her arm and tilted her head to look at Chrysabelle.

Chrysabelle recognized that look. 'I'm fine.' She lifted her bandaged hand without wincing. The scratch on her elbow was almost gone. 'Even my wounded bits.'

Velimai's brows rose. Clearly, she didn't believe that.

'I'm fine, really.' Chrysabelle tapped a finger on the journal. 'Just missing her.'

Velimai nodded and signed, *Me, too, always.*

Chrysabelle nodded. Velimai understood. At least to some extent. 'Sit with me.'

Velimai leaned the tray against the table and took the chaise on the other side. Her hands flew as she sat. *You want to talk?*

'No. Just company.'

The wysper smiled softly, opening her mouth as if to say, 'Ah, I understand,' then sank back into the cushions.

Chrysabelle sipped her juice, a habit she'd yet to break. The fruit's sugariness sweetened the blood, something Algernon had always enjoyed. Would she ever leave that life behind her? Would the day come when no reminders existed? Maybe in another hundred years, if she lived that long.

She opened the journal and began to read again, thankful the lack of vampire interaction in her life had not yet dulled her night vision to the point that she needed more than ambient light to see by.

My visit to the Aurelian was more fruitful and more frustrating than I could have imagined it to be. When I asked my one question, for she would not allow more than that, she answered without hesitation. 'Chrysabelle is your daughter. You've cared for her these many years. Did you not feel in your soul she was your child?' In that moment I felt both elation and chastisement. Thrilled to finally know what I had wondered about for so long, and admonished for not figuring it out myself. Should I have? Self-doubt overwhelmed me. What kind of a mother didn't know her own child? A comarré mother, it seemed. 'No,' I answered. 'I didn't feel it.'

I shall never forget the look on the Aurelian's face when she continued. In her eyes, it was plain that I was completely diminished. 'I should not find it surprising, then, that you did not try to ask about your son.'

'My son is dead. Rennata let it slip once.'

The Aurelian laughed. 'Rennata lies.'

Alive? Coldness swept through me, my tongue numb and useless as I tried to comprehend. I thought back to that day. I'd fought with Rennata, over what I don't remember. We fought often. In a fit of anger, she told me my firstborn, my son, had died at the hands of his patron.

Now, looking back, I can only imagine Rennata wanted to wound me as deeply as possible. She was never chosen to bear, and that weighed heavily on her, among other things.

Chrysabelle, my child, if you're reading this, and I pray that you are, find your brother. Go to the Aurelian and use your one question to get his name and set him free as I have done for you. Please, I beseech you.

'Holy mother.' Chrysabelle breathed out the words like a prayer. She reread the passage from Maris's journal as she sat forward. The same numbness her mother described seemed to sink into her bones, deadening the ache in her palm where she clutched the journal.

A brother. A *brother*. She was not without family. Liquid blurred her vision, distorting the journal's pages.

'Velimai,' she whispered, not trusting her voice to the depth of emotion straining her composure.

The wysper turned her head away from the wash of stars now visible in the night sky and made eye contact. Instantly, she sat up, her hands moving. *What's wrong?*

Chrysabelle shook her head, the words coming in a rush. 'Did you know? Maris, the journal, she says I have a brother. Did she tell you? I have to find him.'

No, Velimai signed over and over, her face reflecting Chrysabelle's feelings. *I'll help you. We'll find him. Maybe Dominic—* Her fingers stopped and she went deathly still, pivoting in the direction of the property's entrance gate. One hand gripped the chaise's armrest, the other signed a single word. *Company.*

The almost imperceptible whir of an electric motor reached Chrysabelle's ears. Someone had accessed the gate and was on the property. She left everything and bolted for the house, Velimai right behind her. Once inside, Velimai smacked the button that closed the glass wall while Chrysabelle darted for her sacres.

Who knew the gate code? Dominic? Was he here to get more blood? She grabbed her swords and ran to the door to check the closed-circuit camera. If not Dominic, then who? Had someone broken the ward? Solomon could do it. But why would he? Unless coerced. Her pulse kicked up a beat and her fingers clenched and unclenched the sacres' red leather hilts. The movement reopened the wound on her hand, and fresh blood seeped through the bandages, but the pain only served to hone her awareness. Her sacre hummed in the dim light, trembling as her blood dampened the hilt, ready to be used.

A sleek black sedan rolled to a stop at the inside curve of the circular drive. That car belonged to Dominic, but the driver who got out wasn't Leo. He opened the door for the passenger and as that person exited, Chrysabelle exhaled the breath she'd held.

Mortalis. She hadn't wanted to talk to him earlier, but she was in a slightly better mood now that she'd— The next figure to exit the vehicle behind the fae made her spine stiffen and her jaw tighten. If Mortalis wanted to force this confrontation, fine, but he wasn't going to like the results.

Velimai flickered, clearly agitated. Chrysabelle waved her back. 'I've got this.'

The wysper scowled at the visitors, but nodded as she moved away.

Sacres still in hand, Chrysabelle threw the door open and stood there, glaring as the two intruders came toward her. She pointed the swords at them, more for emphasis than threat. 'How did you get the gate code?'

Mortalis looked at her like she should have expected them. 'Dominic. Look, Chrysabelle, there's a lot that needs to be discuss—'

She leveled the weapons at him. 'Mortalis, if you want us to remain on speaking terms, I suggest you stay out of this.'

Hands up, Mortalis lagged behind, but Mal kept walking.

She swung the blades to aim at Mal. 'You're trespassing.'

His dark gaze pinned her, the tiniest flicker of silver lighting his near-black irises. 'So sue me. We need to talk.'

'I think you mean *you* need to talk.' She tossed the swords into the air, reversing her grip on the hilts as they came down so she could cross one arm over the other with the points toward the ground. The engraved blades threw soft sparks as they moved with her breathing. 'But that assumes I'm going to listen.'

He stopped on the landing, just shy of the threshold. The invisible barrier from her lack of invitation loomed between them, but the look on his face said he might risk it. She'd once seen a vampire enter a house uninvited. Three days of cleaning hadn't removed all the stains. Mal planted a hand on each side of the door and leaned in until his handsome face was inches from hers. The interior lights cast blue highlights in the black waves of his hair. 'You're going to listen. Then you're going to do some explaining of your own.'

'You can't make me.' Sweet sunlight, what was she? Five? At least she hadn't flinched. Why did Mal's nearness affect her at all? Because he must obviously still be her patron. Sounded good. She'd go with that. Better than admitting it had anything to do with her feelings or his broad, muscled body.

He inhaled, didn't even try to hide it. 'You smell good.'

'You'd know.' She snorted softly, sucking in a nose full of his scent in return. She could almost feel her traitorous body ramping up its blood production. He didn't even have the decency to look like someone had just beaten the shade out of him. But then he'd heal quickly with a belly full of her blood, wouldn't he?

'How's your hand?'

The simple question coupled with the soft growl of his voice nearly undid her, all but unbalancing the perfect blend of righteous anger and justified indignation she'd concocted. 'What? It's fine.'

He glanced at her right fist, his nostrils flaring. 'It's bleeding.'

'Your fault.' Somehow, despite the obvious blood scent she must be putting off, he was maintaining his human face. Something probably also made easier by the blood of hers he'd recently had.

His eyes narrowed slightly and one corner of his mouth twitched. 'Would you like me to kiss it and make it better?'

Heat as unwelcome as he was spiraled through her. As a matter of fact, she wanted him to do just that. Kiss her hand. Then her mouth. No, she didn't. She didn't want that at all. Shoving that horrid thought aside, she asked, 'And risk becoming one of your names? I think not.'

The subtle hints of pleasure vanished from his face. 'Let me in.'

'No.' She shrugged, trying to throw off the urge to speak the words that would give him access. 'House rules.'

Silver edged his pupils. 'Chrysabelle.'

She tapped the left blade lightly against her leg. Suddenly, the game shifted and she was winning. Maybe she shouldn't be enjoying this, but she was. 'Is that the closest you can come to *please*?'

He pushed off the door frame and bent his head to stare at her from under his lashes. Oh, he was good at working the dark-and-dangerous thing, but she was over that. For the most part. He cocked one brow. 'I'll be around back.' He ran his tongue over his teeth behind closed lips. 'Don't make me wait.'

And then he was gone in that lightning flash of speed only a vampire his age could manage.

Every brain cell screamed at her to let him rot out there. Every fiber of her comarré being itched to join him. Somewhere in between, the lonely, hungry female in her wanted to crawl into his arms and forget all the reasons she shouldn't.

Beyond the walkway, Mortalis leaned against the car. He tipped his head to one side, indicating she should follow Mal.

She slammed the door shut.

Velimai waited on the other side, arms crossed.

'I already know what you're thinking, so just don't. Don't say it.' Chrysabelle slipped her sacres back into their sheaths, girded herself mentally, and headed out.

Doc stayed in the cargo hold until Fi had come and gone again. He'd been able to talk to her once more, but her cognition of who he was and what was going on had only improved slightly. Watching her being torn apart didn't get any easier either, no matter how many times he saw it. The gut-wrenching sight strengthened his determination to get Aliza the blood she needed to make all this go away.

He had no real plan to get Dominic's blood, other than to explain to him face-to-face what the situation was. He figured Dominic owed it to him. After all, Fi had died in the attempt to rescue Maris. Not to mention Doc never would have been cursed if not for Dominic's supernatural crank.

The scene outside of Seven was unreal. Around the roped-off entrance, the crowd accosted anyone going in or coming out with the kind of enthusiasm once reserved for rock stars and Hollywood players. Across the street, a small handful carried signs reading FANGS BUT NO FANGS and VAMPIRES SUCK. He stopped at the edge of the swarm, trying to catch the eye of Tec, one of the wolf-shifters who worked the door.

At last, Tec nodded to him and Doc pushed through the crowd. A woman, human by scent, grabbed his arm. 'Are you a vampire? Do you want to bite me?'

Unbelievable. He pulled away, stilling the snarl in his throat but unable to stop his eyes from going leopard.

'Oh,' she cooed. 'Whatever you are, I'm game.'

'Actually, you're prey.' He pushed forward and left her behind, blank-faced and openmouthed.

Tec grabbed Doc's wrist above his outstretched hand as he approached and Doc returned the greeting. 'Long time, man.'

'Yeah, well, you know Dominic and I fell out.'

Tec made a small woofing sound deep in his throat. 'Yeah, Mia told me when you two, you know ... ' He pulled a pack of cigarettes out of his pocket. 'That's some bad juju, man.'

'That's for damn sure.' His curse and Mia were two things he didn't need reminding of, although Fi had erased Mia's place in his heart. Doc glanced around at the crowd and changed the subject. 'I hope you're getting paid extra.'

'Actually, we are. In fact' – Tec jerked his head toward the door – 'if you see Mia, tell her your first one's on me.'

'Thanks, bro.' Doc slapped Tec on the shoulder and went inside. He hadn't counted on Mia being here, but then, why wouldn't she? A good job was a good job, and in Paradise City, good jobs – straight jobs – were as hard to come by as feathers on a fruit fly. Didn't change the fact that he didn't plan on seeing Tec's sister unless absolutely necessary.

Several yards down, the hall ended in a set of steel double doors painted bloodred and decorated with a pair of crouching gold dragons. That was new. What was wrong with dirty and rusted? Guess that didn't go with the new velvet ropes cordoning off the entrance.

A second later, the door swung open and a fringe vamp he didn't know let him through. They nodded at each other, the only greeting needed.

Doc made his way through a set of heavy velvet drapes and entered the throng of fringe, varcolai, fae, and remnants. It had been years since he'd been in this club, since the night of his curse, actually. Besides the doors, nothing had changed. Same gaudy crystal chandeliers, same dark wood, same odor of blood, drugs, sex, and booze. He stopped, his gaze hooked by the petite blonde crossing his path. Scratch that. Something had changed. Dominic suddenly had a whole lot of comarré working for him. The comarré and comar sidled past. On closer inspection, they had none of Chrysabelle's fineness. Dominic was producing fakes, but the fringe didn't seem to care. Or maybe they didn't know better?

Dominic's business was Dominic's business. Doc moved on, searching for the man, but a quarter hour later and he'd yet to find Dominic on the floor. Doc tapped the arm of a passing server, a female remnant with traces of shifter – or drugs – in her eyes. 'Your boss in?'

She tucked the edge of her tray against her side. 'Dominic's always in.'

'What room is he in?' Better to look for him on the floor than go straight to the man's office. The days of belonging to this world were long over, and assuming any of those privileges still existed could have bad consequences.

She shrugged. 'You'll have to ask Katsumi. She's acting manager.'

That explained the new paint job on the doors. 'And I would find her where?'

'Not sure.' The girl looked around. 'I don't see her.'

'Yeah, me neither, which is why I asked.' This was going as well as everything else in his life. 'What about Ronan or Mortalis?'

She laughed. 'Ronan hasn't been here since he got his fangs handed to him in the pit. And Mortalis was here, but ... ' She lifted one shoulder as she glanced around the club again. 'I dunno.'

He exhaled slowly and reminded himself that yelling wasn't going to make the girl any smarter. 'How about Mia?'

The girl smiled. 'She's in Vanity.'

Finally. 'Thanks.'

She slipped back into the crowd and he headed for Vanity. Glistening gold-mirrored hangings draped the entrance, reflecting a thousand images of himself and the golden glow of his eyes. Like he needed the reminder of what he was – and wasn't anymore. Pushing through, he walked into the lounge. Nothing had changed here either. Textured plum silk covered the walls. The seating areas were all gold-mirror backed and done with more purples, this time suede and leather. Peacock feathers decorated everything else, matching the enormous peacock-shaped bar heavily paved in crystals and glass tiles so it sparkled like a disco ball.

The perfect spot for Mia to hold court. Even among all that bling, she stood out. True beauty had a way of outshining glitz. And true beauty was the best way to describe her slim dancer's body, long dark hair, and big brown eyes. Tonight she seemed taller than her usual five foot three, and he wondered if she was wearing platforms. That girl rocked some serious heels. At least she had when they'd been going out. He took the last spot beside the service bar and waited for her to glance up. Didn't take long.

'Well, now, they'll let anyone in here, won't they?' She neatly folded the spotless bar rag she'd been wiping down the bar with and tucked it away before she made her way over. The reflected prisms from the blinged-out bar covered her in speckles of light as bright as her smile. 'I can't believe it.'

'Believe it. It's me.' He smiled back. Hard to imagine a chick that petite could be a threat to anyone, but he'd seen a fae-varcolai remnant purposefully sneeze on her once. Bad idea. Mia's fear of germs bordered on the manic. She'd hit the offender with a blow to the windpipe so fast and hard the creature had required two weeks of ventilation to recover.

She leaned against the counter. 'What are you doing here? I haven't heard from you since your pride ... you know.' Her smile faded, memories flickering in her eyes. 'Well, it's really good to see you.'

'You too.' He dropped his smile as well. 'How have you been?'

'Good. Busy. You know, same old same old.' Her face twisted in the wistful look of pity he'd gotten all too accustomed to. 'How are you doing?'

He paused. Mia wasn't just anyone. They had history. He'd once thought they also had a future, but those days were gone, and the only woman he wanted a future with now was Fi. Still, Mia was a friend. Seemed to still be. 'Things are okay.' He shrugged and sat back, tried to smile away the truth. 'Nothing you need to worry about.'

She tilted her head, her eyes shimmering to their icy wolf blue for a brief second. 'Whatever you say, Maddoc. You want a white Russian?'

She remembered his usual, but he hesitated. Varcolai social laws made turning down food or beverage from another varcolai highly disrespectful, but Mia was a bartender. Offering drinks was her job. 'Just a club soda.'

'You on the wagon?' She made a funny face but snagged a tumbler and started filling it from the gun.

'No. I'm here to talk to Dominic.'

'Ah.' She squeezed in a lime before setting the glass in front of him. 'Sure a drink wouldn't be a better idea?'

'Gotta stay clearheaded.' He sipped, watching her wash her hands. The water beaded on her skin like it was coated in oil. He turned the glass in a small circle, shifting the ice. 'You wearing latex?'

'Spray-on latex is my best friend.' She wiggled her fingers at him. 'But then you knew that.'

He ignored the subtle jab at their past. 'Speaking of Dominic—'

'Which we weren't.'

'But we are now. Where is he tonight?'

'In his apartments, I guess.'

She leaned in and he caught a whiff of vanilla. Flashes of the past, of bare skin and hot nights, flitted through his brain. 'Between us, he's been scarce on the floor lately. Real scarce.'

'What about Mortalis?' He sucked in a chunk of ice, cooling himself down. Mia might still get a little physical reaction out of him, but she'd get that from most men. Fi was where his heart was.

Mia straightened as a server came to the service bar and put in a drink order. Mia nodded and lined up glasses. 'He's usually here, but I haven't seen him tonight. I think he was taking some-body home.'

Since when had Mortalis become the designated driver for anyone but Dominic? He turned, watching the crowd in the lounge while Mia filled the order. Some were barely keeping their clothes on, but that was status quo in Vanity. You didn't come here to fade into the background. One vamp, Middle Eastern and possibly noble-blooded, had a horde of fake comarré around him, but his gaze seemed stuck on Mia. Doc reminded himself it wasn't his place to care anymore, but that didn't stop the protective feelings from surfacing. The server took her drinks and left. He turned back to Mia. 'Who's Sheik Fang over there? He looks noble. And he's staring you down pretty hard.'

She snorted. 'He might be noble, but if he's in Paradise City, he's probably anathema. He intro'd himself as Nazir or something. He tried to kiss my hand. Can you imagine? Dead lips on my skin? Like that's going to happen.' A pair of remnants sat at the end of the bar. She greeted them with a smile, before glancing at Doc. 'Let me get their order and I'll be right back.'

He nursed the soda until she returned. 'I heard Ronan got beat down in the Pits.'

Mia laughed. 'Man, that was beautiful. Well, from what I heard. I wasn't there.' She sighed as she wiped down the bar. 'You're never going to believe who he fought.'

He swallowed the ice he was chewing. 'Who?'

'Remember that anathema who used to fight here all the time, hardly ever won, had those names all over him like tattoos – Hey, you know, I think that's who Mortalis was taking home.'

Mal. Doc dropped the glass. 'I gotta go.'

Within moments, he was back outside and running toward the freighter. If Mal had returned to the Pits, there was a damn good reason why. Not that Mal wouldn't welcome a chance to turn that Irish neck biter into ash. Doc ran with a speed no human could match, but it wasn't nearly as fast as he could have gone in his leopard form. His lungs barely straining, he plowed through street after street. The neighborhood surrounding Seven was about as ghetto as you could get, but the chances of someone giving him trouble were slim. This was fringe country, and the uneasy peace between fringe and varcolai had so far survived the covenant's breaking.

He turned a corner, putting the worst of it behind him. An acrid odor rose up around him, clinging to his skin like spiderweb. He slowed down, scanning the street for the source. He knew that smell from somewhere. It reminded him of ... of ... He came to a complete stop.

Piles of ash dotted the asphalt and sidewalk. The bitter scent reminded him of the way the vampires they'd killed at Tatiana's had smelled when they died, because that's what he was looking at.

Pile after pile of vampire remains.

Chapter Ten

Even with his back to her, Mal felt Chrysabelle with his whole being as she walked toward where he stood by the pool. Her heartbeat, which had ratcheted up the moment he'd stepped out of the car and then again when he'd told her she smelled good, echoed in his veins. Her scent, thicker and more hypnotic with the fresh blood on her palm, draped him in a magnetic haze. Only a few weeks had passed since he'd seen her, but the memory of her preternatural glow and glittering signum paled in comparison to her in the flesh. With her sunny blondeness and eyes that matched the summer sky, she remained the essence of everything he craved.

And like a fool, he'd let her affect him. Had he actually said, 'Would you like me to kiss it and make it better?' Chalk that up to another moment of his life he'd like to erase. *Fool, fool, fool* was the best the voices could do, subdued by ingesting so much blood in such a short amount of time.

Her slippered feet halted a yard or so behind him. 'Well? Talk.'

Without turning around, he could picture her. Arms still

crossed, one hip cocked out, that 'I dare you' look on her face. He closed his eyes, dropped his chin to his chest, and, so help him, he inhaled.

His muscles tensed to steel wire, his nerves pinging shocks of pleasure and need through him faster than he could register. The desire to maintain his human face vanished in a shiver of angled bones and jagged fangs. He rolled his head to one side, mouth open to let the tangible scent of her slide over his tongue. The ache in his gums mirrored the ache piercing his gut. Holy hell. If she'd deliberately given her blood to Ronan, it might be enough to push Mal over the killing edge. Back to that blind hungry rage that had once owned him. *Yessss* ... There was only so much betrayal one man could take. *You're not a man. You're a monster.*

The soft *tap, tap, tap* of her fingers drumming on her arm broke through the sharp, white urgency surrounding him. 'I'm waiting.'

Yes, he was a monster. She would do well to remember it. He spun, knowing how he must look and not giving a damn. 'I am aware, but considering the circumstances, patience might be a better option.'

Surprisingly, she didn't say a word. Instead she walked past him, not touching him but close enough to tighten the noose of desire around his throat. If she hadn't done it deliberately, he'd be shocked. She walked to the chaise, sat, then lifted a glass of juice from the side table. Juice that had barely been touched. Had his arrival interrupted something? Another visitor? One glass didn't mean she'd been alone. Vampires didn't ingest human foods, except alcohol.

She held it up to him in a mock salute, then took a long, slow sip. Her throat worked as she swallowed, her eyes never leaving his.

Hades on a cracker. She was torturing him on purpose. And probably enjoying it. Maybe he deserved it. And maybe she deserved a little in return, except he had no idea how to torture a woman who clearly didn't care if he continued to exist or not. 'What were you doing at Seven?'

She set the glass down. 'I could ask you the same question.'

'I think it was pretty obvious what I was doing there.'

'I meant besides making a spectacle of yourself.'

Is that what she thought? 'I don't owe you an explanation.'

'No, you don't.' She swung her legs over the side of the chaise as if to leave.

'I'm giving you one anyway. Katsumi promised me Dominic's help in exchange for winning.'

Her forehead crinkled. 'His help for what?'

'For removing this curse.'

The muscles in her jaw tightened. She looked down at her wounded hand. Was she hiding shame or anger?

'That was certainly a good reason to fight, then. Also a good reason to drink the blood I sent you.'

'It was good enough for Ronan.'

Her head jerked up. 'What does that mean?'

He saw no injuries on her that might indicate Ronan had taken her blood by force, which meant she'd either given it to him willingly – something he couldn't imagine her doing – or she truly didn't know he'd gotten his hands on it. But how would that have happened? 'Ronan had your blood in his system when he entered the arena. I didn't smell it on him until he started to bleed.' The combination of her blood already ingested and the anticipation of the fight had refocused his senses to the purpose of winning. 'I tasted his blood to be sure. It was heavily laced with yours.'

The shock in her eyes told the truth. She hadn't known.

'How is that possible?' The heels of her palms came down against the chaise's frame as she pushed herself up. She flinched, pulled her wounded hand to her chest, then shook it off like it was nothing.

That nothing drove a small, gold dagger into his shriveled heart. He hated that she hurt almost as much as he despised how pathetic she'd made him for caring.

Hands cupped to her stomach like she felt ill, she paced a few steps toward the pool and stood there, facing away from him. Gleaming with that mesmerizing comarré glow. 'Actually, I know how it was possible.' Her hair spilled down her back like moonlit silk. 'Dominic's driver came by with a letter from Dominic requesting blood. I sent some.'

A hard surge of possessive anger shot down his spine. She *had* given another vampire her blood. This from the woman who had spouted the tenets of comarré law to him as the reasons for so many of her secrets and actions.

Still overlooking the pool, she continued. 'He just seemed so needy in his letter and after all he did to help with Maris . . . ' She shrugged. 'It seemed like the right thing to do.'

He struggled to maintain a level of calm, quickly realizing he was not going to maintain it much longer. He clenched his hands until his knuckles popped. 'What does comarré law say about a comarré giving her blood to a vampire who is not her patron?'

'That it is not allowed . . . ' Her voice faded into the night air and she turned. Her thumb stroked the side of her bandaged hand. 'Yes, I see what you're saying. You're assuming you still own my blood rights, which you very well may. Comarré law doesn't really cover blood rights reversion in a case where your patron gains your blood rights by stealing them, then gives your blood to a ghost who is actually haunting *him*, who then turns human again only to die for a second time.' She stared at him, a small storm brewing in her eyes. 'Yes, that is rather a gray area. One I'm surprised you'd even care about ... Oh, I get it. You're jealous.' A false smile lifted the corners of her crimson mouth. 'Isn't that touching.'

He moved toward her a step. 'I am not jealous. I am simply tired of being betrayed.'

Her smile disappeared. 'I did not betray you.'

'You promised help, got what you wanted, and withdrew.'

The angry sparks returned. She jabbed a finger in the air. 'Just because I haven't helped you yet doesn't mean I'm not going to. Besides, I sent you blood.'

'Was that supposed to mollify me?'

'You refused to speak to me, so I did what any comarré would do in that situation – the best I could.'

'What you did was keep me at arm's length. You could have come yourself, but then you would have had to face the fact that you'd lied to me. Yet again.' She'd lied to him so much when they'd first met that he'd thought her incapable of the truth. Maybe he'd been right.

'I didn't lie about helping you.' She shook her head, her mouth opening and closing as if the right words wouldn't come. 'You don't understand.'

He crossed his arms. 'Then explain.'

Anger and tension spun off her in waves. She tilted her face away from him, and he thought if not for her wounded palm, she would be wringing her hands. Blonde strands swung down to brush her cheek. 'Contacting the Aurelian means a return trip to Corvinestri. I wasn't ready to do that then. I thought you'd understand, give me time to get over Maris's death.' She turned her head just enough to make eye contact. 'But you shut me out almost immediately.'

'I didn't shut you out.' On the flight home, she'd sat alone, curled up and facing the wall. He'd let her be. He understood sorrow. 'I gave you space to grieve. But you stayed silent.'

She rolled her eyes. 'Yes, and you were the epitome of communication.'

He shook his head and angled himself toward the house. 'This is pointless.'

'Do you know where I went before I ended up at Seven that night?' She moved forward a step. 'I went to the freighter.' Then another. 'To see you.' One more put her within a foot of him. 'To tell you I was ready to help. But you weren't there.'

She was too close. The needy ache throbbing in his belly again forced him back in her direction. 'That's convenient.'

'It's the truth.' Her eyes dared him to call her a liar again.

'So help.' He spread his arms. 'I'm right here.'

'I will. Soon. I have to speak—'

'Another delay.' He threw his hands up and backed away. 'How surprising.'

She grabbed his arm with her injured hand. Heat seared his skin. The voices whined at the blood contact, always hungry but always hating her. *Bite her, drink her, drain her.* 'Listen to me. I've found a way to get to the Aurelian without going back to Corvinestri, but it's dangerous—'

'To who?'

'To me. Now shut up and let me finish.'

He cocked a brow. Someone was shedding their sweet comarré image. 'Go on.'

'I just need to speak to someone who's been part of the process before. Maris left some details in her journal, but not enough to make me comfortable.' She scooped up a leather-bound volume from the table and began flipping through it. She stopped and tapped a finger on one of the pages. 'This could be clearer.'

He glanced over her shoulder and snorted. 'I don't know what kind of trick you're pulling, but that page is blank.'

Her face screwed into a questioning frown. 'Are you blind?' She lifted the journal. 'This page isn't blank. Granted, Maris's handwriting is cramped, but it's not impossible to read.'

'The page is blank. You understand the meaning of that word, don't you?'

A short, strangled sound emanated from her throat. She turned the page. 'How about this one?'

'Blank.'

She thumbed through a few more. 'Anything?'

'Nothing.'

'Well, what do you know?' A slow, impressed smile spread across Chrysabelle's face. 'Maris warded her journals against vampires.'

He tried to refocus her. 'Who is this person you need to speak to?'

'Just someone who knows how this works.'

'Who?'

She stared at him, petulant sparks flying off her as if she were flint and he were steel, challenging him with her eyes to say something smart. 'Dominic.'

'No.'

'No? Don't even begin to try to tell me what to do. The way I see it' – she poked him in the chest – 'you need me. I don't need you.' She swept past him and walked toward the house, muttering as she went. 'This is the most unbalanced relationship I've ever had the misfortune to be a part of.'

Unbalanced? Clarity smacked him in the face. She was mad because he'd drunk her blood, but she hadn't gotten her half of the exchange. That was easy to fix. *No.* Unpleasant. *Yes.* But easy. Carefully avoiding her injury, he looped his fingers around her wrist – noting that her wrist blades weren't strapped on – and brought her to a stop.

'What on earth are you—'

His mouth ended her sentence and started the voices howling. He slipped his hands around her forearms and pulled her against him, savoring the velvet warmth that seeped into his skin from hers. He told himself he was kissing her because he owed it to her, but that became a lie the moment his lips touched her carmine mouth. He kissed her because he wanted to.

Because he could.

The voices ratcheted down to a tolerable hum.

He deepened the kiss, careful to keep his fangs from nicking her. She was sweeter and more pliant than he remembered, or maybe her scent intoxicated him, making recollection impossible. Her temperature rose in time with her heartbeat, and she went boneless in his grasp.

She was pleasure in the flesh, heat and softness and every womanly delight he'd done without these past centuries. All he could wonder was why he hadn't done this sooner, why he'd thought this a task worth avoiding. Never again would he—

She stiffened and his bliss-addled brain refused to react in time to keep her from jerking out of his clutches. 'What do you think you're doing?' Her left fist cocked back.

'I'm making up for—' He ducked as she swung. 'Drinking your blood. Your half of the deal, right? Power for power. I thought that would make us even.'

'Even?' She growled the word, swiping the back of her

trembling bandaged hand over her mouth. Her chest rose and fell with each breath. She shook her head, clearly provoked, if the flush across her face and neck was any indication. 'That only works right after you ingest the blood, when your heart is beating. That kiss was ... pointless.' She spun and stomped off toward the house.

Pointless? He thought not. If nothing else, it proved she was a woman who clearly did care if he continued to exist or not. With a smile that would probably earn him another left hook, he sauntered after his comarré. Maybe life wasn't so bad after all.

Fool, fool, fool.

Chapter Eleven

'Varcolai?' Tatiana grimaced as she stepped over the creature's hindquarters and circled around to see the face of the female Nasir had brought her. A shifter. Gah. They were such lowly beings, meant to be servants or watchdogs. Couldn't he have found a fringe? At least they were still vampire. She sighed. The girl would have to do. Tatiana didn't want to waste time sending Nasir back to the club Octavian had found. 'How long before the silver wears off?'

Nasir had followed the girl from the club, then injected her with enough colloidal silver to shut her system down. The result was a return to her true animal state.

'Another few minutes.' Nasir crossed his arms and leaned against the room's arched doorway. 'She is a bartender in the club. That should give you fair access.'

Tatiana nudged the she-wolf with her boot. 'I need her awake so she can shift. I can't do this without seeing her human face.'

Through trial and error, she'd learned the limits of her powers of mimicry. She couldn't create an original image, nor could she take on the likeness of anyone deceased. She'd found that out one painful, lonely night after Mikkel's death. All she'd wanted was to see him one last time. Instead of his beautiful face looking back at her in the mirror, she'd seen . . . something she never wanted to see again.

Death.

The wolf whimpered, stretching her legs against the plastic zip ties binding her. Those wouldn't hold if the creature regained consciousness.

'Octavian, get ready with the restraints,' Tatiana called, then nodded to Nasir. 'Get them on her before she wakes up completely.'

'Of course, my love.' Nasir grabbed the wolf's bound legs and dragged her across the cement floor to where Octavian stood waiting.

The mansion her head of staff had obtained was more than Tatiana had expected. It was shockingly suited to her needs. The kine owners, delicious as they had been while alive, had enjoyed a wide variety of kinks, evidenced by the windowless dungeon in the center of their house. A room they'd obviously used based on the equipment's wear marks and the lingering fragrances of blood and other less-appealing fluids. She'd known mortals engaged in such things but never realized some took it to such an extent. How lucky for her.

The click and scrape of metal against concrete filled the room as Nasir fixed the largest shackle around the wolf's throat. He tugged on the chain, testing where it was set into the wall. Octavian attached two more sets to the wolf's legs. The creature's thin joints barely filled the heavy metal fetters, but the one around the neck would hopefully be enough until the shifter was in human form. After that, Nasir had a drug that would prevent her from shifting again and escaping.

The creature's lids opened, her startlingly blue eyes instantly fixed on Nasir. Her lip curled back and with a snarl, she leaped, grazing his calf before the chain snapped her to a halt.

Nasir spun, his fist raised in anger. Through the tear in his trousers, red oozed from the already mending gash. The bitter spice of vampire blood mixed with the already present scents of leather, sweat, and sex.

'No, Nasir.' Tatiana couldn't have the girl bruised yet. She needed to see her human face as unadulterated as possible.

He relaxed and dropped his hand. 'Filthy creature.'

'Yes, I agree.' Tatiana shot him a look of displeasure. 'And yet you chose her for me to mimic.'

Realization flared across his face. 'I never meant any disrespect. I only thought no one would suspect that such a powerful noble would masquerade as one so lowly.'

Octavian snickered. Tatiana raised a finger in his direction. The small gesture silenced him. He turned away and busied himself as she moved toward Nasir. 'Do I assume to know how your potions and brews should be mixed?'

'No, of course not—'

'Do I tell you what metals to transform?'

'No, but—'

'Then don't do any thinking for me. Understood?'

He bristled at her words but said nothing. Time was running out to appease the ire of the ancient ones. Possessing the ring was paramount. Nothing else mattered.

A shiver of magic unsettled the air. Behind Nasir, the shifter had become human.

Tatiana walked around him to face the creature she was to become. 'She's a lot smaller in her human form. Interesting.'

'You're about the same size, I believe,' Nasir said.

She glared at him.

The girl shook, her brown eyes large and liquid. 'Where am I? What do you want with me?'

Tatiana leaned down, careful to stay beyond the girl's reach. Instantly, the shifter lunged. Her eyes snapped wolfen blue, and her canines jutted longer and sharper. Tatiana didn't flinch. Instead, she shed her human face and snarled back. To the girl's credit, she didn't retreat.

'Shifter, know this. You do not frighten me any more than a bit of refuse blowing in the wind. You are beneath me.' She pointed at Octavian while keeping eye contact with the girl. 'Your life is worth less to me than that human's. Do you understand?'

'I understand.' The girl nodded and trembled with what Tatiana suspected was rage, not fear. 'I also understand you wish to die by varcolai hands, bloodsucker.'

She could break this one if need be. Or let Nasir do it. 'The only one in this room who's going to die by varcolai hands is you, should you choose to take your own life.' She stood, straightening herself to her full height. 'Your name?'

'Go screw yourself.'

Tatiana cracked her palm across the girl's face. 'Your name. Now.'

'Mia.' The girl's head was down, her face hidden in a sweep of brown hair. She lifted her chin. Blood welled from the corner of her mouth, the scent hot and earthy like an ancestral forest after a summer rain. 'You won't get away with this. My pack will come looking for me. My brother works at the club. He'll notice I'm gone.'

'Really, *Mia*? Somehow I think otherwise.' Tatiana laughed and turned to Octavian. Time to remove him from the room. She preferred her servants didn't have a full grasp of her powers. Besides, a little havoc in the city would make things more interesting. 'Set the Nothos free to hunt the comarré. Remind them to return her alive.'

'Yes, my lady.' Octavian bowed and trotted off to do her bidding.

She refocused on the girl and opened herself to the power the Castus had bestowed upon her. Sensation tingled through her. The girl's eyes rounded and her mouth dropped open. Tatiana knew her change was complete and exact.

The shifter scuttled backward until she hit the wall. 'How did you ... You look just like me.' Regaining her composure, she shook her head, her jaw working. 'You'll never pass for me.'

Tatiana pictured the girl's wolf form in her head, and a second later, she was down on all fours looking out through animal eyes. Another second and she was back in the girl's human form. The sudden back-and-forth left her light-headed and queasy, but she hid the ill effects by snapping her fingers for Nasir. He was at her side in a flash, and she grasped his arm as if preparing to leave.

Steadied, she retook her own image before addressing the shifter one last time, holding tight to Nasir as a new bout of dizziness spun her head. 'As you can see, I will pass for you quite easily, and if you don't give me the information I need, no one will even realize you're missing until your carcass turns up as roadkill. Do we have an understanding, or do I need to make myself clearer?'

Mia tucked her knees to her chest and shook her head slowly. 'No. I understand perfectly.'

Right foot, left foot, right foot, left foot. Chrysabelle concentrated on taking steady, even steps back to the house, but the air had become thicker, the earth slightly tilted, and her body traitorously warm since Mal had tried to make up for drinking her blood by kissing her.

Right foot, left foot. She could do this. She could make it into the house without wobbling or sighing or anything else that might give him a clue that what he'd done had affected her exceptionally more than she was ever going to admit.

After his reaction to her sending blood to Dominic, she knew he wasn't going to like her needing to see Dominic about this new way of getting to the Aurelian, but he'd helped Maris through the ritual. Besides, who else was she going to ask?

She wished she could gather enough real anger to match the acting she'd done when she'd pulled away from Mal, but there was nothing to draw from. Painful as it might be to admit, he was right and she was wrong. If he did still own her blood rights – which he most likely did – sending blood to another vampire was the human equivalent of cheating on a spouse.

In noble society, he could demand his blood money back. Or worse. She glanced over her shoulder to see where he was and jumped, a small yelp escaping her before she could stop it.

'Scare you?' he asked from where he walked beside her.

'No.' Yes. Like he didn't know. 'I hate that silent speed thing. Worst vampire ability ever.'

He made a sound like strangled laughter. 'I'll try to make more noise in the future.'

So he assumed they'd be spending more time together? 'No, you won't.'

He tucked his hands into his pockets. 'Have a little faith.'

His tone said he wasn't just talking about making less noise. Had he kissed her for a reason beyond thinking he owed it to her? Had he been marking his territory? The anger she couldn't find before was slowly making its way to the top of her head. 'If you think—'

Loud, repetitive honking broke the night's silence. Someone was at the gate.

'Stay here,' Mal said.

Without bothering to answer, she left him behind and raced into the house to see what was going on, grabbing her sacre as she hit the foyer. The security camera showed Mal's ancient sedan outside her gate, Doc at the wheel. He leaned on the horn again as Mal came speeding into view on the monitor. She hit the button to open the gate and went outside, where Velimai and Mortalis stood by Dominic's car.

What's happening? Who's here? Velimai signed.

'Doc,' Chrysabelle answered.

With Mal jogging behind, the old gasoline-powered vehicle screeched to a stop in the circular drive and Doc jumped out. He twisted to face Mal. 'What were you doing in the Pits?'

'Taking care of business.'

Doc shook his head, clearly incredulous. 'Ronan could have killed you.'

Mal snorted. 'And you care because ... ?'

Doc's hands were clenched, his body a fuse waiting to be lit. 'Because without you, Fi's gone.'

Mal shot Chrysabelle a look. 'Fi *is* gone, Doc. You know that.'

Doc's fist slammed the car's side panel, denting it slightly. 'No, she's not. I've seen her. She's stuck in some kind of nightmare loop. She shows up every night in the cargo hold and then ... ' He glanced down, shaking his head in obvious anger.

'And then what?' Chrysabelle asked as she walked forward.

Doc turned his leopard-yellow eyes to her. 'And then Mal kills her. She's stuck repeating the night she died over and over.' His voice cracked. 'Every night, she stumbles through those ruins and every night' – he leveled his gaze at Mal – 'he rips her throat out.'

'Is she . . . aware of what's happening to her?'

'Yes,' he hissed.

'Holy mother,' Chrysabelle whispered. Mortalis cursed softly in faeish. How awful for Fi. And for Doc, who so clearly loved her.

Mal's jaw went slack and he seemed somehow to pale. She knew those memories weren't easy ones for him. Being reminded of them couldn't be pleasant. How much worse would it be to have them played out for everyone to see? And poor Fi. To die every night, suffering through the pain and fear . . .

'Well,' she announced loudly, as if volume superseded emotion, 'there's got to be something we can do.'

'There is. But I need to see Dominic first and I can't find him.'

'You're in luck.' Her voice sounded a lot more chipper than she felt. 'We're just about to go see him.'

'We are?' Mortalis asked.

'Velimai will stay here, but yes, the rest of us are,' Chrysabelle answered.

Mortalis crossed his arms. 'No. I'll get Dominic, bring him to the club. We can meet there.'

Chrysabelle pointed her blade at the fae. 'I realize you're protecting him, but if you don't get in that car and drive us to his penthouse immediately, so help me, holy mother, I will slice those horns off your head and insert them into a body cavity.'

Mal snorted. Mortalis frowned. 'You've lost your mind.'

She lifted the sacre a little higher, the sword buzzing with her emotion. 'Get in the car.'

He did, muttering more incomprehensible things in faeish.

'Nicely done, comarré.' Doc started for Dominic's car. 'Dominic won't be happy about this, but he should probably know someone is killing off his customer base, too.'

'What?' She stopped, hand in mid-reach for the car door.

Doc paused on his side of the vehicle. 'Yeah, I stumbled onto a fringe graveyard. Must have been eight, nine piles of ash.'

'I can't imagine who would do that.' Other than Creek. Maybe. He'd had no problems knocking off the fringe attacking her. Chrysabelle swallowed down the suspicion. He'd come to her rescue. That made him one of the good guys, which meant they were technically on the same side.

Weren't they?

Chapter Twelve

Creek kept to the shadows while on the streets. Not that he needed the protection, but it helped him blend in with every other mortal brave enough to show their face after dark. Those who went out after sundown in this part of town were either looking for trouble in the form of a score, a woman willing to do the most for the money, or a chance to mingle with the othernatural crowd, or they were plain stupid. Regardless, that made for dangerous company.

His kind of night.

An old nylon windbreaker, pulled over his hair and tugged low so it almost covered his eyes, and baggy jeans, which supplied ample room for extra bolts, painted him as just one more punk out for an evening of mayhem and mischief. The jacket also covered the chest holster carrying his crossbow and halm, the lengths of titanium comfortably reassuring against his ribs. He cruised the section of town surrounding Seven, looking for a chance to run into Chrysabelle again. Meanwhile, he might find an opportunity for a little more practice.

Three working girls of the fringe variety hung on the busiest corner, waving at the cars that slowed as they drove past. Creek shook his head and slipped into a doorway across the street to hunker down and wait. The idiot who picked up one of those hookers probably wouldn't be coming back. Creek's fingers dug into his empty back pocket for a smoke before he realized what he was doing. Old habits died hard.

The tallest of the trio postured as a silver sports car coasted down the street. She flicked her long blue hair over one shoulder and sashayed toward the curb in high-heeled boots. The red glow of brake lights lit up the car's back end. Human curiosity of vampires was hitting a new peak. More and more were coming to believe the fanged monstrosities were real, and those who believed fell into two camps: those who feared the vampires and those who wanted to *be* vampires. The latter tended to be pale-skinned, fake-fang-wearing sycophants who dressed like they were going to a graveside orgy. What did they hope for? To find a vampire who would grant them eternal life? At the thought, the marks on his back itched.

The car pulled up and idled, the passenger side window rolling down. The tall fringe, so narrow-hipped and muscular Creek wondered if she might actually be a he, approached the vehicle and leaned on the door.

After a few minutes of conversation, the fringe got in and the driver eased away. Creek peeled off from his perch and headed after them, a slow lope at first so he wouldn't arouse suspicion. Once they were a few blocks away, he poured on the speed and caught up, then slowed again as the car turned down an alley. He followed, as silent as the vehicle's electric engine.

The car parked and the headlights flicked off, leaving only ambient light to see by, but it was more than enough for him. Anyone who survived the KM rituals got rewarded with a whole heap of amped-up abilities. Speed was one of those. Great night vision, another.

The pair in the car seemed to be chatting. Creek moved closer, keeping low and watching his steps so as not to disturb any debris that might make noise. The john was paying her. How ironic, considering he was about to pay again with his life.

The female stuffed a few bills into her top and laughed, her fangs shining in the moonlight. Time to roll or the man in that car would be a bloodless sack of bones in three ... two ...

Creek sped to her door. His hood fell back. In a single fluid motion, he whipped out a bolt and yanked the car door open. This close, the crossbow was overkill. She was mid-lunge, fangs bared. She snapped around in his direction, spitting like a wet cat.

'Hey!' the human male yelled. He reached for the female. Light glinted off his wedding ring. 'Get your own—'

Creek sank the bolt into her chest. She screeched, her eyes rounded in shock, then she crumbled into ash. He shook the bolt off. A few plastic fifties clung to the end, pierced through. He pulled them off and pocketed them. The john didn't deserve them back. He pointed the bolt at the man. 'You married?'

'What the—' The man scowled. 'Yes.'

'Kids?'

'Yeah, why?'

Creek reached through the car and yanked the man halfway out. 'Because you're a piss-poor excuse for a husband and father, out here trying to score a little vampire tail. Go home and apologize to your family. Do something nice for them.'

The man nodded, his eyes wide.

Creek tossed him back into his seat. 'Don't let me see you here again. I won't be as merciful.'

The man kept nodding. Creek watched until the car pulled away, hard memories clamping down on him. Too bad no one had ever given his father the same warning. But then, some people only understood brute force.

Doc slouched against the cold white marble wall of the foyer while Mortalis went through the retinal scan that would get them into the elevator and up to Dominic's penthouse. His jaw ached from clenching it, but Venetian Island oozed luxury like a head wound oozed blood. It worked his last good nerve. Especially since he'd been one of the mules carrying the heavy load that had paid for this palace. Knowing that made every inch of this upscale ivory tower a personal insult, where a visit to Chrysabelle's didn't bother him one bit. Maris had paid for her crib via Lapointe Cosmetics, not drugs and fake comarrés and pit matches.

The elevator swooshed open, a wood-paneled, sculpted-carpet coffin. Mortalis held the door while Mal and Chrysabelle got on. The fae looked at him expectantly.

Doc followed, his reluctance increasing with each step. He hadn't seen Dominic since the trip to Corvinestri, and that was fine with him. Now he had to ask for help from the very man who'd caused his curse in the first place.

Nothing sucked more than needing your enemy's assistance.

Mortalis moved his hand out of the way, and the doors closed with a soft *ping*. The lift shot up, smooth as old cognac. Which Dominic probably drank by the bucket. Doc flicked a claw out on his pointer finger and gouged a scratch into the mahogany paneling. Petty and childish, but then leopard-shifters weren't known for their personal growth.

'Remember,' Mortalis said. 'I go first.'

'Yeah, thanks, I'd forgotten the other hundred times you told us.' Doc blew out a breath. Tension crackled along his nerves. This was not going to end well, he could feel it. But whatever it took, he'd help Fi. Or die trying. Maybe he could come back as a ghost, too? Then he'd haunt Dominic. And Aliza. And maybe Mal just for funsies.

The doors opened onto Dominic's private foyer. Un-freaking-believable. Even Mal whistled. The ceiling was a mural of some gods and goddesses getting their chow on. Gilding covered everything that wasn't stone or polished wood. Doc snorted. 'Lemme guess, this is from the early Mafia period of history?'

Chrysabelle glanced at him. 'Actually, that ceiling is a copy of *The Feast of the Gods* by Bellini.'

'Feast, huh? Figures.' Perfect for a vampire who devoured life like it was his personal porterhouse.

Mortalis hit the HOLD button on the elevator, then stepped out and approached the penthouse. Doc wondered if he'd be able to restrain the urge to *accidentally* break something once he got inside. Mortalis rapped the lion's-head door knocker hanging off the set of bronze double doors. Once, twice, a pause, then a third time.

The door opened, revealing a slender, lavender-eyed female in a clingy black dress. Everything about her looked human, except for the lack of life in her unnaturally colored gaze and plasticky smooth skin. 'Welcome.' Her voice was an automated purr. 'How may I help you?'

Chrysabelle leaned over to Doc and whispered, 'What is that?'

'That,' Doc answered, not bothering to lower his voice, 'is a symbot.' When he'd still been in the business, he'd seen them at some of the homes of his wealthier clientele, but he hadn't known Dominic had one. Made sense though. A lifeless android was the perfect companion for a lifeless vampire.

Mortalis cleared his throat. 'Isabelle, I need to see Dominic.'

'Of course.' She smiled blankly and pivoted, extending her arm toward the room beyond. 'Please come in.'

'I need you to bring him here.'

'One moment, please.' Like the well-oiled machine she was, Isabelle disappeared into the apartment.

Mortalis glanced back.

'We know,' Doc said. 'Let you do the talking.'

Chrysabelle reached out toward the fae but let her hand drop without touching him. 'Mortalis, if Dominic fires you, you can come work for me.'

'It's not being fired I'm worried about.'

Footsteps interrupted them. Dominic. They heard his voice first.

'Buonasera,' he called out to Mortalis. 'Why didn't you come in?' He came into view, Isabelle behind him. His expression went cold when he saw Doc. His gaze shifted to Chrysabelle, then to Mal, then back to Mortalis. 'Why did you bring them here?' He held a tense hand out toward Chrysabelle. 'No offense, *cara mia*, but you must understand my need for protection.'

She stepped forward. 'Of course, Dominic. That's exactly why we came. Forgive Mortalis. I threatened him with harm if he didn't bring us to you immediately.'

A strange light entered Dominic's eyes. 'You threatened him? With what?'

Mortalis cleared his throat. 'It was nothing.'

Mal stepped out of the elevator. 'She threatened to chop his horns off and shove them into a body cavity.'

Chrysabelle glared at Mal. 'I never used the word *shove*.'

Dominic's laughter interrupted them. 'Bravo, *bella*. You are most assuredly your mother's child.' He sobered a bit. 'If you needed to speak to me, why is it necessary for all of you to be here? Couldn't you deliver the information to Mortalis and have him bring it to me?'

Chrysabelle shook her head. 'Someone stole blood from me in your name, and Ronan ended up with it. That needs a face-to-face explanation.'

Doc wondered how Dominic managed not to react to that news. On the way over, she'd explained to the rest of them what had happened, and the severity of the situation had registered immediately. Had Dominic somehow already known? Maybe he'd given the blood to Ronan after all. Mal looked like he'd come to the same conclusion, judging by the cords tightening in his neck.

'There are other, more private matters I need to speak to you about as well,' she added. 'Doc also has news you should hear.'

Yeah, and a small request for a vial or two of blood. Nothing major.

With obvious reluctance, Dominic stepped out of the way. 'Come in, then, but if I find any of you have shared this location with anyone, you will see a side of me you do not like.'

Doc held back the response burning his tongue.

Many minutes later, when they were seated in Dominic's surprisingly sleek living room, and Chrysabelle and Mal had finished explaining everything that had happened, Dominic finally looked shocked. 'I would never ask you for blood. I know too well what is and what is not appropriate when it comes to comarré.' He looked up for a moment as Isabelle refilled his wine. 'Mortalis, you must find Leo and ask him for the details of the night he went to Chrysabelle's. Who gave him the letter? Where did he deliver the blood?'

'On it.' Mortalis nodded. 'What about Ronan and Katsumi?'

'We can't assume anything until we know more. I'll talk to Katsumi first, then Ronan.'

Mal leaned back in an angular leather chair. 'Both of them lie. How can you believe anything either of them says?'

Dominic waved a hand through the air. 'I have ways.'

'You mean drugs,' Doc muttered. Dammit. That wasn't going to help his case.

Dominic's gaze arrowed in on him. 'Perhaps now would be a good time for us to speak.' He stood, palming the bowl of his wineglass. 'Let's go to the library, shall we?' He lifted his glass toward Chrysabelle. 'If you'll excuse us.' Without waiting for an answer, he headed out of the room.

Doc went after him, staying back until Dominic stopped and twisted the matte steel lever on a black lacquered door.

'After you.'

Books – real books, not just digital copies – filled the floor-to-ceiling brushed steel bookshelves. Was there anything the man didn't spend money on? Doc stood in the middle of the room and ignored the chairs. This was not a conversation you sat down for.

Dominic closed the door. 'Well? What is so important that after all these years you come to me this way? Or have you finally realized that the blame for your curse rests elsewhere? Have you decided to come back to work? I can always use good help.'

Like that would ever happen. Doc unclenched his jaw and blew out the breath he'd been holding. 'Someone's killing off fringe vamps. A few streets away from Seven, there must be eight or nine piles of ash. I thought you should know, given that they're your club's bread and butter.'

Dominic's brows lifted for a moment. 'I appreciate the information. I will have someone investigate further. But that's not what you really came to discuss, is it?'

'No.' Here went nothing. 'I'm here for Fi's sake.'

'Malkolm's ghost? I don't understand.'

Doc explained what had been happening, ending with an abbreviated version of his trip to see Aliza. 'There's one thing she needs to bring her daughter back.'

Dominic swallowed a sip of wine. 'My blood.'

Doc checked his surprise. 'Yes, but how did you know that?'

'Aliza's been trying to get it for years.' He swirled the wine in the glass. 'If I haven't given it to her, what makes you think I'm going to give it to you?'

For a moment, Doc was stunned, but he quickly remembered this was Dominic he was dealing with. The man did nothing unless he stood to gain. 'We're talking about restoring the lives of two women.' Then Doc remembered something Chrysabelle had quoted from her mother's journals. Something Maris had attributed to Dominic. 'Sometimes love is worth the risk.'

Dominic's eyes burned silver for a brief second, but that was all the acknowledgment he gave the words. 'And sometimes it is not. I'm sorry for Fiona, but Aliza's daughter is another story. Her greed got her where she is, the abuse of that which she purchased from me. Not what I sold her, but how it was used. She has reaped what she sowed.' He wandered to a bookcase and leisurely perused the spines, his back to Doc. 'Tell Chrysabelle to come in, would you?'

Just like that, the conversation was over. The flame of hope in Doc's chest went out, replaced by a darker fire. One that blazed hotter. One that burned away the fine line between right and wrong.

One that didn't care who it reduced to ashes.

Chapter Thirteen

Mal leaned his forehead against the wall of glass that made up the north side of Dominic's ultramodern penthouse. Mortalis had already left to follow up with the driver and Chrysabelle had been talking to Dominic in the library since Doc came out looking like murder incarnate. Whatever he and Dominic had discussed, it hadn't gone well.

From this height, the city beyond the bay seemed like a glittering jewel of tranquility. Precious electricity flowed into this part of town without interruption. Couldn't have the inhabitants of Venetian Island being reminded what a dump the rest of Paradise City was. The condo buildings on this secluded haven were well maintained, no signs of vandalism or even the acid rain corrosion that marred most other areas. The streets had an abundance of trees. Mostly palms, but still. No wonder this small island employed their own harbor police to patrol the borders.

It reminded him of where Chrysabelle lived, of the luxury her mother had left for her, and, once again, of how great a delta existed between Chrysabelle's world and his. *And how little you deserve her.*

He rapped his head softly on the glass, the lights beyond blurring, and stared at his reflection. 'Why do you torture yourself thinking about a future with her?' *Because you're a fool.* 'Once she helps you, she'll be gone.' *Good, good, good.* They would go back to their separate lives. Her in her castle. Him in his slowly sinking rust bucket.

He closed his eyes and shut out the scowl on his face. 'She only sends you blood because that's what a good comarré does for their patron. It's an obligation.' *Blood, blood, blood.* And since his curse meant he couldn't drink from her veins anyway, why shouldn't she keep her distance and send it to him? Why not drain her? *Drain her, drain her.* He rolled his forehead against the cool glass, trying to flatten the voices. Those miserable plastic containers of blood lacked her warmth and her smell and the sweet symphony of her breath and her heartbeat and— Enough. He would deal with it, just like he'd dealt with every other wretched aspect of his life.

Mal opened his eyes, the glittering scene in front of him coming into focus. Something about the next island over seemed familiar. No, not the island, but something about it. He looked harder. Big boat. Pool that overlooked the water. Nothing about that unusual for these man-made islands. They'd been created to keep the wealthy a healthy distance from reality.

But the design in the bottom of the pool . . . what was that? It looked like a swirl. Or a starburst. It reminded him of the phoebus signum Chrysabelle had told him all comarré wore on the backs of their necks. It was the same as the logo Maris had used for her cosmetics company. The design Chrysabelle had engraved into Maris's headstone.

His jaw loosened a bit.

That was Maris's pool. Chrysabelle's now. How about that.

Had Maris known? Mal straightened and glanced back to where Doc sat staring daggers into the air. Mal tucked the info away for future reference as he walked over and sat beside the shifter.

'Why do you look like you're going to kill someone?'

Doc shrugged. 'Don't know what you're talking about.'

'I'm talking about whatever happened between you and Dominic just now.'

'With all due respect, what went down isn't your business. Understand?' Doc threw back the last of his drink and stood. 'I'll be in the car.'

If not for Chrysabelle and Dominic returning at the same time, Mal would have gone after him.

She smiled weakly. 'We should probably go as well. Dominic needs to get to the club and we should—'

'We should go check on Nyssa like Mortalis asked us to,' he finished for her. It was a complete lie, but she clearly wanted to go. Had she not had any success with Dominic either?

'Yes, we should.' She nodded, eyes brightening at the out he'd given her.

Dominic paused beside her. 'Perhaps after that, you could investigate this street Maddoc told me about near the club. Supposedly there are piles of fringe ashes there.' He sighed. 'I can't have someone killing off my customers, especially near the club. It's bad for business.' He set his empty wineglass down. 'This city doesn't need a fringe uprising either.'

'We can take a look.' Mal had planned to check that out anyway after dropping Chrysabelle off. If someone was killing vampires, it seemed like something he should know about.

Chrysabelle frowned. 'Won't you need your car back if you're going to the club?'

Dominic laughed. 'I have more than one, *cara mia*. Now off you go. You have much to discuss with your patron, no?' He gave Mal a very serious look. 'You will do as she says. Understood? I will not have the child of my beloved harmed in any way. This thing she proposes to do, it is not easy. The outcome could change everything. And not just for you.'

Mal shot back an equally serious look. 'If you think I would ever let harm come to her, you don't know me very well.' And suddenly Mal wondered how well he knew himself. Was he willing to put Chrysabelle in harm's way in order to remove his curse? She'd been visibly shaken when she'd entered the room. He caught her gaze. 'What exactly does this visit to the Aurelian entail?'

She cleared her throat before answering, lifting her chin slightly. 'Blood sacrifice.'

'Whose?'

Her face steeled with determination like she was preparing for a fight. 'Mine.'

Tatiana entered Seven as easily as if she actually worked there, her guise of the bartender Mia firmly in place. So far, all the information she and Nasir had tortured out of the shifter was accurate. The employee entrance was exactly where Mia had said it would be. Tatiana punched in the code Mia had supplied: 55-21-16. The door clicked open. The little beastie had told the truth. Tatiana smiled. Amazing how powerful the sight and stench of a single Nothos could be.

She paused inside the door and smoothed her hands over the new body she wore. The cheap purple velvet bustier and black pleather pants were an affront to the beauty of her usual haute couture, but Tatiana willingly made the sacrifice. If the night went well, she would find the comarré whore, capture her, and torture her until the twit gave up the ring. Then, so long as her ex-husband, Mal, kept his distance, Tatiana would never have to return to New Florida again.

Seven's back corridors were also as Mia had mapped out. Tatiana tried to walk with the nonchalant confidence of someone familiar with her surroundings. She shivered at the thought of having to hold down such a menial job, of relying on such work to live. In her human life, she'd made her way as a thief, a fortune-teller, and sometimes a whore. That, in combination with being Roma, had led her to the gallows. Then to Malkolm and the role of wife and mother, and ultimately to the transformation into the powerful creature she was now and the life she felt she'd always been meant for.

A male and female pair of fae walked toward her. With their dark eyes, dark hair, and scantily clad bodies covered in henna patterns, they looked like twins. Mia hadn't mentioned anyone fitting their description, so she gave them a brief nod as they approached.

The pair slowed and the female nodded back, eyes bright. 'Hello, Mia. How are you this evening?'

Bloody hell. 'Just great, thanks. Gotta run. Don't want to be late.'

The male laughed as the pair came to a halt, effectively blocking her path. 'No, we don't want that, do we?'

'No.' She was starting to wonder if she should kill them and move on, but hiding the bodies would take time and could arouse suspicion.

The female leaned in, nostrils flaring. Her long-lashed lids fluttered as she inhaled. 'You smell delicious this evening. Is that a new perfume?'

'Yes,' Tatiana answered. 'I just got it. Now if you'll excuse me, can't keep the boss waiting.'

The female wrapped her arm around the male's waist. 'So you've heard?'

'Heard?' She scanned her brain for a forgotten bit of info. What was she supposed to know?

The female lifted her face from where she nuzzled the male's neck. 'Dominic's back and he's questioning all the employees.'

Dominic. Dominic. What did she know about him? He was the dead comarré's lover. Anathema. House of St. Germain, same as Nasir. He might know where the daughter of his former screw lived. Time to find out a little more. 'What's he questioning them – us – about?'

The fae pair shrugged simultaneously, but only the male spoke. 'We can't say, as our turn hasn't come yet, but it might have something to do with that fight the other night.' They laughed conspiratorially. Clearly there was something she wasn't getting.

'Okay, well, gotta run. See you later.' She squeezed past, brushing against the male. He inhaled sharply, as if she'd hurt him. She rolled her eyes. Stupid, sensitive fae. She didn't have time to go back and apologize, regardless of what Mia would have done.

She was around the corner when he called out for her to wait. Ignoring him, she found the employee access for Vanity and slipped inside.

She took her place behind the bar, a monstrosity of crystal bits and glass tiles that was actually shaped like a peacock. She gave a little half smile to the bartender she must be relieving. He was fringe, tall and not unattractive. Mia had insisted she had no amorous relations with any of the other employees, but based on how this one looked at her, Tatiana had to wonder. She wiggled her fingers at him. It seemed the kind of puerile gesture Mia might make. 'Hi, there.'

'You're late.' He winked. 'But in that outfit, I forgive you.' He tossed a small white towel onto the shelf beneath the bar and came toward her. 'Everyone's taken care of at the moment.' He pointed toward the sink in front of her. 'There are a few glasses I haven't washed yet.'

'I'll do those. Don't worry about it.' She picked one up and looked for a rag.

His eyes widened. 'Aren't you going to spray gloves on?'

'No, I'm fine.' Why should she bother with gloves? This wasn't her skin anyway.

He tipped his head and lifted a shoulder. 'Alrighty, then. Well, I doubt you'll be too busy. It's been slow. I think people are a little freaked out about all the missing fringe.'

More nonsense she didn't understand or care to. She just wanted him gone so she could tend to her own business. She scooped up a rag and waved it at him. 'Well, you have a good night. Better get home before the sun comes up.'

He gave her a mock salute, gathered his things, and left through the door she'd come in. As soon as he was gone, she tossed the rag down and surveyed the rest of the lounge. What she saw stunned her. Some kind of cheap imitation comarré. They didn't glow. She inhaled. Didn't have that same sweet blood scent. No, these were clearly kine masquerading as comarré. Was this some sort of parlor trick?

All around the room, idiot fringe indulged themselves with the counterfeits. Didn't they know any better? Or was this their way of mimicking their noble betters? Anger at such posturing churned in her gut. What fools.

The sound of glass shattering tore her attention away from the scene. She glanced down. Her hand was clenched and the tumbler she'd been holding in her right hand lay in pieces on the metal countertop. Bright platinum peeked out where the glass shards had gouged the false flesh she wore. She adjusted her illusion to mend the wounds and swept the pieces aside.

'What kind of beer do you have on tap?'

She tucked her hand behind her and looked up into the face of a remnant. Disgusting mud-blooded hybrid. She'd had enough of this part of the charade. Waiting on these half-wits was getting her nowhere. Time to find someone who could lead her to the girl. 'Taps are dry. Go home and drink there, freak.'

Finding some small joy in the remnant's shocked expression, she flipped up the service bar and headed out into the rest of the club. If tonight proved fruitless and she had to return to this dump, she was going to reward herself by killing a few of the patrons.

She deserved that much, didn't she?

Chapter Fourteen

Chrysabelle extended her stride to keep up with Mal's long legs. They'd dropped Doc off at the freighter, then parked in Dominic's private garage near the club. She'd pushed for driving to the streets Doc had told them about, but Mal had insisted that driving might scare off anyone lingering nearby. Which was exactly why she wanted to do it. Any opportunity to get Creek out of their path. Well, Mal's path. She wouldn't mind another chance to talk to Creek, find out exactly what he was up to without Mal freaking the guy out. Creek might be human, but his speed and weapons said there was more to him than that. What human killed vampires with so little fear?

Which led her to wonder what was going on with the dead fringe if Creek *wasn't* killing them. The deaths could be the result of a turf war. The fringe were getting more territorial lately and definitely bolder. The way she'd been tracked was proof of that.

Maybe she'd run into her friends Frankie and Ruby. She wondered what they'd think of Mal. Probably that she never traveled without dangerous male company. She laughed softly.

'What's so funny?' Mal asked.

'Hmm? Oh, nothing.' No point in telling him. He'd just get all bothered that she'd been in danger, which might have been touching once, but now that she knew it was just his way of guarding his own freedom, it lost some of its appeal. Also, telling that story might lead to Creek and she wasn't up for that conversation with Mal.

'Laughing at nothing is one of the first signs of mental illness, I believe.'

She stared at him. 'Did you just make a joke?'

He clutched at his dead heart. 'I can be funny.'

'I ... I'm sure you can.' Not that she'd ever seen that side of him before. What a change from the man who'd been on the verge of losing control just a few hours ago at her home. Had he forgiven her for sending blood to Dominic? Or was it the possibility of his curse being removed that had him in such a good mood? Whatever the reason, she liked him this way. He seemed almost ... human. Like Creek. Not that she could ever mistake Mal for anything but vampire.

Dawn was less than two hours away and the streets were deserted. She glanced at Mal. Most vamps would be thinking about shelter as the first tendrils of daysleep crept into their systems. He showed no signs of slowing.

'Dawn's coming,' she said, still watching him and knowing that he was probably watching her as well with his exceptional peripheral vision.

Scanning the streets ahead of them, he answered, 'We've got time.'

She knew what he meant. Not just time to check out what Doc had reported, but time for her to explain everything she'd learned talking to Dominic, which she hadn't wanted to do with Doc in the car. And she wanted to let it settle into her own head before she had to explain it to Mal. She still hadn't processed the news that she had a brother.

'I will explain soon. I promise.' The ritual for getting to the Aurelian was not going to be easy. It could kill her. Or push Mal over the edge. What were the chances she could keep him away while she carried it out? The streets of downtown Paradise City just didn't seem the right place to explain how dangerous a thing she was about to do. Or get into another argument.

'I don't like *soon*. I like now.'

'You know what I'd like? To kill Tatiana.' That should change the subject nicely.

'Who wouldn't?' He stopped. 'Look, I've come to realize you don't respond well to pressure. You're stubborn.'

So much for a new topic. She halted beside him, crossing her arms. 'I'm not stubborn. You push too much.' He could be so infuriating when he tried.

'You're determined to do things your own way, without help, and you're not dealing well with the transition from the comarré world to this one—'

'I'm dealing fine.' Was that what he thought? She was trying. She should get some credit for that.

'No, you're not.' He shoved a hand through his hair. It was so long it skimmed his shoulders. 'I'm not a patient man. Not anymore. I'm tired of waiting. So whatever you need to do to get ready, do it. Now.'

She almost laughed at how ridiculous he sounded. So very much like a man of his time. Or a noble commanding his comarré. She uncrossed her arms and planted her hands on her hips. 'Is that an order?'

'It is what it is.' He took a step forward, and a bolt whistled through the space he'd just occupied. It sank into the concrete block of the abandoned storefront behind him, dropping hunks of debris to the ground. Cracks veined out from the impact.

He grabbed her, tossed her over his shoulder, and took off. She fought to catch her breath. Everything around her blurred into streaks of light and muted color. Her braid whipped out past her face like it was connected to a string. Beneath her, he ran with a lethal grace, his muscles moving as oily smooth as a serpent's.

When he stopped, she had little idea how far they'd gone or in what direction. He hadn't run for more than a minute, but at that speed, they could be miles away.

He slipped her from his shoulder but kept his body in front of hers as he turned to glance back the way they'd come. Her heart thumped in her chest as she leaned against the building behind her. From what she could see beyond the hulking vampire in front of her, none of the surroundings looked familiar.

She reached for the comfort of her wrist blades. 'Where are—'

'Quiet,' he whispered.

She quelled the urge to punch him in the shoulder. It wouldn't matter how much or how little noise she made. If that bolt had come from the person she thought it had, there would be small chance of escape. Why hadn't she told Mal about Creek? Maybe she *was* stubborn. Determined to do things her way. No time like the present to make things right. She moved to stand beside him. 'Mal.'

With a stern look, he clamped his hand over her mouth. His cool fingers felt good against her skin, and his scent burrowed into her brain. Neither of which were helping. She turned her head, trying to free herself. His hand didn't budge. Now who was being stubborn? She did the only thing she could think of that didn't involve sticking a dagger into him.

She ran the tip of her tongue across the seam of his fingers.

He yanked his hand away like he'd been burned. He glared, then put her behind him again.

'Listen to me.' Better to tell him about Creek now than—

'C'mon out, vampire. There's no point in hiding or running. Let the comarré go and I won't kill you.' The sound of a crossbow being cocked and loaded echoed from the street, but Creek wasn't visible. 'Well, I will kill you, but I'll make it quick.'

—than to have Mal find out on his own. Which was right now, apparently. She edged out from behind Mal. An unnatural stillness permeated the night. 'Put your crossbow up,' she projected toward the street. 'It's not what you think.'

A disturbing growl emanated from Mal. His human face was nowhere to be seen. 'What's going on?'

'We have company,' she answered.

'I noticed,' Mal snarled back. 'Why do you know more about it than I do?'

'Because . . . ' There was no good, short answer. 'I just do.'

Creek emerged from the darkness to walk toward them, crossbow aimed at Mal. 'You're an ugly cuss, you know that?' He nodded at her without taking the weapon's sight off Mal. 'Walk to me. It's all right – you're safe now.'

'Chrysabelle, stay where you are.' Mal half stepped in front of her and bared his fangs at Creek. 'She's safe right where she is, and she'll stay that way.' The faint moonlight revealed he now gripped a jagged-edged black blade in his right hand. She hadn't even seen him whip it out. 'I wouldn't go so far as to say that about you.'

This was going to get ugly. And then uglier. With a gentle shove, she pushed past Mal to stand between the two men, turning her body sideways and raising a hand to each of them. 'I'm fine. Both of you put your weapons down. No one is killing anyone.'

Neither of them moved except to raise their weapons higher. And Mal thought she was stubborn? 'Creek, I am with Mal of my own free will. He's my patron and as such—'

'What did you say his name was?' The tip of Creek's crossbow dropped a centimeter.

'Malachi,' Mal spat as he made determined eye contact with Chrysabelle. Obviously, he didn't want his real name revealed. She understood, remembering when he'd used that false name with her, but really, Creek wouldn't know vampire history any more than would a rock on the ground.

'As I was saying, Malachi is my patron, and as such, you have no right to come between us, but he has every right to fight you should you choose to do so anyway.' Which she really hoped he didn't. 'Leave us be, Creek.'

Mal twirled the knife through his fingers until it was a blur of black. 'How do you know his name, Chrysabelle?'

Creek answered first. 'Because we've met before, vampire.'

Great. Unsolicited help from the ex-con. She sighed. 'He's right. We did.'

'When?' Mal moved slightly closer to Creek.

'The night I saw you at Seven,' she answered, keeping her gaze on him.

An angry growl came out of Creek. 'Was he the one who cut your hand?'

She whipped around toward Creek. 'No.'

Mal responded a second behind her. 'I would never hurt her.'

Creek came forward a step. 'And yet I had to save her from getting punctured by a gang of fringe.'

She exhaled and rolled her eyes skyward before shooting Creek a hard glare. 'Could you let me tell this story?'

'Is that true?' Mal asked.

'Yes,' Creek answered. 'Her bleeding hand was drawing them like flies.'

Chrysabelle sighed. 'I was holding my own.'

Mal reversed his grip on the blade and dropped his arm to his side. 'Apparently not.' He looked at Creek. 'How many did you take out?'

Creek tipped his crossbow up to rest against his shoulder. 'Five.'

'Five?' Mal stared at her. 'How many were there to begin with?'

'Okay, enough. I'm glad you two have bonded over my perceived inability to fend for myself, but this' – she waggled her finger between Mal and Creek – 'is not why we're out here.'

Mal took a moment to study Creek. His nostrils flared. 'Who are you anyway? Your scent's too sour to be fully human.'

'Don't worry about who I am, vampire. Worry about protecting your comarré. If I have to do it again, you're done with her.'

And just like that, the weapons were back in play.

Mal shook his head, his irises edged in silver. 'She doesn't need anyone's protection. She could take you out with one hand tied behind her back. Whoever you are.'

Internally, she grinned at Mal's assessment. 'He's just a guy who came to my rescue.'

'Actually,' Creek spoke up, 'I'm more than that, Chrysabelle. I didn't plan on telling you this way, but I think you need to know. I'm Kubai Mata. Sent to help protect you.'

Mal threw back his head and laughed. 'Kubai Mata? The secret fairy-tale vampire-slayer organization? Oh, that's rich.'

Kubai Mata? A wash of unease ran through her. Was that possible? She'd been educated to believe that they may have once existed but now were exactly as Mal described. A fairy tale of sorts. How would a human even know about them to make such a claim? Her stomach knotted with the feeling that her world was shifting too fast for her to keep up.

Mal tucked his blade away and looked at Chrysabelle. 'You didn't mention he was mental. Nice company you've been keeping.' His gaze returned to Creek. 'Slayers of any variety have a very short life span, so I guess I won't be seeing much more of you. Kubai Mata.' He shook his head. 'Amazing. Come, Chrysabelle. We have work to do.' He hooked his hand around her upper arm and began to turn them both around.

Creek stuck the butt of his crossbow against his shoulder and aimed. 'Get your hands off her, vampire. I don't care if you believe me or not, but you won't hurt her while I'm here.' His finger found the trigger. 'Last chance.'

Mal rolled his eyes.

Creek pulled the trigger.

Before Chrysabelle could inhale to react, Mal shoved her out of the way, spun to the side, and snatched the bolt out of the air as it blasted past.

Creek fired again, but the second bolt whistled past Mal's charging form, tearing the leather of his jacket under his arm.

Mal leaped at Creek, caught him around the waist, and slammed him to the ground. Together they rolled across the debris-strewn pavement.

'No!' Chrysabelle shouted. She yanked her sacre out of its sheath and ran toward them. Mal's hands squeezed Creek's windpipe while Creek reared back to land a punch. She slipped her sword between them before Creek's fist came down. If Creek really was KM, she needed to talk to him. 'Enough.'

Both men froze, but neither made an effort to disengage.

She unsheathed her second sacre and added it to the mix, easing the points of the swords into the hollows of their throats. 'Let's go. Now. This foolishness is over.'

Slowly, they untangled and got to their feet, glaring daggers at each other.

'If one of you kills the other, I'll kill the survivor, understood?'

Of course, Mal spoke first. 'No, you won't.'

No, she wouldn't, but right now she felt like it. 'Try me.' She pushed them farther apart, opening a tiny nick in Mal's skin that healed in less than a second. She would hear about that later. 'I don't care if you hate each other, I don't care if you get along, but if you're both going to live in this city, you're going to have to find a way to tolerate each other.' Neither of them looked like they'd heard a word she'd said. 'That means no killing. Each other.'

Creek pointed a finger at Mal. 'Killing vampires is part of my job.'

'Not this vampire,' Chrysabelle said.

Mal straightened and stared Creek down. 'Your job's fatality rate just went sky-high.'

Creek shook his head. 'You don't get it. Neither of you do. This city is about to crumble before you – along with the rest of the world. Since the breaking of the covenant, bad things have begun to happen.'

'Like you?' Mal asked.

Creek ignored him. 'Like nightmares coming to life and black magic strengthening and evil's foothold in this world growing larger. The more humans start to believe in the danger around them, the more power that danger has. Things you've never dreamed of will materialize on the strength of those beliefs. I'm not just here to protect humans from vampires. I'm the first line of defense against every unnatural horror about to rise up and take a bite out of this world. Vampires are just the beginning.'

Chrysabelle sheathed one sword. 'Who put you in charge of protecting the human race?' She'd always thought that designation belonged to the comarré.

Creek's scornful look spoke volumes. 'That's always been the job of the Kubai Mata. We've been waiting for the day this would happen, and now that it has, we're here.'

'We? How many of you are there?' she asked.

'Enough.' Creek backed up a step and jerked his chin toward Mal. 'You step out of line toward her again, and you're ash. I shouldn't even allow you that much.'

Mal laughed. 'You think you scare me?' He cracked his knuckles. 'I eat mortals like you for breakfast.'

Creek brought his crossbow back down. 'Thanks for the reminder. Maybe there's no point in giving you a chance.'

'Both of you shut up,' Chrysabelle snarled. 'Mal hasn't killed anyone in years.' A rapid, muted thumping filtered in from the alley behind them. 'What is that?'

Mal and Creek swiveled toward the sound. It got louder, but not much. The wind shifted, washing a sour wave of brimstone over them. Chrysabelle reached for the sword she'd sheathed as the tremble of recognition shook her spine. The sacre whined for blood, quivering to be used.

'Nothos,' Mal spat. 'That can only mean one thing.'

Chrysabelle nodded. 'She's come after the ring, hasn't she?'

Chrysabelle shoved the white-cold fear away and opened herself to the anger over Maris's death, still fresh and close to the bone. Her sacre hummed, hungry, greedy, ready to engrave her pain on someone else's skin.

'You mean Tatiana?' Creek asked.

Before either of them could confirm, the first Nothos came into view, all wrongly jointed and horse-faced, yellow eyes lit like embers, spittle dripping from its crowded jaw.

Creek's smile split his face like a jack-o'-lantern as he nodded. 'Looks like the hellhounds have arrived.' He cocked the crossbow's trigger. 'It's hunting time.'

Chapter Fifteen

'Fi!' Doc burst into the cargo hold, praying he could pull Fi out of her loop even if just for a few minutes. After his disastrous meeting with Dominic, Doc needed to see her more than ever. His mind was awash with revenge fantasies, but he knew those could easily take him down the wrong path. Fi could calm him. Refocus him. 'Fi! If you can hear me, please come out. Please, baby.'

Seconds ticked by. He swept the flashlight down the narrow corridors created by the stacked rows of rusting storage containers. A rat scurried back into the shadows. 'Fi, please, if you can hear me.'

Nothing. Not a flicker. Not a hint of her wispy image. His hand tightened on the flashlight, and the anger simmering in his gut began to boil. He was too late. She was gone and the next time he'd see her, she'd be moments away from being torn apart right before his eyes. And once again, he'd be helpless to stop it.

He slammed the side of his fist into one of the containers. The noise echoed through the cavernous space as he slumped to his knees. His eyes burned.

'Doc?'

The voice brushed his skin. His head came up, his flashlight searching. 'Fi? Baby?'

'Here,' she whispered.

She was a few yards up the passage. She kept her right side to him, strangely shy now that she'd begun to remember bits and pieces. Or maybe it was the way she looked. She'd never let anyone see her in her murdered form the first time she'd been a ghost. He shined his light on her, but it was too bright and she disappeared beneath its intensity. He tossed it away, blowing out a hard breath and offering her a shaky smile. 'I'm so glad you're here. I thought you were gone. Until, you know . . . ' No reason to complete that thought.

'No.' She smiled weakly, floating closer. 'I'm here. It's just hard to make myself visible too far out of the loop.' She wiggled her fingers in front of her. They were as sheer as steam. 'As you can tell.'

'You look great.'

She ducked her head and a curtain of brown hair hid the blood streaking the front of her sweatshirt.

'I don't care about that.' He pointed to the dark stain. 'Or that.' His finger moved in the direction of her throat, where the flesh lay open like some kind of horrible flower.

She twisted, hiding that side of herself. 'Don't.'

'Fi, it's okay.' Shoulda kept his mouth shut.

'It's not okay. *I* am not okay.'

She flickered again and he wondered if she'd rather disappear than deal with her reality. He couldn't blame her. He'd wished that for himself once upon a time. Before her.

'You're going to be fine. You'll see.' He ached to hold her, to pull her against him and tell her everything was going to be okay, even though he was no closer to saving her than he had been a few hours ago. If anything, he was further from his goal.

'You're a bad liar.' But her smile widened. 'How did it go with Dominic?'

He dropped his head. He shouldn't have told her about going to see Dominic, but he'd wanted to give her hope. What an idiot he was.

'Not well, I guess.' She laughed but the sound was almost a sob.

His head jerked up. 'I'll figure it out. I will. Don't worry.'

She flickered, thinner than when she'd first shown up. 'What did he say?'

Doc couldn't bring himself to tell her. 'I'll talk to him again. Make him understand better.' And he realized he meant those words. He would give Dominic one more shot. If he still didn't offer up the required blood, Doc would find a way to get it. By whatever means necessary.

'He won't, though, will he?' She started to cry, her image wavering and blinking in and out.

'He will. He *will*. Don't cry, baby.' Doc had to get Fi back. 'I didn't mean to upset you.'

She shook her head, her hair swinging free where it wasn't clumped together with blood. 'I don't know what's worse – remembering what my life was like before we went to Corvinestri, or not remembering. Too late now, I guess, since it's all coming back.'

His mouth opened, but he kept quiet. She'd gone to Corvinestri because of him. He was to blame for this and he knew it. Sorry only went so far. 'Maybe I should go. Give you some peace.'

'No.' She turned to face him full-on. 'The only peace I have is with you.' Tears shimmered on her lower lids and streaked her pale cheeks. 'Don't leave, please. Not yet. Not until the sun comes up.'

'You got it, baby.' Anything to keep more tears from falling or causing her any more pain. He leaned against one of the storage containers and nodded toward the deck beside him.

She crossed her legs and floated down beside him, the brush of her ethereal form cool against his body. 'Tell me about the first time we met.'

He laughed. 'Again?'

'Yes. I love that story.'

'I'm aware.' He began the story just as he had the last two times. 'It was the second full moon after I'd been cursed, and the first one since my pride had thrown me out. Mal found me in an alley.'

'Saved you from a pack of wild dogs, you mean.'

'Yeah, that. He brought me back here—'

'That was right after I tried to leave him and realized I couldn't.' Her mouth twisted a little.

'I guess he thought fixing me up and letting you keep me as a pet would make you feel better. Course, in my animal form, there was no way for him to tell I was varcolai—'

'And hardly an acceptable pet for a young woman such as myself.' She snickered, pursing her mouth when he shot her a look.

'Or anyone,' he added. Not that he minded being her pet now. 'For the length of the full moon, three nights and three days, I was barely conscious, unable to shift into human form even if I'd wanted to.'

'Until ...' The glee wrapped her voice like a Christmas ribbon, and he felt a thousand times lighter.

'Until one warm afternoon, you carried me out into the sunshine, holding me in your arms like a . . . like a . . . '

'Baby doll,' she whispered, barely controlling the naughty trill that sent her words an octave higher and his spirit soaring. 'Except, I wouldn't normally scratch a baby doll's belly.'

He couldn't help but smile. 'Which is what woke me up and freaked me out into shifting back to my human form.'

The giggling started right on cue. She always cracked up during this part of the story. 'Right in my arms. You knocked me down.' Her laughter faded until she could speak again. 'It's not every day you end up with a large black man lying on top of you.'

'Thankfully,' he added, chuckling at the remembered image of her sprawled beneath him and looking shocked out of her skin.

She sighed and silence settled peacefully between them for a few minutes. He glanced over. Her eyes were closed, her head tipped back, a soft smile curving her mouth. He'd be thrilled, if she weren't so see-through he could count the rivets in the storage container they leaned against. She wouldn't last much longer. The thought stripped away his joy.

'I'm glad you remember me,' he said quietly, wanting to hold on to the moment for fear there wouldn't be many more.

Her eyes opened. 'Me too.'

His hands clenched as fresh anger surged through him. Didn't Dominic understand this was more than just wanting to help a friend? This was the woman Doc loved. Wouldn't Dominic have done the same for Maris? Of course he would have. He would have done anything for that woman.

A pinprick of an idea formed in Doc's mind. As it grew, his sense of hopelessness shrank. He rested his head against the storage container and let his imagination take over until the plan evolved into something concrete. Why hadn't he thought of this already? The way to control anyone was to find their weakness and exploit it. Aliza and Dominic were not that different, they both wanted the same result. Doc had just been too wrapped up in his own needs to see things clearly. He jumped to his feet, ready to put things in motion. 'Fi, I have to go, I ...'

But she had already disappeared.

The twelfth Nothos loped out of the fading fog, and Mal cursed under his breath. Facing down two of them in Corvinestri had been a different story. He'd had Doc, Dominic, and Mortalis to help. Not that Chrysabelle hadn't held her own – she had, but the Nothos she'd killed then *had* gotten his claws on her. Only her body armor had saved her from serious injury, and she wasn't wearing it now.

As a pack, the Nothos began to lurch forward, elongated jaws hanging open, piercing yellow eyes fixated on Chrysabelle. *Let them have her.*

She whipped out her swords. Creek leveled his crossbow. Like that was going to be much help. Mal doubted those bolts would be enough to down a Nothos. *Then let them both die.*

'We each get four,' Chrysabelle said softly. 'I'll take the ones in the middle, you two take—'

'No,' Mal interrupted. 'I'll take them all. You're going to get the hell out of here. You're the one they're after.' He wouldn't allow harm to come to her, no matter what the situation was between them. Besides, with this much blood in his system, he could control the beast, use it, then shackle it up again. Probably.

'Save the great-protector act, Mal.' She kept her eyes on the approaching Nothos. 'We're doing this together. Just like last time.'

'Last time there were two of them and five of us.' He eased his control off the beast within and glanced at the KM. 'Creek, get her out of here now and I won't kill you the next time I see you.'

The slayer looked at him like his brains were leaking out his ears. Or maybe it was the names shooting black tendrils past the collar of Mal's jacket. 'Big assumptions, vampire. But it's your funeral. Saves me some work.' He nodded at Chrysabelle. 'C'mon, my bike isn't far.'

She pulled away, just as Mal knew she would, just as he'd expected the scowl on her face. 'I'm not going anywhere.'

The beast snapped its chains and roared with predatory joy. 'Chrysabelle, they will capture you and take you back to Tatiana, who will torture you until you tell her where the ring is. We were too late to save Maris. I don't want to be too late to save you.'

Her mouth thinned to a hard line. 'I'm not happy about this.'

'So noted.' He shed his jacket to save it from the changes taking over his physical body.

'If I go, you have to promise me not to kill Creek.'

Her desire to protect the slayer angered the beast. 'Agreed.'

But she stayed rooted to the spot. The Nothos spread out into a semicircle, now less than a hundred feet away.

He could see by the look on Creek's face that he hadn't a clue about Mal's curse. Already, the voices were expanding beyond his head, flowing into his muscles and bones. 'Go,' he commanded, his voice now layered with a multitude of others. 'Let me do this.'

She nodded, her eyes soft with concern. 'Be safe,' she whispered.

His T-shirt tore across his broadening form. 'I will. Now go.'

She sheathed her blades and backed into a staring Creek. 'What's happening to him?'

'I'll explain on the way.' She tugged him along and he turned, glancing over his shoulder as they disappeared down the adjacent alley. The Nothos shifted in that direction, but Mal blocked their path. With Chrysabelle out of danger, Mal gave the beast its freedom. It stormed through him, scratching and clawing and leaving only a few fraying strands of control for Mal to cling to.

A couple yards away, the Nothos snarled as if they sensed their new opponent.

The beast snarled back with a mouth that held longer fangs and more teeth, then bent its head and plowed forward. It sliced out, claws shredding muscle and sinew.

Howls filled the beast's ears and the stench of brimstone and blood bathed its nostrils like a sweet perfume.

The Nothos leaped onto the beast, raking its back with sickle-like talons, but it shook them off and shoved a fist into the maw of the closest one. Its fingers dug into the hellhound's throat and tore out its spine. The Nothos crumbled, turning to ash as it fell.

Grabbing two more Nothos, the beast slammed their heads together. Brain matter splattered over its skin, hissing like acid. The beast laughed with a chorus of voices.

The Nothos hesitated. The beast did not. Dawn was coming and there was no time to waste. The host must be protected.

When the carnage was over and Mal had forced the beast back into its chains, he surveyed the ground around him, counting the piles of ash even as his body trembled from the beast's exertion. Eight, nine, ten ... where were eleven and twelve?

Hands dripping with the foul blood of the Nothos, Mal spun toward the alley Chrysabelle had escaped down. The cuts and gouges he'd endured in the fight stung now that he'd become himself again. His body craved the rest necessary to heal, and the pull of daysleep already weighed on him. Even the voices were exhausted. Dawn was minutes away. Going after Chrysabelle and the escaped Nothos was not an option unless he intended it to be his *last* option. There was no way he could find her and shelter before the sun came up.

Wounded, bleeding, and almost comatose with the need for sleep, he took off in the direction of Seven, the closest refuge he could think of, even though every fiber in his body and mind ached to go after Chrysabelle.

But that way lay death. And there was no way he was checking out and leaving Chrysabelle alone in the clutches of a man like Creek.

Chapter Sixteen

The scent of brimstone faded as Chrysabelle ran alongside Creek and away from Mal. She hated leaving him behind almost as much as she hated that he was right about what would happen to her if the Nothos captured her. The disappointment of not fighting side by side with Mal made her wish things were different, but it wasn't safe for her to be near him when his beast took over. The voices hated her and the beast had already come close to killing her once before.

'Explain.'

'What?' She looked over at Creek keeping pace beside her.

'What the hell was happening to him?'

'His beast was coming out. It's part of his curse.' She returned her gaze to the street ahead of them. Her sacre shifted slightly with the rhythm of her stride, *tap-tap-tapping* her back. 'If you're really KM, shouldn't they have taught you about him in Kubai Mata school? I thought it was your job to kill vampires. I'd think he'd be pretty high on the list.'

'You want me to kill him? 'Cause you're making a pretty convincing case.' Creek glanced back the way they'd come. 'And, no, they didn't teach me about every vampire. There's only so much they could cram into my head in two weeks.'

'He's anathema. You know what that means?'

'Yeah. Means dark is the only side he's got.'

'No, it isn't.' Mal was so much more than even she'd guessed. 'He saved my life.'

'Of course he did. He wants your blood.'

She slowed her run to a walk. Let the Nothos come. Killing one might improve her mood. 'You don't have a clue.'

A few paces away, he slowed as well and turned to face her. 'You sweet on him or something?'

She stopped so suddenly she almost fell over. 'You're barking mad.'

Creek took a few steps back in her direction. 'You at least care for him. And he certainly digs you.'

Her jaw went south. 'You *are* insane.'

He held up his hands. 'Fine. You tell me that's not the case and I'll believe you until proven otherwise.'

'Good, because we don't have that kind of relationship.' Maybe that was a lie, but she wasn't about to take some sort of personal inventory to sort out whatever it was she did feel for Mal. Not for Creek's sake anyway. She stalked past him, then realized she didn't know where they were headed. 'Where's this bike of yours?'

'Around the block.'

'Great. How about we make the rest of the trip in silence?' She looked back at him and went deadly still. 'Two Nothos, coming up the street behind you.' Holy mother, what did that mean for Mal? Had they escaped him? Or . . .

Creek had his crossbow out a moment after she drew her sacres. The handle warmed in her grasp. Her personal sacre had been tuned to her during its crafting when the hilt had been filled with her blood, marrying the blade to her as though it were an extension of her arm. Now it vibrated in her hand, ready to taste Nothos flesh once again.

The wind shifted, bringing the sour stench of brimstone and the more subtle spice of blood. She refused to think about whom that blood might belong to.

Instead of waiting for the Nothos to come to her, she attacked first, blades blurring in a figure eight before her body. The Nothos retreated out of reach, leaping onto a nearby building while the second Nothos took three of Creek's bolts to his torso in rapid succession. They barely slowed the creature down.

'You need a blade!' she yelled back to Creek. Those bolts might down a vampire, but they were on the slim side for the demon spawn.

Creek was beside her a few seconds later, a long titanium quarterstaff in his hands. Her hands were too full to tell him that wasn't going to work either. Her Nothos snapped its jaw, spraying burning saliva across her cheek.

She swiped the spittle away with the back of one hand. The Nothos grabbed for her. She ducked. It lunged, catching the edge of her tunic and shredding it. She shoved the creature as it went past, using its momentum to throw it to the ground. The scent of blood increased.

With a guttural growl, she drove her blades into the Nothos's back before it could rise and anchored it to the pavement. The monstrosity planted its hands on the asphalt and pushed up. Its flesh slid along the blades, but the sacres remained fixed in the ground. Caught at the hilts, it stayed hunched over, unable to straighten further.

The Nothos screeched, swinging its double-jointed arms at

her, reaching with its awful hands for the merest inch of skin. Threads of white silk hung from the claws that had almost sliced her belly open.

Behind her, Creek still fought. More than that, she couldn't say. She moved around the Nothos so it couldn't see her and jumped, landing with a foot on either side of its spine. The move slammed it into the ground again. She flicked out her wrist blades and drove one into the spot where the creature's heart should be. A gush of yellow blood and renewed yowling told her she'd aimed correctly. With both hands on the second dagger, she punched the blade downward and severed the Nothos's spine. She worked the weapon back and forth until the head was nearly severed. Finally, the creature went to ash beneath her feet.

Breathing openmouthed and ready to take on the second abomination, she turned in time to watch Creek spear his Nothos through with the quarterstaff. He lifted the staff until the creature dangled off the end like a bit of refuse, then smashed it into the ground with such force the asphalt compressed beneath it.

The Nothos didn't move when Creek yanked his quarterstaff free, but Chrysabelle had doubts it was truly dead. Creek apparently understood that. He slid a long knife from his boot, kneeled, and bisected the spine with greater ease than she'd done. Like he'd had practice.

Nothing remained in the pothole but ash.

On odd lightness filled her head, as if the slowly brightening sky was invading her brain. Creek leaned over, resting his hands on his knees, his chest rising and falling with the exertion. 'Those things are hard to kill.'

'Yes, I know.' She fought the urge to sit. Or sleep. What was wrong with her? 'That wasn't my first.'

'Kill or encounter?' He straightened. His jeans were torn where the side of his leg had been slashed open from thigh to knee. Fresh blood from his movement ran out of the gash. Suddenly she felt queasy. Like she might pass out. What had he asked?

'Uh, both. We ... we ran into them when we tried to' – she swallowed – 'to rescue my aunt. I mean, my mother.' She pointed to his thigh. Her hand shook. 'You're bleeding pretty badly.'

He glanced up. His brow furrowed with abrupt concern. 'So are you.'

'No, it didn't touch me, just ripped my tunic.' Swaying slightly, she looked down at the frayed edge of her shirt. The fabric was deep red. And wet. Three broad gashes scored her stomach. Beneath the open flesh, muscle peeked out. Blood saturated the right side of her trousers all the way down her leg. She wiggled her toes, listening to the squishing sound of her fluid-filled slipper.

'I think I've lost a lot of ... ' Her vision narrowed and a faint buzzing rang in her ears. 'Creek?' Her mouth was so dry. The sun would be up soon. Had Mal found cover?

'Right here.' She felt warm hands supporting her. Then nothing.

Tatiana, still in the guise of Mia, had tried and failed three times to explore the club and find someone who might be able to connect her with the rogue comarré. Each time she had slipped away from her post behind the bar, someone in charge had sent her back.

At the moment, she was standing in a cramped storage room amid cleaning products and bundles of cocktail napkins while some hoity-toity Asian fringe who used too much perfume and obviously enjoyed referring to herself as 'the manager' reprimanded Mia. Katsumi, some other flunky had called her.

'Mia, are you listening to me?'

Tatiana couldn't keep from rolling her eyes. 'Yes, I'm listening.' This whole scheme had gone bollocks up in a flash. Dawn had to be close, although she couldn't feel it like she should. The club probably pumped drugs into the air system to keep the crowds partying. If she didn't accomplish what she'd set out to do, and quickly, she'd be stuck here until nightfall. The very thought of being trapped in this place made her want to retch.

Katsumi narrowed her eyes and scowled. 'Do you think running a club of this size and scope is such an easy thing?' She planted her hands on her hips. One pinky was missing from the knuckle down. Interesting, but not *that* interesting. 'I'm sure you think you could do better, but I assure you, you could not.'

Tatiana smiled. 'That's a marvelous idea. Best I've heard all night.'

'What is?' Katsumi squinted. 'Why are you looking at me that way?'

Tatiana punched Katsumi in the temple with as much power as she could. Katsumi staggered back and caught herself on one of the metal racks. Using the shelving as leverage, she hoisted herself up and drove both feet into Tatiana's torso.

Pain shot through Tatiana's torso as one of her ribs fractured, and the force of Katsumi's kick threw her into a stack of boxes. She leaped to her feet and charged forward, metal hand outstretched. She formed her hand into a collar, clamped it around the fringe's neck, then lifted the woman until her feet dangled off the floor. 'Think you can best me, weakling fringe? Think again.'

Terror-filled eyes wide, Katsumi pried uselessly at the platinum encircling her throat. 'Who are you?' she wheezed.

'That's the least of your concerns.' Tatiana scanned the room for something to secure Katsumi with. Several rolls of duct tape sat on a low shelf. Not a challenge for a noble, but for a fringe it should suffice, at least temporarily. She snatched up a roll, loosened the tape with her teeth, and started a strip.

Katsumi eyed her actions with horror. 'No.' She let out half a scream before Tatiana jerked her upward, slamming her head into the ceiling so hard the plasterboard crumbled. Katsumi's head lolled over the platinum collar. For a moment, Tatiana worried she'd killed her.

Tatiana quickly re-formed her hand, dropping Katsumi to the ground, and then imagined herself as Katsumi. She flattened her metal hand into a mirror and checked her image. Perfect. With renewed confidence, she began to cocoon her captive in numerous layers of silver-gray tape. Once finished, she hoisted the woman's body and dumped her behind a row of stacked chairs.

Then Tatiana brushed herself off, adjusted her new outfit – at least the fringe had the good taste to wear silk – and headed out into the club to finally accomplish what she'd come for.

Chapter Seventeen

Doc stared down the fae before him. 'Mortalis, let me in.' Minutes were ticking by. His patience was gone. Not that he'd had much to begin with.

Arms crossed before the interior doors to Seven, the shadeux didn't budge. 'No.'

'Did Dominic tell you not to? Is that why you scampered out here when Tec let me in?'

'Dominic didn't need to tell me anything. I know what the history is. Look how overjoyed he was I brought you to his penthouse.' Mortalis shook his head. 'And I do not scamper.'

Doc wanted to smash something or someone against the fancy new gold dragon doors that barred his way into Seven. 'You know the history? The whole history?'

Mortalis's face held its stony expression. 'I know enough.'

'Do you know Dominic's stubbornness is costing two women their lives?'

The stone cracked slightly. 'What do you mean?'

Doc explained what Aliza had said and how she'd agreed to

help Fi. 'All I'm asking is one more opportunity to talk to him. Talk. That's all.'

'I'm going to end up working for the comarré,' Mortalis muttered as he stepped aside. 'Dominic asks, you haven't seen me, I haven't seen you, and I have no idea you're here. Understand?'

Doc popped his fist against the shadeux's shoulder. 'You're all right for an uptight son of a—'

'Don't make me change my mind.'

Hands up, Doc backed through the double doors and toward the club's main lounge. 'I'm gone!'

This time, he went straight to Dominic's office via the route he'd traveled when he'd been running goods. In minutes he was at the back entrance to the office. He knocked, shoving down his nerves. This would work. It had to. All that mattered was helping Fi, consequences be damned.

Dominic called, *'Si.'*

Doc eased into the room, hoping to get several steps inside before the vampire saw him.

'Mortalis is getting soft, I see.' Dominic's back was to him. 'I thought we were done talking, varcolai.'

So much for stealth. 'We were. But something new came up when I got back to the freighter and saw Fi again.'

Dominic closed the file drawer he'd been looking through, went to his desk, and sat, turning his chair to face Doc. 'I fail to realize how this interests me. Dawn comes. I must sleep occasionally, despite the rumors.'

Doc forced himself to radiate truth. 'I think you'll find it very interesting. Fi has found she can communicate with—'

Pasha and Satima burst through the door on the other side of the office. A mask of anger distorted Pasha's dark face. 'You let this creature take up your time while we must wait?' His nostrils flared with indignation. 'We have urgent business, not a rehash of the past.' With a haughty look at Doc, Pasha crossed his arms. 'Ignore us at your own peril.'

'Yes,' Satima mimicked. 'At your own peril.' She leaned against her brother, one hand splayed on his stomach.

Dominic steepled his fingers against his forehead as if a killer migraine had just struck. Doc completely understood. He felt a little that way himself. 'Fine. What is this urgent business?'

Eyes glittering, Pasha stared at Doc while he spoke. 'The little varcolai bartender—'

'The wolf-shifter,' Satima interjected.

'Mia?' Doc asked.

Nodding, Pasha turned his attention to his boss. 'She brushed past me on her way in this evening – very rudely, I might add—'

Dominic's hand cracked sharply against his marble desktop. Satima jumped. 'I do not have time to worry about perceived slights against your person. I am done for the night.' He loosened his tie. 'Get back to work, both of you. And you . . .' He pointed at Doc. 'Out.'

Doc stayed where he was. Pasha uncrossed his arms, planted his fingers on the marble, and leaned in as if the vampire hadn't said a word. 'There was skin contact.'

Dominic's agitation faded a little. He worked the cuff links out of his starched white cuffs. 'And?'

Straightening, Pasha lifted his chin and made eye contact with Doc before answering. 'I saw her death.'

Doc snorted. 'You say that every time you touch someone. Get a new line, gemini.'

'Because it's true, little cat. My talent is without question.'

Unclipping his black pearl cuff links, Dominic shook his head. 'How is this important?'

'She also smelled like a vampire.' Satima rested her head in the crook of Pasha's neck. 'Tell them about her death, brother.'

Pasha inhaled as he started. 'I saw her in a dungeon, surrounded by—'

'Have you told Mia this?' Dominic interrupted. 'It is rather inappropriate to reveal someone's future without them present, is it not?'

Pasha frowned. 'That is our habit, yes.'

Dominic picked up a slim silver device, squeezed a button on the side, and spoke. 'Send Mia up, please.'

A voice Doc didn't recognize answered back. 'Yes, sir.'

Dominic replaced the intercom and gestured toward the chairs behind the twins. 'Sit. We will wait.' He waved over his shoulder. 'You, too, Maddoc, as you are now somehow part of this great important interruption.' He looked at his watch. 'You are all infringing on my personal time. What you've come to tell me had better be astonishingly valuable.'

Fortunately, they didn't have to wait long. Mortalis came in, Katsumi trailing him. 'Mia isn't here.'

Katsumi looked around the room as if she were seeing new faces. 'I sent her home. She wasn't feeling well.' Her gaze hung on Doc for a moment, then moved to Dominic. She studied him with an odd intensity. 'Don't let me interrupt whatever is going on.'

'No, that settles it.' Dominic stood. 'This can all wait until tonight. I'm turning in.' He slipped a key into the desk lock and turned it. 'Katsumi, go home. You've been here long enough, too.'

She twisted her hands together, then forcibly stilled them. 'I . . . I can't. The sun is up.'

'You know you have the use of my car.' Dominic tucked the key into his pocket. 'Mortalis will drive you.'

'Of course.' She smiled strangely. 'Long night. Busy. So much on my mind.' She waved her hands around her head like she was stirring up the crazy. Talk about a fringe struggling with daysleep. She sounded like she was tripping.

Doc stood, stretching to his full height. 'I still need to talk to you, Dominic.'

'No. I'm done for the night. Whatever it is can wait.'

'No, it can't.' This was Fi's life. 'Just a few minutes, man—'

'No,' Dominic barked, silver lighting his eyes. 'Enough. Malkolm is in the Donatello suite. You can stay there or go home, but either way, I will not talk to you until I have had some rest.'

Mal was here? Interesting, but his presence didn't stop the rage worming through Doc's spine. He swaggered forward, throwing his hands up. 'You're a cold piece of work, Dominic Scarnato. What if Maris's life were at stake? What then?'

'You leave Maris out of this.'

Mortalis's hand went to the dagger tucked in his belt.

Think of Fi, think of Fi, think of Fi. Doc backed off. 'Can't. Fi's been in touch with her.' Dominic's mouth hung open as Doc twisted to leave. 'See you when I see you.'

'Wait,' Dominic called. 'Stay. Explain. Everyone else out. Mortalis, take Katsumi home, then come back here immediately.'

Doc smiled, then blanked his face and turned back to the group. A very sulky pair of haerbinger fae skulked out of the office first.

'If it's all right with you, Dominic, I will just stay here. I am exhausted.' Katsumi sighed as if to illustrate her weariness.

'Fine.' Dominic waved a hand. 'You may take your usual suite.'

'The ... which one was that again?' She smiled sweetly and made the swirling motions by her head again. 'So tired.'

'Mortalis, escort Katsumi to the Dante suite, please?'

'On it, boss.' Mortalis took Katsumi's elbow and steered her toward the door.

Katsumi went very slowly. 'I would love to hear how this Fi contacted the comarré? Perhaps I could wait until—'

Dominic pointed to the exit. 'Mortalis, now.'

The fae removed the sour-faced Katsumi with impressive efficiency. When the door closed behind them, Dominic took his chair again and motioned for Doc to sit, too. He did, and with the same fervency he'd once used to talk his customers into trying some of the most dangerous drugs on the face of the earth, he began to spin the yarn that was Fi's greatest hope for survival.

Creek gently maneuvered his Harley through the streets, keeping to the smoothest part of the road as best he could. The comarré, still passed out, sat behind him, strapped to him with a couple of bungees. It had taken some maneuvering, but he'd buttoned her into his jacket with her limbs at her sides, then anchored her to him at the waist and upper back with the cords. She rested against his back, her head on his shoulder.

He checked his mirrors for fanged company, then reminded himself it was morning. At this hour, vampires were as good as dead. Even the blood-covered comarré couldn't compete with dawn's pale, deadly light.

Good for Chrysabelle, because her wound required immediate attention. The hellhound's claws had sliced through her skin and the top surface of silvery-white tissue, exposing the bright red muscle beneath. She would need some serious stitches, but if she could handle getting all those signum, she could handle stitches without anesthesia. Didn't mean he wasn't already regretting the pain he would have to inflict on her. He'd deal with the throbbing gash on his leg after she was taken care of.

Killing the engine, he parked the bike and unhooked the bungees, leaning forward to keep her weight on him. He eased upright, holding her arm as he got off the bike, then scooped her into his arms, and opened the door. He took her upstairs to his bed. She moaned softly when he set her down.

'Shhh,' he whispered, fixing the pillow beneath her head. 'You're safe. I'll be right back.' He hurried to walk the bike in and secure the door. The old metal looked rusted, but he'd reinforced it on the inside. Nothing was getting in here without him knowing about it. He grabbed his med kit and returned to her side.

Working quickly, he cut away her blood-soaked clothes, then carried them to the loft railing and tossed them onto the concrete floor of the old machine shop. They'd need to be burned before sundown or he might as well hang a neon arrow by his front door.

He turned around and paused at the sight of the woman on his bed. He was a man and he was weak, that much was starkly clear. He should not be feeling desire for an injured ally, but seeing all that blonde hair spilling across his pillow, her sculpted body in those small white underthings, her skin shining with gold . . .

And *blood*. He mentally begged her forgiveness as he shook off the troublesome thoughts. The Kubai Mata had made him into something more than human, but they hadn't erased the mortal nature he'd been born with. Refocused, he fetched clean

water and towels, laid out the necessary things for what he was
about to do, and sat on the bed beside her.

She murmured something.

'It's all right. You're safe.'

Again, her lips parted in a half moan, half whisper. 'Mal.'

Of course she would ask for the vampire she professed not to
love. 'No, you're with Creek.' The words came out harsher than
he intended.

Her eyes fluttered open. This was not a good time for her to
wake. Not when he had seventy-plus stitches to sew into her
flesh. 'Creek?'

'Yes.' Beneath all that gold, she was pale except for the dark
smudges shadowing her eyes. He put a hand to her forehead, but
even before he made contact, the heat rising off her skin seared
his palm. Fever had set in, brought on by the hellhound's poison.
Poison he'd been sealed against. Delirium could not be far
behind for her. Meanwhile, his leg had already begun to heal.

'Creek.' The word wasn't a question this time. 'The ... Kubai
Mata.'

He dipped a towel into the water and gently wiped away the
crusting blood from her wound. 'That's right. KM.' Maybe keeping her talking would help get her through the pain.

But she said nothing else, nor did she flinch at his touch, even
as he neared the ragged skin. Her eyes stayed closed and her
breathing took on a rhythmic cadence. She hummed softly, a
tune he'd never heard.

Cleaning finished, he threaded a sterilized needle. 'I'm going
to stitch now.'

She nodded in slow motion. He said a quick prayer and made
the first stitch. Not a flinch. Eased by her stoic ability to take the
pain, he proceeded without looking up until the first gash was

closed. Twenty-four of the neatest stitches he'd ever made. His head came up, proud of his work.

Tears streamed from the corners of her closed eyes.

His gut tightened and a small tremor ran through him. He set the needle aside and grabbed a bottle of whiskey. Cap unscrewed, he held it out as he sat back down. 'Here, drink some of this.'

Her eyes opened, her pupils barely focusing on the bottle. 'No alcohol for comarré. Must keep the blood . . . pure.'

'You need it for the pain.'

She closed her eyes again. 'Comarré don't feel pain.' Her voice was thready and weak.

'You were crying.' But he didn't push it.

She didn't answer, instead going back to the repetitious breathing and humming. He took a long pull of whiskey to settle the sudden case of nerves he'd gotten before putting the bottle aside and taking up the needle again. The tears didn't return.

Finally, he finished. He taped gauze over the stitches and sat back. 'I'm all done. I did the best I could, but there will probably be a scar.'

She answered with a sound like faraway laughter. 'Comarré don't scar.'

He covered her with the sheet. 'Get some sleep. I'm going to shower, then I'll be downstairs if you need me.' Maybe her system could work the poison out on its own. Maybe the fever was already burning it away. If not, he'd call Argent. Or maybe take her to his grandmother. She might know how to fix this.

He went downstairs and started a pot of coffee. Then, in the small bathroom, he stripped down and checked his leg. More of a deep gouge now. Already the edges were closed. By the time he'd finished showering, it was a long red weal. Wearing only a towel, he added his ruined jeans to the pile of clothes to be burned, poured the coffee into a thermos, and went back upstairs. He set the thermos on the bedside table – Chrysabelle seemed to be asleep – and turned to dress.

He was wrong.

'Your marks,' she whispered. 'You really are Kubai Mata.'

He glanced over his shoulder. One finger lifted off the bed to point at his back. He'd already dropped the towel, so he stayed where he was. So what if she'd seen his marks? They weren't sacred. Not exactly. Chances were good she wouldn't remember anything after this fever was done with her anyway. 'Go back to sleep. You've got a fever and you need to rest.'

'Musta hurt,' she whispered as she seemed to succumb to sleep again.

Like hell, he wanted to say, but she knew all about that, didn't she? In fresh jeans and a clean T-shirt, he settled next to her on the bed, his back against the plywood-barricaded window that made up the side wall, his shirt sticking to his damp body. He was about to pour a cup of coffee when she started talking softly. He almost couldn't hear her.

'I don't want to die.'

The words were so plaintive, so earnest they gave him a chill. He scrunched down beside her, brushed a few strands of hair from her face. Her skin burned beneath his fingertips. 'You're not going to die, I promise.'

She moaned and struggled to sit. He wrapped his arms around her to keep her immobile until she calmed. 'No.' She tensed. 'I need to find my brother.'

'Your brother is fine.' He pulled back to see her face. Red flushed her cheeks, making her signum stand out like flames. The poison rode her hard. Her mind was suffering. Comarré didn't have family, not in the true sense of the word. Perhaps she spoke of a comar she'd been close to.

She pulled against him, frantic. Despite her injury, she was incredibly strong. Pinpoints of blood leaked through the gauze. He swung his leg over hers to hold her down. Still, she persisted. 'Where is he?'

'He's fine, he's fine. Try to rest.' He used the edge of the sheet to dab the sweat from her face.

She relaxed a little, but he kept his arms around her. 'I need to find him.'

'As soon as you're better, I'll help you look.' For right now, he would just hold her to keep her from pulling those stitches out. Not because she felt damn good in his arms. Not because of that at all.

'You will?'

The heat from her fevered body poured into his. He turned his face into her neck and whispered the words into her hair. 'Of course.' Any promise to keep her safe. That was part of his job. *Just* part of his job.

She exhaled, her body going limp. She moved a little, like she was snuggling against him. His body took notice. 'You're a good man.'

He half smiled and repositioned the sheet over her again. She had no idea.

She sighed, weakly patting his leg where her hand rested. 'Even if you are a vampire.'

Chapter Eighteen

Tatiana prowled the halls, still amazed at how the effects of daysleep barely registered here in Dominic's lair. At her best guess, the sun had been up for two or three hours. She'd rested for an hour in her appointed suite to regain some of the strength used by holding Mia's and Katsumi's images for so long, but now it was time to find Malkolm and get him to reveal the comarré's location. Thanks to the charcoal-skinned fae, Tatiana knew just how to work Malkolm into telling her, too. The fae had told her to leave Malkolm alone, that now was not the time to make things right. Sounded to her like Malkolm and Katsumi had had some sort of lover's quarrel. For Tatiana's purposes, now was very much the time to make things right.

She laughed, almost woozy with power. Not in five hundred years had she forgotten what pleasures her husband enjoyed. Now she would once again use them to bend him to her will. Just as soon as she made sure Katsumi hadn't been discovered.

If only there was a way to let Nasir know she was okay so he wouldn't come looking for her and screw things up. But she would not risk blowing her cover trying to alert him.

The club was quieter at this hour but far from deserted. She kept her head down and the clipboard she'd found in front of her. So far, few employees or patrons had been willing to disturb the busy manager. She walked into Vanity, doing her best to look preoccupied, and headed for the private door that led to the storage room where she'd left Katsumi.

'Katsumi. I didn't expect to see you this shift.' The remnant bartender smiled as he set drinks in front of his customers. His eyes held a hint of wolfen blue, and his hands carried an extra digit. Canine-shifter and fae. Wonderful.

'I'm not really working – just had to check some things in inventory.' That sounded right. She kept going, hoping he'd get the hint and leave her alone.

He didn't. 'While I have you, could we go over next week's schedule? I can't work the Wednesday shift because—'

'Fine. I'll get someone else to do it.' If that didn't work, she'd promise him a raise to shut up. Or drag him into the back room and kill him. Unfortunately, her powers of persuasion didn't work against fae or varcolai, or when she used the mimicry power.

His brows rose. 'You will? Great. Thanks!'

She made it to the exit and slipped through to the maze of behind-the-scenes passages used by employees. She could barely remember how to get to the door she'd first entered, let alone this storage room. Coming back through Vanity had been the best shot.

Using Katsumi's thumbprint, she unlocked the door and cautiously entered. The stacks of chairs she'd dumped the woman behind were moved, and Katsumi had wriggled about half the length of her lower body out. Other than that, the room was undisturbed.

Tatiana locked the door and dropped her illusion. A few more minutes of rest couldn't hurt. She tugged Katsumi back into place and repositioned the chairs to hide her.

'Don't worry, fringe. I'm almost done with you.'

Katsumi squirmed and said something that sounded like a curse but was too muffled by duct tape to be understood.

Tatiana patted her on the head. 'There, there. You're being very helpful. I might let you live.' Not bloody likely.

Back out into the club, she once again used the clipboard and an air of busyness to keep the peons away. Soon she was several levels lower and back in the suites section. Hers was at the end of the main corridor. Although Dominic had referred to the rooms by name, none of the doors were marked. She counted until she came to the fifth door. She opened it. Yes, this was hers. The Dante suite. Would the Donatello be close by? Dante was a writer, Donatello a sculptor. If Dominic considered them both artists, they might be near each other. If not . . . There was no way to tell if his method was based in some sort of reasoning or if he was just another capricious noble.

With no other option she could see, she clung tightly to her guise as Katsumi and started opening doors.

Soft, familiar hands glided over Mal's body, tugging him gently from the grip of daysleep. Swirls of gold and remembrances of silken skin flashed through his fogged brain. The voices buzzed with worry, but they were as distant as the moon. He turned into the warm honeyed scent of woman, slipping his hands around a slim waist, and drew the form against him.

The dream caressed him and kissed his neck, murmuring words of smoky promise. Satiny strands of hair teased his skin. Sunlight danced behind his lids. Hungry sounds left his throat, and the desire for sleep waned as pleasure pulled him to the surface. Something sharp nicked him. His body tightened with desire. Then revulsion.

Fangs.

The coma of daysleep vanished.

He jarred awake to the voices' metallic whine, the sick-sweet scent of jasmine, and the prickle of an unwelcome evil. Every grain of his being stirred with the knowledge that something was very wrong. *Wake up!*

He leaped away from the bed and the body filling the space next to him and flicked on the light.

Sprawled across his bed was the last woman he would have ever imagined and certainly not one he had ever hoped would end up there on purpose.

'What the hell are you doing, Katsumi?' The delicious feeling that had filled him when the woman in his dream had been someone else fled at the sight of Katsumi's naked, tattooed body. *Destroy her*, the voices begged. How he'd like to.

Her laugh was soft, seductive, and completely unwelcome. 'I am trying to atone for all that has gone on between us. I don't want us to fight anymore, Malkolm.' She fluttered her lashes and offered a coy smile. As if she could ever be considered coy.

'You and I will never have that kind of relationship. You need to leave.' He started toward a chair near the bed to get his shirt, remembering too late that his beast and the battle with the Nothos had destroyed it. That thought led him directly to Chrysabelle. Again. He hated not knowing if she was safe. 'Get your clothes and go.'

'Now, now,' she chided him. 'Your body was perfectly willing to have that kind of relationship just a moment ago.' She slid out of the bed and sashayed toward him. Her hair tumbled past her shoulders to brush the top of her hips. The only thing covering her bodysuit of ink was a tiny red silk thong. The tattoos were far more interesting.

She stopped in front of him and rested her hands on her hips. 'You like to look? Go ahead.'

The dragon curling over her shoulder glared at him. He forced his gaze to her face. 'I don't want to look or touch. I just want you to leave.' *Get her out now.*

'You're not even going to let me make up for . . . you know?' Her eyes glimmered with petulant humor. He knew that look from somewhere, but it wasn't Katsumi.

'For poisoning me? For trying to get me killed?' He laughed. 'You think sex is going to make up for that? How cheap do you think I am? Don't answer that.' He shook his head and reached for his jeans. 'Besides, you're bloody mental if you think I have the slightest desire to swim in the same waters as Dominic and Ronan.'

'Dominic?' She looked genuinely stricken.

'Did you think people didn't know? Why else would he have made you manager?' He stepped into his pants, turning away to zip up. The idea of sex with Katsumi made his long-lost soul shudder. The voices agreed.

'You're sleeping with her, aren't you?' The anger in Katsumi's voice was unmistakable. And oddly familiar.

'No,' he answered, already knowing who Katsumi referenced. *The blood whore.*

She shrieked and the air shifted. He spun in time to catch her hand before it raked his back. 'Of course you're sleeping with her. You knew exactly who I was talking about. That filthy comarré whore—'

Anger shot through Mal and he backhanded her. 'I told you never to speak of her that way again. I should cut your tongue out.'

A flicker of silver lit her eyes, gone so fast he wasn't sure he'd seen it. He grabbed for her arm to get a better look, but she snatched her discarded clothes and ran for the door. 'You'll be dead before that happens.'

'Good riddance.'

She slammed the door. Just as well. Daylight or not, he had to find Chrysabelle. He put his jacket on and left. Katsumi had already vanished from the hall. Maybe she'd stormed back to her room. Who cared, just so long as she was gone.

He knocked at Dominic's office door, not sure where else to start.

Doc opened it.

Not the person he'd expected to see, but apparently there was a lot of that going around today. 'What are you doing here?'

'I could ask you the same thing, bro.'

'Chrysabelle and I went to investigate those fringe deaths. Ran into a pack of Nothos on the wrong side of midnight. This was the closest shelter. You?'

'Long story. Where's Chrysabelle?'

'I'm not sure.' But he had an idea, which was the problem. A Mohawked slayer kind of problem.

'You think she went back to the freighter?'

'No.' Call it a hunch.

'Then why didn't she come with—'

'Out of the way.' Mortalis pushed past Mal, a bound female form in his arms. 'Help me get her unwrapped.' He laid her on one of the couches and began to peel a layer of duct tape from the woman's head.

'Who is it?' Mal asked.

'Not sure. No one's been reported missing. I've been helping out with security since Ronan disappeared and heard thumping coming from the storage room by Vanity. Found her.' Every layer of tape Mortalis pulled off revealed another one. 'If she's a breather, she can't have much time left.'

'Stand back,' Doc said. He popped a sharp claw from one finger and scored the casing down the middle.

'Careful,' Mortalis said.

'I'm always careful with the ladies.' Doc stood back. 'I'll unwrap her head while you two finish the body.'

Mortalis worked his fingers under one edge. 'Take the other side, Mal.'

'Got it.' The tape was melded to the woman's clothing, but he dug his fingers between the sticky layers. Together, he and Mortalis worked the tape loose.

'Mother Bast,' Doc whispered.

Mal looked up the same time Mortalis did.

Beneath the cocoon of duct tape lay a frightened and shivering Katsumi. Tear tracks streaked her eye makeup down the sides of her face and into her hair.

Mal shook his head. 'That's impossible. Katsumi was just in my bed.'

'What?' Doc and Mortalis both whipped around to look at him.

'Not what you think.' Mal grimaced. 'And obviously it wasn't Katsumi.'

She shook her head, forehead wrinkling in distress.

'Then who? And why?' Mortalis finished unwrapping the trembling fringe and helped her sit.

She clung to him, gripping his arm until her knuckles

whitened. She swallowed and tried to speak, but nothing came out. Her hand went to her throat.

'Raw from screaming?' Mortalis asked.

She nodded.

'I'll get you some tea.' He looked at Mal. 'Who was in your room?'

With a burning cold certainty, Mal knew how the woman in his bed had known just how to touch him to get the response she had, and how she had understood what the tease of fangs would do to him. Why he'd seen a flicker of silver in her eyes.

The name bit the tip of his tongue with a serpent's venom, so he spat it out.

'Tatiana.'

Chapter Nineteen

Weak knocking roused Dominic. He'd been half awake anyway. He glanced at the clock. Six hours of daysleep. Hardly enough, but these days one took what one could get. He slipped out of bed, pulled a cashmere robe over his silk pajamas, and walked out to the sitting room. '*Si.*'

His manservant, Vertuccio, entered and bowed. 'My lord, Ms. Tanaka is here to see you.'

'*Si, si.* Send her in.' Too bad Katsumi needed to be questioned. He was definitely *arrapato* – in the mood – but curse his libido, he had to find out about the letter sent to Chrysabelle and where the blood thusly attained had gone. If Katsumi was guilty, she'd have to be dealt with.

She walked in and all desire drained from his body. '*Porca vacca*, what has happened to you?'

A wreck of a woman stood before him. Katsumi's makeup was tear-streaked. Her hair, always so sleekly bound, fell to her waist in a disheveled mess. And oddly enough, her skin and clothes bore a random pattern of thin lines of some kind of sticky residue. 'What has happened? Are you all right?'

'No.' Her voice was terribly hoarse. He could have sworn she sniffed. Or perhaps that sound was a sob. Out of Katsumi?

He called Vertuccio back. 'Bring tea and one of the better comars. Ask Jacqueline if you're not sure.'

'Very good, sir.' Vertuccio went off to do as Dominic had commanded, shutting the sitting room door behind him.

Dominic took the large wingback chair across from the electric fireplace. He missed the smell and sound of a real fire, but for a vampire, real fire could also mean death. He contented himself with the artificial smoke smell and synthesized crackling. 'So. Explain what has occurred.'

She relayed how she'd been overpowered, bound and gagged with duct tape, and left in the storage room. About the strange metallic limb that had transformed into a noose. How she'd screamed until she'd tasted her own blood. How she'd been sure of her death until Mortalis had found her. She wept softly and Dominic couldn't remember a time when he'd seen Katsumi cry. Ever.

He nodded as she continued, going on to describe her captor. 'Malkolm believes it was Tatiana.'

'As do I.' In fact, he'd expected it. Tatiana hadn't seemed like the type to forgive and forget. 'Chrysabelle sliced Tatiana's hand off during the battle in Corvinestri, but she must have found someone from St. Germain to build her a new one. An adaptable metal hand such as you described could only be the work of an alchemist.' But to have Maris's killer here, in his club, in his home ... The thought of Tatiana's presence eroded his nerves until they felt raw and exposed. The killing urge rose up in him, as did a new understanding of what Katsumi had been through. She was fortunate to be alive. 'I am deeply sorry you were subjected to this.'

A knock on the door interrupted them.

'Enter.'

Vertuccio came in bearing a tea service on an antique sterling tray. Behind Vertuccio followed one of Seven's best comars. Vertuccio set the exquisite tray down on the center table and gave a short bow. 'Anything else, sir?'

'Yes. I assume Mortalis is already searching the premises for Tatiana. I want a report from him as soon as possible.'

'Very good, sir.' Vertuccio backed out, closing the door as he went.

Dominic gestured to the comar. 'You, sit beside Katsumi.' Then he waved his hand from Katsumi to the comar. 'Go on. Feed. You must fortify yourself. Regain your strength.'

She nodded as the comar offered up his wrist. She accepted it, her fangs descended, and with great delicacy, pierced his skin and drank. The comar shuddered with obvious pleasure.

Dominic helped himself to a glass of Brunello while he waited. He would feed soon enough, but until then, the rich, dark red wine was a close substitute for blood. He stared into the fire as he sipped, letting memories of life with Maris wash over him. They had been so happy, so full of joy, even if it had only been for a short season. He ached for her. The chance to see her, to speak to her once more ... He sighed into his glass. He could not pass that up.

A few minutes later, Katsumi wiped the corners of her mouth with her knuckle, not that there was anything to wipe away. She had always been one of the most fastidious feeders he'd known. She bobbed her head at him. 'Thank you. I do feel better.'

'You may go, *grazie*.' Dominic dismissed the comar and poured Katsumi a cup of tea. 'You'll be your old self in no time.'

She accepted the tea but didn't drink. 'That's part of what I'd like to talk to you about.'

He raised a brow. 'Go on.'

She set the cup and saucer down gently, head bent, chest pulled in like a guilty dog before its master. Her words were quiet, although the hoarseness had begun to diminish. 'I don't want to be the old me anymore. I'm tired of being fringe. I couldn't protect myself against that woman because she was noble. She was stronger, more powerful ... ' She sighed deeply, her fingers interlacing tightly. 'I want you to resire me. I want navitas.'

He'd wondered when she'd make this request. He'd been waiting for it, actually. Humans wanted to be vampires, fringe wanted to be noble, and nobles wanted the power of the ancients. No one was ever satisfied with what they had. He studied her plaintive face, longing bright in her eyes. 'This is not an easy thing you ask of me.'

'I know, but—'

'No, you can't know.' He held his hand up. 'And just because I am noble doesn't mean I am skilled in this ritual. I have never performed navitas, never seen it performed, but I know it is not without risk. You could die. Succumb to madness.' Like Tatiana. He swirled the wine in his glass. 'I must think on it.'

'I know the risks. I don't care. I want to change my life.'

'You want revenge and the power to carry it out.'

'No, Dominic, I swear that's not it.' She shifted, leaning forward. 'I am not the gentlest of fringe. I know that. I am difficult to get along with. Overly ambitious. Conniving. I cheat. I lie.'

A more perfect opportunity he could not imagine. 'And steal?'

Her gaze dropped to her lap. 'I can guess what this is about. Yes, and steal. But I'm done with that. I want to turn over a new leaf. Put this life behind me and rise above my past. Become a better creature.' Her eyes lifted to his. 'A companion more worthy of you.'

But Dominic was not so easily swayed. 'You sent Leo to Chrysabelle's, didn't you?'

Her fingers worried the fabric of her gown. 'Yes.' Her voice went low and soft. Almost repentant. 'I am truly sorry, my lord.'

That honorific rarely crossed her lips. Might she genuinely desire change? 'What was the point of stealing blood from her? And where is Leo?' That fringe would definitely die. An example had to be made.

'I don't know where Leo is. As for the blood . . . ' She sighed. 'Malkolm has had comarré blood these last few weeks. He is much stronger than before. I needed the blood for Ronan, to ensure he would be strong enough to face Malkolm in the fight I had planned.'

'Something else I would not have allowed.' One offense after the other. He began to calculate a punishment that would suit.

'Which is why I didn't tell you. I knew you would have refused me. Again, my apologies.'

'And what of Ronan? Mortalis tells me he's been gone since the night of that fight.'

She sighed. 'After the fight, I took Ronan to my apartment, did what I could for his injuries, then came back here. He was gone when I returned. I don't know what's become of him.'

'Why was this fight between them so important?'

Again, she stared at her fingers. 'The fight quadrupled the club's take that night. I wanted to prove to you I could run this club.' She hesitated. 'I also stood to make a large sum for myself.'

He'd seen the books. The receipts from that night had been astronomical. 'Are your accounts so dismal? I pay you well.'

'You do.' She shrugged. 'But I am greedy. I like nice things. I wanted to live more like you do and less like . . . like a fringe.'

'There is no automatic wealth that comes with nobility. Look at Malkolm. There are homeless in this city who live better.' He'd paid to have her windows helioglazed. Sent Solomon to ward her apartment against intruders. But of course she wanted more. And didn't care about the cost. 'Ambition is one thing. Greed quite another.'

She stared at her hands, her mouth tightening then softening. 'Forgive me.'

'Did it occur to you that either Malkolm or Ronan could have lost their lives?'

'Yes, and they knew it, too, but their past made the fight too hard to pass up.' She stared into the fire. 'Ronan was eager for it. Malkolm not so much.'

He rapped his fingers on the arm of the chair, contemplating all she'd told him. To say he was angry with her behavior was putting it lightly. 'You forged my words. Stole from someone I consider as close as *famiglia*. Violated my trust – what little there was of that to begin with. Caused grave injury to someone I now consider a friend and almost killed another of my employees. One might say it would be well within my rights to mete out whatever punishment I deem fit.'

She nodded. 'It would be. And I will abide by whatever you decide.' She raised her hand, splaying her fingers. 'I would gladly give you my other pinkie if you deemed it necessary.'

He stared in disbelief. This was not the Katsumi he knew. Or had ever known. She seemed truly broken. 'You cannot expect me to believe this change of heart simply because you speak the words.'

She dropped her hand and shook her head. 'No, I cannot. But

I will show you. You'll see. I am different. I . . . I had too much time in that storage room to consider my life and what kind of person I was. What I saw horrified me. There was no wheat to sift from the chaff. Nothing of value. I do not wish to die and leave such a legacy behind. It's not too late for me to change. Please, believe me.'

'I will, once you've shown me. So change. Become this new creature. When I believe you are sincere in both heart and actions, I will offer you navitas.' He paused. Her countenance brightened. 'You may find you no longer need it.'

She moved from her seat to kneel before him, taking his hand and kissing his fingers before pressing it to her cheek. 'Thank you, Dominic. You'll see. You'll see just how different I can be.'

He tried to pull his hand away, but she clung to him. 'Until that time, consider yourself under house arrest. You will not leave Seven without my permission, and when you do, you will be accompanied by someone I assign to you. Your life is no longer your own until I decide how best to deal with your transgressions.'

'Whatever you say, my lord. Thank you.' Still cupping his other hand to her cheek, she slid her free hand up his leg. 'Perhaps there is something I could do to earn your forgiveness now?'

He pointed toward his private bathroom. 'Clean yourself up and we shall see. You may not thank me when I am through with you.'

Chrysabelle's body ached. No, her bones ached. Her body throbbed. Especially across her stomach. She remembered fighting the Nothos and passing out, then time warped into memories both lucid and blurred. She knew Creek had stitched her wounds – holy mother, that pain had been unlike any she'd felt since her last visit to the signumist – but she didn't remember how she'd gotten to his home. Or into his bed.

A few other images flitted in and out of her consciousness. One was crystal clear. The broad expanse of Creek's naked back. Then the awfulness of realizing the words upon his skin had been *branded* there. If she closed her eyes, she could still read them.

Omnes honorate. Fraternitatem diligite. Deum timete. Regem honorificate. Honor all men. Love the brotherhood. Fear God. Honor the king.

It was the code of the Kubai Mata. Just having those sacred words upon his body made his blood poison to the creatures he'd been trained to slay.

Those words also meant there was no denying Creek was who he said he was. She exhaled her last ounce of hope that perhaps he'd just been a misguided soul with a desire to bring a fairy tale to life. More than ever, she believed he must be responsible for the deaths of those fringe Doc had stumbled upon. She would ask Creek point-blank. As a KM, chances were good he wouldn't lie to her.

Hot and sweaty, she flipped the sheet off and groaned softly. For the second time in the last few weeks, she'd woken up in a strange man's bed wearing nothing but her intimates. A swath of gauze covered the right side of her stomach. Dried blood stained the corresponding side of her underwear, but thankfully, Creek had left them on, because she had no doubt he was the one who'd undressed her.

Pushing to her elbows caused a rush of fire to ignite the skin beneath the gauze. She collapsed back to the mattress with a gasp. Okay, she hadn't expected it to hurt quite that much.

'It's the poison.'

She jumped, lighting a new round of searing heat across her belly. Creek stood at the top of the stairs. She whipped the sheet back over herself. 'That's why it hurts so badly, isn't it? And why I'm burning up? Fever from the Nothos poison.'

He nodded and brought a plate of food and a glass of water to the bedside table. He set them down, then pressed his calloused palm to her forehead. 'Most of it's gone now. Fever was a lot worse this morning. Few more hours and the pain should be manageable.'

'It's manageable now.' She needed to get home. To her own bed.

'Want to get up and walk around, then?'

She ground her teeth together.

'That's what I thought.' His hand reached for the plate again. 'You need to eat. Keep your strength up.'

'It's a little hard to eat lying down.'

He held a fork loaded with scrambled eggs. 'All you have to do is chew.'

Her stomach growled. Reluctantly, she opened her mouth. Being fed by someone seemed a very intimate act. At least he could look a little less pleased with himself.

But his enjoyment in the act didn't stop her from cleaning the plate. Or devouring the second course of wheat toast with peanut butter and honey, which she managed to eat by herself without too much honey ending up on her or the bed. Sated, she allowed him to help her sip some water, then felt sleep invade her muscles with its sweet, dreamy pull.

And dream she did. Of a Mohawked warrior and a vampire challenger. Of hellhounds and claws like fiery scythes. Of bodies turned to ash and a mother she'd never see again.

She woke in a panic, but it faded quickly as her surroundings registered. The gold light of afternoon sun gilded the building's interior where it leaked through the dirty skylights. The faint smell of smoke lingered in the air.

'Creek?' Perhaps he'd left. She eased up onto her elbows, the pain bearable now, just as he'd said it would be.

He soundlessly appeared at the top of the stairs. 'How are you feeling?'

'Much better.' And hungry again. But enough was enough. 'I need to go home.'

'You need more rest.'

'Thank you, Doctor.' Nice way to talk to the man who'd saved her life. 'Look, I know I need more rest. I just prefer to do it in my own home.' After a long, hot shower and one of Velimai's steaks. Maybe two.

He nodded. Was that disappointment on his face? No, just a shadow. He should be pleased to get rid of her. Kubai Mata weren't meant to be nursemaids. 'I've got a T-shirt and a pair of sweatpants you can borrow. Riding back on the motorcycle isn't going to be fun for you.'

'I'll call for my driver.'

'I don't have a phone.'

'Motorcycle it is, then.' Even though the thought of being tucked against him that way unnerved her. She would have to wrap her arms around him, press herself against that branded back of his. Did he think she'd forgotten? How could she? A thing like that didn't slip from your mind. It stayed there, layering itself over the image's owner every time you looked at them so that they and the image became inseparable. Her glimpse of Creek was as branded into her memory as the words on his back.

He pulled some clothes off a shelf and set them on the bed. 'Take your time. I'll be downstairs when you're ready.'

I'll never be ready, she wanted to tell him. Instead, she dressed sitting on the edge of the bed, moving slowly as she pulled on the clothes he'd given her. His room was sparse. A side table, a set of shelves made from cinder blocks and boards, a few nails in the wall to hang things on. At the far end, a back alley window led to a fire escape. Surely the KM could do better than this? Or was it a cover?

Her supreme lack of energy brought that line of thinking to a quick close. *Home.* That was the only thing to be concerned with. Her shoes were nowhere to be found, so she padded barefoot down the stairs, holding on to the gritty railing with as much strength as she could muster. At the halfway point, she stopped, light-headed and breathless. While she rested, she surveyed the remainder of Creek's home.

A massive chain and winch hung from the ceiling, and old metal presses and piles of scrap had been pushed against the walls, but in the center of the dingy, concrete-floored room sat a two-wheeled monster. Nothing about the motorcycle seemed remotely safe. In fact, with the matte-black finish and the chromed metal parts, it looked evil. Like something a Nothos might ride. Or Mal.

Mal. She dropped her head and groaned softly. She had no idea what had happened to him after they'd parted ways. *Please, holy mother, let him be safe.*

'You okay? Need some help?' Creek came into view, wiping his hands on a towel.

'No. I'm fine.'

He gave her a suspicious look and stayed where he was, watching her.

She started down the stairs, gripping the railing. She made it to the landing, wincing only at every other step.

He threw the towel over his shoulder. 'If that's fine, I'd like to see what still-in-pain looks like. You should really stay in bed and rest.'

'I will. In my own bed.' Because being in his made her uncomfortable. Just like being in Mal's bed had.

'Suit yourself.' He turned and walked into the makeshift kitchen. 'Coffee?'

Pulling her gaze from his back was almost impossible. 'No, thank you. I just need to get home.' Finally, she looked away and, feeling worn out from her trip downstairs, sat on the landing to wait for him to be ready. She rested her head on her knees, unable to recall the last time she'd felt so exhausted.

'Chrysabelle?'

She woke with a start, earning a punch of pain through her gut. 'What?'

Creek sat beside her on the landing. 'You fell asleep.'

'I was resting my eyes.'

He bit the inside of his cheek too late to hide his grin. 'Look, I know you don't like me, don't want to stay here with me any longer than you have to—'

'No, no, I like you just fine.' She did, actually. Except for the part where he might be a fringe serial killer. Which she still needed to ask him about. 'I'm sorry if I gave you that impression. I'm very thankful for what you did for me. Saving my life and stitching me up and all that.' It *was* nice to be around another human.

His dark, winged brows lifted fractionally. 'But?'

'I don't know what you mean.' She knew exactly what he meant. She wasn't comfortable with him because being around him felt like trying to stick the opposite ends of two magnets together. Too much push–pull. Too much dangerous attraction. One move in the wrong direction and the magnets stuck together like they were meant to be that way.

He leaned in, his blue eyes reflecting flashes of her signum. 'Don't you?'

It was wrong for a man to be that beautiful. 'Don't you think we should ...' She pointed lamely at the motorcycle.

'Uh-huh.' He kept staring. Like he could see her lies. 'You don't feel at all uneasy around me?'

'Don't be silly. You're human, I'm human – what's to be uneasy about?'

Looking away, he picked up her hand as though he hadn't heard a word she'd said. 'You don't have to feel that way, you know.' His thumb stroked the curling gold vine that trailed from her wrist bone to her first knuckle. The dizziness returned with a vengeance. 'I would never hurt you. It's part of my directive to protect you.'

'Good to know.' The words came out much softer than she'd intended, but part of her was surprised she could speak at all. Her heart thudded. At least Creek couldn't hear it. She told herself to pull her hand out of his. Nothing happened.

'Don't be afraid of me. I would never hurt you.' He glanced at her, his face earnest.

She shook her head. Or nodded. She had no idea. There was a wildness about him that frightened her as much as Mal's steely control. He let go of her hand. She looked down for a moment and when she raised her head, he was there. His mouth on hers. Warm and soft and—

Before she could respond to his kiss, he pulled away, stood up, and walked toward the motorcycle. 'You're right. Time for you to go home.'

Chapter Twenty

Chrysabelle was home. Mal could hear the rhythm of her pulse beneath the swooshing palms and the chorus of nocturnal insects. It was faster than her resting heart rate. Maybe she was training. That was a good sign. If she was training, she was okay. Still, he hesitated to knock. She'd be mad he'd climbed the privacy wall and circumvented her security. Or maybe she'd be mad he'd demanded she run from the Nothos. Or maybe she'd still be steamed about him fighting in the Pits or drinking her blood or a whole host of other things he could think of. She was good at being mad at him. *Drain her, then.*

They were good at being mad at each other.

But right now, he couldn't think of a single reason to be anything but concerned. All he could think of was finding out if she'd been hurt by the Nothos. Or that whack job Creek. Kubai Mata. Did he also moonlight as the tooth fairy?

Mal walked to her door and knocked.

Predictably, Velimai answered. With her usual cold glare, she studied him for a moment. Then shut the door.

Cursing under his breath, he knocked again. 'Velimai, get Chrysabelle.'

The bothersome fae opened the door and shook her head. Her hands and fingers flew.

He held a palm up. 'You know I can't understand a word you're signing.'

Velimai rolled her eyes and disappeared into the house, leaving the door open. She returned, writing on a tablet with a stylus. Her mood didn't seem to have improved. She turned the tablet so he could read what she'd written on the screen.

Chrysabelle is resting. Cannot be disturbed. Go home.

So. Not training. Not good. 'No. I need to see her. She won't mind being disturbed, trust me.' Or maybe she would. But she'd get over it. He needed to know she was okay. *You need her blood.*

Velimai hugged the tablet to her chest and shook her head.

'You're not the only one who can yell.' Mal glared back. 'You want me to wake her up my way? Then you can explain why you didn't go and get her in the first place.'

Velimai flipped him a sign he understood perfectly and walked away in the opposite direction. Hopefully to get Chrysabelle.

A hundred hours later, Chrysabelle appeared, skin as pale as the big white robe she was wrapped in, hair loose around her face, and dark circles beneath her eyes. She moved tentatively, like she was in pain. Even at this distance he felt her body temp was off. Too high. He was relieved she was alive and upright, but her condition left a lot to be desired. 'What's wrong?'

'Can we go out to the lanai?' The words were strained.

'Sure.' He could argue a thousand other days to be let in. 'Meet you there.'

It took her ten minutes longer to join him than it should have. She delicately sat onto one of the chaise longues, then eased her feet up and patted the cushion. 'Sit.'

Bite. He did as she asked, welcoming the closeness and instantly wishing for more. 'What happened?'

She smiled. 'I'm glad you're okay.' She reached out and squeezed his hand, knocking his mental balance into a dark crevasse. Her touch made the voices howl.

'Thank you. And likewise.' Except she clearly wasn't okay. 'Please tell me what happened. Two Nothos got away from me. I know they went after you.' If he was lucky, they'd eaten Creek for dinner. *Or you could.*

With a sigh, she rested her head against the chaise's high back. 'That's why I wasn't sure if you were all right. They found us.'

Us, she'd said. Like she and Creek were a couple. He looked away long enough to force the calm back onto his face. 'Then what happened?'

'We fought them. Killed them. We both got wounded, but I took the brunt of it.'

'You should wear that body armor of yours from now on.'

She glanced down and adjusted her robe. 'That wouldn't make it very comfortable for you to be around me.'

That she would care about that detail raised a sense of satisfaction in him. 'I'll deal. How badly were you hurt?'

'I needed a few stitches. Still working the Nothos poison out of my system, which, as I'm sure you've noticed, is why I'm running a little hot and fast.'

'How many is a few?'

'Enough to close me up.'

'How many?'

Her expression darkened. 'I think around seventy.'

The sensation drained out of his extremities. 'Seventy. Seven zero.'

'Yes,' she whispered.

'Son of a priest.' The beast inhaled. The scent of blood was strong. But so was another scent. 'Who gave you those stitches?'

'Who do you think?'

There was no thought. Just a growl and his fist pounding the tumbled marble pool deck. The tile cracked. He got up and walked to the edge of the pool. Stared unseeing into the crystalline water. Listened to the whine of the souls in his head.

'You're upset he saved my life?'

The slayer had touched her. *She probably asked him to. Probably loved it.* '*He* saved your life? I'm sure my sending you away and taking the bulk of those monsters had nothing to do with the fact that you're still here.'

'Mal . . .' Her voice was soft, cajoling.

Now was not the time for his anger. He knew that but let it roil within him anyway. 'Where were you injured?'

'Across my stomach.'

Rage choked him. 'Did he undress you, too?'

'Yes.' Anger replaced the softness. 'Just like you did.'

He had no problem remembering that day. Forgetting it . . . now, that was an issue. He turned. 'If you recall, you undressed yourself that day. I covered you up.'

She scowled, making herself look even more pitiful, and muttered something under her breath that sent an electric skitter over his skin and the voices into a new frenzy.

He cocked one eyebrow. 'What did you say?'

'I said bite me. But I meant it figuratively.'

'Now you sound like Katsumi. Which seems like a good

enough reason to change the subject.' That or he was going to destroy something. 'Tatiana was in Seven. Her hand has been replaced by some metal prosthesis that can change shape. She's hunting you. Sooner or later, she's going to find you. Unless you get your boyfriend to track her down and stake her first.'

'I figured the Nothos were a sign she was here. Now we know for sure. And her being here makes her easier to find and kill.' She laughed. 'It's interesting to see you jealous.'

Damn right he was jealous. 'You confuse jealousy with protecting what's mine. Your blood rights. Or have you conveniently forgotten that again?'

'Conveniently? You mean like the way you're only my patron when it's convenient?' She snorted softly. 'This is a two-way street, Malkolm.'

'Don't you care that Tatiana's after you? That she's in town?'

'Dominic sent Solomon over to ward the house when we got back from Corvinestri. Some kind of extra-strength spell that erased the house's location from Tatiana's memory.' She stared directly at him in a transparent show of bravado. 'Besides, I have every intention of killing her the first chance I get.'

'She found the house once, she'll find it again. You're injured. You're in no condition to fight her if she shows up. Especially if she brings more Nothos with her.'

'She won't have to fight. I'm here.'

At the voice, they both looked up. Mal cursed at the slayer walking toward them. Velimai hovered behind Creek, looking far too pleased to have escorted the KM in. 'What are you doing here?'

'Checking up on my patient. She can't spare the blood right now, so you might as well leave.'

'She's not your patient.' A storm rose up in Mal, a maelstrom of darkness and desperation. *Kill him.*

Creek lifted a brow. 'I put those stitches in. Or didn't she tell you that?'

'I told him.' Chrysabelle's face went from pale to pink. Was she blushing? Not a look Mal recalled seeing on her before. 'What can I do for you, Creek?'

'Like I said, I just came to see how you're feeling.' He glanced at Mal. 'Check on those stitches.'

'You'll do no such thing,' Mal growled. He'd be double damned if he was going to let that mortal touch Chrysabelle again.

'You both need to relax.' Chrysabelle rolled her head from side to side against the chaise's back. 'And stop acting like children.'

Creek laughed in Mal's direction. 'I'm pretty sure he's more of a senior citizen.'

'You're definitely a child.' Mal shrugged off his jacket. 'One who could use a spanking.'

With some effort, Chrysabelle swung her feet onto the ground. 'I'm done with both of you. Go home.'

Mal rushed to her side to help her up. Creek got to her two seconds later. Senior citizen, indeed. 'It's not safe for you to be alone.'

Creek nodded. 'I agree with the old man on that one.'

She pulled away from both of them, her eyes flashing sparks like her signum. 'Fine. Stand guard. Patrol the grounds. Beat each other to a bloody pulp. Whatever makes you happy. Just don't think you're coming in. Either of you.' She headed for the house. 'I have a battle to prepare for.'

*

'I don't see anything but rat droppings and rust down here.' Dominic grimaced as he surveyed the cargo hold.

'She'll be here soon as the loop starts.' Doc rubbed a hand over his scalp. This had to work. He was out of ideas, and this wasn't even a good one.

Dominic eyed Doc suspiciously. 'Why are you so twitchy?'

'I'm not twitchy. I'm anxious. I miss Fi.' Which was true. He ached for her. Hated what she was about to go through. Again. But his nerves were also wired with what was about to go down.

Dominic walked to one of the storage containers and leaned against it. Doc had told him to wear casual clothes. For the Italian, that meant dress slacks and a silk shirt, but at least he'd left the suit at home.

The solar lantern at Doc's feet cast weak shadows into the solid black surrounding them. A bead of nervous sweat zipped down his spine as the prickle of his sixth sense raised the small hairs on the back of his neck.

'She's here,' he whispered.

Dominic straightened. 'Where?'

Doc pointed to the faint glow drifting down the corridor. He was counting on Dominic being mesmerized so he could get into position.

'Doc? You there?' Fi sounded tinny in the cargo hold's expanse.

'Sure 'nuff, baby. Right here. See the light?'

'Who's with you?' Fear edged her voice. Her image emerged as she got closer. She squinted at Dominic.

'Don't worry, sweets. Just a … friend. Dominic. Maris's friend. Remember? We all went to Corvinestri together?'

She scowled. 'He's the reason for your curse.' Suddenly her

ghostly image shifted into something freaky scary. Her face flickered between flesh and bone, her skull showing through the flesh, her eyes like burned-out coals. 'I don't like him.'

'It's okay, Fi. He's not here to hurt either one of us.'

'What's the meaning of this?' Dominic shifted uneasily. 'Tell her I want to speak to Maris.'

'Chill. We're dealing with a lot of unknowns here, you dig? She's not quite herself.' Damn, he was starting to look forward to this. 'Bout time someone took Dominic down a peg.

'You told me she'd had contact with Maris. I want to talk to her now.'

'Soon. Be patient. Fi's got to get through her own stuff first.' As if on cue, Fi screamed and the thin sound moved him into action. The loop had begun.

From the tangible blackness surrounding her, a skeletal figure attacked, grabbing her.

Dominic grimaced. 'No wonder Malkolm has such anger. To be left to rot like that ...'

Doc tried not to watch. He'd seen it too many times. Plus, he had work to do. He reached beneath his jacket to the waistband of his jeans and pulled out the syringe.

Her mouth opened in a second scream. The flashlight fell from her hand and landed with the beam pointed at her.

Hands still behind his back, he moved into position behind Dominic and worked the cap off the needle.

Oblivious to Doc's scheme, Dominic watched with blatant curiosity as Mal's carcass sank his fangs into Fi's throat, shredding her flesh like tissue paper. Blood spurted down her front while Mal gorged.

Doc's anger peaked. With a quick jab, he hammered the syringe into Dominic's jugular and shoved the plunger down, filling his system with a cocktail of laudanum and colloidal silver. Dominic cried out, spinning to face Doc.

The color seeped out of Fi as she fought.

Dominic's hand clenched at his neck. He yanked out the needle. 'What have you done?' He staggered backward through the loop. His true face erased his human one, but his fangs only descended halfway. He dropped the syringe.

Fi's punches bounced off Mal's thin frame. Her feet dangled off the stone floor of the nightmare's ruins.

Doc pulled out the empty second syringe. 'I did what I had to. To help Fi.'

Fi went pale as ash.

Dominic fell, his eyes rolling back in his head. 'Stay away from me. You don't know what you're doing.'

'I know exactly what I'm doing.'

With a groan, Dominic went completely still. Doc got the needle into a vein and pulled the plunger back until the barrel filled with blood. There. Mission accomplished.

Doc looked up. Mal's image in the loop stared back with hazy eyes. A scrap of skin hung from his withered jaw. Once again, Fi lay dead at his feet.

Time to get moving. Once Dominic came to, Doc would have a target the size of Texas on his back. But the repercussions meant nothing. He pocketed the precious vial and returned the specter's dead-eyed gaze. 'Your days are numbered. I'm about to set your captive free.'

Chapter Twenty-one

'Oh, that's it. Right there. Harder. Mmm-hmm, get in there.' Tatiana purred into the massage table's headrest. Octavian's hands were miraculous gifts. And she deserved gifts. Especially after what she'd been through.

Holding the guises of the shifter and the fringe had spent her energy reserves and then some, leaving her drained. She'd barely had enough strength to avoid detection at the club when she'd realized the fringe's body had been discovered. Changing back into the shifter's form had almost caused her to black out, but surviving until sundown had become her singular focus.

Now, back in the safety of the estate Octavian had secured and with twelve comatose hours of daysleep behind her, the time had come to make new plans.

She could have killed Malkolm, but she needed him to get to the comarré. The ring was close. Tatiana could feel it as clearly as she could feel Octavian's glorious fingers kneading the muscles along her spine, working their way down to her tailbone.

'Delicious,' she whispered. 'Don't stop.'

'I won't, my lady.' His thumbs worked in slow circles, eliciting soft cries of pleasure from her.

A darker male scent invaded past the neroli oil Octavian used. She opened her eyes as a pair of masculine feet came into view. Nasir. 'I thought I was the only one who got you to make those sounds.'

Like most men, Nasir was prone to childish bouts of jealousy. Not that Octavian's hands on her naked body were any of his concern. She was an Elder. Her actions were not Nasir's to judge. Nor would she indulge his emotions. Not now. 'What news from the Nothos?'

'No news. None have returned.'

'Call them back, then.' Why must she do everything? Could no one function without her step-by-step input? She closed her eyes, tired of looking at his hairy toes.

'They have been called back. A day ago. None have returned.'

'Call them again. Perhaps they've found good hunting and are too busy gorging themselves to pay attention.'

'I *have* called them again. And again. Every hour on the hour for the past six. They are gone.'

Her entire platoon of Nothos? She wrapped the top sheet around her body and sat up. 'That can't be.'

'It is.'

'Bloody hell.' Her fist slammed the massage table, causing it to creak. '*Bloody, bloody hell*. I need them. I was going to send them out on a new hunt.' She'd brought back a piece of lining from Malkolm's jacket so the Nothos could follow his scent and lead her to the comarré, who was surely with him. Now she was out of Nothos. Only one solution came to mind. 'Take the plane, go back to Corvinestri, and get more. Your comarré will stay with me. I'll wire money into your account, but so help me, if you don't come back, I will stake you to a solar panel and let the sun have its way with you.'

'But I—'

'Octavian, Nasir leaves immediately. You will drive him to the airport and inform the pilots of my orders.'

'Yes, my lady.' Her dutiful servant bowed.

Her less-than-dutiful companion did not. 'Now see here, I have no intention—'

She narrowed her gaze at Nasir. 'You will do as I tell you. I am your Elder. This situation is not open for discussion. Do you understand me?'

'Yes.' The word was forced out through clenched teeth and a jaw so tight Tatiana wondered if it gave him pain. She hoped it did. Ingrate.

Nasir stormed from the room, but Octavian had yet to leave. 'Was I unclear in my directions?'

'No, my lady, not at all. I was just wondering if there was anything else I could do for you since I'll be out. Bring you some breakfast, perhaps?'

Octavian might be a bit of a suck-up, but sometimes more was more. 'No, I'm fine. I have my comar.' She hopped off the table and tucked the sheet more firmly around her. 'Get him to the plane as quickly as you can, then hurry back. I have ... plans.'

'Very good, my lady.' He bowed and scurried out to fulfill her orders.

Octavian was everything she'd ever wanted in a companion. Smart, passably handsome, biddable, willing – nay, eager – to do whatever she asked, regardless of how menial or gruesome a task. There was only one quality he lacked. She smiled and ran her tongue across her fangs. As soon as Nasir returned from Corvinestri and she no longer needed him, Tatiana would remedy Octavian's problem and finally give him the one thing he craved more than life itself.

Death. Eternal and unyielding. And along with it, all the power that accompanied the Tepes family name.

Dominic had gone down faster and with less fight than Doc had expected. Or maybe he'd misjudged the amount of colloidal silver and laudanum to use. Fi studied Dominic's prone form like she'd never seen a vampire that close before. 'Watch out, baby. Never know with vamps.' Doc cringed. Of course Fi knew that. That's how she'd ended up a ghost in the first place.

'Did you kill him?' Fi hovered over Dominic's body, the worst of her loop behind her.

'No.' At least he hoped not. But wouldn't Dominic have gone to ash if Doc had killed him? Doc poked at Dominic with his toe. The man was definitely out. Whether from the colloidal silver or the laudanum, Doc wasn't sure, but the combination had done the job. Even if he had burned his fingers on a few stray drops of the silver.

Fi wavered, biting her lip. 'What did you do to him, then?'

'Knocked him out.' Like a chump.

'Why?'

Just like always, Fi was full of questions. 'To get his blood, sweets. Need that to fix you.'

She smiled. 'I can't wait to be fixed.' A second later, she clapped her hands over her mouth. When she took them away, she was frowning. 'He's going to be mad.'

'That's a sure thing.' Doc hefted Dominic's limp body into his arms and swung the vampire over his shoulder. Better to leave him in one of the small sun-proofed cabins than down here in the grungy, rat-infested hold. Dominic would be furious at what Doc had done, but maybe a little consideration would keep Dominic from killing Doc the first chance he got. Or not. Whatever. It was worth a shot.

Fi quivered. 'Not just mad. He might try to kill you.'

'Not if I can help it.' He gave her a quick, reassuring smile. 'Don't you worry about that. Now, I gotta go. Probably won't be back for a little bit.' He tipped his head against the vampire pitched over his shoulder.

She nodded. 'Not until he leaves. I understand.'

'Good girl. I don't want you to worry. I might be gone, but you know it's because I'm working on making things right for you, okay?'

'I know. Okay. Be careful.'

You too, he wanted to say, but what was the point? No matter how careful she was, she was still going to die every night until he got her free. So instead, he said a quick good-bye and left the light of his life alone in the dark with her demons.

After dumping Dominic in a cabin, Doc hustled out to the Glades. At this hour, Slim Jim, the good ole boy Doc rented air-boats from, was in bed. Most humans were. His shop was dark, locked up tight. Mindful of Slim Jim's itchy trigger finger and bias against trespassers, Doc carefully slid some bills though the mail slot and unplugged one of the boats from its charger. In minutes he was skimming across the shallow water, headed for Aliza's.

He shifted to his half-form, using his leopard-enhanced night vision to navigate and his heightened senses to keep tabs on the strange world unfolding around him.

From the narrow banks and grass thickets, animal eyes reflected the boat's running lights. A large splash greeted him as he rounded an island of cypress thick with Spanish moss. Once, he caught sight of a snake slithering through the water. Damn thing must have been as thick around as his thigh. Reminded him why he hated the Glades. After dark, the place was a nightmare, rife with things that would gobble down a house cat like it was a snack.

No wonder people dumped bodies out here.

A large winged shape passed through the moon's light, casting Doc in shadow for a moment. He glanced up, but the thing was gone. Too big to be a bird. What else lived out here, he didn't really want to know.

Aliza's house rose off the horizon at last. Doc slowed as he approached, happy the lights were on. Waking the old witch would only add to an already crappy evening. And, in a second stroke of luck, Chewie's spot on the dock was empty.

Doc idled the engine and went fully human. Classic rock and laughter spilled from the house. 'Aliza!' he yelled to be heard over the ruckus. He was about to yell again when the screen door opened onto the wraparound porch.

'Well, look what the cat dragged in.' Aliza saluted him with a bottle of vodka and laughed like she'd said something original. A few of her coven members drifted out behind her. Most of them looked as sloshed as she was.

'I'm here to talk about what we discussed.' He recognized one or two of the women standing behind her but none of the men. He wasn't about to air personal business in front of strangers. Especially when it was the kind of business that could be used against him.

'What we discussed?' She took a swig from the bottle. 'Your little undead dead friend?' Her audience laughed.

'Yes.' Once again, a trip to Aliza's was not turning out the way he wanted it to. Surprise.

She leaned on the railing, dangling the bottle over the water. 'I already told you what I need to make that happen.' She glanced back at her friends, then at him again. 'Begging ain't gonna help you.' She snickered. 'Purring might.' Her friends broke out in laughter and she joined them, snorting at her own hilarity.

'I'm not here to beg. I have what you want.' He had both items she'd asked for, including the Medusa.

She spoke to her friends but loud enough for him to hear. 'If I had a fiver for every man who told me that . . . ' More laughter, but she suddenly turned to look at him with more sobriety than she'd showed since she stepped out onto the porch. 'You have the blood?'

The word turned the assembled crowd's laughter into murmurs and whispers.

'Yes.'

'Show me.'

Again, not how he wanted this to go down, but what he'd done wasn't going to stay secret once Dominic woke up anyway. He reached into the interior pocket of his jacket, pulled out the vial, and held it up. Aliza handed off the vodka and adjusted one of the security floodlights anchored to the railing to shine on him directly. The blood glowed like expensive wine. Deathly quiet spread over the crowd.

Aliza, suddenly all business, gestured toward the dock. 'Get up here.'

He moored the airboat, jumped off, and climbed the stairs to the door. Aliza had it open and waiting. The smell of booze, pot, and magic assaulted him as he walked in. Beer bottles and cups littered the flat surfaces. Someone had strung fairy lights around Evie's statue, and a mostly eaten sheet cake sat on the counter next to the sink. Black sugar roses trimmed what was left of it. 'Am I interrupting something?'

Aliza shut the door behind him, her face somber. 'Today is Evie's birthday.'

He handed her the vial and a small packet of Medusa. 'Well, this should mean she'll be here in person next year.'

'Yes.' Aliza nodded, oddly quiet. 'Stay here. I'll be right back.'

As she left, her coven filtered through the kitchen getting drinks, cake, whatever excuse they could to check him out, all the while eyeing him like he might snap them up like field mice. Or turn into a unicorn. Varcolai and witches didn't exactly run in the same circles, but they weren't unknown to each other either. Or maybe they'd just never seen one who'd gotten blood out of a vampire and lived to tell the tale.

A few of them nodded in greeting. He just stared back from where he leaned against the wall. He wasn't here to make friends.

Aliza returned, her face cranked into a scowl. She waggled the vial of blood at him. 'This is no good.' The few coven members left in the kitchen quickly disappeared.

He straightened. 'Like hell it is. I took it out of Dominic myself.'

'Oh, it's that scum sucker's blood all right, but it's tainted. Laced with laudanum and silver.'

Frustration burned in his gut. 'How the hell did you think I was going to get the blood out of him? I tried asking. Trust me. Didn't work.'

'You screwed up, shifter.'

'No, you screwed up.' He jabbed his finger at her. 'You said get Dominic's blood. You never said anything about what it could or couldn't have in it. Now, you find a way to clean it and make it work.'

'Are you threatening me?' She squinted at him, but her gray eyes were too bloodshot to intimidate.

'I'm telling you to live up to your end of the bargain.' If she took that as a threat, she was smarter than he gave her credit for, because if she didn't fix Fi, he would find a way to make Aliza and her whole coven pay.

She glared at him for a moment, then studied the fluid in the vial, swishing it around. 'I can try to clean it, but chances of that working are almost nil. Either way, the blood stays with me.'

'Fine. Keep it. Just figure out a different way if you can't clean it.'

'There is no different way.' Aliza's eyes took on a watery sheen. 'You can't just release the kind of magic Evie's under without wiping it out. It has to be destroyed.'

A thought struck him. 'If you don't, what happens?'

She shook her head, looking drunk and confused once again. 'What happens to what?'

'To the magic. If you don't destroy it, what happens?'

'It would find Evie and turn her into stone again.'

'Just Evie?' He raised a brow, wondering if his idea had any merit. 'Or could the magic be redirected?'

She slumped into a kitchen chair, turning the vial in her hands. 'Sure, but who are you going to get to volunteer to be turned into stone?'

Doc laughed with new hope. 'Who said anything about a volunteer?'

Chapter Twenty-two

'Too bad you can't go in.' Creek nodded toward the house from his side of the gate into Chrysabelle's estate.

Mal snorted. 'She said neither of us could come in. Human hearing must suck more than I remember.'

'I heard her just fine. I meant you're incapable of going in. Couldn't if you tried.' He shrugged, enjoying the night air. It was good to be outside, although he'd prefer to be at Chrysabelle's side. 'Not unless she invites you, which obviously she hasn't. Now, I, on the other hand, could walk right through that front door—'

'What makes you think she hasn't invited me?'

'Has she?'

Chrysabelle was so much the vampire's weakness. Who could blame him? She was beautiful. A comarré and a vampire. Kind of like a mouse falling for a cat. A mouse Creek had a vested interest in.

Mal glowered in response.

'That's a no, then. You scared that wysper she keeps on staff will start singing?' He wasn't sure what Chrysabelle saw in Mal, but he knew too well how good women could fall for bad men. Especially when they'd been brainwashed into thinking it was the right thing to do. The KM could offer her sanctuary if she needed it.

'Velimai doesn't scare me. And Chrysabelle's mother never gave vampires invitation into the house. Chrysabelle has chosen to keep that rule. It's a good one, considering.'

'Considering what?' Creek laughed. 'That you might sneak in and drink her to death?'

Mal's eyes went silver, his voice husky. 'I would never hurt her. She knows that.' He looked away. 'I'm not the one she needs to worry about.'

The vampire seemed sincere. Creek guessed that was possible. 'You mean Tatiana, the woman you were talking about before.'

'Yes. She's after something Chrysabelle has. And she's more than just a woman.'

'She's after the ring.' The focus of his mission. 'I know who Tatiana is. Elder of the Tepes family. Nasty female vamp. Rumored to be Lord Ivan's favorite bed toy.'

If the vampire was surprised by Creek's knowledge, he hid it. 'I mentioned the ring the night we battled the Nothos. All that proves is you're a good listener. And yes, that's the Tatiana we were referring to. Is that all you know about her?'

'I knew about the ring before that night.' Creek checked his mental files. 'As far as Tatiana, there isn't a lot more to tell. She came out of nowhere, appearing on the scene right after she went through navitas. We also know that Lord Ivan is the noble who resired her, but he's not her original sire. She's borderline insane, too, most likely because of the navitas.'

'Borderline? Try over the line. But I'm pretty sure it started before the navitas.'

'How do you know? You weren't ever truly part of the nobility, as far as KM records show.' Truth was, Creek knew nothing about Mal except what Chrysabelle had told him.

'You got that right.' Mal stared toward the house. 'But I know plenty about Tatiana. I know her intimately. She was my human wife. I'm the one who sired her.'

Creek turned to stare at him. 'She was your wife?' He shook his head. 'Dude. I feel for you.' Some choice in women. 'That locket she wears, the one with the portrait of a little girl inside. That little girl mean anything to you?'

Mal's face froze, but sorrow laced his gaze. 'Yes.' He turned his body away from Creek. 'Our daughter, Sofia.'

'What happened, if you don't mind me asking?'

'I thought the KM knew everything.' The vampire crossed his arms, his gaze still fixed on the house. Probably listening to Chrysabelle's heartbeat.

'The KM might. I only know what I've been told.'

'Tatiana was the linchpin in my being cursed. She's also responsible for imprisoning me in the dungeon of a ruined castle for fifty years.'

'Fifty? Damn. I was only in for seven.' He couldn't imagine doing a stint that long. He leaned against the gate, feeling luckier than he had when he'd woken up. 'Time like that changes you.'

'Tatiana meant for me to wither into dust in that dungeon. Lord Ivan was there that night. He helped her. So was another vampire, but he's already been taken care of.'

'Good to know.' He'd had no idea Tatiana had such a history, but she was definitely capable of everything Mal had said.

Mal stepped away from the wall and moved a few paces toward the house. 'Do you know the extent of my curse?'

'Just that you are cursed. That's all Chrysabelle told me.'

Mal nodded. 'I'm sure she'll fill you in over time, but I'll save her the trouble. I can't drink from the vein without killing my victim. The voice of every soul I take inhabits my head.' He yanked his sleeve up. Black script covered his skin. 'I wear their names on my skin.' He pulled his sleeve back down. 'I've drunk from the vein once since Tatiana's curse. That soul manifested as a ghost who haunts me to this day.' His gaze dropped to the ground for a moment. 'She did anyway. She's gone now. Killed because of Tatiana.' He shook his head. 'Long story.'

'Why are you telling me all this?' Not that Creek wanted him to stop. Tatiana was his enemy, and it was good to know more about her and what she was capable of, but Mal's sharing so easily was unexpected.

Mal pointed toward the house. 'Because Chrysabelle wants us to get along. I know you're here to kill me. Up until a few weeks ago, I would have painted a target on my chest and opened my arms to your bolt. I'm not that creature anymore. Because of her. My life, such as it is, has purpose now. To protect her.'

'I'm not here to kill you, unless you present a threat to her. And protecting her is part of my job as well.'

'Then we meet on common ground.'

'Even where Tatiana is concerned.' Creek stuck his hand out. 'Truce.'

Mal stared at his hand. 'Why should I trust you?'

'You shouldn't – not any more than I trust you – but we have the same purpose.' He tipped his head toward the house. 'And the same enemies.'

Mal stilled for a moment like he was thinking, then shook Creek's hand. 'Agreed.'

They went back to leaning on their respective sides of the

gate, passing the time without a word until Mal spoke. 'What were the seven years for?'

'Killed my father.'

A few seconds ticked by. 'Any particular reason?'

'He was choking my sister to death.'

Mal gave him a sideways glance. 'She okay?'

'She is now.'

Mal nodded. 'Tatiana hates me because I didn't save Sofia's life by turning her into a vampire.' He shoved his hands into his pockets. 'Like I would damn my daughter's soul.'

'Hard decision.' Creek wasn't sure what else to say to that, so he chose nothing. Mal didn't need platitudes. The silence stretched out between them until a pale figure appeared in the upstairs windows.

'Speaking of decisions ...' Mal pushed off the wall. 'I just made one.'

Chrysabelle knew she should be in bed, resting, but instead she stood at the French doors that led from the master suite to the large balcony overlooking the front of the estate. With the lights off and if she stood angled just so, her night vision was still sharp enough to pick out the two dark figures standing on either side of the property's gate.

If she walked outside, she could see them even better. But she wasn't going to do that because she didn't want to hear them arguing and threatening to kill each other again. How could two intelligent men be so stupid?

They *had* to find a way to share this world, because she didn't want either of them hurt. They were both good men at heart. Just very different. And equally interesting.

Creek because of his humanity and because she believed he

was a warrior on the side of right. The kind of man she *should* align herself with. She wanted to know him better.

With Mal it was different. They'd been through so much together, and where Creek was a connection to her mortal side, Mal connected her to the side that definitely wasn't. She also believed she served as a link for Mal to his long-forgotten humanity. Mal had fought for her. She wanted to fight for him, too. Even if they weren't currently seeing eye to eye.

And lastly, both men were powerful reminders of the light and dark that lived within her. She had moments when one side definitely pulled her more strongly than the other. Losing touch with one might push her over a line she could never uncross.

She feared that like she feared losing her comarré identity. No matter how much she wanted to leave it behind and become a modern woman the way her mother had, there was comfort in the routines and traditions. It was all she'd known, and for all those years, comarré life had provided her with guidelines and boundaries. Breaking away meant making decisions based on feelings, not rules. Feelings she'd been trained to subvert.

Making those kinds of decisions also meant accepting the consequences when things went wrong.

Things like what might happen with Mal if she gave him a chance at her heart. Or if she chose to get to know Creek better. Both of which appealed to her.

There were more reasons that that, she knew, but *those* reasons, those feelings . . . she had no room for them. No desire to stir them up and acknowledge that her emotions concerning these two men were untried and unfamiliar and wholly frightening.

Both of them had cared for her when she'd been injured. Both of them had joined her in battle and fought beside her. Protected her. And both of them had kissed her.

She bent her head and rested it on the glass. Her breath fogged the pane as she exhaled.

For a woman who had known only order, chastity, and servitude for the last one hundred fifteen years, having these two men in her life was a great deal to take in.

Almost too much.

She sighed, raised her head, and startled. A dark, familiar form leaned against the balcony railing. Her robe lay discarded across the bed, but she opened the door anyway, bracing herself for more complaints about Creek.

Mal's jaw tensed as his gaze traveled from the thin straps of her white silk nightgown to the tips of her clear polished toes.

'Can I help you?' She crossed her arms, hiding her breasts as his gaze returned to her face.

'I see the resting is going well.' Mal punctuated his question with a half smile. 'Tired of being in bed or haven't you been there yet?'

She gave him a little smile in return. This was the Mal she liked most. 'I rested on the couch, but Velimai has taken to mothering me. I couldn't stand it anymore, so I came up here. If she knew I wasn't in bed . . . '

'She's right. Bed is *exactly* where you need to be.' The silver in his eyes added layers of meaning to his words.

She laughed to cover the surge of heat that must be coloring her skin and tried to make light of what he'd said. 'Did I just hear you side with the wysper? Suddenly up is down and black is white.'

He shook his head, grinning. His teeth gleamed feral and hungry. She swallowed and her hand strayed to her throat. 'Go ahead, make fun. I can take it. I have broad shoulders.'

Yes, he did. Among other things. Holy mother, that smile might be her undoing. Just the sight of his fangs revved her heart. Which he undoubtedly heard. 'Why can't we be this way with each other all the time?'

He went still. The smile vanished and his eyes focused on the balcony's tile flooring. 'You realize you're asking that of someone who hasn't had substantial human contact in over fifty years. Before that, well, we both know how my contact with humans ended up. I've never been a people person. Even when I was human.'

She sensed they were approaching rare ground. She had to tread carefully or the conversation would be over before it started. 'Is it that hard? To connect with people?'

'It is when your idea of connecting means sucking the life out of them. I'm never going to be normal. Even by vampire standards. Whatever that means.' He pushed off the balcony and walked toward her. 'I just came to check on you before I leave. I had an idea.' He shoved his hand through his hair and turned away, inches from the invisible barrier her lack of invitation put between them. 'On second thought, never mind. I should go.'

Dawn was an hour away. He had time. 'Tell me the idea.'

He stayed facing away long enough that she assumed he wasn't going to share. At last he turned back. 'I know you're hurting. Nothos poison isn't something to mess around with. If you gave me some of your blood and I kissed you, it would give you a little extra healing power. It would help.'

A delicious shiver went through her. She refused to acknowledge what that meant, because she certainly couldn't deny how it made her feel. Nor could she deny how much she wanted what he was proposing. She struggled to keep those emotions off her face. 'Yes, it would.'

'Just a little blood,' he qualified. 'I know you don't have much to spare after what you must have lost from the injury.'

She gave him a little smirk. 'I'm comarré. Blood production isn't something I have trouble with. I'll be right back.'

Leaving the door open, she slipped into the bedroom, put on her robe, then went through to the sitting room and took a glass from the morning kitchen. When she returned, Mal was back against the rail.

She walked out into the night air and eased onto the all-weather couch, mindful of her injury. The balmy air almost made her thin robe too warm, but somehow two layers of silk seemed better than one between her and the vampire who switched gravity off every time he touched her. She put the glass on the coffee table and held her wrist over the goblet's mouth. Mal turned away and planted his hands on the carved marble railing.

'I don't mind,' she said softly. She almost wanted him to watch.

'I do.'

She nodded, knowing he couldn't see her. She flicked the blade out of her ring and pierced her vein. The pain was brief. As the first trickle of blood filled the glass, Mal groaned. The scent must be overwhelming. Or maybe it was the knowledge that he was about to partake of her blood.

At the sound of stone cracking, he yanked his hands off the railing and crossed his arms over his chest. It would be a lie to say her power over him didn't hold a certain appeal, but that seemed such a base emotion, she didn't want to own it.

Glass filled, she pressed her thumb to the small wound and held her wrist up. 'I'm done.'

Mal flashed to her side a second later, eyes silver, face fully vampire, fangs extended. There was no cajoling to get him to drink, no arguing on his part. Without delay, he lifted the glass and drained it, then set it down and settled back against the cushions as the blood visibly worked its power through him.

His eyes closed, but his mouth hung open like he was panting. Soon, he was, his chest rising and falling as his lungs expanded. His muscles tightened, and he shuddered, jaw clenched with what looked like pain. A few moments later, he relaxed and his hand strayed to his chest. He pressed his fingers there and opened his eyes. 'Never fails to amaze me.' He sat up, took her hand, and placed it over his now-beating heart.

His body was warm beneath her palm, another effect of her blood. She ached to feel his skin against hers, but the act of touching his black-inked body still shocked her. Wicked, wicked comarré. 'It must really be something to feel when you're not used to it.'

'It is.' Still holding her palm to his chest, he moved closer until their thighs touched. Heat penetrated the layers of silk. Such closeness was dangerous. Like him. The heat seeped into other parts of her body, and his scent surrounded her in a haze of spice and earth and possibility. 'Now your turn.'

She twisted toward him and winced. She pulled her hand out of his and pressed it to her stomach. 'Moved too fast.'

'That won't do.' He slid his arms beneath her legs and around her back and just like that she was on his lap. His hands dropped to the small of her back and her knee, but his touch reverberated through her entire body.

The contact made her foolish and eager. And vulnerable. By now she should be used to feeling that way around Mal, but this was something more than just the defenselessness born of his being a vampire. It came from his being a man.

They were at eye level. And for some reason, he was still smiling.

'Better?'

Oh, *better* was one word to describe it, but there were a few others she could come up with in her vampire-addled brain. Breathless. Electrifying. Frightening. 'Yes, that's fine.' *Fine.* Because why not use a word that in no way scratched the surface of her emotion? She was as stunted as Mal when it came to relationships. Although the patron–comarré relationship was something she'd had plenty of experience with, this was nothing like that. Nothing. At. All.

'Good.' He lifted his hands to cup her face as his own shifted back to human, his fangs neatly out of the way. His thumbs smoothed her cheekbones. 'Beautiful,' he whispered. His eyes glittered as if something inside longed to be free, but he said nothing, just brought his mouth to hers.

She closed her eyes, shut out the weight of her past telling her not to enjoy it, and did exactly that. She reveled in the pressure and softness of his mouth. The tenderness with which he caressed her face. One of his hands went to the nape of her neck, gently massaging, then his fingers threaded into her hair. She shivered with the overload of sensation.

No wonder Maris had given up everything for Dominic. At that moment, Chrysabelle understood her mother. She sighed with contented pleasure, allowing herself to feel the bliss in the joining, and wondered what his bite would feel like. The question aroused an ache in her that nearly made her cry out.

She forced the thought away and concentrated on the kiss, because that was all they would ever share. A kiss. Just like the last one she'd had. Except that kiss hadn't been with Mal. It had been with Creek.

Suddenly, guilt stung her, the memory of another man's mouth on hers as sharp and hot as the signumist's needle. She pulled away, her heart pounding. She hoped Mal thought it was because of the kiss and not because there was something unconfessed between them. He would be furious if he knew. Enough to harm Creek.

'What's wrong?' he asked.

'Why do you ... like me?' The question came out before she could stop it, but she was glad it had. She wanted to know. With Creek now in her life, she needed to know what kept Mal coming back to her. 'Is it just the blood?'

His face darkened. 'No.'

'Then what?'

He stared into her eyes, his lips parting, then closing again like he'd changed his mind about what he was going to say. 'The voices tell me not to. That's reason enough for me.'

She dropped her head, nodding.

'And,' he continued, 'I've never known anyone like you. You're ... good. And yet you still like *me*.'

She lifted her head to look at him again, but he turned away so she couldn't see his eyes.

He wasn't a bad man, no matter what his curse had made him do. She caressed his hand. 'Thank you for the kiss. I'm sure that was enough.'

He turned back to her, eyes blazing silver. 'I'm not.' He retook her mouth like he had a right to it.

Another full minute passed before the guilt ate its way back into her brain. She broke the kiss for good. Tried to breathe. 'Thank you for helping me.'

He laughed softly, his face very close to hers. 'Yes, clearly that was all about helping you.' He tucked a strand of hair behind her ear. 'It's okay to take pleasure from life. There's far too little of it for most. You and I especially. Don't deny what comes your way.'

Denying pleasure was not her problem, but he didn't know that. She sighed.

He raised his brows. 'Or perhaps you found no pleasure in that kiss? If so, you should have been an actress, because it certainly seemed you did.'

'No, it's not that. Kissing you' – the very words heated her skin – 'is definitely pleasurable. At least when you intend it that way, it is.'

He sat back. 'Ah, so I'm to be punished for past transgressions?'

'Just making a comparison is all.' Because she was *not* comparing Mal to Creek. Not in any way.

'Then what is it?'

She'd wanted the kiss. Now she must deal with the emotions it had created. She eased off his lap and onto her feet. Already her senses sharpened and the tightness of her wounds lessened. 'It's my past, the last century of my life, lived in a very different way. It weighs on me. Colors my actions. I am still very much comarré at heart, despite the new circumstances of my life. Those rules are hard to discard.' If that was what she even chose to do. Sometimes those rules made more sense than anything else she knew. Having no man was infinitely simpler than having two. She shook her head and walked around the couch to the door. 'Am I comarré? Am I human? What rules do I live by? I'm not making excuses. Or maybe I am.' She rested her hand on the door frame and turned. He stood on the other side of the couch, staring at her. 'I just need time.'

'And as long as you need me, time is all I have.'

She wasn't sure what he meant by that, but she liked the sound of it. 'Give me a couple of days to recover, then come back and we'll talk about what it's going to take to get to the Aurelian.' She'd tell him everything, including the fact that she had a brother.

He nodded, a smile lighting his eyes. 'Two days. I'll be back.'

'Good night, Mal.'

'Good night, Chrysabelle.' And he was gone, disappearing over the railing in a soundless blur.

She closed the door, confident of only one thing. She wanted Mal *and* Creek in her life. How she would accomplish that without destroying them both remained to be seen.

Chapter Twenty-three

Daysleep. Laudanum. Colloidal silver.

Each blanketed Dominic in a thick, numbing fog. His struggle against them had been short-lived. Giving in was so easy. Too easy. The only choice.

And so he had let go of consciousness and fallen into a bottomless abyss of anesthetic blackness. It was peaceful here, like daysleep, but darker and thicker and adrift with strange dreams.

Now something tugged at him from the other side. It pulled at him. Lifted his limbs. Shook him. Slapped his face.

'Dominic.' The voice came and went in the miasma. It flitted in and out, like a tiny white *farfalle* among the lemon blossoms of his mamma's orchard. Again the voice called him. 'Dominic.'

'Mamma,' he answered, unsure if the word left his throat.

'Dominic, wake up.' That voice didn't belong to his dear sainted mother, may she rest in peace. It belonged to ... someone else. His mother's apron was muslin, bleached by the sun when she hung it to dry. He watched it flap in the breeze. Felt the sun on his face.

'Dominic, please.'

The *farfalle* buzzed at him like a bee. It *was* a bee. He tried to lift a hand to swat the pest away. He couldn't tell if he moved or not. He didn't care. The voice left him alone, and he drifted back toward the childhood memories so distant he could scarce remember them until the laudanum had sharpened their edges.

Fingers pried his mouth open, and soft, cold flesh pressed his lips. Scented like flowers. Blood trickled onto his tongue, spilled down his throat. By instinct, he drank.

The memories began to fade as the laudanum and silver slowly lost their grip. The wrist vanished from his mouth. The voice came back.

'Dominic, please wake up.' Not a butterfly or a bee. A woman. Small hands, feminine but incomplete, held his face.

He knew that voice. The woman's image drifted like smoke through his brain. Katsumi. He tried to open his eyes, but they rolled back in his head. He managed to lift a hand to her forearm. 'Drugged,' he whispered.

'I know,' she answered. 'You reek of laudanum and silver.' Alarm framed her words. 'Who did this to you? The varcolai?'

Dominic stayed still. He would deal with Maddoc on his own terms. 'Help.'

'Of course, my lord.' She scooped her arms around him and brought him to a sitting position.

His head lolled against her shoulder. With his face against her neck, he inhaled her jasmine-scented skin. The sweet aroma of blood danced below the perfume. 'Feed me.'

'Take whatever you need. I fed just before I saw you leave.' She turned in toward him, more willing than he had memory of. 'Forgive me for following you. I know I'm supposed to be confined, but I was concerned.'

If she'd followed him, she'd seen the varcolai. 'Leave the cat to me.' He mumbled the words against her flesh.

'Of course.'

All he cared about was fresh blood to wash the poison from his system. He opened his mouth and bit down. Weakness made his bite unsure.

Katsumi cried out softly but held still. 'Again, my lord,' she told him. 'Take the vein.'

So he did, managing to pierce her properly this time. Blood poured into his mouth. He suckled, feeling his strength return with every swallow.

Katsumi's hands found his cheeks. 'Enough, please. You weaken me.'

He released her, barely able to keep himself upright. Rubber muscles clung to lead bones. Movement was almost impossible. His head cleared quickly, but his body would take time. Days perhaps. He needed to be home. 'Get me out of here.'

She pulled his arm around her neck and slid her own around his waist. With only slight effort, she got him to his feet. He shuffled forward, his weight on her. 'Car?'

'Yes, I have a car. No driver, though. I ... I didn't want to alert anyone to what I was doing.'

He nodded. No driver was good. He didn't want anyone knowing what had happened. Weakness could mean death. With each faltering step, his anger increased toward the varcolai. 'Why did you follow?'

'You left with the varcolai. I know that history. I was worried. I see now I was right to think you were in some kind of trouble.'

'*Si,*' he muttered, wanting to waste no more effort on speaking.

They made it to the car without interruption, although

Dominic had partially expected to see Malkolm. Katsumi helped Dominic into the backseat. He lay down on the leather and, while imagining how he was going to kill Maddoc, passed out.

He woke up in his bed in his suite at the club. The clock showed nearly seven – a.m. or p.m., he didn't know. He remembered Katsumi waking him to drink blood, and by the taste of it, it had been from his comarrés. She slept on the chaise near the fire. Judging by the effort it took to move his body, he was right to think it would take days for him to fully recover. He watched Katsumi for a moment. She seemed different somehow. Softer. A little worn around the edges. When he was well, he would reward her for saving his life.

She could have taken advantage of the situation. Could have killed him. Taken control of Seven for herself. But she hadn't. It wasn't proof of her desire to change, but it was worthy of reward. He would give her navitas. Having a noble vampire who was previously fringe on his side would strengthen his hold on Paradise City immeasurably. Especially if war broke out between varcolai and vampires once again, which it very well could when Dominic killed Maddoc. The varcolai might be on the outs with his pride, but Sinjin wouldn't let such a thing go unanswered. Yes, another noble ally could make all the difference.

Provided Katsumi lived through the resiring.

Crouched in the crown of a palm on the property opposite Chrysabelle's, Doc waited until the Mohawked brother had motored out of Chrysabelle's neighborhood. He didn't recognize the guy, but maybe Dominic had sent him over to keep an eye on Chrysabelle. The guy looked human, but he might be remnant.

Either way, the bike was tight. Someday, when this mess was done with, maybe he'd get a bike like that and take Fi for a ride. Anything was better than thinking about the danger he was about to put a friend in.

He hesitated. He should find somewhere else to go. But where? His pride wasn't an option. Although maybe Sinjin would be willing to take him back once he realized what Doc had done to Dominic. But then maybe Dominic would expect that.

No, he needed a vampire-free zone, and Chrysabelle's was the only place that fit that description. Reluctantly, he dropped out of the tree and jogged across the street.

Doc buzzed the intercom at the pedestrian gate leading into Chrysabelle's estate. He gave the security cam a nod. The gate buzzed. Just like that he was in. One step closer to creating chaos. Resigned, he pushed through and headed for the house. What choice did he have? Fi needed him and Chrysabelle's was the only vampire-safe place he could think of to hole up in.

Chrysabelle stood in the open doorway. Her gaze went to the messenger bag slung over his shoulder. 'Hi. Mal need more blood?'

If only it were that simple. 'No, uh, I was hoping you might let me crash here.' *Say no. You really don't want me here.*

She shrugged. 'Sure. You and Mal aren't fighting, are you?'

Relief and regret twisted his gut into a hard knot. 'No. It's a long story you'd be safer not knowing.' That was the straight truth.

Her brows lifted slightly. 'This have anything to do with Fi?'

'Yes.' *Go ahead, ask more questions. Find a reason to turn me away.*

She moved out of the doorway. 'Come on. There's plenty of space.'

'Thanks. I probably won't be here past Halloween.' Or until Dominic found him. Doc walked into the foyer, admiring the house. If he had to hide out, at least he could do it in style. Yeah, because that justified putting a friend in a bad sitch. 'I don't think I've ever seen your joint in the daylight. Nice. Your mother didn't spare the cash, huh?'

'I guess not.' She shook her head, her eyes filled with a faraway glimmer. 'It's a lot of house for one person and a semisolid wysper.'

'Where is Velimai?'

'She went into the city to run errands, get groceries.' She smiled at him. 'If I'd known you were coming, I would have had her stock up on fish.'

'I won't eat much. I—' His stomach growled before he finished speaking. 'I am a little hungry.'

She laughed and looped her arm through his. 'I think there are leftovers from last night's dinner. Let's get you some. You know, it'll be nice to have some company.'

Sure. Until Dominic showed up and she got caught in the middle of this mess. Maybe he should tell her. She'd want to help Fi, wouldn't she? But he couldn't bring himself to confess. Not yet. 'If I can help out around here, I will.' Not that he was good for much besides making things worse.

She led him into the kitchen and disconnected from him to reach for the fridge. 'There is one thing you could do for me.'

Tell you the truth? 'Sure. Name it.'

She took out a large pan of lasagna. Even cold, the aroma of meat filled the air. 'I could use a sparring partner. I'm tired of training alone.'

'I can do that.' The way things were going, he could use the practice. As soon as Dominic recovered, he would come looking for Doc, ready to settle their score.

And the last time a handicapped shifter had bested a noble vampire was never.

Chapter Twenty-four

'I wondered when you'd get here.' Creek snapped the Harley's kickstand into place and nodded at the tarnished green dragon perched on his loft railing. After watching the exchange between the vampire and the comarré on the balcony, Creek's mood had turned foul. Not even a day's worth of hunting had erased the image of Mal's mouth on Chrysabelle's. Creek had to pull it together fast. The sector chief didn't need to know about that.

Argent blinked the inner membrane over his unnerving green eyes and shifted into his half-form. 'Creek.'

'Sector Chief.' Despite the overwhelming urge to watch the varcolai's every move, Creek walked out of Argent's sight line and into the kitchen. He'd learned the hard way not to show fear in front of the dragon-shifter. He opened the fridge. 'Beer?'

'No.' A soft *thunk* indicated Argent had returned to the first floor. 'I've been waiting for you almost all day. Do you not come home at sunrise?'

'Daylight is the safest time to look for nests.' Or stand guard over the comarré. Creek had stayed long after dawn had chased Mal away. He glanced over. Argent crouched beside the bike and stroked the transmission, one of the few chromed pieces on the custom V-Rod. The engine was blazing hot, but dragons had a weakness for shine and a high tolerance for heat.

'True. How goes it?'

'Not a social visit, then.' Like Creek had thought for half a second that's what this was about. 'It goes fine.'

'You have the ring?'

Creek wrenched the cap off the bottle and took a long swallow. 'It's not going that fine.'

Argent straightened and turned to face Creek. 'The grand masters would like to know how things are proceeding. What should I tell them?'

He leaned against the workbench that served as his kitchen table. 'That I've found the comarré. She was injured fighting some hellhounds, so things are going slow until she heals.'

The section chief nodded. 'Has she mentioned the ring? Does she at least still have it? The grand masters are anxious to recover their property.'

'I'm sure they are. Having such a valuable piece stolen from their archives must really bite the big one.'

Argent tensed. 'Answer the question.'

'She's mentioned it. No idea if she knew her patron Algernon was a KM double agent or not. She doesn't seem the type to have been working a scheme like that with him.'

'Do you think she'll give the ring back willingly, then?'

'Can't answer that. Remind me what the ring does again?' Not that he'd even been told in the first place.

'That information is need-to-know only.'

'And I still don't need to know.' He chugged half the beer.

'No, you do not. Just work your end with the comarré.'

'Like I said, I'm only just getting to know her.'

Argent's forked tongue flicked out. The mythical shifters had a hard time staying fully human. 'She's been here recently. You must be getting to know her well.'

'Not yet, no.' And certainly not as well as the vampire. But Creek was patient.

Argent's narrow pupils latched onto him. 'Then work harder.'

He gave a weak salute. 'Aye, aye, Section Chief.'

'Don't blur the line between protector and friend, Creek.'

He took a pull from his beer and let it cool the temper heating his words. 'Wouldn't dream of it.'

Argent walked back to the V-Rod, strolled around to the other side, and squatted to better see the shiny bits on the engine. 'Tatiana is here.'

'So are her Nothos. That's how the comarré was injured.'

Through spaces in the engine, Creek watched Argent trail his fingers over the chrome parts. 'You must work harder. Samhain approaches. With their parties and their costumes, humans will unwittingly call up a myriad of creatures that will have to be dealt with. Having that power-hungry vampiress running loose will not help the situation.'

'I understand.'

Argent stood. 'Good. Because I would hate for your sister to lose her scholarship.'

'So would I.' Just like he'd hate to serve the rest of his sentence for a brand-new murder. He ground his teeth together to keep from saying something he'd regret.

'Very well.' Argent slid the cargo door open. The sun hung low in the afternoon sky. 'I'll be in touch.'

'I'm sure you will.' Creek nodded his good-bye, glad to get the shifter out of his space so he could crash for a few and be rested for tonight's hunt. He'd have to stay away from Chrysabelle's for a few days, no matter how much he wanted to see her. Long enough for Argent to get bored and move on.

With a shiver, Argent switched to his dragon form, spread his massive wings, and disappeared into the sky.

Dominic stared through Katsumi's helioglazed windows at the dying sun. The time was nearly at hand. He turned to face her. She lay prone on her bed. They'd decided her own apartment was the best place to perform the navitas, lest anything should go wrong. 'This is your last chance to leave things as they are.'

'No.' She shook her head and reached for Dominic's hand. 'I want this change. I accept that permanent death is a possibility and madness a risk. I am willing.'

He nodded, coming to her side and taking her hand. 'Your instinct will be to fight me, especially as death enters your body. You must give in. Die completely. Or there will be no rebirth.'

'I understand.' She was pale, her face devoid of its usual makeup. Instead of one of her high-necked gowns, she wore a simple robe that bared her throat. The finely drawn petals of a chrysanthemum peeked out from among her myriad of tattoos. She trembled.

'Don't be afraid, *cara mia*. I'm here with you.' He offered her a smile and squeezed her hand.

Her eyes went liquid as she squeezed them shut and tipped her head back to expose her neck. 'Please. Now.'

'Patience. I cannot begin until the sun sets.' He watched the ball of killing light sink. At last, it touched the horizon. Without another word, Dominic shifted his face and plunged his fangs into her neck. She jerked, but made no sound as she held her arms at her sides. He drank, sampling each swallow for the bitter dregs of death. She cried out as her fringe life drew to a close, bowing against the bed, struggling with the nearness of the end. At last the taste of dust and carbon and burned sugar crossed Dominic's tongue. He pulled away.

Katsumi lay gray and limp. Working quickly before she went to ash, he scored his wrist and forced it against her mouth, flexing his fist to pump the blood. 'With this blood, I make you flesh of my flesh.'

But she didn't move.

'Drink,' he urged her. 'Drink.'

Still nothing. Why had he done this? Why had he agreed to this foolishness? The gash on his wrist closed. He tore it open again and put it to her mouth. '*Dai*,' he begged. 'Live.'

He opened her mouth farther with his fingers, making sure the blood was getting down her throat. Her skin was cold and powdery to the touch. He cursed himself. He had lost Maris, now he was going to lose Katsumi as well.

The sun slipped lower, the last of its orange light bronzing her lifeless form. He opened the vein on his wrist a third time and tried to feed her again. If he couldn't revive her before the sun set completely . . .

The apartment door burst open and Ronan barreled through. He looked from Katsumi to Dominic. His hand strayed to the knife secured to his belt. 'What happened? What have you done to her?'

'Nothing.' How *stupido* to think he could perform navitas. He'd never seen it done, only understood it from the texts he'd studied ages ago. Before he'd offered to turn Maris. Why had he been such a fool? He pulled Katsumi into his arms and held her, petting her hair to assuage the distress of what he'd done. Any second now she would disintegrate in his arms. Gone forever.

Instead, she coughed. A hard shudder wrenched her body as she coughed again. Her eyes opened. They were as bright silver as a new lira. She cried out as her face shifted, her hands coming up to clutch her cheeks.

Ronan, mouth slightly open, stepped back, shaking his head. 'Fringe can't do that. What did you do to her?'

Katsumi cleared her throat and ran her tongue across her new, longer fangs. She laughed, her eyes sparkling, then kissed Dominic on the mouth. 'Navitas,' she whispered to Ronan, kissing Dominic again. 'I am no longer fringe.'

The smile on Dominic's face caused his cheeks to ache. 'No, *cara mia*, you are nobility now. House of St. Germain.' He kissed her back. 'How do you feel?'

'Like I could devour a small nation.'

He rose from the bed. 'Get dressed and we'll go to the club and you can have your fill of any comar you wish.'

'Wonderful.' She slid off the bed on the other side and dashed into her closet. A second later she stuck her head out, yelled, 'Welcome back, Ronan,' and then ducked back inside.

The fringe lamely raised his hand, then let it drop to his side. He palmed the crown of his head. 'I didn't even know that was possible.'

Dominic crossed his arms. 'Don't ask. I have no intention of ever doing that again.'

Ronan snorted and lost his blank expression. 'Don't worry, I won't. Nobility is the last thing I want.'

'Is that so?'

'Yeah.' He jerked his thumb at his chest. 'I'm the bloody new king of the fringe.'

Ronan was too brash to lead anything more than a parade. Dominic didn't like the idea of him in charge of a good portion of his workforce and customer base. He cocked one eyebrow. 'I wasn't aware the fringe had a king.'

Ronan grinned. 'They do now.'

Chapter Twenty-five

Tatiana paced anxiously. Patience was not one of her virtues. Two days was enough time to get to Corvinestri, gather more Nothos, and return. She wanted Nasir back so she could send her new Nothos out, then begin Octavian's transformation. Her plan was perfection. She'd already set the stage, had all her props in place. The thought of what Octavian might become, of how much better he would be, how endlessly loyal ... She laughed at her own cunning.

But until that happened, she needed the shifter girl alive. Not that Tatiana had any desire to take the guise of Mia upon herself again. Rot it all, but if that were her life, she'd have walked into the sun ages ago. Bartender. How humiliating.

Outside, a car door slammed. Then another. At last.

She hurried to the great room and stopped at the sight of the vampire standing there. She bowed to allow herself a moment to cleanse the rage from her expression. This was *not* part of her plan. 'Lord Ivan, I did not expect you.'

'Didn't you?' A faint bruising marked his left eye and cheek. Only a blow from one of the Castus could mark a vampire of Ivan's age. 'How long was I supposed to wait for you to make things right? The ancient ones are not pleased and neither am I.'

Nasir strolled in behind Ivan. Octavian followed next, his arms laden with bags. He shot her an apologetic look. As if there were something he could have done to keep Lord Ivan from coming. Denying that blighty ratbag could mean death for a kine like Octavian. But that would all change very soon.

She nodded, but inside, acid boiled in her belly. 'I am on the verge of setting things right. I just needed a few more Nothos.'

He stalked closer. 'How exactly did you go through a dozen of them?'

'I'm not sure. They just never returned.'

He rolled his eyes. 'This kind of incompetence is unbecoming, Tatiana.'

'Incompetence?' Some of the acid erupted. 'Should I have babysat them? Held their ugly little hands until they got the job done right? We use Nothos because they normally accomplish the tasks they are sent to do without supervision.'

'You forget your place.' His hand seized her throat and tightened, crushing her larynx. 'Speak to me that way again and I will cut off your other hand.'

Octavian's eyes bulged. Nasir had the bloody gall to look pleased.

'Yes, my lord.' She dropped her gaze, realizing too late that Nasir had been Ivan's puppet from the beginning, meant to keep tabs on her. How had she not seen that sooner? That weasel would get his. 'Forgive me. I am as upset at my failure as you are.'

He released her, brushing his palms against each other as though he'd dirtied himself. 'What plan do you have to remedy this?'

To kill every last one that opposed her. 'I have a scrap of the anathema's clothing. I will give it to the Nothos and release them. Malkolm will either lead them to the girl, or his capture will draw the girl to us. Either way, success is at hand.'

Lord Ivan nodded, stroked his chin. 'Very good. Carry on.' He snapped his fingers at Octavian. 'Put my bags in the best room, then give my driver directions into town.'

With scowling eyes, Octavian clicked his heels together and headed upstairs. She hated Lord Ivan's treatment of her pet. Octavian was hers to command.

Lord Ivan turned back to Tatiana. 'I shall be taking your car and going into the city. They say Americans are the other white meat.' He laughed wickedly. 'I intend to find out. I'll expect progress when I return.'

'Yes, my lord.' There would be progress, but not the kind he'd expected. Pompous old fool. She happily watched him leave, then gave Nasir the sweetest smile she could manage. No point in tipping him off. 'I'm so glad you're back. I missed you terribly.'

His dark brows lifted. 'You did?'

'Of course.' She swatted him playfully on the arm. 'Let me go deal with the Nothos, then I'll meet you upstairs and show you just how much.'

His face went positively electric. 'I'll be waiting.'

'Preferably on the bed and undressed?'

He laughed. 'That's my girl.' He kissed her and dashed up the stairs, passing Octavian on the way down. Anger contorted her manservant's face. Sweet Hades, she adored that kine far more than was prudent.

She put a finger to her lips and shook her head, indicating he shouldn't say anything out of line. 'Show me where the Nothos are.'

He led her to the guesthouse, where the gruesome beasts were already destroying what their brothers hadn't. A few of them paused to train their yellow eyes on Octavian.

'Food?' the closest one asked, coming closer to the kine. Octavian ducked behind her.

'No,' she snarled. Malformed idiots. 'Pay attention.' She pulled the scrap of fabric from Malkolm's jacket out of her pocket and held it aloft. 'Trace this scent to the vampire it belongs to, then follow him until his path crosses that of the comarré your useless brothers couldn't track down. Bring her back to me alive. Understood? Not half dead. Not partially devoured. Alive.'

Heads nodded in unison. One sneezed, spraying mucus across his brothers. Bloody hell, they were repulsive creatures. 'If you cannot capture the girl without fighting, then don't. I need you alive as well. Come back and get me and I'll take her alive. Any breach of my instructions and I will personally hunt you down and disembowel you.' Filthy beasts.

She tossed the fabric into their gathered midst. They descended upon it like the ravening beasts they were. 'Octavian, open the door and get behind it.'

He nodded, his gaze never leaving the Nothos. As soon as he was protected, she shouted, 'Go!' and pointed out the door.

The Nothos streamed into the night, whining and chuffing, their clawed hands and feet tearing up the flooring and leaving gouges in the cobblestone drive. The last one melted into the dark like a wisp of smoke.

'It's safe now.'

Octavian came out from behind the door. 'I cannot abide those creatures.'

'No one can. But they serve a purpose.' She looked around.

Lamps lay shattered, sofas upended, curtains shredded. They were creatures of destruction, true to their twisted roots.

He sniffed. 'I will do what I can to straighten things, my lady.'

'Don't bother.' She stared at him, studying the man she saw before her. The time was right. Perhaps overdue. 'I have a much more important task for you.'

'My lady?'

She held out her hand to him. 'I need you to die.'

Creek stayed away from Chrysabelle's for almost two and a half days, just to be sure Argent wasn't hovering nearby. No matter what power this ring had, no matter if she chose to give it up or keep it, Creek wanted her safe.

Sunset was still a few hours away, guaranteeing he'd have time alone with her.

Chrysabelle had put his name on her visitor list, something the gate guard confirmed with a quick ID check. At her estate's private entrance, the security cam scanned his face, then the gate opened and let him through. He parked opposite her front door.

As he walked up, the door opened. Chrysabelle wasn't as alone as he'd thought she was. Behind Velimai, an enormous, ebony-skinned man stood in the doorway. Sweat covered his shaved head and his eyes flashed gold. Feline varcolai. This was new. The man stepped in front of the wysper. 'I got this.'

The fae nodded and left.

Creek studied the varcolai. 'Chrysabelle here?'

'Who are you?' The man's gaze swept him from head to toe and back.

'Creek. She knows me. And you?'

'Yeah, she knows me, too. What's your business?' He rolled one muscle-rounded shoulder. His hands were taped like he'd just stepped out of a boxing ring. Judging from his sweaty T-shirt, maybe he had.

'My business is with Chrysabelle.' Creek squared his body and narrowed his eyes. No one intimidated a KM.

'Hey,' a female voice called out. 'You coming back up or are you tired of me whaling on you?' At least he knew Chrysabelle was home now.

The black man looked off to the left. 'Man here says he has business with you. Name's Creek.'

'Be right there.' And a few moments later, a flushed and glowing Chrysabelle appeared. Her white tank top was sheer with perspiration, showing her sports bra beneath it. The gleam of sweat on her skin set her signum on fire. She pushed tendrils of hair off her face with one forearm and wiped her forehead with the other. Her hands were taped just like the varcolai's.

'It's okay, Doc.' She patted his arm. Maybe Doc was some kind of trainer. 'Hit the shower if you want. That's enough for today.'

Doc grunted, gave Creek a look of pure warning, and disappeared into the house.

Creek waited a few seconds longer to be sure he was gone. 'I don't know how you stand all that friendly.'

Chrysabelle smiled. 'Doc's a great guy. He's just been a little on edge lately. What brings you by?'

'I need to talk to you about something. Can I come in?'

'Can't stop you, can I?' She moved to let him in. 'It's not like you're a vampire.'

Not by a long shot. 'I won't come in if you don't want me to.'

She shrugged. 'It's fine.'

He walked into the foyer, waited for her to close the door, then followed her into a large sitting room. White and ivory dominated the decorating. Very comarré. She sat at the edge of a snowy leather sofa. He took a seat across from her. She lifted the hem of her tank top and wiped sweat from the hollow of her throat. The gauze covering her stitches was gone, leaving three pink sutured lines visible on her skin. They seemed to be healing well. And fast.

'I'm sorry,' he said. 'I realize I'm intruding. You'd probably rather be showering.'

She laughed. 'Is that your way of telling me I smell?'

'No. Hell, no. I've always been partial to a healthy sweat on a beautiful woman. It's the ones who never exert themselves you have to worry about. I take it you were training?'

She nodded. 'Have to stay sharp. Doc makes a great sparring partner.'

'So would I.'

She smiled a little. 'I'm sure you would.'

He gave her an out by pointing at her stomach. 'You should probably get those stitches out if you're healing as quickly as you seem to be.'

She flushed, or maybe she'd been that shade of pink already. 'It's not hard, right? Just snip and pull? I can get Velimai to do it.'

'I'm glad you've got her. Wyspers are good to have around.' Very good. Particularly if vampires dropped by unexpectedly. Which gave him a way into the real reason he was here. 'Especially if there's something in the house worth protecting.'

Her brows furrowed. 'What's that supposed to mean?'

There was no point in skating around it. 'I – that is, the Kubai Mata – we know about the ring.'

She pushed back, her jaw tensing. 'Does everyone know about that wretched thing? I suppose you think I should give it to you for safekeeping, right?'

That answered the question of whether she'd be keeping the ring or not. He leaned his elbows on his knees. 'Not me, but back to the Kubai Mata, yes.'

'Back to them? You make it sound like it was theirs to begin with.'

'It was. Your patron, Algernon, was working with the KM as an inside source. Somehow he found out about the ring and stole it from the archives. Flipped on them. The grand masters are not happy.'

'Algernon?' Her hands unclenched. 'I never would have guessed that about him, but our relationship wasn't exactly deep.' She shook her head, taking it all in. 'Do you know what the ring's power is? Why Tatiana wants it so badly?'

'No.' He snorted out a breath. 'I may be KM, but I'm also just a grunt.'

'What does that mean?'

'I'm not high on their trust list.'

She tipped her head and looked at him like she was seeing him with new eyes. 'I trust you.'

He hadn't expected that. 'You don't know me well enough to trust me.' Although he wanted her to. Very much.

'You saved my life. I trust you until you give me reason to do otherwise.'

He bowed his head. 'I hope that doesn't happen.' And he meant it. Someday she'd understand that what he was doing was for her good and the good of mankind. He lifted his chin and looked into her eyes. 'Do you feel that way about Malkolm?'

She narrowed her gaze. 'You mean do I trust him?'

'Do you?'

She hesitated. 'Yes.'

'But?'

Her fingers wound around each other. 'No *but*. I trust him.'

'What about that thing he becomes?'

She dropped her chin slightly. 'No, I don't trust that part of him.'

Creek couldn't blame her. 'Do you think he would ever attack you when he's like that?'

She stood, walked to the back wall of glass doors and looked out. 'He has.'

Anger pushed Creek to his feet. 'When?'

'About a month ago.' She shook her head. 'It's nothing to worry about now.'

He went to her side. 'If he did it once, what makes you think he won't do it again?'

'Mal won't.' The glass reflected her scowl. 'He has better control now.'

Creek had pushed her far enough. A seed of doubt existed in her. That was all he needed to know. He backed off. 'You know him better than I do, I'm sure you're right. Other than the beast part of him, he seems like a . . . decent guy.'

'He is.' She looked at Creek with sudden curiosity. 'Although you're the last person I'd expect to say such a thing.'

'We're trying to be civil. For you.'

'Thank you.'

What other thoughts rolled through her head? He knew what was going on in his own, and it didn't have anything to do with the vampire. This close, not touching her felt impossible.

'I need to ask you a question,' she said. 'And I want you to answer me honestly.'

'Of course.'

She looked at him as though she were trying to see into his soul. 'Have you been killing off fringe vampires?'

'What do you mean killing off?'

'Numerous piles of ash have been found in your neighborhood. All in the same area.'

'Not me.' A comarré caring about fringe? 'But I have killed a few who were putting human life in danger.'

She nodded and looked outside again, the faraway glaze returning to her eyes.

He jerked his chin toward the vast lanai beyond the sliding glass doors. 'That's some pool.' And some luxury yacht parked in the deepwater slip a little farther out.

She tipped her head like she was seeing it for the first time. 'I hardly ever use it.'

'How come?'

Her mouth quirked to one side. 'I'm not a great swimmer.'

Genuinely shocked, he laughed. 'I thought swimming was a comarré prereq.'

'It is, but I never seemed to get the hang of it. I did enough to pass my classes, but that was it.'

He unlocked the latch on the slider. 'Never too late to learn.'

'Yes, I think it— Hey!'

But he had the door open and his shirt off before she'd set one foot after him. 'Last one in's a rotten egg.' He shucked his jeans on the run, almost tripping in the grass, and dove headfirst into the cool blue.

He bobbed to the surface, swam back toward the shallow end, and waited for her. 'Coming in?'

She stayed on the edge, staring at him with disbelieving eyes that were very clearly not focused on his face. 'You don't have a bathing suit on.'

'Boxer briefs are close enough.' He winked and a hot, wicked surge charged through him like a freight train. 'I've already seen you in your underthings, so quit stalling. I won't let you drown.'

'Drowning isn't what I'm worried about.' Her gaze remained downstream.

He planted his feet. 'Plus, you could use a bath.'

'What?' Her head came up and her hands went to her hips. 'I thought you said I didn't smell.'

He shrugged. 'My mother taught me better than that.' He ducked underwater as her tank top sailed at his head, then broke the surface laughing. His laughter died the moment her fingers went to the drawstring of her loose pants.

She untied the string and let them drop.

It was a very good thing the water was on the cool side. He'd seen her tangled in the sheets of his bed, her body broken and bruised, but this ... this was ... very different. She stood at the pool's edge, glazed by the sun's dying light. Her blonde hair, her pale skin, her signum all a thousand shades of gold. He ached at the sight of her. At being so close to such beauty, and in that moment, his insides clenched with a powerful hunger.

He wanted her. Not just because he'd been seven years without a woman, but because of the woman she was. Didn't hurt that Mal wanted her, too, but that was just the alpha male in him. Chrysabelle was the only woman who might ever really understand his purpose as a Kubai Mata.

'You're staring,' she said.

'Yes, I am. Because you're beautiful.' He moved toward her and patted the tiled edge. What he was about to do bordered on inappropriate, and he didn't give a damn. 'Sit. Let me have a look at those stitches.'

She dipped her head, her hair swinging forward as she sat, almost hiding the color rising in her cheeks. She dangled her legs in the water. 'This feels very much like you're trying to seduce me.'

'Maybe I am.' He moved between her knees. 'Can you blame me? I'm a man.' He checked the wounds. The flesh had knit seamlessly back together and was as new and unblemished as the rest of her body. The stitches no longer served a purpose.

'Who hasn't had a woman in a long time,' she added.

That was for damn sure, but he'd had plenty of practice keeping his libido in check. 'These stitches really need to come out.'

She pulled one foot out of the water. 'I'll get some scissors.'

'No need.' Hands on her hips, he pulled her to the very edge and leaned in toward her stomach.

Her fingers tightened on his biceps and she arched away from him. 'What are you doing?'

'Removing the knots. Hold still.' He brought his mouth to her warm skin, found the knot with his tongue, and bit it off. She inhaled, body tensing. He leaned back, pulled the knot out of his mouth and showed it to her. 'See?'

Her eyes had the look of a woman drunk on something she'd never tasted before, but there was conflict there, too. 'We shouldn't do this. *I* shouldn't do this.'

He held on to her. 'Then tell me to stop.'

She swallowed. 'I don't want to, even though I think I should.'

'Because of Mal?'

She didn't reply or try to leave. Enough of an answer for him. He took longer this time, trailing his tongue over her salty-sweet skin. Her nails dug into his flesh and she moaned softly.

'Oh,' she breathed. 'That feels . . .'

'Good?'

'Wrong.' She exhaled. 'We shouldn't be doing this.'

'You said that already.' He kept his hands on her hips. The heat from her skin melted into his palms and traveled through his veins, sparking a fresh blaze within him.

'It goes against everything I was raised to believe.'

A tick of desperation tensed his jaw. 'The covenant is broken and you no longer live under comarré law.' Despite the fact that she clung to many of the old ways. He forced the frustration out of his voice. He understood she was still finding her path. He brushed his thumbs over her ribs before taking his hands off her completely. 'No one owns you. Not anymore.'

'You mean Mal, don't you?' she said softly.

'I just mean you're free to make your own decisions.' The pool lights switched on, surrounding them in a pale blue glow. He wanted to kiss her. Not a halfhearted peck like the last time when he'd been short on courage and long on doubt. A real kiss. The kind that would stay with her well after he'd left her for the evening.

But more than that, he wanted *her* to kiss him. For the intimacy to be her idea. Even now, he could see the temptation playing in her eyes.

She put her hands on the edge of the pool and lowered herself into the water, then planted her hands on his chest. 'You're smoother than I thought you'd be.'

She'd thought about what he would feel like. Knowing that made standing still a test of his control. Not pulling her into his arms was nearly impossible. He shivered with pent-up energy but let her do as she wished. Her fingers mapped the hollow of his throat, the crevices of his collar-bone, the valley of his chest.

'Turn,' she directed him.

He did, feeling the weight of her gaze on him, on the words branded into his skin. He stood for her, letting her look her fill.

After a bit, her fingertips found the raised lines and began to trace them. *'Omnes honorate,'* she whispered.

'Honor all men,' he answered back.

'Do you?'

'The ones who deserve it, yes.'

Her fingers traveled on, sending small electric shocks through his body. *'Fraternitatem diligite.'*

'Love the brotherhood,' he translated, knowing full well she could read the words.

'Have the Kubai Mata been good to you?'

'They've brought me to you.'

She sketched the next phrase. *'Deum timete.'* A smile played in her voice.

'Fear God.'

'What else do you fear?'

More things than he could count. 'Nothing.'

'Regem honorificate.' Her fingers stopped there, making the rest of his body ache for the same attention.

'Honor the king,' he responded.

'Who is your king, Creek?'

He turned to face her. 'Who's yours?'

Her eyes held a rebellious sparkle. 'I have no king. Now answer the question or I'll alert the KM that you don't uphold your vows.'

No longer willing to wait, he pulled her into his arms. 'You glitter like a king's ransom. That should satisfy them.'

He kissed her, the way he'd been longing to. He was not disappointed.

She kissed him back.

Chapter Twenty-six

'I see you're busy.' *And not with you,* the voices taunted Mal. If thoughts could kill, Creek would be headless and missing his genitalia. The pair sloshed apart and Mal noticed the flush of pleasure across Chrysabelle's very exposed upper body. She was not the innocent in this situation as he'd first perceived, but certainly Creek had kissed *her*, not the other way around. *Guilty, guilty, guilty* . . .

Creek looked like a cat fat with cream. Chrysabelle looked like she'd just accidentally drop-kicked a kitten. Mal fought a tempest of emotion, none of it good. The voices laughed at him, told him this was what he deserved. What he should have expected from any woman in his life. Betrayed. Again.

She fiddled with the strap of her sports bra. 'I didn't expect you.'

'You asked me to come.' Had she meant him to see this? *Yes.* Fine. He'd seen it. *Remember it.* He didn't need to be hit with a sledgehammer to get the hint. She liked Creek. *Anyone but you.* He was human, Mal understood that. He couldn't compete with a human. And apparently, his answer to why he liked her hadn't been enough.

'I did, didn't I? I remember that now.' She nodded as she waded toward the steps. 'Let me get a robe.'

'You do that. I'll wait here.' As difficult as it was not to watch her exit the pool, dripping wet in only a sports bra and a pair of small white underwear, Mal found it even harder not to dive in and hold Creek under until he stopped breathing. *Kill him or he'll kill you.* What kind of a truce was this? Had it been some kind of plan to wheedle Chrysabelle away from him?

As soon as the sliding glass door closed behind Chrysabelle, Creek leaped out of the pool and scooped up his clothes. The movement put him toe-to-toe with Mal. He shook his head with a degree of condescension that made Mal's fists throb with inactivity. *Hit. Drain. Kill.* No, for Chrysabelle's sake, he wouldn't kill Creek. However ... Mal hauled back and nailed him across the jaw.

The punch took Creek to the ground. On hands and knees, he shook his head, popping his jaw to one side. 'I take it you're not happy.' He pushed to his feet, clothes in hand.

Mal scraped his gaze down Creek's body, stopping at his groin. 'I hope for your sake the water was just cold.'

Creek tugged on his jeans and leaned in. 'Punching me is a pretty jealous move, don't you think?' He pulled his T-shirt on over his head. 'Interesting, considering you told me you don't love her.'

Mal didn't answer, unable to deny the words. His hands balled into fists again.

'That was a lie, then.' Creek nodded and took a step back but made no signs to retaliate.

'I can't love her. I'm not human.'

'Vampires are incapable of love?'

'Not the kind she needs.'

'How do you know what she needs?'

Mal walked away and sank into one of the chaises. 'I can't be with her during daylight hours.'

'Everyone needs to sleep.'

He frowned, fingers flexing. 'Don't you get that I'm not human? Not anymore.'

'Neither am I. Not exactly.'

'But I'm a monster on the inside.' And the outside, if he dropped his human face.

'Most men are.'

'For someone who was just kissing her, you're trying awfully hard to give her away. What game are you playing?'

'No game. And I'm not trying to give her away. I'm trying to keep her happy.' Creek took the chaise across from him. 'I think we both could.'

'You want to share her.'

'I want to keep her.' He shook his head. 'After my father was out of the picture, my mother changed. It was like she rediscovered being a woman. My sister would write to me about all the different men my mother was dating – good men, but men just the same.'

'You think Chrysabelle's going to sow some wild oats.'

'She's putting her comarré life behind her more each day. Things that have always been forbidden aren't any longer.'

Chrysabelle, out in the world, tasting what it had to offer. The men who would come after her … Mal didn't like the idea of sharing her with Creek, but at least he was a known quantity. There were worse choices. *Like you.*

It didn't hurt that Creek could be available during daylight hours if she needed something, either. He studied the man across from him. 'She deserves better.'

Creek nodded. 'Too bad. She's getting us.'

The glass door slid open. Both men turned as a frowning Chrysabelle strode toward them. She was dressed in a simple white top and pants, her hair tied back. 'You two aren't beating the crap out of each other.'

'Disappointed?' Mal asked. Because he could start.

'Pleasantly surprised. And a little befuddled.' She hugged her arms around her body. 'Mal, I promised you we'd talk. Creek, if you could give us some privacy?'

'Sure.' Then he whispered under his breath to Mal, 'By the way, I've been in the house.' With a parting smile, he went to Chrysabelle's side. 'I won't be far. Yell if you need me.'

'I won't, but thank you.' She walked past Mal, toward the chaises. 'So we're back to this, are we?'

'I have no idea what you mean.' Actually, he had a pretty good idea of what she meant, but he wasn't about to give her that. If she wanted to talk about it, she could spell it out.

'I mean you being angry at me.'

'I'm not angry. I'm here so you can uphold your end of our deal.'

'So seeing Creek and me together like that didn't bother you?'

Like salt in an open wound. But Creek had a point about the possibilities. 'He's not the worst choice you could make.'

Her brows shot up. 'You feel okay?'

Feelings weren't something he wanted to discuss. 'What did you find out from Dominic?'

She hesitated, seeming a little sad. 'You remember how I was able to open the portal into Tatiana's estate?'

'Yes.'

'I may be able to access the Aurelian through the same means, but it also requires a blood ritual.'

The very sound of that made the voices whine with an eagerness that turned his stomach. The beast clawed to be free. 'There has to be another way.'

'There isn't.' She looked at him, eyes distant. 'And I don't want to keep owing you. You deserve your answer.'

'If Creek hears about the blood ritual, he's going to want to know more. And maybe he should. As a precaution,' Mal said. He hated admitting his weakness, but he'd hate hurting her more.

'As a precaution for what—'

'Did I hear my name?' Creek called out as he approached.

'Yes,' Mal answered. Humans didn't hear that well, but KM probably did. Creek might actually be telling the truth about who he was. 'We need to talk.'

Upstairs in the guesthouse in one of the few bedrooms not destroyed by the Nothos, Tatiana gazed down at Octavian's outstretched form. He trembled upon the bed with an ecstasy so palpable it coated her tongue like warm treacle. He seemed on the verge of orgasmic bliss.

That, she imagined, would disappear rather quickly as death took hold of his mortal brain. She would not pamper him through this experience. The vampire that had taken her mortal life had devoured her like food. If Octavian wanted this existence, he must learn its harsh realities.

Her staring seemed to make him twitch. 'Your mortal life ends tonight. You understand that?'

'It will be my greatest joy,' he panted. 'I am ready, my lady. Take me now.'

She laughed. 'You are such a whore, Octavian. I believe that will serve you well in the centuries to come.'

Before he could utter another sycophantic word, she fell on him, thrusting her fangs into his tender neck. His breath ruffled her hair as he cried out in pleasure, but those sounds eroded into strangled gasps the more she drank. There was pain now, she knew that, but worse, he would feel the press of death's shadow upon his soul. The promise of immortality would seem a very distant thing at this moment. She expected him to fight, but he went utterly quiet as the last of his sweet, life-filled blood drained down her throat. She took one last draw to be sure. The mouthful tasted of death.

She spat the bitter draught onto the floor and checked his pulse. Thready and fading. She jagged one fang across the inside of her wrist, then pressed it to his lips.

He came alive so quickly she wondered if she'd taken him down far enough, but there was no mistaking the death she'd tasted in his veins. This was just his eagerness to change on display. He lapped greedily at the blood she offered him.

He drank and drank until a faint buzzing rang in her ears. 'Enough.' She yanked her hand away and counted down. Three ... two ...

With a cry, Octavian convulsed like a bolt of lightning had struck him. His body arced between tense and limp as the invisible currents of life and death surged through him. As with all turnings, death – the permanent kind – occasionally came out the victor. She had no doubts this time. Octavian's will was too strong.

At last, he lay still. The color drained from his skin. Facial lines smoothed. His slightly crooked nose straightened. The fine polish of nobility settled upon him as though he'd been born that beautiful. She studied him. A fine creation. She would train him to be the loyal companion she'd always deserved.

His lids fluttered and he opened his eyes. They'd gone from dull brown to a luscious cognac that matched his now-glossy hair. 'Am I . . . ' His chin quivered as if he couldn't bear to speak the words lest they somehow become untrue.

'Yes, you are. Welcome to the glorious and powerful Tepes Family, Octavian.'

He sat up, blinking his eyes like he'd gotten dizzy. Running his hands over his face, he felt the new angles and edges of his vampire visage. His fingers went to his teeth. He pricked one on a fang and stared at the pearl of blood shimmering on his fingertip. He turned to her. 'I'm hungry.'

She nodded. 'You want to feed, don't you?'

'Yes.' His face darkened with the pleasure of anticipation. 'I want to kill.'

Delight bubbled up inside her and she clutched at her dead heart. 'Oh, my sweet, that is exactly what I'd hoped you'd say.' She took his hand and licked the blood from his finger. 'Because I am the most wonderful sire, I have prepared something for you.' She patted his leg. 'Wait five minutes, then come back to the house. Stay downstairs. When I call you, come up.'

Busy running his tongue over his teeth, he nodded. She left and hurried into the house and upstairs to the bedroom.

Nasir was naked on the bed, just as she'd anticipated. 'What took you so long?'

Bloody prat. 'I had to deal with the Nothos. I told you that.' She shut the door behind her and walked toward him, swaying her hips in a way she knew distracted him.

She trailed her fingers up his leg. 'You've been a naughty boy being away from me for so long, haven't you?'

'Yes, very naughty.' He nodded eagerly.

'Then you should be punished.' And punished he would be, but for an entirely different reason. She unbuttoned her blouse and let it fall to the floor. Nasir reached for her, but she moved away. She wriggled out of her skirt, keeping her expensive French bra and panties on along with her heels. Nasir was suitably distracted. From under the bed, she took the black briefcase she'd planted earlier.

Nasir's eyes widened with pleasure. His body tightened and he tried for her again. She slapped his hand away. 'You are a bad, bad boy. Lie back and do as you're told.'

Biting his lip, he stretched out on the bed. She took out the lengths of rope and teased them across his stomach and groin.

His eyes shuttered at the sensation. 'You're killing me.'

'You have no idea.' But he'd find out soon enough. She tied his arms and legs to the bedposts, planting nips and bites on his skin as she went. She'd miss him in her bed, but Octavian would be a willing student.

He tugged playfully at the rope. 'That's it, nice and tight. You wouldn't want me escaping and ravishing you sooner than your little game allows, now, would you?'

'No, we can't have that.' She almost laughed. The rope might look like simple silk, but its core was woven silver encased in gold to hide any telltale buzz. There was no breaking it. Not for him. 'I think I'd like some wine. Octavian, can you come here, please?' There was no need to shout. Octavian's new hearing would pick up every word.

'How dare you let that kine in here when I'm like this.' Nasir's nostrils flared. He pulled at the rope. 'What is this? Why can't I break this?' He struggled harder.

She stood at the foot of the bed and watched him serenely.

'You've been Ivan's pawn from the beginning. You shouldn't have brought him back here.' She shook her head and strolled around to the side so she could lean in and whisper the words into his ear. 'Your betrayal must be punished.'

'What are you doing?' His eyes were wild now, his body limp.

Octavian came in. He seemed shocked at Nasir's condition, but smiled when he saw Tatiana's outfit. He quickly looked away. 'My lady, I did not expect—'

She clucked her tongue. 'Octavian, we are family now. You must not call me *my lady* anymore.'

Nasir rambled in Arabic. Perhaps he was cursing, for surely he understood his fate now.

She walked to Octavian and took his hand. 'Do you like what you see?'

'You mean ...' His gaze ran the length of her. 'Yes, very much, my – Tatiana.'

'Are you still hungry?'

His eyes never left her. 'Yes. A thousand times yes.'

She cupped his chin and kissed him softly on the mouth. 'Then go and have your supper. Your dessert will be waiting.'

He glanced at Nasir and grimaced. 'But to drink from another noble ...'

'Don't make such a face. And I don't intend for you to just drink from him. You are to drain him dry.'

Nasir howled and struggled harder.

Octavian leveled his gaze at her. 'Besides causing the death of another vampire, which I know is the unforgivable sin, may I be so bold as to ask why you wish me to do this?'

She laughed over Nasir's ranting. 'Your naïveté is charming. I believe, as do many of our kind, that the first meal after one's turning is crucial. In this case, I am hoping that by draining

Nasir, you will obtain some of his powers as well. You'll be sort of a hybrid of Tepes and St. Germain, although you must hide the alchemy powers from the other nobles. We mustn't tip them off to what we've done.'

'Of course not. But what of his death? Lord Ivan will know. There are others in Corvinestri who also know Nasir is here with you.'

'Those at home are fully aware of how dangerous the Southern Union is, full of varcolai and fringe and remnants. Unfortunate things happen in a place like this.' She shivered for effect. 'As for Lord Ivan, you leave him to me. Now, do as you're told.'

He bowed slightly, then fell upon Nasir with a viciousness that warmed her. Nasir's struggles faded quickly. She went to stand beside the bed. 'Be careful now. You mustn't drink his death or you'll cause your own.'

Octavian lifted his head from Nasir's ruined throat. Blood coated his chin. Vamplings were always such messy eaters. 'How do I know?'

'You'll know. The taste changes. Becomes bitter.'

He drank a moment longer, then sat back on his heels and wiped his face with the back of his hand. 'I swear I can feel his power within me.'

'Good.' She gestured toward Nasir. 'Watch out. He should—'

With a sound like sand rushing through an hourglass, Nasir went to dust before them.

'Turn to ash any moment.' She folded the coverlet up and over, packaging Nasir's remains neatly, then set the bundle aside. 'Now then . . .' She smiled at Octavian and climbed up on the bed to kneel across from him. 'Are you ready for your dessert?'

Chapter Twenty-seven

'Assistance is all we ask,' Ronan repeated.

Dominic mulled the request over. He stared into the fire, its electric crackling soothing him. Ensconced comfortably in his suite with Katsumi at his side, a glass of Brunello in his hand, and a bellyful of comarré blood, Dominic could almost forget the chaos his world was in.

Almost.

But there were too many wrongs to be righted, too many irritants to be dealt with for him to relax and go about his life. He sipped his wine before answering Ronan. 'The fringe may have anointed you king, but in my eyes, nothing's changed. They are still an unorganized group of rabble-rousers.'

'Indeed,' Katsumi added with the kind of laziness that came from being well fed. Three comars and she'd almost gone for a fourth. Apparently navitas built a powerful appetite.

Ronan smacked his fist into his palm. 'Fringe make up the bulk of your customers. Until you help us stop these killings, we will boycott Seven. Your income will dry up. Not to mention your employee list.'

Dominic laughed. 'You clearly don't understand the bulk of my business. Seven provides some of it, *si*, but there are many other aspects to what I do. What I provide.'

Ronan sat back, his mouth a thin, tight line. 'We will interrupt your runners. Keep your products from reaching their destinations. And what of your comarré? Who will pay for their blood when the club is empty?'

Dominic leaned forward. 'Where will your subjects get their blood if not from my sources? Will they ravage the human population and risk turning the city against them? Or do the fringe plan on adopting a more vegetarian way of life?'

Katsumi covered her mouth and laughed softly. Dominic gave her an appreciative glance. Whether it was her fresh nobility or her self-induced change, he very much liked the new Katsumi. He squeezed her knee through the purple kimono she wore.

'Vegetarian? Like hell. There are plenty of humans in the city who are willing to be bitten.' Ronan preened. 'It's a good age to be a vampire.'

'You invite trouble going that route. There may be humans who worship our kind, but there are many more who fear us. Fear is a powerful emotion. Powerful enough to unite them against us.'

'Now you understand how the fringe feel. We are being slaughtered.'

'And if I decide to help you? What do I receive in return?'

'What do you want?'

'To locate a noble vampire by the name of Tatiana. She's here from Corvinestri. She's the one who killed Maris.' He paused. 'I have another, more delicate issue that needs dealing with first.'

Ronan's brows lifted. 'If you're asking for secrecy on this

matter, I'm willing to swear a blood oath – in exchange for your oath that you'll help us.'

Dominic tapped a finger on the side of his glass. A broken blood oath meant death. No questions. 'Katsumi can witness.'

'You got a set of plums asking for that. She's on your side now.'

'Ronan, we are all on the same side. You think it's going to make any difference to the humans if we're noble or fringe?'

'She's not witnessing. Not alone.'

'Who else, then? Vertuccio?'

Ronan snorted. 'Like he would be fair. No, I choose Mortalis.'

'You know he's loyal to me.'

'Yes, but I also know he's not one to let a broken oath go unpunished.'

Dominic shrugged. 'Fine. Vertuccio, come in, *per favore.*'

The manservant entered and stood awaiting instruction, hands clasped behind his back. 'My lord?'

'Send Mortalis in.'

'Right away, sir.' Vertuccio nodded and left.

Ronan shook his head. 'Must be nice, being waited on hand and foot.'

'You say that like I don't deserve my wealth or what it's afforded me.'

'Bloody right,' Ronan snapped back. 'You've made your money off the backs of the likes of me and the rest of the fringe.'

'You're a fool, Irish.' Katsumi tsked. 'You want Dominic's help and then you insult him?'

Ronan propped his ankle on his knee. 'You're one to talk. Look at the guff you've pulled and now you're sitting here, high and mighty.' He pointed at Dominic. 'You don't know the half of what this article's been up to.'

'Actually, I know the whole of it and I'm dealing with it in my own way.'

'By making her a bloody noble?' He shivered in mock fear. 'Oh, please, punish me, too.'

Anger set Dominic's jaw. 'Ronan, you're out of line. Shut your mouth before I change my mind about helping you. You're the one who doesn't know the half of what's been going on. While you were off becoming king, Tatiana nearly killed Katsumi. And then there is the incident I've not yet spoken of.' Wrath over Aliza having his blood shot Dominic to his feet with such force that Ronan flinched.

Ignoring the man, Dominic walked to the carafe and topped off his wine. 'Dead fringe are the least of my concern when Maris's killer is treating this town like her personal playground. I will help you because your help will make my job easier. I do not require your help to accomplish my goals, however.' So long as the fringe didn't abandon him as Ronan promised. If they did, his resources would be sorely tried. 'But one more word out of you and you will regret the day you were turned. Am I clear, Your *Highness*?'

Ronan glanced at Katsumi, then back at Dominic. 'Yeah, you're clear.'

Vertuccio opened the door and stepped to the side. 'Mortalis, sir.'

The shadeux entered. He nodded at Dominic, then Katsumi, but Ronan garnered a rare raised brow. 'I thought you were dead.'

Katsumi rose to hand Dominic her glass for more wine. 'Not only is he alive, he's king of the fringe now.'

Mortalis grunted. 'So. Not just a rumor.'

Surprise widened Ronan's eyes. 'You knew?'

Mortalis shrugged. 'I'm well connected.' He approached Dominic. 'What can I do for you?'

'We need you to witness a blood oath.'

Mortalis crossed his wrists in front of his body, a very soldier-at-ease position. 'Whenever you're ready.'

'I'm ready,' Ronan said. He stood and stripped off his jacket.

Dominic set his wineglass down, removed his cuff link, and rolled up his sleeve. 'As am I.' He moved into position across from Ronan. Katsumi came to stand at his right side, Mortalis on his left.

Ronan and Dominic thrust their bared wrists out to the other, then Dominic spoke. 'This blood oath is between Ronan and myself. I vow to give him aid in uncovering whoever is killing fringe vampires in Paradise City.'

Ronan took his turn. 'This blood oath is between Dominic and myself. I vow to give him aid in finding Tatiana and the unspoken request he has yet to reveal.'

Mortalis nodded. 'Seal the oath.'

Each man grabbed the other's wrist, brought it to his mouth, and bit. Dominic swallowed a mouthful of Ronan's blood as Ronan did the same with his. Finished, they disengaged.

'This blood oath is sealed and witnessed,' Mortalis said.

'Sealed and witnessed,' Katsumi added.

'Anything else?' the shadeux asked.

'No.' Dominic unrolled his shirtsleeve. 'Escort Katsumi to her suite. Ronan and I require privacy.'

Katsumi kissed his cheek. 'Come to me when you're through?'

'Perhaps.' Depending on how things went with Ronan, Dominic thought it best not to promise anything.

She left with Mortalis, then Ronan retook his seat. Dominic returned to the bar for his wine.

'So, Dominic, what's this great unspoken wrong that's been leveled against you?' Ronan's tone made it clear he expected some minor insult.

Wine in hand, Dominic returned to the couch. 'My blood has been stolen.'

'How?' Ronan's curt expression disappeared. 'By who?'

'The how is not important. The who is Maddoc, but I don't know if he still has it. If he doesn't, it's already in the hands of the witches.'

'Aliza? I assume this is about that whole cock-up where her daughter got turned to stone. She must have promised to undo Doc's curse.' Ronan scrubbed a hand over his face. 'The dark power she could conjure with your blood . . . ' He swallowed and looked at Dominic. 'But, then, you know that.'

'I do.' Dominic nodded, sipped his wine. 'Which is why I want it back. No matter the cost.'

'Collateral damage acceptable?'

'By any means.' Dominic leaned forward. 'Just keep Maddoc alive. I want to kill him myself.'

Chrysabelle settled onto the chaise beside Mal. Creek sat across from them. A KM slayer, an anathema noble, and a comarré. It was like the start of a bad fringe joke.

'What do you want to talk about?' Creek asked.

'The blood ritual Chrysabelle is going to perform,' Mal said. 'If it's as dangerous as she says, you should know about it. In case.'

Creek nodded. 'I agree.'

'What exactly do you think is going to happen?' Chrysabelle asked. It wasn't like either of them was going to be present during the ritual.

Mal looked at her. 'I don't know. Maybe you should explain just how dangerous this ritual is going to be.'

Ignoring the oddity of the sudden cooperation of the two men, she answered. 'I said it was *potentially* dangerous. Mostly because of the amount of blood that must be spilled. It will weaken me temporarily.' She stood, walked to the edge of the pool, and turned her back on the water she and Creek had just been sharing. The skin across her stomach felt tight where it was healing. 'I will not discuss the details of the ritual with either of you. All I have to do is perform it, get the answers Mal needs, and I'm done.' Done with her bargain with Mal. And ready to begin finding her brother. And hunting down Tatiana.

'What answers does he need that this ritual will provide?' Creek asked.

She held her hand up before Mal could respond. 'I'm going to see the Aurelian. To find a way to release Mal from Tatiana's curse. It's my end of a deal, and I need to uphold it.'

'Wait a minute,' Mal said. 'It sounds like you intend to do this alone.'

'Of course I do.'

He shook his head. 'No. Not alone.'

Creek sat straighter. 'Yeah, from what I understand, the Aurelian can be moody.'

She laughed, because it was better than screaming. 'As though either of you has a say. This ritual is a primal comarré secret. That you know it exists means I've already said too much. What makes you think I should share it with either of you?' Even though Maris had shared it with Dominic.

Creek crossed his arms. 'We're all on the same side. There's no harm in sharing comarré knowledge with us.'

Mal rolled his eyes at her. 'I could fill a book with the comarré secrets you've told me. What's one more?' He pushed off the chaise and came to stand by her. 'Besides, you're doing this for me. I should be there to protect you.'

'I can protect myself.' Not that those words ever penetrated his brain.

'Then to provide backup. Either way, you're not going alone.' Creek stretched out on the chaise and folded his arms behind his head. 'I'm not leaving until you agree.'

Mal looked at the slayer, then back at her and nodded. 'I'm not leaving either.'

Her nails bit into her palm from clenching her fist. How were they suddenly teamed against her? 'Then I won't do it.'

Mal's irises silvered around the edges. 'You'll do it. Because you owe me.'

He was right about that. Having that debt over her head bothered her immensely, plus there was no way she was going to pass up a chance to find out about her brother. 'Fine. You can both watch the ritual and remain by the portal after I open it. But you cannot come through with me. No one may enter the presence of the Aurelian but a comarré, and even then I may not be exactly welcome.'

'Why?' Mal asked.

Her fingers worried the edge of her silk tunic. 'After the way I disobeyed Madame Rennata in Corvinestri? I led vampires through secret comarré passageways. I used my fighting skills in front of noncomarré. I defied her order to let Maris become a sacrifice for the greater comarré good. I am sure she is not pleased with me. I'd be surprised if she ever granted me entrance into the Primoris Domus again.'

Mal glanced over at Creek, then back at her. 'So this ritual might be the only way you could access the Aurelian?'

'Safely? Now, yes.' Safe was really more of a guess. Blood rituals were never sure things. Although Maris had survived this one. The thought boosted Chrysabelle's mood.

'When will this happen?' Creek asked.

That was the question, wasn't it? She took a breath. 'I need a little time, but I can be ready by tomorrow night.'

Mal nodded. 'Good. What do you need to prepare?'

'Nothing you have to worry about. Be here within a half hour after sundown. I'm starting whether you're here or not, got it?'

He frowned. 'I'll be here.'

Creek hopped off the chaise. 'Me too. Might even come early. Bring some takeout.'

She brushed past Mal, stopping in front of Creek. 'This ritual isn't a game. It's deadly serious. You of all people should know that.'

He nodded, repentance in his eyes, and put his hand on her arm. 'I do know. Just trying to lighten the mood. I'm sorry.'

She sighed and massaged the back of her neck. 'It's all right. I'm just anxious about the whole thing.' She'd never been to the Aurelian. It was a daunting thought, a face-to-face with the woman who knew the entire comarré history, who knew answers to questions comarré had not yet even thought to ask. It was said she was as old as time and that age had made her capricious, prone to whims as variant as the breeze.

Chrysabelle wanted to read Maris's journal entry again. 'I'm going in. I need to start my preparations.'

The sliding doors opened and Doc stuck his head out. Behind him, Velimai vibrated like an oncoming hurricane. 'We got trouble.'

'What are you doing here?' Mal asked.

Doc shook his head. 'Another time.'

'What's the matter?' Chrysabelle rushed toward him, Creek and Mal on her heels.

Doc shifted to his half-form and sniffed the air. 'Nothos.'

Mal shook his head. 'I don't smell anything.'

'Wait till the wind shifts.' Doc jerked his thumb toward the front of the house. 'I went out to check the gate was secure and I smelled brimstone. They're definitely in the area, if they're not jumping the gate yet.'

'Son of a priest.' Mal's hand went to the small of Chrysabelle's back. 'Get inside. It's you they want.'

Creek whipped out his crossbow. 'He's right. Stay inside.'

'It's not me Tatiana really wants.' Chrysabelle shook her head. 'It's the ring. She knows I have it.'

Mal pointed to Doc. 'You and Creek take the front. Velimai can guard the house. I'm going to get Chrysabelle out of here.'

'You got it,' Doc answered. 'You,' he said to Creek. 'This way.'

Chrysabelle looked at Mal. 'How are you going to get me out of here?'

He glanced back at the *Heliotrope*, unmoved from its moorings since before Maris's death. 'Can you pilot that thing?'

'No way.'

He cursed again. 'Then I'm driving.' He grabbed her hand. 'Let's go.'

Chapter Twenty-eight

From his perch atop the estate's stucco security wall, Doc watched a pack of Nothos lope down the street toward the house. He pointed toward them and whispered, 'There.'

The man, Creek, had an air about him Doc didn't like. Or maybe his distrust came from seeing Creek all up in Chrysabelle's business out in the pool. The man was overstepping. That girl was meant for Mal, whether she or Mal knew it or wanted to acknowledge it. Not that Mal showed it, acting the fool like he had. Dumb bloodsucker.

'I see them. My eyesight's as good as yours, varcolai.' Creek leveled his crossbow and took aim.

Doc's weapons were limited to a few knives. Once again, his inability to shift handicapped him. A noise from the other side of the street caught his attention. He inhaled. Over the stench of sulfur, the faint scent of vampire came through. He glanced back toward the house. Mal was nowhere in sight.

He chalked the noise up to nerves and refocused on the problem at hand. The Nothos were close enough now that the glow of their yellow eyes shone through the darkness. The smell of brimstone gagged Doc. Damn, those things were ripe.

Creek pulled the trigger. The bolt whistled home, thunking into the shoulder of one of the beasts. It screeched, causing the group to turn. A crapload of yellow eyes gazed up at Doc and Creek. Jaws unhinged, dripping saliva. Doc's stomach rolled. Nasty. A few of the creatures sniffed the air, whining softly. Their elongated heads bobbed and they shuffled back and forth restlessly. A few of them trembled with what seemed like excitement.

Suddenly, one Nothos lurched forward, scrabbling up the wall toward them.

Doc whipped out a blade and Creek lined up his bow, but before either of them could react, a second Nothos lunged, grabbed hold of its brother, and yanked him off the wall. Words Doc didn't understand were exchanged, then with a round of snarls and hisses, the Nothos retreated and headed back the way they'd come.

'We scared them off,' Creek said, shouldering his weapon.

Doc snorted. 'You don't scare Nothos off. Fear isn't something they understand, it's what they create. Something's up.' He jumped down to the grass shoulder. 'I'm going after them.'

'On foot?'

Doc shot Creek a look. 'What? You can't hang?'

'I can hang as long as you can.' Creek dropped onto the grass beside him. 'Don't you want to shift?'

Doc almost laughed. 'I'd love to shift.'

'Then do it. Won't bother me.'

Like upsetting him was even a concern. 'I can't shift. Not fully.' He morphed to his half-form. 'This is as far as I can go.'

'What's up with that?'

'Don't worry about it.' Doc took off in a long, easy stride after the Nothos. Creek kept up without much effort. When they got too close, they slowed until the distance between them and the Nothos stayed safe and unnoticeable. Every once in a while, Doc glanced over his shoulder. His hackles were up, but he couldn't figure out why. If there was a Nothos behind them, it was doing a killer job of staying hidden.

Over the Mephisto Island bridge and into Paradise City, then across another causeway and into a different neighborhood. Nice, but not as primo as Mephisto. They'd traveled almost an hour. Creek showed no signs of tiring. Doc reassessed the man beside him. 'Chrysabelle says you're a slayer.'

'Mmm-hmm.'

'She says you're Kubai Mata. I thought the KM was a kiddie tale.'

'Nope.'

So that's how it was going to be? One-word answers? What kind of chump did this player think Doc was? He stopped short and grabbed Creek's arm. 'Listen to me, slayer. I don't know what game you're running, but you hurt Chrysabelle and I will rain hell down on you.'

Creek had enough sense not to laugh. 'I'm not here to hurt her. I'm here to protect her.'

'Then keep your hands and your mouth off her.'

Creek jerked his arm out of Doc's grasp. 'My business with the comarré is no concern of yours.'

Chrysabelle's kindness in opening her home had brought out a protectiveness Doc hadn't felt for anyone but Fi in a long while. 'It is when she's my friend. She's not meant for you, slayer.'

That got Creek to laugh. 'Oh, who is she meant for? Mal?'

'Yes.'

'You really believe that, don't you?'

'Yes. And so does Mal.' Again the feeling of being watched ran over his skin like ants.

'Who she's with is her choice.' Creek started after the Nothos, now no longer in sight.

Doc let it drop, picking up his pace to match the slayer's. Minutes passed in uncomfortable silence, but they covered more ground, finally catching up to the Nothos again.

'They're slowing,' Creek whispered.

More than slowing, they were scaling the wall of another estate, disappearing one by one over the side. 'They're going home.'

'Back to Tatiana.'

'Yes.' The last Nothos vanished over the wall. Doc turned to Creek. 'I'm going to do some recon. You in?'

In answer, Creek leaped to the top of the wall. No way could a human have done that. The brother was definitely enhanced. He looked down at Doc expectantly.

A second later, Doc stood beside him. He inhaled, catching the stench of the Nothos. He tapped the side of his nose, then pointed forward. Keeping to the top of the wall, they followed the odor.

Once the wall veered away from the roadside, palms and magnolias clustered against it, giving them cover. They slunk forward, now on all fours, moving cautiously. The smell of brimstone grew stronger.

Through the trees, they watched the Nothos file into the property's guesthouse. On the driveway connecting the two, a male vampire carried a bound and gagged female toward a high-end sedan.

Doc pushed some palm fronds out of the way to see better and caught sight of the woman's face. His blood chilled. Mia. Despite the bruises on her face, he recognized her. Pasha's claims of seeing her death filled Doc's head.

The vampire threw her onto the backseat, slammed the door, then got in behind the wheel. The car headed for the gated entrance.

Doc grabbed Creek's arm. 'I know that girl. I'm going after her. You get back to Chrysabelle's, tell her we found Tatiana.'

Without waiting for an answer, Doc threaded past Creek, under the palms and back to the road. The car was already through the gate, its taillights red as embers a few yards up the road. Wherever that vampire was taking Mia, it couldn't be good.

He jumped down, ready to run. A hand closed over his arm. He whirled around to see Ronan. 'What are you—'

Ronan clamped a rag over Doc's nose and mouth. 'Time to pay the piper, shifter. Imagine finding you and Maris's killer in one night. Dominic is seriously going to owe me.' Powder on the cloth clung to Doc's mouth and nostrils, the bitter taste an instant warning. He struggled not to breathe, but his heart jackhammered in his chest. He thrashed out at Ronan, but the fringe dodged him. At last Doc inhaled, choking as the powder clogged his airway. His throat burned and the taste of dirty nickels coated his tongue. The back of his brain went numb.

Ketamine.

A thick, heavy curtain closed around him. The ground under him fell away and he slipped down, down, down into a blackness as endless as death.

Chapter Twenty-nine

Mal adjusted the *Heliotrope*'s speed down to a crawl. By now, Creek and Doc had probably fought off the Nothos. Or had died trying. What had Doc been doing at Chrysabelle's house anyway? *Maybe she's kissing him, too.*

'I think we're far enough out. I can't even see the house.' Chrysabelle had stayed quiet while Mal piloted her mother's yacht through the waters of the Intracoastal, but now she kicked her feet up onto the leather sectional. 'You could have let Creek drive the boat and gone after the Nothos yourself.'

He grunted in response. Did she really prefer Creek? The voices cheered as his stomach sank. *She wants him, not you. Good riddance.*

'Or I could have fought alongside all of you.'

Yes, because the last time she'd faced the Nothos, she'd done so well.

'Of course, I realize because of our deal you have a stake in my protection.'

That wasn't the only reason. Should he tell her how he felt? How could he when he wasn't even sure. *Liar. Fool. Coward.*

'How'd you learn to drive a boat like this anyway?'

'You pick up a lot in five hundred years.'

'Oh good. For a moment I thought you'd gone mute.' She jumped up and walked toward the control panel, where he stood between the wheel and the captain's chair. She reached for a red button. 'What's this do?'

He grabbed her hand before she made contact with the distress locator. 'Not that one.'

'You feel a little cold. Time to feed soon.'

He let her hand go as his fangs shot down. Not the proper response. Especially when she'd made her choice and it hadn't been him. *Never will be you.* 'I'm good.' He backed away, needing distance. 'Take the wheel.'

'And do what?' The narrowest ribbon of panic curled through her voice.

'Just hold it steady.' He stayed far enough away that her perfume didn't wind around him like the serpent that had beguiled Eve. Why had he thought being in a confined space with her was a good idea? *Close enough to bite. To drink. To drain.* She'd probably get bored and head out to the deck any minute.

Instead, she grabbed the wheel. 'You should teach me to drive in case I ever need to.'

A second later he was behind her.

She jumped, backing into him, then pulling away just as fast. 'I hate when you do that.'

Was it him that made her jumpy? Someone with her experience with vampires should be used to the speed at which they moved. Or maybe his closeness bothered her because she wasn't entirely sure Creek was the right choice. From his spot behind her, he put his hands on her shoulders and steered her into the captain's chair, then planted his hands on the armrests. He leaned in and almost sniffed the curve of her neck. Almost. The whining in his head kicked up a notch.

'See this?' He brushed his forearm against hers on the way to the instrument panel. 'This is the fuel gauge.'

She nodded, pulling her arm into her side. 'Got it. Fuel gauge.'

'And this' – he reached around her other side to tap the compass – 'tells you what direction you're going.' Her warmth radiated into his skin from where his chest touched the back of her shoulder. Her pulse sang in his ears, an angel's voice with a siren's song. The voices whirled into a frenzy. *Drain her, drain her.*

His mouth grazed the tender spot beneath her ear before he realized he'd moved.

She stilled. Then jerked away. 'What are you doing?'

What he wanted to, that's what. He spun the black leather chair until she faced him, about to tell her the truth of his feelings, even though he wasn't sure himself. Then he saw guilt in her eyes.

'Don't.' She put her hands up. 'I have to tell you something.'

The tiniest shard of fear burrowed into his gut. 'What?'

Her eyes stayed fixed on the horizon. 'Kissing Creek was my choice. I *wanted* to kiss him.'

So she'd made her decision. He moved, trying to catch her eyes, but she refused to look at him. 'It's because he's human, isn't it?'

She shook her head as she lifted it. 'No. Maybe. I don't know why. I just wanted to.' Her chin jutted out defensively. 'I can kiss whoever I want to.'

'Yes, you can.' He pushed off the chair and took a few steps back. His hands shook with the memory of seeing them together. 'I understand and I'll leave you alone.'

She lifted her chin farther, her eyes clouding over. 'What? No. I wasn't trying to push you away. I just didn't want you to think Creek had forced himself on me.' She slipped out of the chair. 'I don't want you to leave me alone.'

'What about Creek?'

She twisted to put her hands on the wheel. 'I want both of you,' she whispered. 'That's horrible, isn't it?' She moved away from the console. 'I'm done driving. And ready to go home.'

'It's not horrible.' Except for him. 'I get that things are changing for you. Creek and I will deal with whatever you decide.' He slid in behind the wheel and adjusted the boat's speed.

She nodded. 'Thank you for understanding. I'm going outside for a bit.'

He stared down at the control panel. He didn't understand at all. But keeping part of her was better than losing all of her. When he looked up, Chrysabelle stood at the railing on the lower deck. Her hair flowed out behind her and the wind molded her white silks against her body. From this distance, the glow about her was soft and ethereal, reminding him of the first time he'd spotted her.

That night at Puncture seemed years ago now. She'd been frightened and looking for help. Not much had changed. She still had plenty to fear, plenty she needed help with. Her life was no better for knowing him.

Once this trip to the Aurelian was done, his curse would be broken. The time would be right for him to move on. Start fresh. Let her do the same.

He stared past her, into the black waters of the Intracoastal. He'd been starting fresh for almost five hundred years. He could do it again.

Up ahead, the dock came into view. At the end of it, Creek

stood alone, looking very much like a man with nothing good to report.

'Doc's gone.' Creek shook his head, knowing the news wouldn't go over well.

Chrysabelle rushed down the gangway. 'What do you mean he's gone?'

'We made the first strike against the hellhounds, but they retreated—'

Mal shook his head. 'Nothos don't retreat.'

'These did.' Creek ignored Mal's incredulous look and continued. 'We tracked them back to Tatiana's – she's about an hour from here – then we saw another male vamp stuff a female varcolai into a car and take off with her. Doc said he knew the girl and went after her. I watched Tatiana's a little longer, but got back to the street in time to see a fringe male throw an unconscious Doc into his trunk and peel off. I came back here as fast as I could.'

Mal cursed. 'What did the fringe look like?'

'I only saw him from the back. Short hair with flames carved into it, earrings—'

'Ronan.' The word came out of Mal's mouth like a curse. 'Head of security at Seven. Or was.'

Chrysabelle turned to Mal. 'What would he want with Doc? You think he's going to use him to get back at you?'

'Get back at you for what?' Creek asked, already imagining a few things.

'Ronan and I have never seen eye to eye.'

'Last time they fought was the night those fringe attacked me and I met you,' Chrysabelle offered. 'Mal beat Ronan up pretty badly. He'd want revenge.'

Mal shook his head. 'Going after Doc isn't his style. That kind of plan requires more thinking than Ronan has the capacity for.'

Chrysabelle crossed her arms. 'Then what?'

'The night we went to see Dominic, Doc talked to him about more than just the dead fringe he'd found.' Mal shot Creek a look but kept talking. 'I'm sure it had something to do with Fi. And the conversation didn't go well.' He paused. 'Why was he staying at your house, Chrysabelle? Why would he leave Fi alone?'

Her gaze drifted downward. 'I asked him if you two were fighting. He said no. He said it was a long story I was better off not knowing. I asked him if it involved Fi. He said yes.' She looked up, tension playing across her pretty face. 'Doc's in trouble, isn't he?'

Mal nodded, then jerked his thumb at Creek. 'Where we need to go, he probably shouldn't come.'

'You mean Seven?' Chrysabelle asked. 'I think they let a few humans in now.'

'It's not the human part that concerns me. It's the slayer part.'

'He's going.' Chrysabelle headed for the house. 'He's the only one who saw what Ronan did.'

Mal cursed under his breath and took off after her, so Creek did the same. Both men caught up to her in a few steps, but Mal kept the argument going. 'You want to take a slayer into Dominic's club? You really think that's the best thing to do? Dominic might not appreciate it.'

She glanced back at Creek like she was reconsidering. 'Dominic doesn't need to know what Creek is.' She pointed at Creek. 'And you're not going to say a word about being KM.'

He held his hands up. 'My lips are sealed.'

Her gaze shifted to Mal. 'Neither are you.'

'Not a word,' Mal said.

Getting inside the club could be invaluable for future missions. 'In fact,' Creek added. 'I'll be on my best behavior.'

Even if his best behavior meant a few fringe got ashed.

Chapter Thirty

Doc floated and fell. Up. Down. Up. Down. In the abyss of ketamine, everything was nothing, and nothing made sense except the push and pull of unseen forces. His body had abandoned him, leaving him with the feeling of perfect weightlessness. The universe swirled around him, through him. He became the universe. The Creator. The destroyer of all. Darkness filled his mouth and ears, scaled his eyes. He tried to grasp hold of something, tried to pull himself out, but he had no fingers. No hands.

He drifted.

Drifted . . .

Drifted . . .

The scalding scent of ammonia burrowed down through the darkness and yanked him out by the roots of his consciousness. He sputtered awake as he resurfaced. The ketamine sank its velvet claws a little deeper. He fought harder. Blurred images replaced the nothing. He lifted his sandpaper lids. Focused. Then wished he hadn't.

Dominic stared down at him, the silver glow of his eyes

almost blinding. 'So, Maddoc, it appears your day of reckoning is at hand.'

Doc groaned and struggled to sit so he wouldn't die lying down. His brain told his arms and legs to move. They didn't. Then he realized his hands and feet were bound. Without the drug in his system, he probably would've been able to snap the rope, but he was too weak. His tongue was missing. Or made of cotton. Why was he fighting the universe's embrace? He relaxed. The dark curtain began to close around him again.

A hand slapped his face. 'Wake up.' Then a sigh. 'How much did you give him?'

'Enough,' answered an Irish lilt.

'Ketamine,' Doc said, his voice protesting even as he was unsure why he was speaking at all. The powder had left his vocal cords raw, his throat like a slab of meat. Ketamine affected feline shifters the way laudanum did vampires. Maybe worse.

'*Si*,' Dominic answered. 'Not nearly so harsh as the combination you injected into me. But my mercy has a purpose.' He strolled in and out of Doc's field of vision. 'I need you alive. At least a little while longer. Until my property is returned.'

It all came down to the blood. Life for Fi. Death for Doc.

'I don't have it,' he ground out. He'd known this day would come from the second he'd shoved that needle into Dominic. He just hadn't imagined it would come this soon.

Mind-numbing disappointment threatened to pull him back down into the k-hole. His eyes burned. This wasn't supposed to have happened until he knew Fi was safe. He wanted to cry. If he couldn't help her, he deserved death.

'Where is it?'

Doc shook his head, a surge of emotion stealing his voice.

A fist slammed his jaw into the couch he'd been laid out on.

The pain woke him up more than the ammonia had, but he played it off. Let them think he was still whacked. Might give him a shot to break free.

Ronan leaned over, blocking the ceiling's mural. His fist was cocked. 'Where is it?'

'Ronan, enough. I need him conscious,' Dominic said. 'Who has the blood, Maddoc? Aliza? Tatiana? Ronan told me where she is.'

Ronan. How did that limey get to be a part of this? Then Doc remembered that's who'd bagged him out in front of Tatiana's. He spat out a mouthful of blood, bitter with the drug coursing through his system. He wondered what had happened to Mia. If she was still alive. The sinking feeling returned, but this time anger came with it. Why not tell? Wasn't going to make things any worse. 'Aliza.'

A tirade of Italian spewed out of Dominic. Then a loud noise, like a fist pounding on a desk. A few moments later, Dominic was back in Doc's face. 'Since you gave my blood to the witch, you will get it back.'

'Why should I? You're going to kill me either way.' He wiggled his toes, and for the first time since he'd woken up, they responded.

'Get the blood back and help me put an end to Tatiana and I may not.'

Doc barked a laugh, raking pain down his throat. 'Liar. You're going to kill me first chance you get.'

Dominic grabbed a handful of Doc's shirt and jerked him up. 'Get the blood back for me, aid me in killing Tatiana, and I'll let you live.'

Doc stilled, but kept his fingers working on the knots at his wrists. 'How do I know you're telling the truth?'

'I swear it on Maris's grave.'

Doc still didn't trust him, but it meant buying time. He nodded. 'Deal.'

'We get the blood first, before the witch can do anything with it.' Dominic dropped him and the weight of Doc's body crushed his arms into the cushions, ending his attempt to free his hands. Dominic walked away, but Doc could move his head enough to keep track of him. Dominic nodded to Ronan, then tilted his head at Doc. 'Get the walking shackles on him. I want to leave as soon as possible.'

Ronan nodded. 'I'll take him out through the garage.'

Good. Maybe Ronan would screw up, give Doc a chance to bolt. He went back to work trying to loosen his hands.

'No,' Dominic said. 'Take him out through the employee entrance. I want everyone who works here to be reminded of the consequences of crossing me.'

Ronan scowled. 'Are you threatening my people?'

Since when did Ronan have people? Doc snorted in amusement. Ronan glanced over and Doc rolled his eyes back into his head, fluttering his lids for effect. When he checked back, Ronan was ignoring him. Doc took the opportunity to work one hand free.

Dominic pulled on his suit jacket. 'You may be the fringe's king, but I'm still their employer. I will do as I see fit in that capacity. You still want my help, you'd better move. *Capisce*?'

Snarling as Dominic strode out of the office, Ronan headed for the couch. Doc faked a moan as Ronan released his feet and then reached to his belt to unhook the leg chains. Thank you, Mother Bast. Doc shoved his knee into Ronan's head with as much strength as he could gather, rolling himself off the couch and onto Ronan.

With his now-freed hands, he grabbed Ronan by the ears and slammed his head into the floor until the fringe stopped twitching. Then Doc dragged him to Dominic's desk and used the leg shackles to attach Ronan to one of the carved legs. It wouldn't keep Ronan from escaping when he came to, but it would slow him down. Any damage done to Dominic's beloved desk was just a bonus.

He bolted from the office and headed for the employee exit that Ronan had meant to take. It was risky, but time mattered. As soon as Doc reached the door, he yanked it open and ran through.

Something tripped him and he fell hard onto his hands and knees. He turned to see what he'd stumbled over as the smell of death rose up around him.

Blocking the entrance was the body of wolf, a dark pool of liquid framing her familiar shape. *Mia.* Was that what Dominic had meant about the consequences of crossing him?

Doc's body went taut with rage. All deals were off.

Tatiana waited by the car for Octavian. He'd just returned from dropping the shifter's body at the nightclub, something she hoped would divert the attention of the comarré's friends. Now Tatiana would capture the comarré. Octavian wanted to try his hand at making her talk. Tatiana smiled. Her child was so eager. If she had a heart, it would have warmed with his enthusiasm.

The property gates opened and Lord Ivan's sedan pulled into the drive. The vehicle rolled to a stop and he stepped out, wobbling slightly. He lurched forward, grinning like the fool he was. Still, the expression seemed woefully out of place on his normally austere face.

'Home so soon?' Tatiana asked. She'd erroneously expected him to stay out until dawn. 'The night has barely begun.' And she had much to accomplish.

Ivan laughed. 'I've forgotten the wicked pleasure of human blood. How the substances they douse themselves in can affect our kind.' He hiccupped. 'I've not only drunk my fill, but also gotten extraordinarily drunk.' His brow rumpled in thought. 'It seems I may have also imbibed an generous amount of narcotics.'

He laughed again, his voice high-pitched and verging on giggly. 'I think I can hear the grass growing.'

Octavian came out of the house. 'All ready to go after the comarré,' he announced, then paused when he saw Ivan. He frowned apologetically at Tatiana. 'I didn't realize . . . '

Ivan staggered toward Octavian, who folded in on himself like a child awaiting punishment. 'What's this? Tatiana's lapdog is now one of the family?'

Tatiana braced for the rebuke. 'Yes. I needed more help than Octavian could give me in human form. I thought it best—'

Ivan clapped Octavian on the back. 'Splendid! Welcome to the fold, old man.' He collapsed in a fit of soundless laughter.

Octavian caught Tatiana's gaze and lifted an eyebrow. She shrugged in response. She'd never seen Ivan like this, but then she wasn't aware that he'd had anything but comarré blood in his system for ages. Human blood carried consequences. If the host had indulged in alcohol or drugs of any kind, the vampire who drank from them would feel the effects as well. Obviously.

Ivan straightened to wipe the tears from his eyes. Then a curious look crossed his face. 'Say, did you mention you were going after the comarré?'

Tatiana angled a look at Octavian, but what was done was

done. 'Yes, Lord Ivan. The Nothos located her. We were just on our way to retrieve her and bring her back to—'

Ivan clapped his hands, then nearly skipped to the car Tatiana stood beside. 'Marvelous! Let's go. I'm starving.'

She exhaled a ragged breath. 'I thought you were full? We can't drain the comarré until she gives us the necessary information.'

'Of course, wouldn't dream of it. Just a taste, then.' He half fell, half slid into the car.

Out of his sight, she rolled her eyes at Octavian. This was *not* how she'd planned to do this. At least intoxicated Ivan was easier to handle than lord-of-all-he-surveyed Ivan. She gestured to Octavian. 'Let's go.'

'But . . . ' He nodded at the car, clearly indicating their unexpected passenger.

She shrugged and shook her head. She had a feeling that even in this state, Ivan could turn vicious if provoked. Telling him he couldn't come meant risking him taking his anger out on Octavian. There was no choice but to let Ivan accompany them. 'I can handle him.'

Octavian sighed in acceptance, but the tightness around his mouth betrayed his nerves.

An hour later, he pulled the car onto the shoulder in the shadow between two streetlights outside the comarré's estate. She'd persuaded Ivan to stay in the car until they came back with the comarré. Octavian turned off the engine and got out. She joined him, both of them keeping close to the wall.

'Ready?' he asked.

Tatiana nodded and closed her eyes, picturing the one person she was sure could get the comarré to come out of the house. Her former husband. Power swept through her and she opened her eyes. Judging by Octavian's face, the transformation was successful. 'Let's go.' Her voice came out in Malkolm's low growl.

Octavian swallowed. Was Malkolm that intimidating?

The soft whir of mechanics lilted through the night air. The estate's gate opened. She and Octavian flattened against the wall. A car pulled out and as it turned through the streetlamp's pool of light, she caught the face of the man whose body she currently wore. The comarré sat next to him. She caught sight of a third person, but she didn't recognize him.

'Bloody hell. Back in the car. Follow them.'

Octavian kept up without being too close. If they knew they were being followed, they either didn't care or were leading her somewhere on purpose.

Ivan fell asleep, a sure sign his system was not handling the kine drugs very well. Vampires never voluntarily slept at night.

Twenty minutes into the trip and she knew exactly where they were headed. Octavian glanced into the rearview mirror, making eye contact. 'Seven.'

'Indeed.' She cursed under her breath. With the shifter girl dead, she no longer had a cover to go in under. 'Park close to them. We'll wait in the car.'

He canted his head toward Ivan's slumped form. 'He's a lot of help.'

She flared her nostrils in disgust. 'Isn't he, though?' Too bad she couldn't just open the door and shove him out. Maybe she'd get lucky and he'd sleep where he fell until the sun came up and flamed him to ash. Wouldn't that be nice—

'Tatiana?'

Apparently, Octavian had said something. 'What?'

'We've arrived.'

So they had. Up ahead, Malkolm, the comarré, and the other man got out of their car. Octavian had parked two lengths behind. She leaned back into her seat and prepared to wait. Already she itched for activity. If idle hands were the devil's workshop, she was ready to open a factory.

Chapter Thirty-one

Chrysabelle stayed between Mal and Creek but kept her eye on the KM. There was no telling how the crowd might react to him. Humans had only just begun to work at Seven. Human patrons were rarer still and then only as the guest of an othernatural. She saw no one on the floor she recognized, including Pasha and Satima.

Mal pulled them into one of the quieter corners. 'We need to go to Dominic's office, but you waltz in there with a slayer and you're going to make enemies.'

Chrysabelle sighed. 'Mal, no one knows what he is.'

Mal narrowed his eyes. 'Dominic will know he's not exactly human.'

'Hey, no big deal.' Creek crossed his arms and leaned against the wall. 'I can stay out here.' His gaze wandered over the crowd, taking in the patrons like he was cataloging them. 'What's with those comarré?'

Chrysabelle didn't bother looking over her shoulder. 'They're counterfeits. The vampire who owns this club is St. Germain.'

'Interesting use of alchemy,' Creek said. 'Do the patrons know they're fake?'

'I don't think the patrons care.' She faced Mal. 'I'll take responsibility for bringing him in.'

Mal shrugged. 'Lead the way. I'm just here for Doc.' He tensed suddenly, his body straightening, his gaze zeroing in on something over her shoulder. He swore softly.

She turned to see what had caused such a reaction.

Katsumi strolled toward them, her eyes silver.

Behind Chrysabelle, Mal cursed again. 'Dominic's a fool.'

'Agreed.' There was only one explanation for Katsumi looking the way she did. 'Navitas.'

Katsumi saw them, smiled slightly, and headed their way. She stared intently at Creek but acted as though he was no one of importance when she stopped before them. 'Malkolm, Chrysabelle, nice to see you.'

Nice to see you? Maybe Dominic had turned Katsumi into a symbot. Mal snorted as if he were thinking the same thing. 'Is Dominic here? We were hoping to speak with him.'

Katsumi's smile didn't waver. 'I'm sorry, he's not available. Is there something I can help you with?'

Mal stepped forward. 'What's going on with you? Last time I saw you, you were in rough shape.'

Her nostrils flared and she swallowed, but somehow she kept her perma-grin in place. 'I am fine. As you can see.'

Chrysabelle elbowed Mal aside. 'Where can we find Dominic? This is important.'

Katsumi looked at her, a hunger in her eyes Chrysabelle found soulfully disturbing. 'I assure you, he is nowhere you can reach him. I would be happy to help—'

Mal interrupted. 'Then how about you tell us where Ronan is?'

A flicker of something passed through Katsumi's gaze. Her mouth thinned to a straight line. 'I'm sorry, but I cannot help you. Come back tomorrow.' She bowed slightly and hurried off.

'That was helpful,' Creek muttered. 'You two are well liked, I see.'

Chrysabelle was about to say something when the glint of a silver-tipped horn sparkled at her. 'Mortalis.' She pointed across the room. 'Mal, see if you can get him to help us.'

Mal took off through the crowd, returning a few minutes later with Mortalis in tow. Unfortunately, Katsumi was right behind them. Mortalis shook his head very slightly as if to indicate he couldn't help them.

Katsumi forced herself between Mal and Mortalis. 'I've told you Dominic isn't available. I'm going to have to ask you to leave immediately.'

'We're not going anywhere until we get some answers,' Mal said.

'You leave me no choice.' Katsumi turned to Mortalis. 'Escort them out. Tell the front door they are not to be let in again this evening.'

The shadeux nodded and put his arms up as a barrier between them and the club. 'I'll see you to the front.'

Katsumi stayed put as Mortalis herded them out the way they'd come. Heads turned and curious stares followed them. 'Keep moving,' Mortalis whispered. 'I'll explain when we're clear.'

Once they were beyond the double dragon doors, he took them off to the side of the wide hall. 'I take it you're looking for Doc. He was here. Ronan snagged him. Loaded him up with ketamine and brought him back to Dominic.'

'What?' Chrysabelle asked. 'Why?'

Mortalis sighed. 'Doc stole Dominic's blood. And gave it to Aliza.'

'That damned fool.' Mal shook his head in disgust. 'I knew he was going to do something stupid.'

Creek nodded. 'That cat's got some big ones.'

Mortalis narrowed his eyes. 'Who are you? I assumed you were okay since Mal and Chrysabelle don't seem to mind your company, but I'd like a name at least.'

'Creek,' Chrysabelle said impatiently. 'Back to Doc. Where is he?'

'Doc said Aliza promised to help make things right with Fiona if he brought her Dominic's blood. So now Dominic and Ronan are escorting Doc out to Aliza's to give him a shot at getting the blood back.' He shook his head. 'I've never seen Dominic so angry.'

No wonder Doc hadn't wanted to tell her what was going on when he'd come to her house. And no wonder he'd wanted to stay with her. Where else could he have gone that would be vampire-free? He knew she'd adhered to her mother's policy of not giving invitations.

Mal's eyes were almost completely silver and the muscle in his jaw ticked. 'And you were just going to let them take him out there without telling me?' He lunged forward, his voice menacing. 'You know they're going to kill him.'

A sharp pain pierced Chrysabelle's heart. She grabbed Mal's arm. 'We'll go after him.'

'Yes, we will,' Mal said, still looking to Mortalis.

'You have no idea what I'm dealing with here. I have more reports of dead fringe than I can follow up on.' The shadeux held his ground. 'Look, I was about to head out to tell you, but . . . ' Mortalis looked away, his eyes darkening. 'Mia's body was found dumped at the employee entrance. Her throat was slit.'

Mal's mouth dropped. The tension visibly drained from his body. 'Mia as in Doc's old girlfriend? She worked here as a bartender, right?'

Chrysabelle's hand went to her mouth. This was the first she'd heard about Mia or had a glimpse of Doc's past.

Mortalis nodded. 'Doc found her when he tried to escape. Ronan recaptured him in the alley. Doc had her in his arms.' Mortalis cleared his throat. 'You should go. There's time to catch them.'

Mal shook his head. 'I don't know how to get to Aliza's. You'll have to come with us.'

'I can't. Not with Katsumi watching me like a hawk.'

Creek stepped forward. 'Her coven lives in those stilt houses out in the Glades, right?'

'Yes,' Mortalis answered.

'I can guide you,' Creek said. 'I know that area. My grandmother lives out there.'

'Great,' Chrysabelle said. 'Let's get moving.' All that mattered was saving Doc's life.

Mal had been cautious about letting Creek drive, but it had been easier than trying to follow the KM's directions through the Glades' maze of dirt roads while the voices attempted to throw Mal off track.

Creek parked the car and looked over at him. 'Let me do the talking.'

'Your turf, your show.' Mal popped the car door and slid out. The water here smelled a lot cleaner than that surrounding the freighter. Chrysabelle followed from the backseat, staying near Mal.

'Okay.' Creek nodded. 'Stay here until I call.'

Mal leaned against the car, still ready to move at a split second's notice. 'I'll be watching. And listening.'

'I get it. You don't trust me yet. The feeling's mutual.' Creek glanced at Chrysabelle but she didn't say anything. 'I didn't sign on to the KM with the thought that I'd be traipsing through the Glades trying to rescue a shifter who'd done one of the stupidest things I can think of, so cut me some slack.'

'He's right.' Chrysabelle put her hand on Mal's arm. 'We'll be fine here.'

'Shouldn't take long.' Creek approached the cabin up ahead cautiously. The place was dark. Maybe whoever owned it wasn't home. Or didn't like Creek. *Or hates vampires.*

Mal leaned down to Chrysabelle. 'Maybe I should have gone.'

'I can hear you,' Creek muttered. Chrysabelle nudged Mal with her elbow and gave him a disapproving but slightly amused look. Mal shut out the droning voices and listened as Creek walked onto the cabin's porch.

Creek knocked and stood back to wait. Footsteps shuffled inside. The porch light came on and the door opened. The barrel of a Bushmaster assault rifle greeted him. Mal nodded. He'd been right about the owner not liking him.

Creek held up his hands. 'Slim Jim, it's Creek.'

Slim Jim stepped out onto the porch wearing overalls and a Florida Gators ball cap. The man was almost as short as he was wide with more gray than rust in his beard. He grinned, showing off a missing tooth. Slim Jim tipped the Bushmaster back onto his shoulder and chuckled. 'Well, I'll be. Little Tommie Creek.'

Tommie? Mal's chagrin at being wrong was salved with that new slip of info.

Slim Jim scratched underneath his cap. 'How are you, son? Last I heard you were doing a stretch at FSP.'

'Yes, sir. I'm on parole now.'

Too bad he hadn't stayed there.

Slim Jim clucked his tongue. 'Damn shame, that business. Shoulda shot the cuss myself.' He squinted, making his tiny eyes almost disappear. 'What brings you round here so late? You in trouble?'

'You might say that.'

'Lot of that going around. I just rented a boat to another fella seemed like he was in a fix.'

Creek held his hand about six inches above his head. 'Tall, skin like midnight?'

Slim Jim nodded. 'You know Doc?'

'A little. I'm more surprised you know him.'

So was Mal, but then, Doc's drug-delivery service must have taken him out here many times.

Slim Jim continued. 'I been rentin' him boats for years. I know what he does, running the devil's candy out to those witches, but times are hard. Little extra comes in handy.'

Creek nodded. 'Yes, sir, it does. Was there anyone else with him?'

'You betcha. Two a them damn bloodsuckers. He didn't seem that het up to have their company, neither.'

'How long ago did they leave, and do you have a boat we can rent?'

'About ten minutes ago, I guess.' He paused. 'We?'

Creek turned and motioned with his hand at Mal and Chrysabelle. 'I have some friends with me. They're friends of Doc's, too.'

'Go first,' Mal said to Chrysabelle. Chances were good no red-blooded man would shoot a beautiful woman until he at least found out her name. Mal waited until she was a few lengths ahead until he followed.

Slim Jim whistled long and low. 'Ain't that something.' He stepped forward and adjusted his cap. 'Never seen the likes a you.' He started to extend his hand, then snatched it back when Mal stepped out of the shadows. 'Now, you, I know all about your kind.' His Bushmaster fell into his hands again.

The voices began to chant for the man to shoot.

Chrysabelle put her hands out and stepped squarely in front of the rifle. If Mal had breath to hold, he would have. Instead he stepped out of the way. She would not be his shield. Suddenly she smiled at Slim Jim like Mal had never seen before. Her entire face seemed lit from within, and her signum sparkled and shimmered like a coating of diamond dust. He'd never believed the comarré had magic until now.

'Hello.' Her voice was a soft, breathy purr. She reached one delicate hand toward Slim Jim. 'I'm Chrysabelle.'

Slim Jim's mouth hung open. Mal felt a little slack jawed himself. Slim Jim let go of the rifle and took her hand. 'James Chiles. Pleasure to make your acquaintance, miss.'

She held his hand and came closer, her smile never wavering. 'Mr. Chiles, our friend is in horrible danger.' She closed her other hand around his, capturing his old weathered paw between her palms. A twinge of jealousy rose up in Mal that she would embrace the old man that way, but he knew she was doing it for Doc and for that, the jealousy gave way to pride. 'I would consider it a great personal favor if you could help us.'

Five minutes later, they were in an airboat and headed after Doc.

Chapter Thirty-two

Tatiana watched the boat carrying Malkolm and the comarré shrink into the distance. Something buzzed near her ear. She swatted at it. From the small side road where they'd pulled off, the kine's cabin was visible. Another of the boats with the big fans on the back sat parked along his dock. They'd stuck the car behind some sort of three-sided shed. Octavian had called it a hunting blind.

He came jogging back down the path that led from the kine's cabin. 'There aren't any more boats.' He stopped beside her. 'The kine who rents them out is smarter than he looks. His cabin is circled in salt, silver, and iron filings. He's obviously done business with othernaturals before.'

She didn't care one iota about the kine and what he knew or didn't know. She needed a boat to go after the comarré. 'I can see a boat from here.'

'The motor's missing out of it.'

She pounded her fist on the car hood. 'Bloody hell,' she snarled.

The car rocked. A bleary-eyed Ivan opened the door and nearly fell out. 'Where are we?'

'Everglades,' Octavian answered.

'And we're wasting time,' Tatiana said. She clenched her fists, wishing she had something more to pummel.

'We'll have to go back to the comarré's house and wait for her to return.' Octavian shrugged.

'No,' she hissed. 'We're going after them. I am tired of waiting. Tired of being so close I could reach out and grab her gaudy little neck and yet, she still escapes me.'

'How will we follow them with no boat?'

She loathed leaving Octavian behind, but he might not be able to follow. 'We'll scatter and go after them that way.'

Ivan perked up from where he'd slumped against the car. 'Who are we following again?'

She sighed. Babysitting a Dominus was ridiculous. 'The comarré, Lord Ivan.'

He climbed to his feet and stretched. 'It smells like sewage out here. I'd be happy to scatter if it means not smelling this swamp anymore.'

Tatiana didn't bother explaining that they'd be heading deeper into it.

Octavian frowned. 'I guess I'll stay with the car.'

She went to his side. 'You should try to scatter. You come from a line of vampires who hold the power in great abundance. I scattered the very day Lord Ivan resired me.'

Octavian sniffed. 'But you'd been a vampire for years already.'

'Makes no difference. Try.'

Octavian shook his head. 'I don't know how.'

Tatiana turned to her inebriated sire. 'Lord Ivan, would you scatter and show your grandchild how easy it is?'

Lord Ivan puffed up like a bloated pigeon. 'Quite.' He took a few paces away from the car, stopped, and stood very still. A moment later his body dissolved into a swarming mass of black flies. They held his shape for a second, then buzzed into a low, undulating cloud hovering near the car.

'See?' Tatiana asked. 'Easy. Just imagine you can and you will.' She hoped. Not all vampires could, and lineage was no assurance. Just like she'd never been able to duplicate Malkolm's talent. None had. She'd always thought it was some kind of abomination due to him killing his sire.

Octavian nodded and stepped back. He squeezed his eyes shut and looked like he was holding the breath he no longer required.

Not surprisingly, nothing happened.

'You're trying too hard,' she told him. 'Just imagine yourself lifting off the ground, as light as the air around you but ... part of it.' Describing the ability to scatter was harder than doing it. She reached out and squeezed his hand. If he didn't get it this time, he would have to stay behind. Time was running out. 'Relax.'

He shook himself, loosening up, and kept his eyes open. 'Light as air,' he whispered.

And gasped as he broke apart into a shining cluster of click-ing metal scarabs. The tiny gunmetal wings whirred around her with what she imagined was Octavian's joy at achieving what he'd wanted so badly. But metal scarabs? She glanced at her arti-ficial hand. How much of Zafir's magic had spilled into her when he'd attached her hand?

Something to think about later. Right now, she had a comarré to capture. She scattered into a cloud of wasps and joined Octavian's scarabs in the night sky. With Ivan's fat, buzzing flies lagging behind, they started out over the water.

The comarré would never know they'd followed her until it was too late.

*

'Slow down,' Dominic directed Maddoc. Having the varcolai drive the airboat was probably not the best idea, but he was the only one who knew how. Not that it seemed so difficult now. 'Any unnecessary noise and I'll feed you to Chewie.' Dominic didn't want to alert Aliza to their presence until the last possible moment. Fortunately, the boat slipped silently across the water's surface.

Maddoc grunted in response. Ronan adjusted the shotgun across his lap. The bullets might not slow a vampire, but they'd do a good job of stopping a witch.

The stilt houses loomed ahead. A few lights twinkled through the windows, but for the most part they seemed quiet. Still, he expected Aliza would be up. She'd kept odd hours since he'd known her, which was far too long for his liking.

Her dock came into view, her horrid guard alligator, Chewie, sprawled near the base of the stairs leading to the living quarters. That creature would be better off as shoes. Dominic reached into his pocket, feeling the tops of the stashed vials to be sure he had the right one. Satisfied with his selection, he pulled two out, keeping his pinky and ring finger curled around one while he tossed the other toward the creature. It fell with enough force to shatter against the boards. Thin wisps of green vapor seeped out of the vial's remains.

The gator lifted its head, but before it could hiss in warning, it went limp. The sleeping gas had done its job.

The boat bumped the dock and Dominic glared at Maddoc. The varcolai shrugged like it had been an accident, but Dominic doubted it. He motioned for Ronan to tie the boat up, then he went to work shackling Maddoc's hands behind his back and muffling him with a gag. The varcolai reeked of blood, but there'd been no point in letting him change after Ronan had recaptured him. He was going to die. He didn't need clean clothes for that.

Ronan stepped onto the dock, keeping a safe distance from Chewie. He kept his shotgun aimed in the creature's direction while Dominic got Maddoc out of the boat. The gator never moved as Dominic marched Maddoc over Chewie and up the stairs. Ronan stayed behind to watch Dominic's back as they'd discussed. Ronan wouldn't be able to enter Aliza's anyway without an invitation, something that Dominic didn't have to worry about.

Anyone who used his products automatically provided him with entrance into their homes. Granted, none of them knew his products carried this implied consent, but he'd never felt the need to label his goods that way. Building in fail-safes was the sign of a smart alchemist. Dominic hadn't gotten to where he was by being a fool.

He kept Maddoc in front of him as they approached the front door. 'Try anything and I'll toss you over the side,' he whispered as he leaned past to rap on the door.

More lights came on and a slightly built older man answered the door. He took one look at Maddoc, then his gaze skipped to Dominic. 'Aliza, I think you better come here.'

Dominic shoved Maddoc forward, crossing the threshold with ease. 'Yes, she'd better. She's got something that belongs to me, and if it isn't returned, I am going to lose my temper.'

Aliza came rushing into the room. She skidded to a stop when she saw Dominic. 'How did you get in? You don't have an invitation.'

He glanced at the stone figure of Evie. 'Your daughter gave me one years ago.'

Aliza's breath hitched. 'Get out of my house, vampire. You're not welcome here.'

Still holding tight to Maddoc's shackles, he advanced. 'But my blood is, isn't it? I'm not leaving until you return the blood this creature' – he shoved Maddoc to the floor – 'stole from me.'

The man who'd opened the door charged. Dominic tossed the second vial he'd secured in his hand. It smashed to the floor and the man couldn't stop in time to avoid the cloud of chemicals rising up from it. He tripped through them, coughing as he emerged. He dropped to his knees and passed out.

Aliza's gray eyes darkened in anger. 'You're not the only one with power, leech.' She raised her hands. They glowed with the luminescence of witch magic.

Dominic laughed. 'But I am the only one who can bring your daughter back.'

Chapter Thirty-three

Mal had half expected Creek to try something, like veering the boat sharply to one side in an attempt to pitch him off, but Creek did nothing of the kind. *Too bad.* Most likely because such a move would have affected Chrysabelle as well. The spell she'd cast – because what she'd done back there was nothing short of magic – hadn't only affected the old man. Creek had clearly been swayed by it, going quiet and moony-eyed like a lovesick schoolboy. *Like you.*

Mal stared at the boat's wake, losing himself in the curl of white against the black water. If Dominic killed Doc, everything would change. Mal would not let the shifter's death go unavenged. *Yes, kill, kill, kill.* Doc had saved Mal's hide more than once. He was the closest thing to a friend Mal had. But more than that, Mal understood why he'd stolen Dominic's blood, and Dominic should, too. If saving Maris had meant taking Doc's blood, Dominic wouldn't have thought twice about it. Mal would do it for Chrysabelle, too. *She wouldn't do it for you.*

Dominic had always been a cruel, concise man. Things with him were black and white, with few shades of gray. Although

Mal had no idea how Dominic justified giving Katsumi navitas after all she'd done. He straightened a little as the plan for Doc's defense began to solidify in his head.

If Dominic refused to see reason and let Doc go, Mal would claim the right to take Katsumi's life as equal justice for her stealing Chrysabelle's blood. It was the same thing, except Katsumi's reasoning had nothing to do with saving the life of someone she loved and everything to do with greed.

That woman deserved navitas the way Tatiana deserved the ring of sorrows. Maybe Katsumi would go insane just like Tatiana had. Dominic would then be forced to deal with what he'd done.

The boat slowed and Mal looked up to see a cluster of stilt houses looming ahead. Lights blazed in the first one. Ronan stood on the dock opposite a large alligator-shaped lump. Through the front windows, a stone statue faced the water. Then Dominic moved into view. A second later, Doc staggered to his feet. Ronan spotted them and lifted a shotgun.

Mal forced himself in front of Chrysabelle. 'Creek, fringe with a shotgun on the dock. Dominic and Doc are inside.'

'I see them.'

'Ronan,' Mal called out as the boat neared the dock. 'Shoot and you're dead.' He leaped the last ten feet from the boat to the dock, landing close enough to grab Ronan's shotgun, wrestle it away, and toss it into the water. The alligator-shaped lump wasn't just alligator-shaped. As the fringe swung, Mal grabbed Ronan's fist and yanked him around to face the beast while Creek tied the boat up. 'That thing alive?'

'Why don't you get close and find out?' Ronan snarled. 'Get your hands off me, you knacker. I'm king of the fringe now. Screw with me and I'll bring the whole bloody lot down on your head.'

'King of the fringe? And you're still doing Dominic's dirty work?'

'Sod off.' Ronan twisted, trying to break Mal's grasp.

Mal kicked Ronan's legs out from under him and drove him to the boards with a knee in his back. The resounding crunch satisfied Mal greatly.

Creek helped Chrysabelle out of the boat, then joined her. Mal nodded toward the stairs. 'You two go. I'll be up as soon as I take care of this a little more permanently.' He didn't actually know how he'd get in without an invite, but Dominic had managed it. Maybe the witches were some kind of vampire loophole. *Or maybe they'll kill you.*

He looked around for something to restrain Ronan with but found nothing. Nothing but fifteen feet of Jurassic lizard. He dragged Ronan to the gator, planted his knee into Ronan's back again, then pried the beast's mouth open. The smell was best described as ripe.

Above him, all hell broke loose. Shouting, cursing, the sound of weapons being drawn, and something shattering told him it was time to move. *Fight, fight, fight.*

In as few motions as he could manage, he shoved Ronan headfirst into the gator's mouth, then clamped the jaws back down. That should keep Ronan busy for a few minutes. 'I wouldn't squirm too much if I were you. I'm pretty sure he just blinked in a very hungry way.' The creature seemed to be passed out, but judging by Ronan's original distance from it on the dock, it probably wasn't dead. Maybe Mal would get lucky and it would awaken in the next few minutes. A distant buzzing filtered through the other sounds of the Glades. He leaped off the dead-still fringe and took the steps two at a time until he made the front door. It was open.

Chrysabelle's swords and Creek's crossbow were aimed at Dominic. Dominic had a blade to Doc's throat, and the albino woman who must be Aliza stood over the body of an unknown man. Her hands were lit with the strange incandescent glow of witch magic and were pointed at Dominic. The remnants of a pottery lamp lay at her feet.

'How dare you, Dominic,' Mal growled from the door. The buzzing sound grew louder, competing with the drone in his head. 'Let Doc go.'

'Stay out of this, Malkolm. The varcolai must die for what he's done.'

Mal braced his hands on the door frame. He *could* go inside, but he had no idea how long he'd last until the lack of invitation took its toll. *Try it.* Long enough to get Doc out? Or just a few steps in? 'If you kill him, I will exact the same vengeance on Katsumi.'

A moment of confusion crossed Dominic's face. 'She's done nothing to you.'

'She stole blood from Chrysabelle, and not because she was trying to save someone she cared for, but out of greed. You kill him and I will serve her the same justice.'

Dominic hesitated, then shook his head. 'This is different. Katsumi may have acted for less noble reasons, but Maddoc has done the greater damage.'

'What damage? You're the one with the knife to his throat.' The anger in Doc's golden eyes struck Mal as the most intense he'd ever seen. One wrong move on Dominic's part and he'd be the one who ended up dead. Something landed on Mal's hand. The voices yowled. He flicked it away.

Dominic snorted. 'He gave my blood to this sorceress. The true damage has not yet begun.'

Aliza jabbed a finger at him, causing sparks to leap into the air. 'I need that blood to free Evie. If you'd just given it to me when I asked—'

'Evie knew what was at risk when she perverted the goods she bought from me. There are consequences to actions. That is life,' Dominic snapped back.

Aliza shook her head, sorrow and anger fighting for dominance on her face. 'I want my daughter back. That is all.'

Mal addressed Aliza as soon as she took a breath. 'And Doc wants Fi rescued from her current situation.'

'I've already said I would do what I could.'

Mal shook his head. 'Not enough. I want your word you *will* help her.'

'Her word?' Dominic laughed.

Aliza nodded. 'I promise.'

Mal took a step away from the door frame, now dotted with insects. 'Then let me in and I will help you get Evie back.'

She raised one hand toward him while keeping the other trained on Dominic. 'You swear it?'

'I do.'

She nodded. 'Then I grant you entrance, vampire.'

Mal stepped across her threshold. At the same time, an unholy swarm of insects deluged the house.

Tatiana came back together in a whirl of wings and stingers in the spot she'd deemed would give her the most leverage. Behind the comarré. Not even Malkolm yet realized she was in the room. She hooked her arm around the girl's throat and, transforming her fingers into a short blade, pressed them into the comarré's flesh. 'Drop your blades,' she purred into the girl's ear. 'And maybe I'll spare your life once I've gotten what I came for.'

At the words, Malkolm and the others turned. Tatiana tightened her grasp until the comarré's pulse weakened. 'Any of you makes a move and she dies. She may yet if she doesn't drop her weapons.'

The swords fell to the ground. The looks on the faces around her grew more horrified as Ivan materialized behind the Mohawked kine standing beside the comarré. He clubbed the kine on the temple, catching him off guard and dropping him to the ground. Perhaps killing him. The kine's heartbeat stopped. Ivan picked up the crossbow the male had been holding and hefted it. He smiled, seemingly pleased with the weapon.

Octavian appeared a few seconds after him, returning to his body at Tatiana's side. She nodded to the witch. 'My thanks for the invitation. Your timing was impeccable.'

'Indeed.' Lord Ivan brushed himself off as he looked around. 'Although it still smells like the swamp in here.' His lip curled. 'Swamp witches. How utterly vile.'

The white witch sputtered. 'I didn't invite you in. Just him.' She pointed to Malkolm, who glared daggers at Tatiana, but thanks to Ivan and a deftly aimed crossbow, he made no move.

'Octavian, kick the comarré's weapons out the door,' Tatiana directed him. He moved around her and did as she asked, kicking them back through the kitchen and the open door. Twin splashes followed his actions.

'Very good.' Tatiana blew him a kiss on his return, then refocused her attention on the witch. 'Stupid git. For all your magic, you don't know enough to offer invites by name only? Such a novice mistake. When you said vampire, you flung wide the mystical door to those of us waiting on the other side.'

With a cry, the witch conjured a sphere of flames and hurled it at Tatiana. Octavian gasped. Instantly, Tatiana switched arms around the comarré's neck, thrust her metal hand up as she flattened it into a shield, and deflected the fire back at the witch.

The witch ducked in time to avoid being burned. She stayed crouched on the floor near a male witch who'd been sprawled there when they'd entered.

With her knife fingers at the comarré's throat again, Tatiana poured persuasion into her voice. 'You will not do that again, will you?'

'No,' the witch whispered.

'Good. Get up, witch. I wish to see this thing you've discussed performed.'

Confusion clouded the witch's eyes. 'You're going to allow me to bring my daughter back?'

'My fight is not with you. Proceed.' Although Tatiana would never admit to such emotion, she knew the wrenching pain of losing a child and empathized with the witch. She studied the small group. 'Any of you try anything and I will slit the comarré's throat.'

'Like you did Mia's?' the varcolai asked, his mouth twisting in rage.

'Yes,' Tatiana answered with a smile. 'Exactly like that.' She got the feeling the varcolai would have lunged if not for the blade at his throat. Someone in this room would be dead by sunrise, of that much she was sure.

The witch nodded and got to her feet. 'I need some things to work the spell.'

'Hurry,' Tatiana snapped. Her sentimentality had its bounds.

The witch ran out of the room. Tatiana frowned at Malkolm. 'Quite a motley crew you've gathered, husband.'

At the word, a flash of anger lit his eyes. He sneered. 'Not under the pain of a second death will I acknowledge that title.'

She jerked her arm around the comarré's neck, causing the girl to wheeze. 'How about under the pain I could inflict on your little comarré whore?' She laughed. 'Or should I say the pain I *will* be inflicting?' She smiled at the girl. 'You'll be coming with me when this game is over.'

'No, Tatiana,' the comarré rasped. 'I won't. When this is over, you'll be a pile of ash.'

'How dare you speak to her that way,' Octavian snarled.

Tatiana gave him a reassuring look. 'You may take your upset out on her later. Her threats are empty. I am in control of what happens now.'

The witch returned, ending the discussion. In her hands, a collection of vials and jars. She hurried toward the stone statue of her daughter and began mumbling words of little consequence. Witch magic was weak compared to the power the noble houses wielded.

As the witch began circling the statue with powders and earth and such, Tatiana nodded toward the other anathema, the one holding a knife to the varcolai's throat, but directed her words to her faithful companion. 'Octavian, procure that knife.'

Octavian took it from him with no small struggle and returned to her. The varcolai got up but didn't move any farther. The anathema glared at Tatiana. 'If Malkolm or Chrysabelle don't kill you, I will.'

She ignored him and shoved the comarré toward Octavian. 'Guard her.'

The girl flew out of her arms, flipping bone blades into her hands. Tatiana grabbed her around the neck again, making a metal collar with her hand as she'd done to the female fringe in the club, and lifted the comarré off the ground. 'Drop the weapons.'

'Not a chance.' The girl kicked and slashed. One blade splintered against the metal.

'You bore me.' Tatiana shook the girl hard. Her head snapped back and the second blade dropped from her hand. A little more shaking and the girl went limp. Tatiana opened the collar. The girl fell to the ground in a boneless heap. 'Octavian, take her into the other room and search her for the ring. Restrain her any way you see fit.'

Malkolm growled, watching as Octavian grabbed the comarré by the arm and dragged her back into the kitchen.

That accomplished, Tatiana strolled toward Malkolm. She could almost see the wisps of anger curling off him. She stood before him, enjoying the heat of his gaze, letting his fury fuel her pleasure. 'You realize if she'd given me the ring, none of this would be happening.'

'You'll never get it. And if you hurt her—'

'It touches me that you care for the girl, but your affections are foolishly spent on a servant.'

His jaw was so tightly clenched, his words came out in a gravelly slur. 'I *will* kill you.'

She laughed as she turned to face the witch, still preparing her craft. 'Tell me exactly what this spell of yours will do.'

Bent over her work, the witch answered, 'The spell I am going to perform will loose the magic holding my daughter, but not dissolve it.' She finished the circle of earth she'd drawn around the stone statue and started adding crystals at measured intervals. 'The magic is too powerful. It must be given a new place to rest instead.'

'And that new home is to be?' Tatiana leaned forward in an attempt to encourage the witch to explain things more fully.

'The one who caused this.' The witch stopped work on a

second earth circle, sat back on her haunches, and pointed at the anathema who'd been holding the varcolai hostage. 'Dominic.'

'*Maronna!* You cannot mean for me to take your daughter's place,' Dominic said.

'Why not?' the witch asked. She shook her head, the beads and shells sewn into her white dreadlocks rattling. 'It's what you deserve.'

Dominic's face contorted. 'The only one who deserved retribution was your daughter, for perverting my goods. I will not take her place.'

'No, you won't,' Tatiana interrupted. What a serendipitous opportunity. 'Malkolm will.' She nodded to the witch, gesturing with her metal fingers to her errant husband. 'Use the other anathema.'

'Like hell,' Malkolm snarled. 'I had nothing to do with this.'

The witch shook her head. 'No, he didn't. My beef is with Dominic. He did this to my Evie.'

Dominic began to mutter in Italian again. Tatiana stomped her foot. 'Witch, you will do what I say.' She charged toward Malkolm. 'And you will do what I tell you or your whore will die. Octavian, bring me the girl.'

He came out from the kitchen with the comarré over his shoulder. The girl had regained consciousness, but he'd used electrical cords to bind her upper arms against her body while her legs were secured at the calves and thighs. Once again, Octavian proved his usefulness. He deposited the girl at Tatiana's feet.

'Did she have the ring?'

'Not on her.'

Chrysabelle spat at Tatiana. 'You'll never get it. I'll die before that happens.'

'Yes, you will.' Tatiana held her hand in the air and formed it into a thin, sharp blade. It gleamed in the light.

Malkolm stilled. 'Don't touch her. I'll take Dominic's place if you leave her alone.'

'Just as I thought. How pathetic,' Tatiana said. 'Lord Ivan, would you be so kind as to escort my feeble ex-husband into his proper place?'

Ivan, still hefting the weapon he'd taken off the Mohawked kine, gave a short nod. 'If it means this circus will be over sooner, then by all means.' He stepped over the kine's body and pointed the crossbow toward the unfinished circle. The kine reared up, yanked a blade from his boot, and jammed it into Ivan's leg. With a yowl, Ivan twisted and pulled the bow's trigger twice, putting a bolt through the kine's shoulder and another through his thigh, pinning him to the floor. Cursing, he collapsed, unable to free himself.

'Creek!' the comarré cried out.

'Bollocks,' Ivan snarled, tugging the dagger from his thigh. 'I could have sworn the kine was dead.'

So had Tatiana. He had no heartbeat or breath sounds. What human managed that? 'Lord Ivan, if you could get Malkolm into the circle?'

'Yes.' He stared a second longer at the kine, now oozing the most bitter-scented blood Tatiana had ever smelled, before giving Malkolm a shove with the reloaded crossbow. 'In you go.'

Malkolm refused to budge. 'I owe you death.'

'I'll help you,' the bleeding kine added.

Ivan sighed. 'Such tedium.' He goaded Malkolm with the bolt tip until he moved, and kept it up until Malkolm stood inside the circle of earth. 'There,' he said to the witch. 'You have your pawn. Go about your business.' Ivan kept the crossbow up and just at the edge of the magic circle as the witch finished her spell and placed her crystals.

Next, she extracted a vial of blood.

'That's mine,' Dominic hissed.

Now in an almost trancelike state, the witch ignored him and added a drop of blood to each of the crystals, starting with the circle around her daughter.

Malkolm gazed at the comarré with such woeful eyes Tatiana thought she might lose her accounts right then and there. How had that lowly creature captured the affections of a man who'd once been the greatest fear of all five vampire families? It was as preposterous as the lamb seducing the lion. Malkolm should just eat her and get it over with. Bloody fool.

'Per cruor quod terra, vita revert. Per cruor quod terra, vita revert. Per—'

'Aliza,' Malkolm hissed. 'Don't do this.'

'Yes, Aliza,' Tatiana crooned to the witch. 'Do it.'

'Cruor quod terra, vita revert.' Aliza flicked a drop of blood onto the statue, then turned toward Malkolm. A brilliant white vapor leaked out of the statue. It reared back, reminding Tatiana of her late albino cobra, Nehebkau. Aliza dipped her finger in the blood and lifted it to shake a drop on Malkolm. The vapor shifted toward him as well. In a move faster than any human eye could follow, Malkolm jumped out of the circle, grabbed Ivan, and dropped him into it. Aliza released the drop of blood. It splattered Ivan's chest.

The vapor struck, pouring into Ivan like quicksilver and catching him in a net of lightning. He opened his mouth to scream and froze that way. Lips curled back. Fangs extended. Hands clawing against the inevitable. Stone from head to toe.

Beside him, Aliza's daughter, now flesh and blood, fell limply to the ground, coughing and gulping air in great gasps. 'Ma,' she whispered hoarsely.

Aliza gathered her child in her arms, tears streaming down her white skin. 'Evie, Evie, Evie,' she chanted over and over.

Bitter regret washed through Tatiana. There had been no saving her child. No magic words or sacred blood or second chances.

She straightened and took stock of the situation while the rest looked on in shock. Malkolm was unscathed, but in saving himself, he'd done her an enormous favor.

Ivan was out of the picture in a way she could never have even hoped for. She walked toward the statue of her Dominus. Aliza had brought her daughter out of it, which meant there was hope for Ivan yet.

That could not be. Ivan was all that stood between her and the next position of power she so desperately craved. The rest of the House of Tepes would have no choice but to side with her when she held the title of Dominus.

Hope had to be eliminated.

She forged her hand into a sledgehammer and with a cry that shook the house to its foundations, swung it round her body with the strength of centuries and slammed it into Ivan's stone form.

The stone cracked slowly like ice, fractures webbing across his body. His pinky fell first. Then an arm. More chunks followed until rubble covered the floor.

She scooped up the largest remaining piece of his face and tucked it and a handful of smaller shards into her coat pocket. The council would want proof. And she wanted a souvenir of her latest victory.

'Tatiana.'

She spun. Octavian's face was awash in panic. The knife he

held to the comarré's throat trembled. 'Don't fear, my love. Malkolm has done us a great favor.'

'No.' He shook his head and pointed past the weeping witch and her daughter, toward the porch windows. 'Look.'

And she did. Orange edged the horizon line.

Dawn had snuck up on them.

Chapter Thirty-four

With her hands behind her back and the distraction of dawn's approach, Chrysabelle had managed to extract her Golgotha steel and saw through the electric cords binding her hands. She'd almost dropped the blade when Tatiana smashed Ivan to bits, but she'd hung on, just like she clung to the hope she might yet slip the blade into Tatiana's chest.

She was about to yell for Mal and Dominic to get out while they still could when Tatiana grabbed her tunic front and hauled her to her feet. 'I will come for you tomorrow and you will give me the ring.' She tore off a piece of Chrysabelle's tunic and stuffed it into her pocket. 'There's no point in running.'

Tatiana dropped Chrysabelle. Pain shot through her shoulder. Tatiana snapped her fingers at her companion and yelled, 'Scatter.' A moment later, a swarm of insects buzzed out of Aliza's house and back into the swamp.

Mal was at her side instantly. He broke the rest of her bindings. 'Are you all right?'

She nodded, gently rolling her shoulder. 'Yes, but I don't

think Creek is.' He'd worked his thigh free of the bolt pinning it, but his shoulder was still stuck fast.

Mal didn't bother looking. 'How are you?'

'You need to leave,' she told him. 'Dawn is coming.'

'Not without you or Doc.' Mal turned as if to grab his friend, but Dominic snatched the weapon Octavian had discarded and jumped on top of Doc, pressing the blade into his throat. 'Daybreak or not, this isn't over. There is still the matter of the blood I'm owed.'

'You would die over the matter of a little blood?' Doc snarled.

'If need be, yes.'

'Then go to ash.' Doc stared at Aliza. 'Forget his blood. You got what you wanted. You owe Fi help.'

Aliza nodded. 'So I do.' She kissed Evie's head as she got to her feet. She dug in her pocket and produced a small bundle wrapped in white paper. She held it up so Doc could see it before tossing it in his direction. 'Burn that and get her to pass through the smoke. Your Fi will be restored.'

Doc reached for the bundle but Dominic pressed the blade harder. Blood welled up around the metal. 'The remainder of my blood, witch. Return it now. Or I will kill Maddoc.'

Aliza shook her head. 'What do I care if the shifter lives or dies? The blood was my price for what he required. All of it. I'm not returning any of it.'

'Then he dies.' Dominic lifted slightly, as if prepping for the killing blow.

'No!' Chrysabelle shouted. 'Don't you dare!'

Mal held her back, but he was seething. 'You kill him and Katsumi dies. I promise you that.'

'Both of you stay out of this,' Dominic warned. 'This is between Maddoc and me.'

Chrysabelle shook her head, angry tears burning her eyes. 'I wish Maris were alive to see how right she was.'

Dominic stayed his hand. 'How right she was about what?'

'She wrote in her journals that leaving you was the hardest decision of her life, but she knew you'd never give up the dark power being vampire gave you. She couldn't be with you because loving her wasn't enough for you.' She swallowed down the hurt knotting her throat. 'Look at you. She was right. You're so caught up in your own sense of justice.' She looked away for a second, blinking hard to clear her vision. 'If you kill Doc, you and I are through. Your last link to Maris will be gone completely.'

'You don't understand,' Dominic said. 'There is power in a vampire's blood. Power I cannot allow the witch to have. This isn't about justice – it's about self-preservation. Maris would understand that.'

'The woman who gave her life to save mine? No.' Chrysabelle shook her head. 'I don't think she would.'

Aliza pulled a subdued Evie to her feet and held her close. 'This is all very touching, but I'm not giving up the blood, no matter who dies, so stop asking. The deal's done. It's mine.'

Mal stood and stepped forward. 'Would you return Dominic's and take mine in exchange?'

Aliza looked at him with great curiosity. 'You'd give yours up freely?'

'Not freely. Dominic's must be returned.'

Aliza glanced at Evie. The two exchanged a peculiar look before Aliza nodded. 'I'll do it. On one condition.'

'What?' Mal asked.

'What is the ring Tatiana spoke of?'

'The ring of sorrows,' Chrysabelle volunteered. What did it

matter if Aliza knew the ring's name? Time was running out. 'Do you agree?'

Aliza nodded. 'I do.'

Mal held his hand up and spoke to Dominic. 'You must also agree that the return of your blood settles things between you and Doc.'

With great hesitation, Dominic sighed, slowly shaking his head. 'He stole from me.'

'As Katsumi did from Chrysabelle.'

'You will consider that matter settled as well or there is no deal.' Dominic didn't take his eyes off Doc for a second. 'And I want the vial in my hand before I drop this dagger.'

Mal looked at Chrysabelle. She nodded. It seemed like a small price to pay for Doc's safety. 'Then it's done.' Mal shucked his jacket and held out his arm. 'You're wasting time, witch.'

Moments later, Mal's jacket was back on and Aliza held a syringe filled with his blood. Doc stood next to him and Chrysabelle, Doc's eyes bright gold with predatory sharpness.

Dominic's vial was already stowed. 'You're a fool, Malkolm, but I appreciate what you've done.'

Doc grunted, a twisted sound of gratitude and skepticism.

'You may both be fools,' Chrysabelle said. 'The sun will be up in minutes. You should have left when Tatiana did.'

'*Cara mia,* would I be so careless as to put myself in such danger?' Dominic reached into his pocket and retrieved two stoppered metal tubes. He tossed one to Mal. 'Drink it.'

Mal eyed the tube suspiciously. 'What is it?'

'My own version of SPF.' Dominic wrenched the top off, tipped the contents back, and swallowed. 'It will protect you from ultraviolet light for twenty-four hours. Should you wish to end the protection sooner, which you may, you have only to drink blood.'

'What's the catch?'

'For every minute of the twenty-four hours the potion is in your system, you'll age one day. If you partake of mortal sustenance within that time, you will become irrevocably mortal. The aging, however, will continue.' He pulled out a third vial. 'Now if you'll excuse me, I must gather Ronan and be on my way. I have no wish to age any more than necessary.' He left, but his footsteps halted after the screen door swung shut. 'Ronan?'

After a few seconds without a response from Ronan, Dominic yelled again. 'Malkolm!'

Mal downed the tube's contents and tossed it aside. He jerked his head toward Creek as he addressed Doc. 'See to Creek, would you? I have a feeling Dominic isn't happy about the way I left Ronan.'

'Sure.' Doc went to unpin Creek, but Chrysabelle went after Mal.

'What's the problem?' Mal asked, pushing through the door. He held it open for Chrysabelle. Fog clung to the swamp's surface, making the land look like the mythical home of the fae. She expected to see Mortalis or Solomon walk out of the mist at any moment.

'Where's Ronan?' Dominic asked, his gaze suspiciously probing Mal.

Doc and Creek came out behind them. Creek limped slightly and looked angry enough to kill. She squeezed his hand and gave him what she hoped was a reassuring and calming smile. His wounds appeared to be healing already.

Mal shrugged. 'Last I saw, he was getting friendly with the locals.'

'That's what I'm worried about.' Dominic peered over the railing and down through the haze.

Mal, Doc, Creek, and Chrysabelle joined him. Mal pointed toward the dock where the airboats were moored. 'He was right there.'

The fog shifted and the dock came into clearer sight. There was nothing on the boards but a streak of blood.

By the time they'd ditched Creek, who, despite his injuries wouldn't let Mal closer to his apartment than a few blocks, dropped Doc off at the freighter, and were headed to Chrysabelle's house, nearly three hours had passed.

The sun blazed in the amazingly blue morning sky, a sight Mal had not seen in almost five centuries. He knew in his gut that the fiery ball had not changed. It only seemed brighter. More brilliant. More frightening.

He'd found a pair of Doc's sunglasses in the car and appropriated them. The darkness comforted him in a way that made him ache. He had been nocturnal for so long, just the warmth of the sun on his skin made him anticipate pain.

The car provided enough shade that he could almost ignore the oddness of the situation. Almost. The effects of Dominic's potion weighed as heavily as the smell of rotting plant life clinging to him and Chrysabelle after recovering her swords from the muck.

For nearly five hundred years, he'd been ageless. Now aging a hundred eighty days in such a short span of time felt like being reborn.

And that wasn't the half of it. Based on his body's response, he wasn't entirely convinced aging was the only side effect of Dominic's SPF. Mal's bones, muscles, and joints ached with the sudden press of time. It reminded him of human illness. Being warm without the ingestion of blood was wrong. His stomach growled with the hunger for food, a feeling he'd not had since the night he'd been sired. Even his heart beat sluggishly, something that never happened without a draught of comarré blood.

Worst of all, he'd begun breathing.

Chrysabelle glanced at him from the passenger's seat but turned her head away quickly when he tried to make eye contact. Her mouth quirked in a strange way.

'What?' He was in no mood for another argument.

She looked back at him, and he realized the strange expression was an attempt at not smiling. 'You should see yourself.'

'No thanks.' If he looked as bad as he felt, he would pass.

'Well, in case you were wondering, you've gotten a little ... shaggy.' She bit her lip, then laughed.

He pulled down the visor and reluctantly checked the mirror. His hair hung well past his shoulders, and a thick beard covered his face. More startling was the face under the beard.

His human face. No sign of the fanged demon that dwelled within. Come to think of it, the voices had been silent since he'd drunk Dominic's potion.

'Sidewalk!' She grabbed the wheel and jerked it. 'Pay attention, please. I'd hate to survive Tatiana just to die because you're a bad driver.'

He nodded and tried to refocus on the road, but his eyes kept shifting to the mirror. 'Something isn't right.'

'Besides your driving, you mean?' She sighed. 'Yes, you look like a mountain man.'

'Besides that.' The lack of voices, the beating heart, the breathing, seeing his human face reflected back ... an eerie prickle crawled up his spine as he slowed the car at Chrysabelle's front gate. She held still while the facial-recognition scanner did its thing. The gates swung open. He parked the car on the inside curve of the drive and got out. He waited while she retrieved her swords from the trunk, then followed her to the door, lost in the possibility of what it all meant. Velimai opened it as they approached. She stared wide-eyed at him before looking to Chrysabelle for an explanation as to how he was daywalking.

'One of Dominic's potions,' Chrysabelle said as she entered the house.

Velimai peered at him, her nostrils flaring as she inhaled. She shook her head like something about him confused her.

Mal stayed on the porch. 'I'll wait here, but leave the door open in case I need you.' The plan was for Creek to join them as soon as he'd patched up his injuries; then he, Mal, and Chrysabelle would board the *Heliotrope*, where she would perform the rite necessary to get to the Aurelian.

'It might be a while. I have to clean my sacres, get the smell of the swamp water off my body, and then dress according to the tenets of the ritual. You can wait on the boat, if you like, get a shower, whatever you want. The windows are helioglazed.' She smiled. 'I guess that doesn't matter at the moment.'

'I'll be fine. Do what you have to do.' He hung back until she and Velimai left. Oddly, he couldn't hear them or sense Chrysabelle as he might have just a few hours prior. It only made him more impatient to test his theory.

When he'd given them enough time to get upstairs to Chrysabelle's suite, he positioned himself on the edge of the threshold, took a breath, and extended his hand toward the line of invitation.

His hand passed over the threshold with ease. A shiver tripped through him. He exhaled hard and stepped through the doorway.

He stood in her foyer, almost trembling with the realization of what his entrance meant.

One more test. He slipped the knife from his belt and pulled back the sleeve of his jacket. He dropped the knife at the sight of his bare skin. His mouth hung open. Not a swirl of black, not a dot of ink, not a single name. As blank as the day he'd been born. His heart raced as he ripped off his jacket and shirt, grabbed up the knife, and ran for the mirror on the living room wall. Watching his reflection, he ran the knife's edge across his palm.

Behind the fresh line of pain, blood welled. The wound stayed open.

Dominic's potion hadn't just made him immune to sunlight.

It had made him mortal.

Chapter Thirty-five

Something clattered on the floor downstairs. Chrysabelle looked at Velimai, who shrugged and signed, *Stupid vampire.*

'I'll check it out.' Wishing Velimai would cut Mal some slack, Chrysabelle ran back down to see what the noise was. She skidded to a stop on the marble tile of her foyer. Mal stood in her living room. Bleeding. And half naked. Literally. Not a spot of ink decorated his body.

'What are you doing? What happened? Where are your names?' The words tumbled out of her mouth faster than she could make sense of him. 'How are you in here?'

Bewilderment rounded his eyes as he continued to stare at himself in the mirror. He shook his head, dazed. 'I'm mortal.'

Two words. Two impossible words. She stumbled toward him. 'No. It's just Dominic's potion. You can't be mortal.'

'But I am. I'm in your house, uninvited. My cut hasn't healed. The names and voices are gone. My senses are dulled. I can't hear or smell or—' He turned toward her. A flash of pain flickered in his gaze. He swallowed. 'You don't glow anymore.'

'Dominic said you only turned mortal if you ate something.' Mortal. Her insides twisted with the impact of what that meant. But that was foolishness, wasn't it? He wouldn't stay that way. Couldn't. The aging was a death sentence. She shook her head. 'Whatever this is, it's only temporary. Dominic said it would wear off in twenty-four hours.'

He laughed. The sound chilled her with its recklessness. 'Not if I eat.' He spun, scanning the room. A bowl of apples gleamed red on the kitchen table.

'Mal, don't.' Panic closed her throat. The thought of life without him – of watching him die – staggered her. 'The aging will kill you in a few weeks. Maybe less.'

'You don't get it. I've lived long enough. The chance to be human again . . .' Liquid rimmed his lids. 'Without these voices, this constant desire to kill.' He threw his head back and exhaled. 'Already I feel so clean. Reborn.'

Her hands clenched in useless fists. 'Dominic knew you'd feel this way. This is his way of getting back at Doc. Don't you see? By taking you away, he can go after Doc without your interference.'

'Then Dominic wins.' Mal shrugged and met her gaze once more. 'You'll be free, too. Free to do whatever you want with your life.'

He launched toward the apples, but his vampire speed was gone. She beat him easily, tackling him to the hard tile floor and pinning the warm length of him there. Every ounce of her being screamed for him to stay. 'I don't want to be free of you.'

He struggled to get up, but she outmuscled him now. He got one hand on the table leg. 'Let me go, Chrysabelle.'

'No.' She tried to pry his grip loose, but her sweat-slicked fingers slipped. 'I need you.'

'No one needs the monster I am.' He jerked the table. The bowl tipped, showering them in apples.

She batted one away. 'I do. And I can free you of that monster. I'm going to the Aurelian tonight. You'll have your answer.'

'And what if she can't help?'

'She will. I know she will.' Her cheeks were wet, her hands were trembling, and her heart was crying for her to do whatever she had to do to keep him from killing himself.

His hand closed around a single sphere of murderous red. 'Let. Me. Go.'

'I can't let you die when we're so close to finding an answer.' Especially when she might love him. With no other option, she bit her lip until it bled, then leaned down and kissed him.

With only bruises left from his injuries, Creek parked his bike and climbed the gate into Chrysabelle's estate. He knew he should have waited to be buzzed through, but he wasn't in the mood to wait. After everything that had gone down, he wanted to be sure she was okay.

He rounded the massive fountain in the center of the circular drive and stopped. The front door stood wide open. He reached for his halm, cursing the loss of his crossbow. Telling Argent it had been stolen by a noble and turned to stone after being used against him was going to be fun. Argent would question why Creek hadn't ashed every vampire involved. Creek would not let the KM strip him of his assignment. He couldn't let his family down. Not after everything they'd been through. He'd find a reason for the KM to keep him.

A horrible bellow erupted from the house.

Creek had heard the sound before. It was the sound of a

vampire dying. Maybe Tatiana had come after Chrysabelle earlier than expected.

He burst into the house, following the noise to the source. He found it. Mal. Shirtless and pinned to the floor under the comarré. Apples littering the tile like land mines. The wysper vibrated in the corner. What the hell had happened, Creek could only imagine.

Mal opened his mouth for another deafening roar. Blood oozed from his pores. His muscles strained, corded and taut so that every line of sinew strung out like piano wire. The names covering his body writhed and twisted. Sunlight spilled through the kitchen's plantation shutters, and where Chrysabelle's body didn't cover him, wisps of smoke curled off his skin.

'What the hell is going on? I thought he was safe from sunlight?'

Chrysabelle shook her head. 'He had blood.'

Her bottom lip was smeared with red. Creek clenched his jaw so hard it popped. If Mal had hurt her, Creek would kill the bastard with his bare hands.

'Help me get him out of the sun.' She tried to climb off the vampire, but he gripped her forearms so tightly bruises already formed under his fingers.

'Invite me,' Mal ground out. Cracks opened in his flesh, spilling more blood. The names began to merge, covering him in darkness and crawling over his skin. He arched against the floor, almost bucking her off.

To keep Chrysabelle from igniting along with the vampire, Creek grabbed Mal's booted feet and dragged them both into the room's shadowed interior.

'Malkolm, I invite you in,' Chrysabelle whispered.

At the words, Mal let go of her, slumped flat onto the bloody tile, and canted his head away from her and Creek. His wounds began to close and the names stopped moving. Creek grimaced. Wearing your sins on your skin that way was a heavier burden than he could imagine.

She cupped Mal's face in her hand, trying to get him to look at her. 'Are you okay?'

He said nothing, just kept his head turned. Creek could understand the man needed a moment. He extended a hand to Chrysabelle. 'Let me help you up.'

'Thank you.' She got to her feet and let go. She smelled of blood and the Glades, her whites dingy with the latter and gory with the first. The wysper glided toward her, hands and fingers forming shapes he couldn't read. Chrysabelle nodded. 'You're right. I should get ready.' She glanced back at Mal. 'Just tell me you're all right.'

He pushed to his side and sat up with a slowness Creek had never seen a vampire display. He kept his back to her and again didn't answer.

Chrysabelle reached for him, then stopped and pulled her hand away. 'I'll be ready as soon as I can. We'll get your answer.'

Mal cleared his throat. He expelled a hard breath. 'I can't get to the boat without cover.'

She nodded. 'We'll come up with something.' She turned to Creek. 'Won't we?'

'I'll take care of it.' He gave her a nod and tucked his halm away. Befriending a vampire had seemed like dubious business at first, but now he wondered if the partnership could pay off after all. The KM might think twice about getting rid of a slayer who had the trust of a vampire like Mal.

'I'll get ready as soon as I can.' With a last look at Mal, Chrysabelle left and went upstairs.

Creek waited until she was out of earshot. 'You okay to move?'

'No.' Mal shivered and he spoke through clenched teeth. 'I feel like hell.'

He looked like it, too. Getting pulled apart from the inside would do that to a person. 'Take your time. I'll figure out a way to get you on that boat.' Creek took off for the garage, suddenly understanding what it meant to have sympathy for the devil.

Chapter Thirty-six

Now aboard the *Heliotrope* thanks to Creek's help and the protection of a large tarp, Mal still hadn't looked Chrysabelle in the eye since she'd wiped his brief mortality away with a single bloody kiss. Becoming vampire again, in her house, without invitation, had almost killed him. *Good.* Waves of pain still echoed in his bones. The voices had returned with a vengeance. For nearly three hours, he'd sat on the floor of her kitchen letting his body heal to the point where he could move without feeling like he was going to pass out. Or disintegrate. Maybe dying would have been better, but the ache in her voice when she'd said she'd needed him had made him hope for the future. She'd promised the Aurelian would have an answer. *Lies, lies, lies.*

He hoped for Chrysabelle's sake that was true. If he'd lost the chance to die with his brain and body at peace, he would not forgive her. Or himself.

'I'm going to begin now.' She spoke with the same voice she'd used to charm the human into giving them an airboat. Mal distrusted that voice. It sounded false. *It is.* 'Once I start, you must not touch me or interrupt me or you will break the ritual and I will have to start over.'

In the *Heliotrope*'s salon, she kneeled on the gleaming teak floor. Her white silk gown pooled over her knees and feet, the fabric so delicate he could tell she carried no weapons. The only thing between her and the silk were her signum. From shoulder to shoulder, a strand of braided fabric kept the backless dress from falling off, and with her hair twisted up, the length of her spine was visible. Too visible. The gold runes engraved into her skin shimmered with her breathing.

Mal ground his teeth together, despising his weakness for her beauty. *Pathetic. Fool.* Getting lost in her loveliness wouldn't save him, but he still couldn't look away.

At her side was a scrap of paper and a long, narrow pouch of red leather, like the kind that wrapped the handles of her swords. With her head bowed to her chest, she chanted softly for what seemed like an hour or two. The shadows moved around her as the sun sank lower, but she stayed in her place, never wavering.

At last she raised her chin. He rose from his seat and moved a few steps to the side so he could see what she was about to do. Opposite him, Creek did the same.

Her eyes stayed closed a moment longer. When she opened them, she took the small slip of paper and unfurled it across her lap. On it were the runes that decorated her spine. She took up the pouch, unfastened it, and removed a thin gold pipette. One end tapered to a needle-thin point.

She bent her head again in what looked like prayer, but briefly this time. With her right hand, she lifted the pipette, the pointed end facing her. What little color she had drained away.

She inhaled.

Wrapped her left hand over her right.

And plunged the pipette into her chest.

Doc paced the freighter's hold, the small wrapped bundle from
Aliza as heavy as bricks in his pocket. The sun would be down
soon. Just a few more minutes. He'd never seen Fi until after
sunset. There was no reason tonight would be different.

He exhaled, trying to calm his nerves. At Aliza's, Dominic
had told Mal things were square, but Doc didn't believe
Dominic. He knew the man, and the man liked his revenge.

'Fi! Fi, you there?' The sooner he could do this thing, the
better. He flicked on the lighter in his hand, but the small flame
was powerless to chase the hold's gloom. Even the solars, strong
at this hour, didn't do much more than fill the cavernous space
with extra shadows.

'Fi!' he shouted one more time. 'Where are you, girl?'

'Here,' came the weak response.

He whirled around but saw nothing. 'You there?'

'Yes. Trying to be.' She stood a few feet away, so soft and
transparent he could see only the brightest parts of her. The
Cheshire glow of her eyes and teeth, the faintness of her pale
skin. 'It's hard. I feel . . . like I'm not really here.'

Excitement zipped through him. He pulled out the bundle.
'I've got the cure for all that, baby. Stay with me now.'

'You got it?' she asked, growing brighter for a moment.

'Sure do.' He cleared a spot near her, making sure there was
nothing but metal where he planned to start the fire. He'd
brought a bucket of water with him, but if things got out of hand,
that bucket wasn't going to put out much. He pulled out the
bundle and showed it to her. 'I'm going to light this, then you
have to pass through the smoke. Can you do that?'

She disappeared entirely, then flickered back into view. 'Maybe we should wait until a little later so it's easier for me to stay visible. You know, if this works and things go back to the way they were, I could get snapped back to Mal's side, wherever he is.'

'Well, at least we'll know it worked, then, won't we? We gotta do this now.' If Dominic still had that potion in his system, he could be headed here now. Doc listened a minute, trying to see if any odd noises filtered through, but the ship seemed quiet. 'Try for me, okay? For us?'

'Okay.' She smiled. 'For us.'

He set the bundle down and lit the end. The gathered paper ends burned slowly until they hit the fat part. Whatever Aliza had packed in there went up with a bright flare. Greenish gray smoke rose in a thick column. He sat back on his haunches. 'Go ahead, baby. Go through it.'

She gave him a weak smile. 'Here I go.'

As thin and wispy as she was, she nearly vanished into the smoke. For a second, it seemed she and the smoke were one. She bathed in it, closing her eyes and cupping her hands full of it like it was water. 'It's soft. And cool.'

'Not too long now. The witch just said pass through it, not spend all day.' He grinned to soften his words.

She floated through the smoke and stopped in front of him. 'Do I look any different?'

He nodded, hesitant hope filling him. 'You do. You look . . . more solid. Try it. See if you can get corporeal.'

Nodding, she blinked hard. The wound on her throat disappeared along with the bloody sweatshirt, replaced by smooth skin and some funky off-the-shoulder top. She fell to the floor of the hold with a thud. *She was solid.* Laughter echoed through the space. 'You did it. I'm me again! And I'm still here!'

'You sure are.' He scooped her up and squeezed her tight, thrilled there was a tangible body to hold on to, a warm neck to bury his face against. He inhaled until his head swam in the perfume of her. 'I'm never letting you go again, I swear.'

She wrapped her legs around his waist, then pulled away enough to get face-to-face with him. 'Thank you. From the bottom of my heart, thank you.' She kissed him, hungry and crazy and careless. Then she stopped as suddenly as she'd begun. 'You know what?'

'Hmm?' He planted a few kisses on the curve of her neck, his mind already lost in the scent and taste of her.

She twisted, looking over her shoulder. 'If that smoke can fix me, I mean really fix me, like detach-me-from-Mal fixed, maybe you should go through it, too.'

He paused. Her logic wasn't half bad, but the fact that Aliza may have counted on him trying to remove his curse with the smoke was a very real possibility. Would the old witch have anticipated him going through the smoke, too? Could she have planned for it? 'I don't know, baby. What if something goes wrong?'

She ran her nails over his shaved head in long, lazy scratches. 'It could be your chance, but if you don't feel right about doing it ...'

He stared into the smoke. The fire was almost out. *Courage*, he told himself. This could be his one shot to be whole again.

Fi traced the line of his ear. 'If you don't want to, then don't. Doesn't change the way I feel about you.'

'No, you're right. What do I have to lose?' He put her down. 'I'm going to do it.'

She squeezed his hand. 'Go ahead, kitty cat. I've always wanted to snuggle with a big ole leopard.'

He kissed her once for luck and stepped into the smoke. It curled over his body like a cool mist, as soft as she'd said. Peace filled him and he understood why she'd stayed in it so long. Reluctantly, he walked on through.

'Well,' she asked. 'How do you feel?'

He turned and shrugged. 'Good, I guess.' But he'd felt good as soon as Fi had gone solid and he'd known Aliza had done what she'd promised.

'Go ahead,' Fi urged. 'Change.'

New nerves tripped along his back. He nodded and stepped away from her to get some space. Just in case things went ... wrong. He winked at her. 'Here goes.' And gave himself over to his true form.

The shift came easy and smooth in a way it hadn't for years. Almost too easy. Suspicions crept over him, but he shook them off. This was a good thing. No point spoiling it by giving in to crazy guesses that Aliza had somehow tricked him.

Not with the way Fi was looking at him. Her eyes lit up and her grin took over her face. She let out a tiny squeal and clapped her hands.

At the noise, Doc blinked. Instead of being level with her calves, his sightline was at her ribs. He took a step toward her. The paw stretched out in front of him was the size of a bread plate. He flexed his toes. Claws like talons dug into the floor. Mother Bast, his curse was gone.

Fi retreated a step. 'I didn't know you were going to be so ... big.'

The joy at being himself again welled out of him in a loud, guttural yowl.

The look in her eyes changed to something a little less happy. She flickered back to her ghost form.

He shook his head, trying to tell her not to be afraid.

She swallowed. 'You wouldn't hurt me, would you?'

Not in a million years. He just had to let her know that no matter what form he was in, he was all about protecting her. Always. He'd nearly gotten killed trying to rescue her from the hell she'd been stuck in, hadn't he? But that was behind them now. He laughed, which came out like a sneeze, flopped onto the dirty floor, and rolled over, showing her his belly and looking at her upside down.

That got him a laugh. 'Silly boy.' She took a baby step forward. 'I'm going to touch you, okay?'

He kneaded a paw in the air. Her fingers brushed the tip of one ear. He held very still. Her hand traveled to the top of his head, caressing the width of his skull. 'Wow, you're so soft.'

Human, ghost, whatever she was, he adored this female.

She kneeled beside him and buried her face in his neck. 'I love you, Maddoc.'

I love you, too, Fiona. He started to purr.

Chapter Thirty-seven

'What the hell?' Creek rushed forward to stop Chrysabelle, but Mal blocked his way.

He leaned in toward Creek. 'She said not to touch her.'

Creek's whole body thrummed with the urge to stop her. 'She's doing this for you. Anything happens to her' – he stabbed his finger into Mal's chest – '*anything*, and I blame you.'

'Nothing's going to happen to her. I won't let it.' Mal stalked away.

In an almost trancelike state, Chrysabelle seemed not to notice them. With her index finger over the open end of the pipette, she slid it out of her chest and inhaled. Blood bloomed from the wound, but the stain spread no more than a few inches.

She started chanting again, so softly it was hard to hear. Maybe that was on purpose, to keep them from understanding the words she was using. From what Creek could make out, it sounded like the Aramaic the KM recited in their rituals. Using the pipette like a fountain pen and her blood for ink, she drew a perfect circle on the floor in front of her. At the top of the circle, she drew the phoebus, the sun symbol that was every comarré's first signum.

He glanced at Mal. The vampire was practically salivating. His eyes were silver, his fangs visible as he watched open-mouthed. Who could blame him with that much blood? No wonder she'd been reluctant to do this in front of him. She probably worried his beast would break free and devour her. Creek exhaled hard. He'd die before he let that happen.

Circle completed, she bent forward, supporting herself on one hand. With the other, she continued with the pipette, this time writing inside the circle. Creek and Mal shuffled a few steps closer. She copied the runes from the paper into the circle, whispering the name of each one as she went.

After the last one, she set the pipette aside and stood, arms outstretched, palms up. The runes sketched in blood began to expand. Blood flowed from them and filled in the blank spaces within the circle until an almost solid pool of red shimmered before her. The blood expanded until the last empty spot was covered.

A flash of golden light gleamed across the surface. The blood rippled like water. Creek took that to mean the portal was open. Chrysabelle picked up her skirts and stepped forward.

Creek caught movement out of the corner of his eye. Mal shifted nervously. Like he meant to go with her. Creek wasn't willing to take that chance.

He lunged to grab Mal and hold him down. Chrysabelle's foot touched the portal. Mal jumped forward out of Creek's way, his hand snagging the trailing sleeve of her gown. Creek snatched the back of Mal's jacket. Blinding light surrounded them, then plunged them into darkness. A stone wall slammed into Creek and new lights danced in front of his eyes. He shook himself.

Correction. Not a wall. A floor. Mal was a few feet away. Slightly ahead of them stood Chrysabelle, head bowed. Books and scrolls covered the shelves lining the walls. He followed the volumes around until he saw a woman unlike any he'd ever seen before.

Seated at a massive table, its edges overflowing with more scrolls, charts, and star maps, was a tall, slender Persian. The kind of woman who might devour her mate. He wanted to look away, but her coal-black eyes held an age and wisdom that bored into his core and mesmerized him. His body felt screwed to the floor. His joints ached and he knew somehow that she controlled him.

The Aurelian.

Her mouth twisted cruelly as she glowered at him, then at the vampire. She rose, hefted a sword few mortal men would have been able to lift, and pointed it at Chrysabelle. 'You have violated the rules of my sanctuary.'

'What? No, my lady.' Chrysabelle shook her head. 'I did everything as I was instructed.'

'You brought a mortal and a vampire into my presence.' The Aurelian's voice shook the intricately carved walls and rattled the candelabras lighting the enormous room.

Chrysabelle spun to look behind her. Horror marred her expression. 'You fools,' she breathed. 'What have you done?'

Mal answered. 'It was an accident. Creek's fault. He grabbed hold of me at the last minute.'

'Idiots,' she hissed. 'Both of you. Do you think this is a game? This is my life.' Her hands fisted as she closed her eyes and inhaled. When her eyes opened, they held as much anger as the woman hefting the sword.

The Aurelian strode to the front of the table, sword still pointed at Chrysabelle. 'None but comarré are allowed here. This trespass must be dealt with.'

Chrysabelle nodded and turned away from them to face the woman. 'Yes, my lady, of course. My deepest apologies. I instructed them not to follow me through.'

The woman lowered the sword a fraction. 'Then you know them?'

'Yes, I know them, but I told them not—'

'They were present during the ritual?' Fresh sparks glinted in the Aurelian's eyes.

Chrysabelle dropped her chin, her hands tightening until her knuckles went white. 'Yes.'

The Aurelian walked toward Mal. 'The penance for this act is death.'

Tatiana motioned for Octavian. He joined her behind a clump of bushes in the side yard of the comarré's home. 'Anything?'

'No. That side of the house is dark top and bottom. What about here?'

She pointed toward the kitchen windows. 'The wysper. Disgusting creature.'

'Any sign of the girl?'

'No. If Malkolm or that kine is harboring her, it's going to take longer to track her down. Fortunately, with the scrap of fabric I took from the comarré, the Nothos *will* find her.'

He tipped his head toward the back of the property. 'What about the yacht? There are lights on there.'

She turned to look. So there were. She'd been so fixated on the wysper she hadn't noticed. Suddenly the lights within the boat flared brightly. Like a flash going off. 'Come. Let's see what that's about. Unless someone calls that vessel home, we should be able to get in without a problem.'

They kept to the property line until they were at the water's edge, then they snuck across to the dock. She glanced back toward the house. Nothing had changed. She listened for signs of life on the boat. No heartbeat. That meant no comarré or kine were present on the yacht. She sniffed the air. The scent of comarré blood made her mouth water, but past that she picked up the subtle spice of vampire and the earthy sweet smell of a kine but with a lingering sourness.

The scent of the Mohawked kine who'd hidden his heartbeat at the witch's. He and Malkolm could be on the boat, but there was no comarré. So what had caused that flash? Had Malkolm done something to the girl? If he'd killed her to get the ring for himself, Tatiana would kill him for it in turn.

She motioned for Octavian to follow. Together they boarded the craft, weapons drawn. Octavian held the short blade that had once been Nasir's. She fashioned her hand into a smaller version of the headsman's sword she'd come to favor. She opened the first door she came to and slipped in.

In the center of the empty salon, a perfect circle of blood shimmered with an unnatural gleam. The blood scent rushed her, almost knocking her back. Behind her, Octavian growled low. She glanced at him. His fangs were out, his nostrils flared, and his face a warrior's mask of hard angles and sharp bone. For a vampling like him, this much blood scent would be overwhelming. 'Focus. You'll feed soon.'

He nodded, sniffing hard. His eyes rolled back into his head slightly.

She punched his shoulder. 'Control it.'

'I'm trying,' he grated, shaking himself.

'Try harder.' She slunk toward the blood, weapon ready even though they were alone. Some kind of ritual had been performed here. Near the circle lay a sharpened gold straw. The pointed end leaked blood. At the top of the circle was the sun sign she'd come to recognize as the mark of the comarré. That symbol had first led her to the old comarré, and now it would lead Tatiana to the young one and more importantly, the ring.

She leaned in and held her natural hand over the circle, lowering it closer and closer until the buzz of power bit into her skin. She stood and nodded. 'A portal. See that symbol? It can only mean the comarré's run home.' Tatiana laughed sharply. 'If she thinks the Primoris Domus can protect her, she's wrong.'

Morphing the gleaming sword at her side back into a hand, she turned to Octavian. 'Time to return to Corvinestri and end this game.'

'But how do you know she won't just slip back through the portal?'

'Because she can't come through a portal that isn't here.' She glanced around the vessel. 'Set the boat on fire.'

Chapter Thirty-eight

Chrysabelle fell to her knees in front of Mal, arms outstretched. 'No, please, I beg you, my lady. Spare their lives. They came only to protect me. I'm sure of it.'

The Aurelian raised her brows. 'You think a vampire wishes to protect you? Are you ill, child?'

'He's saved my life more than once. He isn't like the rest of his kind, I assure you.' Although he and Creek were surely the biggest meddling idiots she'd ever known. How dare they violate her trust and follow her here? Hadn't she specifically told them not to touch her or interrupt her during the ritual? She'd never wish them death, but they'd earned some kind of punishment.

'Hmph.' The Aurelian pointed her blade at Creek. 'And this one?'

'He's Kubai Mata.'

The Aurelian took a harder look at him. 'Is he?'

'Yes, I swear it.' Chrysabelle prayed for mercy, despite what the two fools behind her had done. 'Please. They don't deserve death.'

'Neither do they deserve leniency.' The Aurelian rested the flat of her blade on her shoulder. 'But for your sake, I will allow them to live. They will not, however, be a party to our discussion.' She strode back to her table, laid her weapon down, and took up an ornate octagonal box. She removed the lid and the perfume of myrrh spilled into the room. 'Until I release them, they will be bound in complete silence, unable to hear or see us.'

'As you wish.' *Thank you, holy mother, for sparing them.*

The Aurelian stood before Creek. 'Rise.' He did as if lifted by an invisible force. Still, he said nothing. She tossed a handful of the powdered substance toward him. It dropped in a perfect circle around his feet. A column of weak light, like sunlight filled with dust motes, rose from the circle until it touched the ceiling.

Creek put his hands up and looked around. He opened his mouth and shouted. Not a sound escaped his conjured prison. He cocked his fist back, muscles bunching in his shoulder, and punched the column to no effect. The rise and fall of his chest increased. He crouched down, splayed his fingertips on the ground, and closed his eyes.

The Aurelian moved to Mal. 'Get up, vampire.'

He got to his feet, but unlike Creek, his posture stayed defensive. He glared at the Aurelian like he was trying to warn her. Like he was trying to protect Chrysabelle.

The woman snorted softly and looked at Chrysabelle. 'This one truly believes he is your protector, doesn't he?'

Chrysabelle wanted to say *I told you so* but stuck with, 'Yes.'

The Aurelian tossed the myrrh at his feet and the process repeated itself, enclosing him in the strange magic. Mal scowled and crossed his arms, looking around and up before settling into the odd perfect stillness only a vampire could achieve. He looked like a statue. A beautiful, dangerous, boneheaded statue.

The Aurelian went back to her table, replaced the lid, and set

the box aside. 'Now, comarré, we begin. You may call me Nadira.'
She took her seat, propped her elbows on the table, and laced her
fingers beneath her chin. 'You are Chrysabelle. House of Primoris
Domus. You've found a way to access me that few comarré have,
although all who accept my signum bear it. Someone guided you.
Another comarré. One you are very close to. You also hold a
piece of powerful magic. One the nobles would very much like
to have. Is that why you've come? To find out the real power of
the thing you've hidden away?'

'No.' Nadira's information didn't surprise Chrysabelle. It was
the woman's job to know the unknown.

'What, then?'

Chrysabelle hesitated. The Aurelian hadn't yet limited her
questions as she'd done to Maris. Perhaps she would allow more
than one. 'I've come because I wish to help the vampire.' She
tipped her hand toward Mal. 'To find a way to remove the curse
he lives under.'

Nadira laughed. 'Oh, child, you know not what you ask or
you would not ask it. I can supply you with this information, but
you must understand that removing his curse will not help him.'

'Why not?' The Aurelian *had* the information to remove it,
just as Chrysabelle had suspected she would. Victory was at
hand.

'He lives under two curses, yes? One that he earned by draining the monster that sired him, the second given to him by the
nobility to restrain him. If you remove the second curse, the one
that fills his head with voices from the souls he's taken, then the
first curse returns in full force. He will no longer think twice
about killing but will once again become the ravening beast
whose only thoughts are death and destruction. What little
humanity is in him will vanish.'

The weight of defeat squashed Chrysabelle's chest, forcing out the joy that had just blossomed there. Faintness overwhelmed her and the air in the room thickened until each breath became a chore. She shook her head, trying to shake the numbness out of her head. 'No, that ... that can't be. I told him I would help him. There must be another way. What if the first curse is removed as well?'

'There is no undoing the first curse, only the second. Do you wish to know how to remove this curse, accepting what he will become?'

Chrysabelle inhaled a deep, shuddering breath and looked at Mal. Part of her wanted to scream at the unfairness of it. Instead, she walked to him and put her hands on the invisible wall between them. 'I'm sorry,' she whispered. 'I can't let you go back to that. I can't lose you that way.' She cared for him too much. And feared that side of him unlike anything she'd ever known. He would understand, wouldn't he?

She studied him a moment longer, wishing she could touch him, explain, lessen the burden of this decision. She faced Nadira. 'Just because I know how to remove his curse doesn't mean I will allow him to do so.'

'Very well. To remove the curse placed upon him by the nobility, he must right a number of wrongs equal to the names on his skin. One for every life he has taken. Only then will his curse be removed.'

Chrysabelle's hope for helping Mal disappeared. How many acts of repentance must he perform? Ten thousand? Twenty thousand? And to what end? So he might become a killing machine again? The bleakness of it soured her stomach. 'You're sure there is no cure for the curse of killing his sire?'

Anger flashed in Nadira's eyes. 'You question me?'

'Only out of concern for him, not because I doubt you.'

Nadira shrugged. 'If there is a cure, I do not know it. Is there anything else you would ask? Your time here grows short.'

'Yes.' She watched Nadira carefully. 'I understand I have a brother.'

Nadira's eyes narrowed to slits. She stared until Chrysabelle felt like a butterfly about to be pinned and placed under glass. 'Who gave you this information?'

'So it's true, then?'

'I asked you a question.'

'I don't wish to say.'

Nadira stood. 'You would refuse to answer me? Your lack of respect astounds me.'

'I mean no disrespect. Only to protect the one who gave me the information.' Maris might be dead, but there was no reason to spoil what was left of her name. Nor would Nadira's knowing make any difference in the question's answer as far as Chrysabelle could see.

'What you mean and what you do are two very different things.' Nadira came around the front of the table, her long robes swaying with an angry tremble. 'I am more than just the keeper of records for the comarré. I am your creator. My husband was Balthazar, one of the Magi who followed the star.' She paused. 'I alone held the Child in my arms. Such power you will never know.'

Chrysabelle bowed her head. She'd known the Aurelian was old, but her true age was staggering. 'No, my lady, I will not.'

'Even then, Samael's dark forces followed us. Under his orders, his children killed my husband and his fellow Magi. I alone escaped, saved by the holy magic surrounding me.'

At the mention of the Castus Sanguis's leader, Chrysabelle

shivered. The Aurelian's chambers would be safe from such intrusion, but the name still chilled her core.

'Without me, you would not exist. Yet you dare not answer me?'

'Yes, that is what I dare.' Chrysabelle raised her head. 'If power cows me, how will I survive the forces against me? I truly mean you no disrespect, but I need answers. The Primoris Domus has done little to help me.' She pointed toward Mal. 'This vampire you think so little of? He has done me more good than my own kind. I came here for answers. If you cannot or will not provide them to me, I bear you no ill will. But the covenant *is* broken. A new age is upon us. The rules of the past must change to reflect that.'

Nadira lifted her chin. 'You have more courage than I thought. Fewer brains perhaps, but courage sometimes counts for more.' She crossed her arms and leaned against the table. 'Yes, you have a brother. He is closer than you think. Always has been.'

'How will I know him? What's his name?'

'You will know him by his signum.' She paused. 'Are you not interested in your father?'

'By his signum? How? My father?' Chrysabelle almost staggered backward with the weight of the unknown. 'Yes, of course, if you are willing to tell—'

Nadira waved her hand dismissively. 'You have asked too many questions already. I am done answering. Leave me.'

'Please, my brother's name.' Chrysabelle wrung her hands together. A name would make things so much easier.

Nadira pointed over Chrysabelle's shoulder.

She turned as the columns of light surrounding Mal and Creek disappeared. They stumbled forward, blinking. Behind them was a massive bronze door. Chrysabelle shook her head.

'Please, we must return through the portal by which we came. Where is it?'

Nadira didn't bother to look up. 'That portal was destroyed from the other side not long after you arrived.'

'Tatiana,' Mal snarled.

'Leave now or your companions die,' Nadira said.

'Do as she says.' Chrysabelle shoved them both toward the door. She refused to come this far only to lose them. Together, they burst through and left the Aurelian behind. The room they entered was stunningly bright compared to the dim confines of Nadira's realm. Slowly, it came into focus.

'Where are we?' Creek asked.

'Bloody hell,' Mal growled.

Dread almost brought Chrysabelle to her knees. They were in the Primoris Domus.

Tatiana stared past her reflection in the plane's window and into the comfort of the night sky, her hand closed around her locket. Soon she would be home. And soon after that, on the doorstep of the Primoris Domus. She would get what she'd come for, too, because Madame Rennata had much to atone for. Tatiana's level of displeasure had reached a new high upon discovering her comar and the comarré recently purchased for Nasir had fled the estate. Tatiana had had no choice but to leave them behind in Paradise City.

Octavian settled into the seat beside her and handed her a goblet of blood. She took the unexpected offering. 'Where did you get this?'

He smiled. 'Was I not the most proficient head of staff you ever had?'

She nodded, her mood lightening. 'You were that in spades.'

'I've always kept your plane stocked with blood.' He clinked his glass to hers. 'We must be sure your next head of staff does the same.'

'Replacing you will be difficult.' If not impossible.

He smiled and sipped his blood. 'Not as warm as you like it, but better than nothing.' He frowned. 'I recognize that look. You're thinking about the lost comarré, aren't you?'

She swallowed. 'How dare those simpering little cows run away?' She growled in frustration. 'Do you know how much money I have invested in them? Mark my words, Madame Rennata is going to hear about this. One more reason to head home as soon as we can.'

'We'll be in Corvinestri soon. Is there anything I can do for you until then?' The silver in his eyes gave his intent away.

'You can promise me I never have to return to Paradise City again. I loathe that place.' She shuddered. 'And I hate living without servants.'

His mouth wrinkled in a poorly suppressed grin. 'You'll enjoy knowing that I turned the Nothos loose before we left.'

For the first time in many hours, she laughed. 'Bravo! I adore you.' She kissed his bloody mouth. 'Maybe there is something you can do for me after all.'

He kissed her back, taking her free hand and pulling her to her feet. He walked them backward toward the bedroom. 'I've always wanted to join the mile-high club. I just didn't think I'd do it when I was dead.'

Chapter Thirty-nine

Madame Rennata walked toward them, the same sour old bag Mal remembered from his last trip here. Except then she'd had a marked limp and a cane. Ignoring the heady, swirling scent of comarré blood, he stepped in front of Chrysabelle. 'We were just leaving.'

She ignored him. 'Chrysabelle.' Her tone held a malice that raised the small hairs on Mal's neck. Laughter rippled through the voices. 'You have violated several laws. You were warned about bringing this creature into our home, and yet you've done it again.' She glared at Creek. 'And now another—'

'He's Kubai Mata,' Chrysabelle interjected.

'I don't care if he's the pope. A violation is a violation.' She narrowed her gaze. 'Worse yet, you took them into the Aurelian's sanctuary.'

Mal glanced behind them. The door they'd come through was gone. Comarré tricks made his skin crawl.

Comars gathered behind Rennata. Big, burly males that looked like they'd be more at home in the Pits than at the beck and call of some vampiress. 'I hereby renounce you, Chrysabelle Lapointe. You are disavowed. No longer comarré.'

'What?' Chrysabelle's entire being shuddered. 'You cannot—'

'I can. And I have.' Rennata snapped her fingers. 'Seize her.'

'Touch her and I'll kill you.' Mal grabbed Chrysabelle first, Creek a second after him. Together they put her between them and faced the comars.

Rennata's nostrils flared. 'If anyone is to be killed, vampire, it will be you.'

'You want her?' Mal snarled. 'You'll have to go through me.' *Drain them. Kill them.*

'Make that *us*,' Creek said, snapping out his halm.

Chrysabelle squeezed Mal's shoulder. 'It's okay,' she said, her voice thick with determination. 'I'll go with them. Rennata is right. I am in violation. I have not come this far to become a coward now.'

'No one would ever call you a coward,' Creek said.

'Not twice anyway.' Mal turned to her. 'I say we fight.' The voices yowled in agreement.

'I'm game,' Creek said.

She shook her head. 'No.'

'You're sure you want to do this? Creek and I will get you out of here if that's what you want.'

Creek nodded. 'In a heartbeat.'

'I'm sure. And I know you both would.' She smiled grimly. 'What's the worst they can do? Take the name comarré from me? They cannot change who I am.' She lifted her chin and stared Rennata down with a fierceness that made Mal proud. 'I am done being comarré anyway.'

'If you're sure,' Mal said one last time.

'I am.' She cupped his face, kissed his cheek, then shifted and did the same to Creek. 'Thank you both. But I must see this through.'

She slipped from between them and into the grip of the comars. Fear flashed in her eyes, belying her brave smile. Mal's gut told him he was a fool to let her go. Beside him, Creek radiated anger, no doubt feeling the same way. But Chrysabelle was a stubborn woman, and if he'd learned anything about her, it was that she would choose her own path, regardless of what anyone else said or did.

Rennata glared at them as all but two of the comars disappeared with Chrysabelle down a hall. The remaining comars brandished swords that matched Chrysabelle's, leveling them at him and Creek. Rennata pointed to the door. 'Outside. Now. You may wait for her there.'

Creek approached the woman, his arms tensed at his sides. 'The grand masters will be interested to hear your treatment of Chrysabelle.'

'Tell them what you like,' Rennata said with a shrug. 'I don't report to them.'

Mal snarled at her, snapping his fangs. The beast stared out through his eyes.

She twitched, then sniffed. 'You don't scare me.' With a twirl of her robes, she marched after Chrysabelle. The comars closed in on him and Creek. Another went ahead and opened the door, gesturing for them to leave.

Creek pushed past them, muttering under his breath. Mal followed behind to join him on the portico. Thankfully, it was dark out. One of the comars slammed the door behind them.

'You have some knowledge of their rituals. What are they going to do to her?' he asked the slayer. Every fiber of his being wanted to rush back in there and find a way to get her out.

Creek clenched his fists. 'Some comarré rituals I know. This is one I don't.' He stared through the windows, but even Mal couldn't see beyond the sheer curtains. 'I say we go back in, bust some heads, and get her out of there.'

'I can't get farther than the main hall. Wards.' A million rescue scenarios played out in Mal's head, none of them making him feel any better, since he couldn't act on them. He needed something else to think about. 'We should figure out how we're going to get back.'

Creek was about to speak when the door opened. Two comars held Chrysabelle under her arms. She was limp, almost lifeless. They dragged her through the door and dropped her at Mal's feet.

Creek swore as the door shut.

Mal had no words for what he saw. Whining flooded his brain. Red haze clouded his vision. As red as the blood drenching her back. She moaned softly. Mal went to his knees beside her. The runes along her spine, the signum that had gotten her in to see the Aurelian, were gone.

They'd cut them out of her skin.

Doc ran because he could and because he hadn't run, really flat-out run, since the curse had taken away his true form. Now, as a leopard, he flew over the cracked sidewalks and pitted downtown streets. Those who saw him were either othernaturals who didn't look twice or humans out to see something exciting. Tonight was their lucky night.

Block after block disappeared until he started to run out of the neighborhood most othernaturals considered safe. He neared Little

Havana, the smell of vampire spice teasing his sensitive nose. He rounded the next corner to loop back around. A small group of brawling fringe cluttered the street. Weapons clanked and flashed as they fought. He ducked into an alley and climbed the fire escape like it was a metal tree. From the roof, he took another look. The fringe were getting ashed fast. Two down. Now three.

They fought one of their own. Sort of. The fringe in the fatigues was Preacher. Doc would have recognized that shaved head, cross-wearing freak of a vampire anywhere. He'd long been on a mission to 'cleanse' Mal, but Preacher hadn't shown himself since their last run-in.

The fourth fringe went up in a cloud of ashes. The last one took off running. Preacher flipped a dagger into him and brought him down, adding a final pile of ashes to the asphalt.

Preacher's fighting abilities against Mal weren't so hot, but against fringe he did pretty well. Or had he gotten better? Was he practicing on the fringe to hone his skills to come after Mal? Why kill them off so close to his home, then?

Preacher collected his weapons, crossed himself, and took off in the opposite direction. Doc followed, keeping to the rooftops to avoid being noticed. His leopard mind loved the height almost as much as the chase.

He stayed with the ex-marine until they were deep in Little Havana. Preacher was headed home, if you could call an abandoned Catholic church any kind of home for a vampire. But Preacher wasn't a typical vampire.

Sure enough, Preacher ducked inside the old cathedral. Doc made his way down to the street level and, staying to the shadows, followed through the same side door Preacher had used. Normal vampires couldn't enter without searing pain, but fae and varcolai didn't share that characteristic.

There was plenty of darkness to hide in, but he remained cautious. No matter how strange Preacher was, he was still fringe with all the inherent abilities, including night vision and excellent hearing.

Doc crawled under the pews. Dust tickled his whiskers. His lip curled. He hated being dirty. A strange cry, almost animalistic, reached his ears. He headed toward it, nudging open a door with his broad nose and peering through.

In the room beyond sat a young girl decorated with gold marks like Chrysabelle's but without the refinement. One of Dominic's comarré. She smiled at Preacher and he back at her. He bounced in an odd rhythmic way, until he turned and Doc realized what he was doing.

Rocking a baby.

The comarré handed him a bottle of what looked like strawberry milk. For a baby? Preacher shook a couple drops onto the inside of his elbow. Doc inhaled. Not strawberry. Blood.

A chilling thought ripped through him. If that child was Preacher's and the comarré's ... if it was half vampire ... Doc shook his head. That shouldn't be possible, but why else would they put blood in the milk? He crept backward slowly. No wonder Preacher was killing off fringe left and right. Doc could think of about a million different people who'd like to get their hands on a vampire child. None of them good.

Chapter Forty

Mal could be thankful for two things. One was that Creek had gotten them a ride home. The plane was old but seemed serviceable, much like the man Creek had forcibly persuaded to fly it for them.

The second and most important was that Chrysabelle was still alive. Barely. But she was. *Too bad.*

Other than that, he wanted to destroy things until the pain he felt over what had been done to her went away. Pain he had caused.

If she hadn't gone to the Aurelian to find a way out of his curse, she'd be fine, not bleeding out in the back of a cargo plane. *All that blood . . .*

And he'd accused her of being selfish and stubborn.

The voices, overjoyed at how close she lay to death, raged in his head until their ranting turned into a sharp, white drone. He shoved it down and did his best to ignore it.

She lay on her stomach on a makeshift bed of tarps and packing blankets. She'd not regained consciousness long enough to do more than ask for water once and mumble something he couldn't understand when he'd lain down beside her and stroked her hair.

He was only vaguely aware that he wept. He'd been a fool not to tell her how he felt. That he cared for her. Deeply. The confession frightened him. Caring for someone made you vulnerable. Worse, it made them vulnerable, too. And tonight had proved that Chrysabelle's vulnerability was a very difficult thing for him to endure.

She moaned and opened her mouth, but said nothing. He brushed the hair off her cheek, sticky with sweat. What they'd cut her with, he didn't know, but the wounds Rennata – because he had no doubt she was the one who'd carved away Chrysabelle's signum – had left seemed unchanged in the hours they'd been airborne. Not even the slightest sign of healing yet. Chrysabelle was suffering and there was nothing he could do. Nothing. Even after they got back to Paradise City, what then?

Helplessness was not a feeling he enjoyed, but it trumped knowing he was the reason her life was bleeding out of her. The pain she'd endured . . . he couldn't imagine it.

He reached down and slipped his fingers through hers. 'I'm sorry,' he whispered. He closed his eyes and wished he could pray.

He woke when the plane's hum deepened. How could he have slept? He lurched upright. Creek sat across from him.

'How is she?'

Mal listened hard over the plane's engines. 'Her breathing is shallow, and her pulse is pretty weak. She's not doing well.'

Creek frowned, stress lines creasing his face. 'Good thing we're landing soon.'

'How soon?'

'Half an hour. We'll need a car.'

'I'll find one.' He'd hot-wire whatever was available. 'I don't understand why she isn't healing.'

'Has to be from whatever the bastards cut her with.' Creek stretched, rolling his head from side to side. 'When we land, you take her home. I'm going to get my grandmother. She's a healer.' He shrugged. 'Can't hurt.'

Mal nodded, surprised to feel such gratitude toward the slayer. 'Worth a shot.'

The landing gear dropped with a loud *thunk*.

Creek grunted. 'Hold on to her. This may not be the smoothest landing.'

Mal shifted her so she lay braced between his legs, her upper body resting on his thighs, her cheek on his hip. He looped his arms under hers and held on as best he could. Creek held on to her legs. Mal tipped his head back against the metal shell of the plane, letting the vibration rattle through his brain and compete with the voices.

Blood scent pierced every part of him, needling into his senses and burying him in a rock slide of hunger. Her body suffused warmth into his skin, making it impossible to ignore. Eyes shut, eyes open, made no difference. There was no escaping the building need.

And yet, he did, forcing it aside, because a part of him had become stronger than that need. The part of him that cared for her. He would do whatever was necessary to heal her and no matter what the voices whispered, he would protect her. From himself, if necessary.

'Here we go,' Creek yelled.

The creak and shudder of the plane touching down felt more like it was coming apart. He held on to her as they jolted onto the

tarmac. The tires squealed in protest and the smell of burning
rubber permeated the air. They were home.

Night was heavy on the city, dawn hours away. He left her
with Creek while he found a limo not far from where they'd
landed. It reeked of Tatiana. If she'd destroyed Chrysabelle's
portal, had she meant to trap them in Corvinestri? Maybe she'd
already left in pursuit of them. Either way, the vehicle was his
now.

The car was unlocked, so he threw it into neutral and yanked
the parking brake into place, then he jumped out and wrenched
the hood up, tearing the latch off the frame. Using the metal sup-
port bar meant to hold the hood open, he touched the solenoid to
the positive battery post. Sparks bit his skin, but the engine
purred to life.

An hour later, he eased Chrysabelle off the long backseat,
carefully putting her over his shoulder. The acrid tang of smoke
saturated everything. Velimai ran out to meet him. For once, the
wysper didn't seem to care he was a vampire.

Without understanding her signs, he knew she wanted to
know what had happened to Chrysabelle. He carried Chrysabelle
into the house without waiting for Velimai's approval and did his
best to explain quickly. 'She made a portal to go to the Aurelian.
She was punished for bringing me and the slayer with her. The
comarré disavowed her and cut away the runes that got her in to
see the Aurelian.' He stopped at the stairs. 'This way to her
room?'

Velimai nodded and went ahead, leading him.

'Why does it smell like smoke? Did Tatiana try to burn the
house down?'

Velimai shook her head, made a sign with her hand like
rolling waves.

'Tatiana burned the boat.'

Velimai nodded.

Which was how she'd closed the portal.

Velimai pushed open a set of double doors. The master suite. She continued through the sitting room, pulling back the linens on a king-size bed.

Before he was close enough to set Chrysabelle down, the wysper signed something and ran into a different part of the suite. He maneuvered Chrysabelle off his shoulder and onto the bed, keeping her on her stomach. She whimpered as he broke contact, so he took her hand. Her eyes flickered open, but they seemed unfocused.

'Shhh, it's all right now. You're home.'

'Hmmm.' Her eyes closed, apparently satisfied.

Velimai returned, towels draped over her shoulder, a basin of steaming water in her hands and a pair of scissors dangling off one finger.

'Good.' Mal sighed. 'I guess I should go downstairs and let you clean her up. Creek will be here soon with his grandmother. She's a healer.'

Velimai shook her head and held out the basin, nodding like he should take it.

'You want me to help?' He took the basin and set it on the nightstand.

Velimai put the scissors and the towels on the bed, then clapped her hands and pointed at his arm.

He held it toward her. 'What about my—'

She swiped her fingers across the palm of his hand. Trails of blood welled up, then faded as his skin healed. She picked up the scissors, handed them to him, and gestured at Chrysabelle.

He'd had no idea wysper skin was so abrasive. 'You need me to do it.'

She nodded, frowning as her gaze drifted to the unconscious comarré.

'She'll be okay.' He hoped. 'Scarred maybe, but okay.' Scars that would be a permanent reminder of what he'd cost her.

With Velimai watching, he cut Chrysabelle's blood-soaked gown off and began the arduous process of cleaning her wounds without hurting her further. She cried out weakly a few times but never fully woke up. At last, he'd cleaned as much of the blood as he could. He covered her to the waist with the sheet, then pulled a chair to the bedside and sat, waiting. Velimai did the same on the other side. They sat in silence, watching Chrysabelle. He was sure the wysper had as little idea about what else to do as he did.

The ticking of the clock on the nightstand filled the room.

From downstairs, a voice called out, 'Hello?'

Mal started. 'That's Creek. Velimai, will you—'

The wysper was already out the door. A minute later, she was back with Creek and his grandmother.

'Any change?' Creek asked.

'No.' Mal's gaze went to the woman beside the KM. Hanks of brightly colored beads surrounded her neck. A loose bun held back her gray hair, and behind thick glasses, her dark eyes watched him intently without a trace of fear or judgment.

Creek took the hint. 'This is my grandmother, Rosa Mae Jumper. She's a healer from the Seminole nation.'

'You can help her?' Mal asked the woman.

She tilted her head back like she couldn't see all of him. 'You live in shadow, dark one.' She walked past him to the bed and held her hands over Chrysabelle. 'This one is full of light. Too much light. She is unbalanced.'

'Can you help her or not? All this mumbo jumbo does nothing—'

'Watch your tone, vampire.' Creek rested a hand on his grandmother's shoulder. 'Mawmaw, what do we need to do to help her?'

She gave him a look that made him remove his hand, then turned back to Mal. 'Peace, dark one. I am here to heal, but I cannot do it alone.'

He leaned in. 'What do you need? Just tell me.'

'It isn't what I need. It's what she needs. Blood. Yours.' Her eyes were unblinking. 'Are you willing?'

He straightened. 'What do you mean?'

'Your blood can balance the light in her. Your darkness can give her reason to fight. The strength of your blood will heal her wounds and give her a chance to live.'

He took a step toward her. She didn't move. 'In English.'

She removed her glasses and cleaned them with the edge of her blouse. 'Cut yourself. Fill her wounds with your blood. Is that clear enough, blood eater?'

Velimai hissed. Mal backed away, shaking his head. 'You don't know what you're asking.'

She put her glasses back on. 'Yes, I do.'

Sharing blood with Chrysabelle could change her. She was comarré, she already bore certain characteristics given to her by the presence of vampire saliva in her system. What would blood do to her? He was afraid of the answer.

Creek approached. 'Are you sure this is safe, Mawmaw?' Nothing about his demeanor said he thought the old woman's proposal was a good one. 'She's a daughter of light. Putting his blood into her . . . ' He scowled.

She sighed. 'You asked me to help, Thomas. I can only offer what the spirits bring me.'

'I don't like it,' Creek said.

'You think I do?' Mal asked.

Rosa Mae walked toward the door. 'She's fading, isn't she? Listen.'

Mal stilled, doing as the woman suggested. Chrysabelle's pulse was weaker, her heartbeat sluggish. Tired. 'If this goes poorly, if *something* happens to her—'

Creek nodded. 'We both take the blame. We both protect her.'

Mal sighed. Reluctantly, he lifted his wrist to his mouth, tore his fangs across his skin. Blood dripped down his arm. He held it over the first gouge along her spine until the bleeding stopped and he had to open his flesh again. He repeated the process until his blood filled both of the raw grooves in her back.

She shivered as his blood seeped into her body. Her pulse strengthened. The edges of her wounds began to pull together.

'She will heal,' Rosa Mae announced.

'Yes,' Mal answered. 'But will she still be herself when she wakes up?'

'She will be who she is meant to be,' Rosa Mae said. 'Take me home, Thomas. Give the blood eater some peace.'

'I'll be back,' Creek said as he escorted her out.

Mal slumped into the chair and settled in to wait for Chrysabelle to wake up. Peace? Not hardly. Never in his life had he had such a bad feeling about something.

He hoped Chrysabelle made it through this unaffected and proved him wrong, but if she didn't . . . if he'd turned her . . . He dropped his head into his hands. She balanced him. Made him feel as close to sane as he'd been in a long while. Turning her into a vampire was unacceptable. There were only so many burdens he could bear.

That was not one of them.

The waning moon shed its pale silver over Aliza's porch, giving them just enough light to work with.

Evie came out of the house, shutting the sliding door behind her. She'd regained enough strength that their work could go forward. 'Midnight hour, Ma. At last.'

Aliza smiled. Her daughter was whole again. Her sweet Evie, well and standing beside her. Aliza nodded at her precious child, thankful she held no hard feelings over the length of time it had taken Aliza to free her. 'So it is.'

'Did the shifter go through the smoke?'

'We'll know soon enough. For now, let's light the candle and start this new spell.'

Evie struck a match and touched it to the wick, lighting the black anise-scented candle. She placed it in the center of the salt and earth pentagram they'd outlined on the scarred picnic table.

Aliza took the vial of blood from her apron and set it beside a wide strip of willow bark on the table. 'Hold that flat for me.'

'I never imagined we'd end up with *his* blood,' Evie said, securing the willow at both ends with her fingertips. She twitched, a subtle jerking of her whole body. She'd been doing it since being released. Aliza hoped it would go away. 'Should be better than Dominic's, don't you think?'

'For sure. Malcolm's blood holds more dark power.' And power was exactly what they were after. Had been, ever since the night Evie had turned herself to stone. They'd just never figured it would take them so long to get the blood to make it right. Aliza uncorked the vial and dipped a glass fountain pen into the blood. On the willow bark she wrote the unholy name. 'This will change everything.'

Evie laughed softly. 'I want a penthouse in the city.'

'Child, we will own the city.' She took the bark and held it over the candle and spoke the simple spell. 'Ancient spirit, now at rest, heed my call and manifest.' Slowly, the bark began to burn. Smoke curled off the papery wood until the fire hit the name written in blood. In a flash, the piece flamed brightly, then went to ash in a puff of smoke.

The smoke grew into a cloud, heavy and dense and viciously red. Evie shivered.

'It's okay,' Aliza assured her. 'The pentagram contains it.'

The smoke spun out and lengthened. Curled into a humanoid shape. Put down hoofed feet. The form towered over them until, at last, the being before them had a voice. 'Who summons me?'

'I do,' Aliza said. 'I and my daughter.'

Hard red eyes peered back at her. 'Mortals?'

'Witches,' Aliza corrected.

'Do you know who I am?' Disgust razed the voice into something like metal against metal.

'You are Samael, the ancient one, he who fell, head of the Castus Sanguis, the creator of the noble race of vampires.' *And,* she thought gleefully, *mine to command.*

He seemed mollified by her acknowledgment of him. 'Why do you summon me?'

'Power,' Aliza answered him.

He laughed. The glass doors rattled and something in the house shattered. 'All beings want power. What do you want from me?'

What they had originally wanted and what they wanted now

had changed since the night Evie had been restored. 'We want the ring the vampiress Tatiana seeks. The ring of sorrows.'

Samael laughed a second time. 'You are not equipped to command such a thing of power. Release me and I will teach you how.'

'I summoned you, didn't I?' She'd expected this response. Known he'd want to be released. No demon wanted to do the bidding of a mortal. It only made her want the ring, whatever its power, that much more. 'And because of that, you must give me what I want and answer my questions.'

His smile vanished. 'I do not have the ring.'

'Then who does?'

'A blood whore. One of the comarré. The one Tatiana seeks.' He growled, the sound like thunder. 'Release me!'

'You mean the girl with the gold tattoos?' Evie asked. She nudged her mother.

He nodded, eyes like fiery slits.

Aliza smiled. 'Then give her to us.'

'I can't.' He scowled. 'I cannot touch her. Why do you think I sent the vampiress after her?'

Evie stepped forward. 'What is the ring's power?'

'Bring it to me and I will help you rule the world.' He leered at her. 'All you have to do is release me.'

Aliza shook her head. 'Not enough, demon. What does it do?'

He raged, arms outstretched, clawed fingers splayed. 'Mortal fools! With that ring, you can raise an unconquerable army. Now, free me.'

An unconquerable army was far more than Aliza had ever hoped for. Plans began to form in her head. Why rule Paradise City when she could have the world?

'Not yet, demon. Not yet.'

Glossary

Anathema: a noble vampire who has been cast out of noble society for some reason.

Aurelian: the comarré historian.

Castus Sanguis: the fallen angels from whom the othernatural races descended.

Comarré/comar: a human hybrid species especially bred to serve the blood needs of the noble vampire race.

Dominus: the ruling head of a noble vampire family.

Elder: the second in command to a Dominus.

Fae: a race of othernatural beings descended from fallen angels and nature.

Fringe vampires: a race of lesser vampires descended from the cursed Judas Iscariot.

Kine: a vampire term for humans, archaic.

Kubai Mata: an ancient secret society designed to protect mankind against othernaturals should the covenant be broken.

Libertas: the ritual in which a comarré can fight for their independence; ends in death of comarré or patron.

Navitas: the ritual in which a vampire can be resired by another, to change family lines, or turn fringe noble.

Noble vampires: a powerful race of vampires descended from fallen angels.

Nothos: hellhounds.

Patron: a noble vampire who purchases a comarré's blood rights.

Remnant: a hybrid of different species of fae or varcolai.

Sacre: the ceremonial sword of the comarré.

Signum: the inlaid gold tattoos or marks put into comarré skin to purify their blood.

Vampling: a newly turned or young vampire.

Varcolai: a race of shifters descended from fallen angels and animals.

Acknowledgments

I must thank my editor, Devi; her assistant, Jennifer; Alex, Jack, and the entire publishing team at Orbit for making this book a reality. You're an awesome group!

Big thanks to the folks who provided me with translation help: Alessandro and Kimberly Menozzi for their Italian translations; Bob Rivera for his Latin translations; Ahmed El Anjanar for his Arabic translation. Any mistakes are mine.

And then there is the crew that supports me, reads for me, gets me writing, helps me brainstorm, talks me off ledges, and keeps me encouraged: Richie, Matt, my parents, Jax, Laura, Leigh, Carrie, Carolyn, Briana, Dayna, Emily, the staff at Romance Divas, my truly amazing agent, Elaine, and the two writers who inspire me daily with their dedication, their work ethics, and their skill with words, Rocki and Louisa.

Lastly, thanks to all the readers out there for taking a chance on one more vampire series.

extras

www.orbitbooks.net

about the author

Kristen Painter's writing résumé boasts multiple Golden Heart nominations and advance praise from a handful of bestselling authors, including Gena Showalter and Roxanne St. Claire. A former New Yorker now living in Florida, Kristen has a wealth of fascinating experiences from which to flavor her stories, including time spent working in fashion for Christian Dior and as a maître d' for Wolfgang Puck. Her website is at kristenpainter.com and she's on Twitter at @Kristen_Painter.

Find out more about Kristen Painter and other Orbit authors by registering for the free monthly newsletter at www.orbitbooks.net

if you enjoyed

FLESH AND BLOOD

look out for

SOULLESS

by

Gail Carriger

CHAPTER ONE

In Which Parasols Prove Useful

Miss Alexia Tarabotti was not enjoying her evening. Private balls were never more than middling amusements for spinsters, and Miss Tarabotti was not the kind of spinster who could garner even that much pleasure from the event. To put the pudding in the puff: she had retreated to the library, her favorite sanctuary in any house, only to happen upon an unexpected vampire.

She glared at the vampire.

For his part, the vampire seemed to feel that their encounter had improved his ball experience immeasurably. For there she sat, without escort, in a low-necked ball gown.

In this particular case, what he did not know *could* hurt him. For Miss Alexia had been born without a soul, which, as any decent vampire of good blooding knew, made her a lady to avoid most assiduously.

Yet he moved toward her, darkly shimmering out of the library shadows with feeding fangs ready. However, the moment he touched Miss Tarabotti, he was suddenly no longer darkly doing anything at all. He was simply standing there, the faint sounds of a string quartet in the background as he foolishly fished about with his tongue for fangs unaccountably mislaid.

Miss Tarabotti was not in the least surprised; soullessness always neutralized supernatural abilities. She issued the vampire a very dour look. Certainly, most daylight folk wouldn't peg her as anything less than a standard English prig, but had this man not even bothered to *read* the vampire's official abnormality roster for London and its greater environs?

The vampire recovered his equanimity quickly enough. He reared away from Alexia, knocking over a nearby tea trolley. Physical contact broken, his fangs reappeared. Clearly not the sharpest of prongs, he then darted forward from the neck like a serpent, diving in for another chomp.

'I say!' said Alexia to the vampire. 'We have not even been introduced!'

Miss Tarabotti had never actually had a vampire try to bite her. She knew one or two by reputation, of course, and was friendly with Lord Akeldama. *Who was* not *friendly with Lord Akeldama?* But no vampire had ever actually attempted to *feed* on her before!

So Alexia, who abhorred violence, was forced to grab the miscreant by his nostrils, a delicate and therefore painful area, and shove him away. He stumbled over the fallen tea trolley, lost his balance in a manner astonishingly graceless for a vampire, and fell to the floor. He landed right on top of a plate of treacle tart.

Miss Tarabotti was most distressed by this. She was particularly fond of treacle tart and had been looking forward to consuming that precise plateful. She picked up her parasol. It was terribly tasteless for her to be carrying a parasol at an evening ball, but Miss Tarabotti rarely went anywhere without it. It was of a style entirely of her own devising: a black frilly confection with purple satin pansies sewn about, brass hardware, and buckshot in its silver tip.

She whacked the vampire right on top of the head with it as he tried to extract himself from his newly intimate relations with the tea trolley. The buckshot gave the brass parasol just enough heft to make a deliciously satisfying *thunk*.

'Manners!' instructed Miss Tarabotti.

The vampire howled in pain and sat back down on the treacle tart.

Alexia followed up her advantage with a vicious prod between the vampire's legs. His howl went quite a bit higher in pitch, and he crumpled into a fetal position. While Miss Tarabotti was a proper English young lady, aside from not having a soul and being half Italian, she did spend quite a bit more time than most other young ladies riding and walking and was therefore unexpectedly strong.

Miss Tarabotti leaped forward – as much as one could leap in full triple-layered underskirts, draped bustle, and ruffled taffeta top-skirt – and bent over the vampire. He was clutching at his indelicate bits and writhing about. The pain would not last long given his supernatural healing ability, but it hurt most decidedly in the interim.

Alexia pulled a long wooden hair stick out of her elaborate coiffure. Blushing at her own temerity, she ripped open his shirt-front, which was cheap and overly starched, and poked at his chest, right over the heart. Miss Tarabotti sported a particularly large and sharp hair stick. With her free hand, she made certain to touch his chest, as only physical contact would nullify his supernatural abilities.

'Desist that horrible noise immediately,' she instructed the creature.

The vampire quit his squealing and lay perfectly still. His beautiful blue eyes watered slightly as he stared fixedly at the wooden hair stick. Or, as Alexia liked to call it, hair *stake*.

'Explain yourself!' Miss Tarabotti demanded, increasing the pressure.

'A thousand apologies.' The vampire looked confused. 'Who are you?' Tentatively he reached for his fangs. Gone.

To make her position perfectly clear, Alexia stopped touching him (though she kept her sharp hair stick in place). His fangs grew back.

He gasped in amazement. '*What* are you? I thought you were a lady, alone. It would be my right to feed, if you were left this carelethly unattended. Pleathe, I did not mean to prethume,' he lisped around his fangs, real panic in his eyes.

Alexia, finding it hard not to laugh at the lisp, said, 'There is no cause for you to be so overly dramatic. Your hive queen will have told you of my kind.' She returned her hand to his chest once more. The vampire's fangs retracted.

He looked at her as though she had suddenly sprouted whiskers and hissed at him.

Miss Tarabotti was surprised. Supernatural creatures, be they vampires, werewolves, or ghosts, owed their existence to an overabundance of soul, an excess that refused to die. Most knew that others like Miss Tarabotti existed, born without any soul at all. The estimable Bureau of Unnatural Registry (BUR), a division of Her Majesty's Civil Service, called her ilk *preternatural*. Alexia thought the term nicely dignified. What vampires called her was far less complimentary. After all, preternaturals had once hunted *them*, and vampires had long memories. Natural, daylight persons were kept in the dark, so to speak, but any vampire worth his blood should know a preternatural's touch. This one's ignorance was untenable. Alexia said, as though to a very small child, 'I am a *preternatural*.'

The vampire looked embarrassed. 'Of course you are,' he agreed, obviously still not quite comprehending. 'Again, my apologies, lovely one. I am overwhelmed to meet you. You are my first' – he stumbled over the word – 'preternatural.' He frowned. 'Not supernatural, not natural, of course! How foolish of me not to see the dichotomy.' His eyes narrowed into craftiness. He was now studiously ignoring the hair stick and looking tenderly up into Alexia's face.

Miss Tarabotti knew full well her own feminine appeal. The kindest compliment her face could ever hope to garner was 'exotic,' never 'lovely.' Not that it had ever received either. Alexia figured that vampires, like all predators, were at their most charming when cornered.

The vampire's hands shot forward, going for her neck. Apparently, he had decided if he could not suck her blood, strangulation was an acceptable alternative. Alexia jerked back, at the same time pressing her hair stick into the creature's white flesh. It slid in about half an inch. The vampire reacted with a desperate wriggle that, even without superhuman strength, unbalanced Alexia in her heeled velvet dancing shoes. She fell back. He stood, roaring in pain, with her hair stick half in and half out of his chest.

Miss Tarabotti scrabbled for her parasol, rolling about inelegantly among the tea things, hoping her new dress would miss the fallen foodstuffs. She found the parasol and came upright, swinging it in a wide arc. Purely by chance, the heavy tip struck the end of her wooden hair stick, driving it straight into the vampire's heart.

The creature stood stock-still, a look of intense surprise on his handsome face. Then he fell backward onto the much-abused plate of treacle tart, flopping in a limp-overcooked-asparagus kind of way. His alabaster face turned a yellowish gray, as though he were afflicted with the jaundice, and he went still. Alexia's books called this end of the vampire life cycle *dissanimation*. Alexia, who thought the action astoundingly similar to a soufflé going flat, decided at that moment to call it the Grand Collapse.

She intended to waltz directly out of the library without anyone the wiser to her presence there. This would have resulted in the loss of her best hair stick and her well-deserved tea, as well as a good deal of drama. Unfortunately, a small group of young dandies came traipsing in at that precise moment. What young men of such dress were doing in a *library* was anyone's guess. Alexia felt the most likely explanation was that they had become lost while looking for the card room. Regardless, their presence forced her to pretend that she, too, had just discovered the dead vampire. With a resigned shrug, she screamed and collapsed into a faint.

She stayed resolutely fainted, despite the liberal application of smelling salts, which made her eyes water most tremendously, a cramp in the back of one knee, and the fact that her new ball gown was getting most awfully wrinkled. All its many layers of green trim, picked to the height of fashion in lightening shades to complement the cuirasse bodice, were being crushed into oblivion under her weight. The expected noises ensued: a good deal of yelling, much bustling about, and several loud clatters as one of the housemaids cleared away the fallen tea.

Then came the sound she had half anticipated, half dreaded. An authoritative voice cleared the library of both young dandies and all other interested parties who had flowed into the room upon discovery of the tableau. The voice instructed everyone to 'get out!' while he 'gained the particulars from the young lady' in tones that brooked no refusal.

Silence descended.

'Mark my words, I will use something much, much stronger than smelling salts,' came a growl in Miss Tarabotti's left ear. The voice was low and tinged with a hint of Scotland. It would have caused Alexia to shiver and think primal monkey thoughts about moons and running far and fast, if she'd had a soul. Instead it caused her to sigh in exasperation and sit up.

'And a good evening to you, too, Lord Maccon. Lovely weather we are having for this time of year, is it not?' She patted at her hair, which was threatening to fall down without the hair stick in its proper place. Surreptitiously, she looked about for Lord Conall Maccon's second in command, Professor Lyall. Lord Maccon tended to maintain a much calmer temper when his Beta was present. But, then, as Alexia had come to comprehend, that appeared to be the main role of a Beta – especially one attached to Lord Maccon.

'Ah, Professor Lyall, how nice to see you again.' She smiled in relief.

Professor Lyall, the Beta in question, was a slight, sandy-haired gentleman of indeterminate age and pleasant disposition, as agreeable, in fact, as his Alpha was sour. He grinned at her and doffed his hat, which was of first-class design and sensible material. His cravat was similarly subtle, for, while it was tied expertly, the knot was a humble one.

'Miss Tarabotti, how delicious to find ourselves in your company once more.' His voice was soft and mild-mannered.

'Stop humoring her, Randolph,' barked Lord Maccon. The fourth Earl of Woolsey was much larger than Professor Lyall and in possession of a near-permanent frown. Or at least he always seemed to be frowning when he was in the presence of Miss Alexia Tarabotti, ever since the hedgehog incident (which really, honestly, had not been her fault). He also had unreasonably pretty tawny eyes, mahogany-colored hair, and a particularly nice nose. The eyes were currently glaring at Alexia from a shockingly intimate distance.

'Why is it, Miss Tarabotti, every time I have to clean up a mess in a library, you just happen to be in the middle of it?' the earl demanded of her.

Alexia gave him a withering look and brushed down the front of her green taffeta gown, checking for bloodstains.

Lord Maccon appreciatively watched her do it. Miss Tarabotti might examine her face in the mirror each morning with a large degree of censure, but there was nothing at all wrong with her figure. He would have to have had far less soul and a good fewer urges not to notice that appetizing fact. Of course, she always went and spoiled the appeal by opening her mouth. In his humble experience, the world had yet to produce a more vexingly verbose female.

'Lovely but unnecessary,' he said, indicating her efforts to brush away nonexistent blood drops.

Alexia reminded herself that Lord Maccon and his kind were only *just* civilized. One simply could not expect too much from them, especially under delicate circumstances such as these. Of course, that failed to explain Professor Lyall, who was always utterly urbane. She glanced with appreciation in the professor's direction.

Lord Maccon's frown intensified.

Miss Tarabotti considered that the lack of civilized behavior might be the sole provenance of Lord Maccon. Rumor had it, he had only lived in London a comparatively short while – and he had relocated from Scotland of all barbaric places.

The professor coughed delicately to get his Alpha's attention. The earl's yellow gaze focused on him with such intensity it should have actually burned. 'Aye?'

Professor Lyall was crouched over the vampire, examining the hair stick with interest. He was poking about the wound, a spotless white lawn handkerchief wrapped around his hand.

'Very little mess, actually. Almost complete lack of blood spatter.' He leaned forward and sniffed. 'Definitely Westminster,' he stated.

The Earl of Woolsey seemed to understand. He turned his piercing gaze onto the dead vampire. 'He must have been very hungry.'

Professor Lyall turned the body over. 'What happened here?' He took out a small set of wooden tweezers from the pocket of his waistcoat and picked at the back of the vampire's trousers. He paused, rummaged about in his coat pockets, and produced a diminutive leather case. He clicked it open and removed a most bizarre pair of gogglelike things. They were gold in color with multiple lenses on one side, between which there appeared to be some kind of liquid. The contraption was also riddled with small knobs and dials. Professor Lyall propped the ridiculous things onto his nose and bent back over the vampire, twiddling at the dials expertly.

'Goodness gracious me,' exclaimed Alexia, 'what *are* you wearing? It looks like the unfortunate progeny of an illicit union between a pair of binoculars and some opera glasses. What on earth are they called, binocticals, spectoculars?'

The earl snorted his amusement and then tried to pretend he hadn't. 'How about glassicals?' he suggested, apparently unable to resist a contribution. There was a twinkle in his eye as he said it that Alexia found rather unsettling.

Professor Lyall looked up from his examination and glared at the both of them. His right eye was hideously magnified. It was quite gruesome and made Alexia start involuntarily.

'These are my monocular cross-magnification lenses with spectra-modifier attachment, and they are invaluable. I will thank you not to mock them so openly.' He turned once more to the task at hand.

'Oh.' Miss Tarabotti was suitably impressed. 'How do they work?' she inquired.

Professor Lyall looked back up at her, suddenly animated. 'Well, you see, it is really quite interesting. By turning this little knob here, you can change the distance between the two panes of glass here, allowing the liquid to—'

The earl's groan interrupted him. 'Don't get him started, Miss Tarabotti, or we will be here all night.'

Looking slightly crestfallen, Professor Lyall turned back to the dead vampire. 'Now, what *is* this substance all over his clothing?'

His boss, preferring the direct approach, resumed his frown and looked accusingly at Alexia. 'What on God's green earth is that muck?'

Miss Tarabotti said, 'Ah. Sadly, treacle tart. A tragic loss, I daresay.' Her stomach chose that moment to growl in agreement. She would have colored gracefully with embarrassment had she not possessed the complexion of one of those 'heathen Italians,' as her mother said, who never colored, gracefully or otherwise. (Convincing her mother that Christianity had, to all intents and purposes, originated with the Italians, thus making them the exact opposite of heathen, was a waste of time and breath.)

Alexia refused to apologize for the boisterousness of her stomach and favored Lord Maccon with a defiant glare. Her stomach was the reason she had sneaked away in the first place. Her mama had assured her there would be food at the ball. Yet all that appeared on offer when they arrived was a bowl of punch and some sadly wilted watercress. Never one to let her stomach get the better of her, Alexia had ordered tea from the butler and retreated to the library. Since she normally spent any ball lurking on the outskirts of the dance floor trying to look as though she did not want to be asked to waltz, tea was a welcome alternative. It was rude to order refreshments from someone else's staff, but when one was promised sandwiches and there was nothing but watercress, well, one must simply take matters into one's own hands!

Professor Lyall, kindhearted soul that he was, prattled on to no one in particular, pretending not to notice the rumbling of her stomach. Though of course he heard it. He had excellent hearing. *They* all did. He looked up from his examinations, his face all catawampus from the glassicals. 'Starvation would explain why the vampire was desperate enough to try for Miss Tarabotti at a ball, rather than taking to the slums like the smart ones do when they get this bad.'

Alexia grimaced. 'No associated hive either.'

Lord Maccon arched one black eyebrow, professing not to be impressed. 'How could *you* possibly know *that*?'

Professor Lyall explained for both of them. 'No need to be so direct with the young lady. A hive queen would never have let one of her brood get into such a famished condition. We must have a rove on our hands, one completely without ties to the local hive.'

Alexia stood up, revealing to Lord Maccon that she had

arranged her faint to rest comfortably against a fallen settee pillow. He grinned and then quickly hid it behind a frown when she looked at him suspiciously.

'I have a different theory.' She gestured to the vampire's clothing. 'Badly tied cravat and a cheap shirt? No hive worth its salt would let a larva like that out without dressing him properly for public appearance. I am surprised he was not stopped at the front entrance. The duchess's footman really ought to have spotted a cravat like *that* prior to the reception line and forcibly ejected the wearer. I suppose good staff is hard to come by with all the best ones becoming drones these days, but such a shirt!'

The Earl of Woolsey glared at her. 'Cheap clothing is no excuse for killing a man.'

'Mmm, that's what you say.' Alexia evaluated Lord Maccon's perfectly tailored shirtfront and exquisitely tied cravat. His dark hair was a bit too long and shaggy to be de mode, and his face was not entirely clean-shaven, but he possessed enough hauteur to carry this lower-class roughness off without seeming scruffy. She was certain that his silver and black paisley cravat must be tied under sufferance. He probably preferred to wander about bare-chested at home. The idea made her shiver oddly. It must take a lot of effort to keep a man like him tidy. Not to mention well tailored. He was bigger than most. She had to give credit to his valet, who must be a particularly tolerant claviger.

Lord Maccon was normally quite patient. Like most of his kind, he had learned to be such in polite society. But Miss Tarabotti seemed to bring out the worst of his animal urges. 'Stop trying to change the subject,' he snapped, squirming under her calculated scrutiny. 'Tell me what happened.' He put on his BUR face and pulled out a small metal tube, stylus, and pot of clear liquid. He unrolled the tube with a small cranking device, clicked the top off the liquid, and dipped the stylus into it. It sizzled ominously.

Alexia bristled at his autocratic tone. 'Do not give me instructions in that tone of voice, you . . . ' she searched for a particularly insulting word, ' . . . puppy! I am jolly well not one of your pack.'

Lord Conall Maccon, Earl of Woolsey, was Alpha of the local werewolves, and as a result, he had access to a wide array of truly vicious methods of dealing with Miss Alexia Tarabotti. Instead of bridling at her insult (puppy, indeed!), he brought out his best offensive weapon, the result of decades of personal experience with more than one Alpha she-wolf. Scottish he may be by birth, but that only made him better equipped to deal with strong-willed females. 'Stop playing verbal games with me, madam, or I shall go out into that ballroom, find your mother, and bring her here.'

Alexia wrinkled her nose. 'Well, I *like* that! That is hardly playing a fair game. How unnecessarily callous,' she admonished. Her mother did not know that Alexia was preternatural. Mrs. Loontwill, as she was Loontwill since her remarriage, leaned a little too far toward the frivolous in any given equation. She was prone to wearing yellow and engaging in bouts of hysteria. Combining her mother with a dead vampire and her daughter's true identity was a recipe for disaster on all possible levels.

The fact that Alexia was preternatural had been explained to *her* at age six by a nice gentleman from the Civil Service with silver hair and a silver cane – a werewolf specialist. Along with the dark hair and prominent nose, preternatural was something Miss Tarabotti had to thank her dead Italian father for. What it really meant was that words like *I* and *me* were just excessively theoretical for Alexia. She certainly had an identity and a heart that felt emotions and all that; she simply had no soul. Miss Alexia, age six, had nodded politely at the nice silver-haired gentleman. Then she had made certain to read oodles of ancient Greek philosophy dealing with reason, logic, and ethics. If she had no soul, she also had no morals, so she reckoned she had best develop some kind of alternative. Her mama thought her a bluestocking, which was soulless enough as far as Mrs. Loontwill was concerned, and was terribly upset by her eldest daughter's propensity for libraries. It would be too bothersome to have to face her mama in one just now.

Lord Maccon moved purposefully toward the door with the clear intention of acquiring Mrs. Loontwill.

Alexia caved with ill grace. 'Oh, very well!' She settled herself with a rustle of green skirts onto a peach brocade chesterfield near the window.

The earl was both amused and annoyed to see that she had managed to pick up her fainting pillow and place it back on the couch without his registering any swooping movement.

'I came into the library for tea. I was promised food at this ball. In case you had not noticed, no food appears to be in residence.'

Lord Maccon who required a considerable amount of fuel, mostly of the protein inclination, had noticed. 'The Duke of Snodgrove is notoriously reticent about any additional expenditure at his wife's balls. Victuals were probably not on the list of acceptable offerings.' He sighed. 'The man owns half of Berkshire and cannot even provide a decent sandwich.'

Miss Tarabotti made an empathetic movement with both hands. 'My point precisely! So you will understand that I had to resort to ordering my own repast. Did you expect me to starve?'

The earl gave her generous curves a rude once-over, observed that Miss Tarabotti was nicely padded in exactly the right places, and refused to be suckered into becoming sympathetic. He maintained his frown. 'I suspect that is precisely what the vampire was thinking when he found you *without a chaperone*. An unmarried female alone in a room in this enlightened day and age! Why, if the moon had been full, even I would have attacked you!'

Alexia gave him the once-over and reached for her brass parasol. 'My dear sir, I should like to see you try.'

Being Alpha made Lord Maccon a tad unprepared for such bold rebuttals, even with his Scottish past. He blinked at her in surprise for a split second and then resumed the verbal attack. 'You do realize modern social mores exist for a reason?'

'I was hungry; allowances should be made,' Alexia said, as if that settled the matter, unable to understand why he persisted in harping on about it.

Professor Lyall, unobserved by the other two, was busy fishing about in his waistcoat for something. Eventually, he produced a mildly beaten-up ham and pickle sandwich wrapped in a bit of brown paper. He presented it to Miss Tarabotti, ever the gallant.

Under normal circumstances, Alexia would have been put off by the disreputable state of the sandwich, but it was meant so kindly and offered with such diffidence, she could do nothing but accept. It was actually rather tasty.

'This is delicious!' she stated, surprised.

Professor Lyall grinned. 'I keep them around for when his lordship gets particularly testy. Such offerings keep the beast under control for the most part.' He frowned and then added a caveat. 'Excepting at full moon, of course. Would that a nice ham and pickle sandwich was all it took then.'

Miss Tarabotti perked up, interested. 'What do you *do* at full moon?'

Lord Maccon knew very well Miss Tarabotti was getting off the point intentionally. Driven beyond endurance, he resorted to use of her first name. 'Alexia!' It was a long, polysyllabic, drawn-out growl.

She waved the sandwich at him. 'Uh, do you want half of this, my lord?'

His frown became even darker, if such a thing could be conceived.

Professor Lyall pushed his glassicals up onto the brim of his top hat, where they looked like a strange second set of mechanical eyes, and stepped into the breach. 'Miss Tarabotti, I do not believe you quite realize the delicacy of this situation. Unless we can establish strong grounds for self-defense by proving the vampire was behaving in a wholly irrational manner, you could be facing murder charges.'

Alexia swallowed her bite of sandwich so quickly she partly choked and started to cough. 'What?'

Lord Maccon turned his fierce frown on his second. 'Now who is being too direct for the lady's sensibilities?'

Lord Maccon was relatively new to the London area. He had arrived a social unknown, challenged for Woolsey Castle Alpha, and won. He gave young ladies heart palpitations, even outside his wolf form, with a favorable combination of mystery, preeminence, and danger. Having acquired the BUR post, Woolsey Castle, and noble rank from the dispossessed former pack leader, he never lacked for a dinner invitation. His Beta, inherited with the pack, had a tense time of it: dancing on protocol and covering up Lord Maccon's various social gaffes. So far, bluntness had proved Professor Lyall's most consistent problem. Sometimes it even rubbed off on him. He had not meant to shock Miss Tarabotti, but she was now looking most subdued.

'I was simply sitting,' Alexia explained, placing the sandwich aside, having lost her appetite. 'He launched himself at me, totally unprovoked. His feeding fangs were out. I am certain if I had been a normal daylight woman, he would have bled me dry. I simply had to defend myself.'

Professor Lyall nodded. A vampire in a state of extreme hunger had two socially acceptable options: to take sips from various willing drones belonging to him or his hive, or to pay for the privilege from blood-whores down dockside. This was the nineteenth century, after all, and one simply did not attack unannounced and uninvited! Even werewolves, who could not control themselves at full moon, made certain they had enough clavigers around to lock them away. He himself had three, and it took five to keep Lord Maccon under control.

'Do you think maybe he was forced into this state?' the professor wondered.

'You mean imprisoned until he was starving and no longer in possession of his faculties?' Lord Maccon considered the idea.

Professor Lyall flipped his glassicals back down off his hat and examined the dead man's wrists and neck myopically. 'No signs of confinement or torture, but hard to tell with a vampire. Even in a low blood state, he would heal most superficial wounds in' – he grabbed Lord Maccon's metal roll and stylus, dipped the tip into the clear sizzling liquid, and did some quick calculations – 'a little over one hour.' The calculations remained etched into the metal.

'And then what? Did he escape or was he intentionally let go?'

Alexia interjected, 'He seemed perfectly sane to me – aside

from the attacking part, of course. He was able to carry on a decent conversation. He even tried to charm me. Must have been quite a young vampire. And' – she paused dramatically, lowered her voice, and said in sepulchral tones – 'he had a fang-lisp.'

Professor Lyall looked shocked and blinked largely at her through the asymmetrical lenses; among vampires, lisping was the height of vulgarity.

Miss Tarabotti continued. 'It was as though he had never been trained in hive etiquette, no social class at all. He was almost a boor.' It was a word she had never thought to apply to a vampire.

Lyall took the glassicals off and put them away in their little case with an air of finality. He looked gravely at his Alpha. 'You know what this means, then, my lord?'

Lord Maccon was not frowning anymore. Instead he was looking grim. Alexia felt it suited him better, setting his mouth into a straight line and touching his tawny eyes with a determined glint. She wondered idly what he would look like if he smiled a real honest smile. Then she told herself quite firmly that it was probably best not to find out.

The object of her speculations said, 'It means some hive queen is intentionally biting to metamorphosis outside of BUR regulations.'

'Could it be just the once, do you think?' Professor Lyall removed a folded piece of white cloth from his waistcoat. He shook out the material, revealing it to be a large sheet of fine silk. Alexia was beginning to find the number of things he could stash in his waistcoat quite impressive.

Lord Maccon continued. 'Or this could be the start of something more extensive. We'd better get back to BUR. The local hives will have to be interviewed. The queens are not going to be happy. Apart from everything else, this incident is awfully embarrassing for them.'

Miss Tarabotti agreed. 'Especially if they find out about the substandard shirt selection.'

The two gentlemen wrapped the vampire's body in the silk sheet. Professor Lyall hoisted it easily over one shoulder. Even in their human form, werewolves were considerably stronger than daylight folk.

Lord Maccon rested his tawny gaze on Alexia. She was sitting primly on the chesterfield. One gloved hand rested on the ebony handle of a ridiculous-looking parasol. Her brown eyes were narrowed in consideration. He would give a hundred pounds to know what she was thinking just then. He was also certain she would tell him exactly what it was if he asked, but he refused to give her the satisfaction. Instead he issued a statement. 'We'll try to keep your name out of it, Miss Tarabotti. My report will say it was simply a normal girl who got lucky and managed to escape an unwarranted attack. No need for anyone to know a preternatural was involved.'

Now it was Alexia's turn to glare. 'Why do you BUR types always *do* that?'

Both men paused to look at her in confusion.

'*Do* what, Miss Tarabotti?' asked the professor.

'Dismiss me as though I were a child. Do you realize I could be useful to you?'

Lord Maccon grunted. 'You mean you could go around legally getting into trouble instead of just bothering us all the time?'

Alexia tried to keep from feeling hurt. 'BUR employs women, and I hear you even have a preternatural on the payroll up north, for ghost control and exorcism purposes.'

Lord Maccon's caramel-colored eyes instantly narrowed. 'From whom, exactly, did you hear that?'

Miss Tarabotti raised her eyebrows. As if she would ever betray the source of information told to her in confidence!

The earl understood her look perfectly. 'Very well, never you mind that question.'

'I shall not,' replied Alexia primly.

Professor Lyall, still holding the body slung over one shoulder, took pity on her. 'We do have both at BUR,' he admitted.

Lord Maccon elbowed him in the side, but he stepped out of range with a casual grace that bespoke much practice. 'But what we do not have is any *female* preternaturals, and certainly not any gentlewomen. All women employed by BUR are good working-class stock.'

'You are simply still bitter about the hedgehogs,' muttered Miss Tarabotti, but she also bowed her head in acknowledgment. She'd had this conversation before, with Lord Maccon's superior at BUR, to be precise. A man her brain still referred to as that Nice Silver-Haired Gentleman. The very idea that a lady of breeding such as herself might want to *work* was simply too shocking. 'My dearest girl,' he had said, 'what if your mother found out?'

'Isn't BUR supposed to be covert? I could be covert.' Miss Tarabotti could not help trying again. Professor Lyall, at least, liked her a little bit. Perhaps he might put in a good word.

Lord Maccon actually laughed. 'You are about as covert as a sledgehammer.' Then he cursed himself silently, as she seemed suddenly forlorn. She hid it quickly, but she had definitely been saddened.

His Beta grabbed him by the arm with his free hand. 'Really, sir, manners.'

The earl cleared his throat and looked contrite. 'No offense meant, Miss Tarabotti.' The Scottish lilt was back in his voice.

Alexia nodded, not looking up. She plucked at one of the pansies on her parasol. 'It's simply, gentlemen' – and when she raised her dark eyes they had a slight sheen in them – 'I would so like something useful to do.'

Lord Maccon waited until he and the professor were out in the hallway, having bid polite, on Professor Lyall's part at least, farewells to the young lady, to ask the question that really bothered him. 'For goodness' sake, Randolph, why doesn't she just get married?' His voice was full of frustration.

Randolph Lyall looked at his Alpha in genuine confusion. The earl was usually a very perceptive man, for all his bluster and Scottish grumbling. 'She is a bit old, sir.'

'Balderdash,' said Lord Maccon. 'She cannot possibly have more than a quarter century or so.'

'And she is very' – the professor looked for a gentlemanly way of putting it – 'assertive.'

'Pah.' The nobleman waved one large paw dismissively. 'Simply got a jot more backbone than most females this century. There must be plenty of discerning gentlemen who'd cop to her value.'

Professor Lyall had a well-developed sense of self-preservation and the distinct feeling that if he said anything desultory about the young lady's appearance, he might actually get his head bitten off. He, and the rest of polite society, might believe Miss Tarabotti's skin a little too dark and her nose a little too prominent, but he did not think Lord Maccon felt the same. Lyall had been Beta to the fourth Earl of Woolsey since Conall Maccon first descended upon them all. With barely twenty years gone and the bloody memory still strong, no werewolf was yet ready to question why Conall had wanted the bother of the London territory, not even Professor Lyall. The earl was a confusing man, his taste in females equally mystifying. For all Professor Lyall knew, his Alpha might actually *like* Roman noses, tan skin, and an assertive disposition. So instead he said, 'Perhaps it's the Italian last name, sir, that keeps her unwed.'

'Mmm,' agreed Lord Maccon, 'probably so.' He did not sound convinced.

The two werewolves exited the duke's town house into the black London night, one bearing the body of a dead vampire, the other, a puzzled expression.